What Readers are Saying

"This deeply moving work is a must read for anyone interested in the intersection between mental health and spirituality. I loved that the author boldly addresses generational trauma and its damaging effects on families who continue the cycle of repression and secrecy. Through her compassionate style, the author offers hope to her characters and to her readers who may be struggling with healing trauma in their own lives. This book inspired me to work through my own difficult familial relationships and rediscover what is possible when we offer radical acceptance, love and forgiveness. This is a truly unique work in a sea of ordinary. I know I will revisit *Feathers from the Fire* over the years as a call to action in my own life."

Thomasina Goltzer, M.A.Ed.
Mother, Educator

"Whew! Reading *Feathers from the Fire* allowed me to release the breath I didn't even know I'd been holding regarding my own son, my original misunderstandings about his "gifts," the desire to hide and protect, and all the pat answers and excuses I perpetually had ready for those with questioning looks. Karlyn's knowledge, experience, and captivating storytelling ability enabled me to stay engaged and take the incredible journey with the mother in the story. By the end, I was totally intrigued with the historical foundation used for this beautiful work of fiction (causing me to do a little research on my own) and filled with tears of gratitude for the awareness and understanding this book will bring to the world."

Theddee Rheyshelle
Grateful Mother, Author, and Storyteller

"*Feathers from the Fire* left me feeling hopeful for those hurting or experiencing the world in a way that deviates from what others consider the norm. The reminder that children inherit the weight of generations and unconditionally love adults anyway brought forth hopeful tears. There's a beauty about it that left me wanting even more of the story behind the story."

Sandy Ingle, PsyD
Retired School Counselor

"Karlyn Pleasants is rewriting the rules of our cultural perception of mental health in this spiritually-dynamic, mystery-driven saga; and the new rules of curiosity, compassion, and leaning in are just what our society needs. This is an undeniable necessity for those whose being has been stirred from within and by the world beyond and for those who have always known and still have yet to understand that there might be another story behind the story."

Alyssa Noelle Coelho
Bestselling Author of *CHOSEN*

"What an amazing read! I didn't want to put this book down! The way the author wove history and generational trauma into the Driscoll family's storyline gave me a new awareness of how the past can hold answers to today's family crisis and a better future if we are willing to take a chance and look."

Lori Giesey
Author of *A Moment In Time* and Collaborator of
*You Can't Make This St*ry Up*

Feathers from the Fire

by

Karlyn Pleasants, PsyD

Feathers from the Fire

Published by
Saved By Story Publishing, LLC
Prescott, AZ

www.SavedByStory.house

Edited by Joyce Walker
Cover by Alyssa Noelle Coelho
Interior Design by Dawn Teagarden
Photo/Illustrations by Özlem Dalyan

Library of Congress Control Number: 2023903333

Paperback ISBN: 979-8-9869578-7-6

eBook ISBN: 979-8-9869578-8-3

Printed in the United States of America

www.SavedByStory.house

To Linda
Thank you for watching over me.

Contents

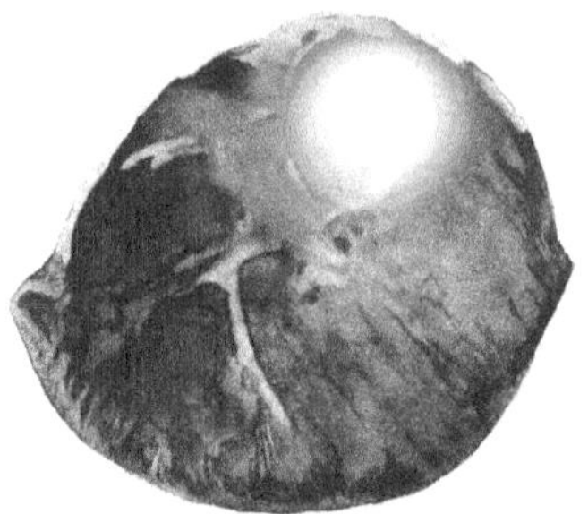

SINCE THE BEGINNING of time, we have searched for clues to illuminate the sometimes-shadowed path of meaning and, therefore, purpose.

Each quest is full of confusing twists and unexpected turns as we gather up and sort through the pieces of our lives until everything locks into place to reveal a bigger story waiting to be told.

It is a serendipitous gift to discover that our journeys are and always have been divinely intertwined with others', as if by the delicate hands of a universal intercessor.

Please tell me this is nothing to be concerned about, Klare silently implored the doctor she had yet to meet. She still hadn't worked out how to tell her husband, Nic, about the incident from last night or how she'd come to make this appointment. *Maybe I won't have to. If the doctor says it's nothing, just normal teenage behavior, problem solved. Move on. If it's something more… well, I can't think about that right now…*

A wisp of a woman introduced herself as Peggy and guided Klare and her son, Finn, to a small waiting room. Peggy's scrubs, the color of weak tea, and her brown wedge orthotics reminded Klare of being in a dental office. The space smelled sterile, and Klare half expected to hear torturesome drilling off in the distance. *Are we in the right place?* Looking around, she was about to ask when she noticed the groupings of diplomas and licenses hung haphazardly on the wall, listing Charles M. Myles, MD, as the lone recipient.

With a sigh, Klare took one of the four plastic office chairs, and Finn chose the one furthest away from her. *What's happened to my son?* she wondered as she watched him drop his unanimated body into his seat. Finn hadn't asked any questions on the way, but it was obvious they weren't going to his pediatrician's office. He had ignored her attempts to make small talk, and uncomfortable with the awkward silence, she stopped trying.

Generic office art of sepia-toned nature scenes dotted the stark white walls. Klare guessed the images of trees and sunsets were meant to be soothing and peaceful for those needing to frequent a psychiatrist's office, but the brown hues came off as lifeless and drab. *Depressing.* Beige and tan throw pillows that had long lost their fluff leaned sloppily against the plastic chair backs. An ordinary commercial wall clock ticked loudly, and Klare felt the acidic rise of doubt and anxiety. A withered, neglected plant sat lonely on a corner shelf. *How hard is it to water a plant?* She shook a few antacids into her palm, ironically noticing how the chalky pastel tablets were the only spots of color in this dreary room. A couple of old *Ohio* magazines from 2014 lay next to a dented tissue box, their once glossy covers marred with the sticky fingerprints of other hands just as sweaty as hers. With nothing else available to offer decent distraction, Klare trained her eyes on the single piece of silvery tinsel that wiggled lazily from the wall vent, indicating that the flat air in the room was indeed circulating.

You can't leave now, Klare warned herself. She closed her eyes, the hazy memory of running down the hall toward the scent of danger reminding her why this appointment was so important.

After gathering up the battered comforter along with its malodorous wreckage, Klare rushed to the trash bin on the side of the house to dispose of what oddly felt like tainted *evidence.* Once rid of its terrible weight, she warily went back inside.

For a split second, she thought about returning to Finn's room, but she found herself unable to take those steps, flooded by some inexplicable jumble of shame, fear, anger, and confusion that seemed to command she seek asylum in her bedroom. She left the door open a crack.

Just in case.

Her phone revealed a text from Nic that he would be even later than expected due to an emergency at the clinic. She was relieved. Somehow, she already knew she wouldn't be telling him about what had happened, at least not tonight.

Veins still racing with adrenalin, Klare paced back and forth, confined within the cage she had chosen, suddenly uncertain how to escape.

Nobody. There is literally nobody I can call right now.

"Well, there's…" whispered a voice that sounded like her own but not quite.

I am not calling her *again!* Klare indignantly rejected the suggestion her mind offered up. *I can hear it now: "I told you this would happen! If you'd done what I said, you wouldn't be in this mess to begin with!"* Then the lecture on the dangers of quacks, charlatans, and nosy neighbors would begin, and how the only safe bet is to not tell a soul. *"Keep it in the family,"* her mother had always said. *"It's no one's business but ours."*

"Okay, okay. Pull it together," Klare instructed herself and took a deep breath.

Okay, so I don't have anyone to talk to right now—maybe after I get some answers. Looking at her laptop, Klare settled slightly at the possibility of a way out of a conversation she didn't really want to have.

Browser open, she stared at the screen, her mind suddenly void of what she could possibly search for. It was as though her brain had gone dark, keeping her from seeing the words she couldn't bear acknowledging. Squeezing her eyes shut, she drew a long, slow breath and then another, until a few scattered ideas emerged.

Smoke? Smoking? No. Well, with smoke comes fire, but I didn't see an actual fire… I don't think. But there was smoke. And there wouldn't be any without fire.

Eyes open again, her quivering fingers hovered above the keyboard, some part of her strangely fearful that the keys would singe and scorch her fingertips upon their touch.

Oh, stop it. Squaring her shoulders, she risked the burn and began.

"Son possibly playing with fire" didn't quite cut it, yielding links for home fire-safety tips and articles about the dangers of children using lighters and matches unsupervised. Adding "teenage" to the search, Finn having just turned thirteen, produced very different results: teenage fire-starters… juveniles who damage property… professional help for behavioral problems. Her stomach gripped and twisted, and she heard her mother's voice of reprimand: *"What do you think you are doing? Are you trying to ruin his life? All our lives?"* She closed her eyes and internally turned her back on this familiar persecutor.

Klare could not bring herself to click on any of the links that suggested delinquency. That just simply wasn't her son. *Painfully shy, overly cautious, yes. But delinquent, not a chance.*

But…

She wasn't sure exactly what was in the pile she squashed, having ripped the comforter from Finn's bed in a flash of panic. But the smoke was real; the memory of it still lingered bitterly in her nose.

I need answers.

Opting for the seemingly softer *"behavior problems"* link, Klare shook her head at many of the "signs" listed—harming animals, stealing, drug use, hostility. None of these fit. She kept reading and came across a few that possibly could: isolation, secretiveness, trouble at school, property destruction. *Well, Finn didn't technically destroy any property, but that's only because I got there in time.* Klare shuddered at an image of what could have happened if she hadn't smelled the smoke or been home at the time. A painful cramp twisted in her belly, and Klare fought against the urge to abandon this agonizing search.

Then one sentence caught her eye: "If you are unsure but wondering if you or a loved one needs help, talking to a specialist could help put your mind at ease." She kept reading. A link for a "juvenile fire setting" program on the sidebar stole her attention. *Oh my God, is that actually a thing?* Her fatigued brain hurled an image of her brother, Scott, onto the screen of her mind's eye, and she recoiled, instinctively squeezing her eyes against this random and quite unwelcome vision.

"Ugh!" Klare grumbled. *How irritating.*

She opened her eyes to continue her research. More clicks revealed a pdf on youth fire setting, an advertisement for a juvenile fire safety program, yet another about arson awareness. *Arson? Ridiculous.* She sighed and pressed her hand against her complaining stomach.

"An assessment is important to determine the underlying reason your child may be displaying behavioral problems," one article stated.

Klare stopped and affirmed the path before her. *The underlying reason. That's it.* She scanned the list of possibilities, divided by "nonpathological causes," such as curiosity or a cry for help, and "pathological causes," like delinquency and psychosis. Gritting through another nauseating spasm, she homed in on "*curiosity*" as the least disagreeable suggestion. *Maybe that's it… maybe he was just being curious? About what though? What do they mean by "a cry for help"? Help for what?* The face of her brother materialized once more.

Stop it! Klare shook the image away and straightened her spine. *This isn't about him; this is about Finn.*

Following the "for more information" link, Klare finally landed on a list of juvenile behavioral specialists, sorted by location. Dizzying vertigo mottled her vision as she sifted through the list, the shockingly frequent "psychiatric hospital" references disintegrating in the blur. She took some sips of her flat, stale tea and willed herself not to slam her laptop closed while she waited for her vision to clear.

The closest was nearly four hours away. That would take all day, and how would she explain that to Nic, to Finn? While there were no immediate local experts, a cursory search revealed several psychiatrists who advertised working with children and adolescents, and Klare decided that would have to do. *This can't wait.* Moving down the list, one doctor in nearby Akron listed a 24-hour emergency number to call. Ten minutes later, she had an appointment set for first thing in the morning.

"Mrs. Driscoll? Finneas? Dr. Myles is ready to see you now. Please, follow me."

The pair followed the soft-soled Peggy down a barren hallway. Finn was ushered into a small room while Klare was motioned into an adjoining one. She felt uneasy at the separation but assumed it was because the doctor would want to talk to her without Finn present. She stood alone in the quiet space, looking through a thick-paned tinted window that divided the two offices. Klare could see Finn and hear the quiet shuffles as he settled into one of the flimsy plastic chairs. He ignored the magazines and half-assembled puzzle on the narrow coffee table and instead closed his eyes and folded his arms over his middle. The bulky sweatshirt he'd taken to wearing, even in this balmy weather, made him look even smaller than he already was.

"We can see and hear him, but he can't see or hear us." She startled at the sound of his voice and glanced up; she hadn't heard the doctor come in. "This is a two-way mirror. A discreet way to observe without being so obvious. Most parents like to keep an eye on their child during meetings."

Dr. Chuck Myles looked nothing like his picture on the website. That doctor looked poised and distinguished. This one, all gray and puffy, had to turn sideways to squeeze his fleshy form between the wall and his desk and scoot the distance to the worn leather chair that groaned under the weight of his bulk, the effort clearly winding him. Of the two small chairs opposite the doctor's desk, Klare chose the one closest to the mirror, and Finn. She waited while the doctor caught his breath and flipped through the forms she had filled out online. Time had not been kind to Dr. Myles.

"So, how can I help you today?" the doctor asked, finally.

Klare's right eye twitched as she wondered again if she was in the wrong place. *I'm not here to check out a library book or order a coffee. Did he even read the forms?* She pulled her shoulders down from her ears, took a breath to steady herself, and peeked over at her son to help her fight the urge to walk out.

When she didn't respond promptly, Dr. Myles looked back at the contents in the folder on his desk and offered, "You listed 'concerns about recent behavior'." He chuckled. "I assume you mean about your son and not yourself?" More chuckling. "Can you give me some examples?"

Klare thought, *That's a bold assumption. And not funny.*

Unclenching her teeth, Klare replied. "Sure. I wrote it on the form there. Finn, my son, had an episode of sorts a while back and, in my opinion, he hasn't really been the same since."

"An episode?"

Yeah, he definitely didn't read it.

"Yes. In May. We were at lunch—Finn, myself, and my husband. Finn got up to use the restroom and after about five or so minutes, my husband went to check on him and he wasn't there. We looked all over and ended up finding him a few blocks away. Apparently, he had become disoriented and wandered off. We took him to the ER to make sure he was okay. They ruled it dehydration."

When Klare didn't continue, the doctor asked, "Was he okay? Hurt?"

Klare shrugged and thought, *No, he wasn't okay. He's still not okay. I'm not okay. Nothing is.*

"No, he wasn't hurt," she offered instead of sharing her true thoughts.

Dr. Myles probed, slightly more gently this time. "Besides the dehydration, has anything else happened?"

Klare scoffed silently and tried to answer with what she thought the doctor needed to know. She felt herself teetering between two parts of herself—one part that wanted to concede to what her mother would be saying right now, *"They're all swindlers just looking to make a buck,"* and running out of there, and the other part that wanted—needed—another opinion. "When we got there, we looked him over and didn't see any signs of injury or anything like that, but we took him to the ER just to be sure. My husband said with severe dehydration, you can sometimes see confusion and disorientation."

The doctor bobbed his head and looked like he was concentrating. "Do you have some other thoughts about what might have happened?"

Here it goes.

"When we found him, he seemed to have passed out. He came to, but was almost… incoherent. He was mumbling and looking around as if there were someone else there. We reassured him that it was just us. We thought that would help him settle down, but it actually seemed to upset him. He started crying and shaking his head, like he didn't believe us. After that, he clammed up and didn't say anything else about it."

"Has he brought this up since or said anything more about that day?" Dr. Myles inquired.

"He says he doesn't remember, but honestly, I don't believe him. He wouldn't share anything at the ER. He says the last thing he remembers is heading to the bathroom and then us shaking him awake when we found him."

"Okay." The doctor jotted a couple of notes, his bloated face pensive under his scraggly salt-and-pepper brows. "Why don't you believe him?"

Defenses rising, Klare reminded herself again that she needed answers today. She was scared about exposing her son in a way that her mother warned would be ruinous, not just for him but for the entire family.

"Well, when he came around, he was *really* distraught. He looked… *worried.* It seemed to me like he wasn't just looking, but like he was *searching* for someone or something that wasn't there. We asked him about it later, but he denied it." Klare looked through the window at Finn, who hadn't moved. "Can dehydration cause hallucinations?"

Dr. Myles paused to give Klare a moment as she took some sips from her water bottle, hands trembling as she tried to replace the lid. "Mrs. Driscoll, this sounds like a very scary situation. It's rare, but yes, sometimes one can experience hallucinations and delirium in cases of extreme dehydration. Have you noticed anything else with Finn that makes you wonder about hallucinations?"

Despite the care apparent in the doctor's voice, Klare's gut seized. A hot flash of fear rose in her chest, and the veins in her temples throbbed. She suddenly felt *in trouble*—a sickening shamefulness discordant with the doctor's reasonable query. She flashed back to the ER doctor's asking Finn a series of nonsensical questions, to which Klare had felt maliciously judged and wildly offended, interrogating the doctor right back. "Do you ask *everyone* these questions? What are you saying? That my child is *mentally ill?*" Nic's reassurances that it was standard screening protocol for anyone presenting with Finn's symptoms had done nothing to assuage her bitter umbrage.

Answers. Remember, you're here for answers.

"He just hasn't been the same since then. He's always been quiet, sensitive, and tends to keep to himself, but since that episode, he's been withdrawn and doesn't engage much. He seems lost in thought, like he's daydreaming but not aware of it. And then last night, I think, um, I think he might have been playing around with fire in his room. I smelled smoke and rushed in there, and he had a pile of things on the floor… I just stamped it out and got rid of it, so nothing really happened, but he's pretty much shut down since then. Hasn't said two words." Glancing over to Finn, still lifeless and limp, Klare's heart squeezed with dread. "I don't know what's going on."

"A fire, hmmmm…" The doctor's voice turned somber and trailed off into silence as if to confirm Klare's worst fears. She didn't realize until this breath-stealing moment how much she'd been hanging on to the hope that the doctor would dismiss this part of the story as inconsequential, as unrealistic as that now seemed. *No, this can't be.*

After several painful moments of watching Dr. Myles nod his head in pensive consideration, Klare cleared her throat. *I can't stand this.*

Delivered more like statements, Dr. Myles asked, "Why don't we bring Finn in and see if we can get him to open up a little? Fill us in on what he thinks about all this?" He planted his swollen hands on his desktop and hefted himself out of his chair to retrieve Finn.

I can't believe this is happening. Klare held back tears of disbelief and wondered for a moment if any of this was even real.

Finn slumped down in the chair next to his mother's and resumed his slouched, arms-crossed, head-down brooding. The part of his face not obscured by his hood sagged with a sullenness Klare didn't recognize in her typically mild-mannered son. Shamefully embarrassed over her son's disheveled presentation and the dark circles under his eyes, her belly lurched and her chest flushed with heat. *This guy must be wondering what kind of mother I am.*

Dr. Myles asked Finn about his hobbies and interests, his best subjects in school, and his favorite books and movies, clearly trying to warm him up for the bigger questions to come. Dread invaded her body as she watched her son simply ignore the doctor's bids to engage.

"Finn, please answer the doctor's questions." Her voice was more disapproving than she intended. "He's just trying to help."

Finn lifted his weary eyes to meet hers, letting his cold stare linger for an extra beat before lowering his gaze again to his lap.

I don't even know this child. This isn't my son, she thought to herself with a flash of fearful irritation.

After several more minutes and just as many failed attempts to connect with Finn, Dr. Myles ceded defeat. He thanked Finn for his time and invited him to return to the adjoining room.

Klare watched her son pause and look through the two-way mirror, then turn back to her for the briefest moment. She swore she could read Finn's reproachful thoughts slipping out through his flat, vacant eyes, "*How could you?*" He turned his back again and left. Sharp beaks of guilt and fear pecked hungrily at Klare's suffering heart.

Dr. Myles sighed and looked at Klare with a sympathy that seemed to say, *I'm sorry, Ma'am. This is really bad.*

Peggy escorted Klare and Finn back down the hall, her soft words floating past Klare's ears and evaporating into the stale ether. Klare gripped the cool, glossy file folder of brochures and information the doctor had given her, barely conscious of her feet moving her toward the exit.

Peggy opened the door for them and whispered in a sympathetic tone, "Please don't hesitate to call us if you have any questions, okay?"

As soon as they were in the car, Finn curled himself into the corner of the backseat, pulled his hood down over his face, and collapsed into sleep. Klare sat still, trying to steady herself so she could drive safely. Snippets of what Dr. Myles said after Finn had left the room already haunted her: "*extremely concerning… dangerous… formal evaluation… assess for deeper underlying issues… more serious conditions… possibly command hallucinations… a symptom of schizophrenia… there are certain medications available for…*" Unable to assemble the pieces of what happened in this clandestine appointment, let alone how she was going to tell Nic about it—*if* she was going to, all she could do was stuff the file folder into her bag and start the ignition.

2

A thin stream of sweat trickled down Finn's back. He knew the heavy, hooded sweatshirt didn't help, but he didn't have the energy, or the care, to take it off. The atypically sticky July air, in perfect concert with his suffocated and smothered soul, corroborated the misery of this terrible day. He coiled himself into the car behind the driver's seat—a more difficult angle for his mother to see him.

Finn had felt himself collapsing bit by bit over the past few days, pieces of himself disintegrating and falling away like pebbles on an eroding cliff. He had been certain things could not get any worse: the girl was gone. Not just gone, but dead. His once constant and resonant companions had gone cold and silent. He no longer had the community center—no Zeb, no Cassie, no Koko. His father was pretty much gone all the time, and his mother had become someone he no longer recognized. No way it could get any worse. But then it did.

On the folder his mother crammed into her bag, the words "*Comprehensive Psychiatric Evaluation*" glared in sickish red ink. He didn't know exactly what that meant, but he knew enough to know it wasn't good. *Psychiatric. Like crazy, mental, schizophrenic.*

He pulled the hood down over his feverish head and closed his eyes. *She thinks I'm crazy. So does that doctor. Maybe Dad does too, and that's why he's never home.*

Finn felt for the small stone that hung from a thin leather cord around his neck. It had been lifeless and dull the last few days, but he could not bring himself to take it off, to give up hope. While it seemed impossible that things could ever be good again, he just couldn't concede. *It is part of me, even if it's dead now too.*

The stone had gone cold the day his mother told him he would not be returning to the community center, the very day he'd decided he was finally ready to tell Zeb about the girl.

But everything changed. He tightened his eyes against the confusing memory of a day that was dreadful in more ways than one.

Finn had turned thirteen in May, and the family had celebrated by attending a community gathering at Duncan Plaza in downtown Massillon and then going out to lunch. They had participated in the local gardening society's event to plant red begonias, white cyclamen, and blue hydrangeas in preparation for Memorial Day. Everyone was happy and, after a couple of hours of digging and planting, famished. Finn rarely accepted his athletic dad's invitation to race, but it seemed like a fun thing to do, and the café was only a few blocks away. Between the warm weather and the sprint to lunch, Finn arrived flushed and out of breath. He excused himself to splash some water on his face while his parents grabbed a table on the patio.

The cool water helped, and he felt better. Tawny eyes stared back at him in the mirror above the sink. *Thirteen. I don't look any different.* He shrugged and turned to join his parents when a faint whisper slipped into his ear—a soft and faraway voice, barely perceptible. He stopped to listen more closely, but it was gone. *That was weird*, he thought, and looked around, although he knew he was alone. Stepping outside, he heard it again. Still far off, but a little clearer now. Not just a voice. A girl's voice. She was singing.

Finn did not recognize the voice or the lilting melody she intoned, but somewhere deep down, he had a peculiar sense that he *knew* her. A sea-green shimmer crystalized at the edge of his vision, and with it came a warm, humming vibration that wrapped around his slight five-foot frame. Noises from the street and the café faded to a low muffle and then vanished beneath her soft song. The glittery emerald aura enfolded Finn in an airy bubble that seemed to lift him off his feet and absorb him inside, as if drawn into a cocoon. Within, weightless, he was held, suspended in what he could only describe as *one*. He could tell he was drifting. No, more like he was being carried. She was singing to him and, mesmerized by her honeyed harmony, he allowed himself to be led.

He was uncertain how long he had been with her when his mother's panicked cries pierced the cottony sea-green cocoon while his father's clammy hands squeezed and snatched him from that sacred space. *No!* He did not want to leave. He wanted to stay swathed in the iridescence, to hear more of her sweet song, to see her. But in one terrible instant, she was gone. Lifted, his breath found his lungs with a force that caused his eyes to snap open. As the shouts and touches of his parents burrowed into his ears and body, he looked around, desperately scanning for any glimpse of her. He could feel her lingering presence but knew, in his aching heart, that she was no longer there. Finn clutched at his chest and gulped lungfuls of air. "*No! No! No!*" rang over and over in his ears, but he had no idea these were his own cries.

By the time the doctor entered the curtained alcove in the emergency room, the atmosphere of crisis had simmered down to a tempered concern. Pumped full of fluids and electrolytes, Finn frequently needed the bathroom, which the nurse said was a good sign. The volumes of blood they took from his tiny veins evidenced no infection or sign of toxicity. A meticulous head-to-toe examination revealed no physical injury or trauma. In an abundance of caution, a cranial CT scan was ordered, explained as an added screening measure for inexplicable fainting, seizures, or sudden behavioral changes. The scans came back clear, and the doctor said she only had a few more questions before they could discuss releasing Finn.

Dr. Andor was an exceptionally tall woman who resembled a swan in both appearance and movement. A head of feathery white hair sat atop her long, thin neck from which hung a delicate gold chain that displayed a single gold feather. Her voice was gentle and her limbs graceful as she pulled up a swivel stool, smoothed out her long white lab coat, and nestled into the seat next to Finn's bed for her final examination.

"So far, Finneas, everything suggests nothing serious and probably nothing more than a nasty little bout of dehydration. Did the nurse explain what that means?" Dr. Andor asked in a petite but lively European accent.

Finn's dad, also a physician, jumped in to assure that not only had nurse Stella been exceptionally attentive, but she had also thoroughly explained all the exams and reasons for them along the way.

Finn was glad his dad was taking the lead because it meant fewer questions for him to have to answer.

"That is excellent to hear," the doctor replied, listening to Nic but keeping her eyes on Finn. "I have a few more questions for you. Then we can talk about getting you home, okay, Finneas? By the way, you have a lovely name."

Finn offered a weak smile and nothing more. He liked Dr. Andor. She had a calm and gentle energy about her, and although comforted by this, he didn't want to answer any more questions. Nic had fielded most of the inquiries about the who, when, what, and how details. No one really pressed Finn beyond his responses to what he remembered *(not much)* and how he felt *(fine, just tired)*. But he had a lot of feelings that he did not want to say: curious, wishing, happy, wanting, aching, miserable… and loved. And many others for which he had no words.

When they had first arrived at the ER, and after he'd been placed in his assigned examination bay, Finn could not help listening for *her*. He carried with him the faint memory of her voice and halfway expected it to re-emerge. He hadn't actually *seen* her as much as he had *felt* her, but he knew if she appeared, he would recognize her instantly.

Instead, he saw his mom's pinched and nervous face that flared a dangerous purple. A couple of times, she followed Finn's searching eyes and, seeing nothing, curtly asked him who he was looking for. But something about her clipped tone and stiff body language did not convey curiosity; it communicated something very different—something that made his breath catch in his throat and his heart hurt. *Suspicion.* Finn instinctively refrained from any more searching; he didn't like seeing his mom this way.

Dr. Andor continued in her gentle lilt. "Finneas, I'd like to ask you some questions that may seem rather silly or strange, but they are simply to make sure that your sharp brain is working exactly the way it's supposed to, okay?"

Finn nodded and, without a single hitch, quietly named the year, season, and date, repeated back words spoken a few moments prior, counted in reverse, and precisely folded a piece of paper according to the doctor's instructions. Finn was pleased that Dr. Andor seemed pleased. His mom, however, did not seem to share that sentiment. In fact, with every question, his usually easygoing mother became more and more agitated, although he could not fathom why. She brusquely interrupted the doctor and asked, although it sounded more like an accusation, the point of "these ridiculous questions."

Nic replied before Dr. Andor could. "Klare, this is standard protocol to rule out any cognitive impairment. It's called a mental status exam, and it's super routine, and obviously Finn is fine. What are you so concerned about?" Finn watched his dad tug on his earlobe.

Klare snapped, "Impairment?! Mental?!" then turned on the doctor. "Are you saying that our son has some sort of mental illness? Why don't you just say that instead of slipping in those weird questions about dates and what city he lives in? That just seems really odd and—"

It was Nic's turn to snap back. "Klare! What on earth has gotten into you? I just told you this is routine and standard. No one is saying anything about mental illness!"

Already taken aback by his mother's frightfully perplexing demeanor, Finn was further puzzled by his typically docile dad's sharp tone. *I've never seen them like this.* Anxiety squeezed his belly.

Finn watched his parents in this foreign, strange dance while Nic apologized to Dr. Andor, who then patted Finn's hand. "Excellent, Finneas, that was spot-on." She rose from her stool. "Well, I believe we are ready to send him home. I'll get the discharge paperwork and some instructions for follow-up."

Suddenly, Finn wasn't so sure he wanted to go home. He couldn't keep his eyes from his mother's angry face and the chill that hung in the air, even after Nic and Klare stepped into the hall to continue their heated conversation. Nurse Stella came in to remove Finn's IV and give him a clear bag containing his clothes and shoes.

The bag of rumpled garments felt like a sad reminder of how the day had crumbled. All traces of *her*—the glow he had felt inside, her sweet voice, her invisible presence—were gone. Finn was miserably back in his body, tired and lonely, and his mind could not erase the image of his mother's hard, accusatory eyes.

Twisted into an impossibly small knot and wedged as far down as he could get without being on the floor, Finn cracked one eye open to catch a glimpse of the side of his mother's face. Her eyes were vacant… distant.

What happened to her? He used to be able to talk to her, but that vanished that day in the emergency room. *She hasn't been the same. But maybe today, I finally got my answer. She thinks I'm crazy—that there's something wrong with me. And there is no one to talk to about it, especially now that I lost Zeb. I know he could have helped me, but that chance is gone now.*

THE PSYCHE'S CLEVER capacity for surreptitiously sending us into well-conditioned routines that shield us from any number of unpleasantries can produce an almost trancelike state of oblivion that may require a blaring horn, a forceful shake, or sometimes a surprise encounter to break the spell and guide one back into reality.

Groaning, Nic let out one of those *it hurts but in a good way* moans as he switched to his right side for another standing quad stretch, his left arm steadying him against the kitchen counter. He'd pushed himself extra hard during his lunchtime run, hoping to burn off some of the irritation left over from his morning argument with his wife.

Surprised to have found the house empty, he couldn't remember what time Klare had said Finn's appointment was, but he'd assumed it was in the morning and that they would be home when he arrived.

She would have called if it was something worse than a cold, he had thought. But she didn't, and when his calls to her went unanswered, an apprehensive pit opened inside his sternum.

He stared out the small kitchen window, waiting uneasily for his wife's car to pull into the driveway.

She would have called. He tried to reassure himself and pulled irritatingly at his earlobe. *Damn tinnitus.* The near-constant peal had ratcheted up after his and Klare's tense exchange about taking Finn to his pediatrician, and it had only gotten worse as the day progressed.

She would have called.

Thinking about his wife's uncharacteristic behavior of late, Nic felt a disturbing reality wiggle its way into his mind.

But she didn't.

The moment his son came through the door, head hidden under the heavy hood of a thick sweatshirt Nic recognized as his, he knew something was seriously wrong.

"Hey!" Nic called out to his son. "Is everything okay? How are you feeling?" A faint panic bubbled inside.

Finn halted midstride and flashed the briefest of glances at Nic, but not so brief that Nic didn't catch his son's red-rimmed, hollow eyes and his grim, downturned mouth. Without a response, Finn continued his course up the stairs and disappeared down the hall to his bedroom. Nic half expected a door slam, which would have been a first for his mild-natured son, but then again, that look on Finn's face was certainly a first. When no slam resounded, Nic turned to his wife with his mouth agape.

"What happened?!" he demanded. "What was that? What's wrong?" The piercing ring in Nic's ears and the building pressure of panic threatened to overrun his senses. His mind could not reconcile the image of his son's dejected face with that of his wife nonchalantly opening the pantry door and beginning to arrange the cans to perfectly align their labels.

"Klare! What are you doing?! Stop it with the cans!" Nic felt like he had entered some upside-down bizarro world where nothing made sense. He watched incomprehensively as his wife continued classifying containers, now by content, as if he weren't there.

The aural scream erupted, a volcano inside his eardrums. Utterly stunned and nearly immobilized by both the blast and Klare's outlandish behavior, Nic froze for a moment, then turned and made for the front door.

I need to run.

"Oh, shit! I'm so sorry!" Nic stumbled backward after hard-clipping the cinder block shoulder of the fellow runner heading the opposite direction. When he recovered from the recoil, the last thing he expected to see was his best friend, Dennis, doubled over in laughter.

"Dude, I saw you coming down the block but didn't think you'd run right into me," Dennis razzed in his deep baritone voice, rubbing his left shoulder from the impact. "You looked a million miles away."

"I guess I was… wait, what are you doing up here? I thought you had something at the club." Nic mirrored his friend, massaging the spot of the collision.

They ran together several times a week, usually at lunch, down at the track of Dennis' training facility, but he'd canceled that afternoon for work.

"Yeah, it ended early. I thought you would have already run today. Otherwise I would have called. Sorry about that."

Dennis was a towering six-foot-five first-round draft pick who never made it to the NFL. A rollover crash at the end of his final year in college cost him his right arm, and no matter how much of a fan favorite, no team was going to pick up a one-armed quarterback. While such a tragedy would have sent most into dour despair over the loss of would-be greatness and fame, that simply wasn't the way of this gentle giant. Dennis was a walking paradox: a kind and sensitive soul encased within a chiseled, intimidating exterior.

"No worries," Nic sighed. "I went earlier today. This is round two."

"Hmmm. That bad, huh?" Dennis was aware that things at home hadn't been going well for Nic, who periodically confided about Klare's recent standoffishness and Finn's continued avoidance.

They moved off the main path to an unoccupied bench and took a seat. Dennis listened closely as Nic explained what had happened only minutes earlier.

"What would they be hiding?" Dennis wondered out loud and then continued even when he noticed Nic stiffen at the comment. "I'm not suggesting anything malicious, Nic, but I've seen this. When I was a kid. With my own kids. Kids are protective of their parents. They've got this built-in radar for sensing when something is wrong and will do all sorts of things to take the pressure off. Distract, overdo it, underdo it, even take the stress on themselves. Anything to ease the burden and not make matters worse. Question is, what's happening that has Finn avoiding you like the plague and Klare acting like nothing's going on?"

Those words… "*anything to ease the burden*"… clashed in Nic's head like a cymbal.

I did that, Nic thought. *I did it all the time. For my mother… when Elem was sick.*

A nauseating wave rolled through Nic's belly.

"Oh my god, do you think it's Finn? She took him to the doctor today. But she would have told me if something was wrong. Right?" Nic despised the doubt and uncertainty evident in his words and even more palpable in his heart.

"Only one way to find out, dude," Dennis said. "Off you go."

When he arrived home, both Finn and Klare were in their respective beds reading, obviously well enough to suggest there was no immediate health crisis. He bid them both an early good night, opted to sleep on the couch downstairs, and resolved to talk to his family first thing in the morning before Finn, if he was feeling better, left for the community center.

Klare knew her uncharacteristic snubbing of her husband's questions was not only mean but also not the kind of conduct he would just let drop.

At least I have a little more time to think, she thought with a small, shame-tinged measure of relief.

Still unsure how on earth she was going to tell Nic about what happened in Finn's room, Klare revisited for what seemed like the hundredth time the surreal memory of the baffling event that occurred barely twenty-four hours ago.

Klare shuttered as another chill rippled up her spine and landed at the base of her neck. She sighed and stretched, irritated at her inability to get through a single page of her book. It was an uncanny sensation, like her body had developed a mind of its own, controlled by some invisible operator maniacally flipping switches and mashing the buttons of her nervous system at random.

It was exhausting.

Solitude had always been her go-to option for recharging, but recently, it had been a requirement—a ravenous need to help her get through each depleting day. Glancing at his side of the bed, she was glad it was Nic's late night at the clinic, although recently, he'd been running late most nights.

I love him, she thought. *But his sidelong glances and questions about my day are simply too much.*

She returned to her book and willed her brain to refocus on the page.

There it is again! Dammit! Goose bumps crawled across her arms while the tiny hairs on the back of her neck sizzled. She slammed her book closed and took a deep, jagged breath to ease the clutch in her belly. Reaching for the Costco-size bottle of Tums on her nightstand, Klare froze midmove as her internal alarm system blared, sirens deafening and inexplicably familiar.

Her body leapt off the bed before her brain registered the movement. She disappeared for a moment, only to materialize on the other side of her bedroom door. At once both in her body and outside of it, she watched herself as if on an old, choppy film reel, in a scene both novel and known. She was running through a hazy hallway, gasping and confused. Her hallway, but not hers. Doors where there weren't supposed to be any. Shaggy rust-orange carpet even though they had gone with the soft-gray Berber years ago. The smell of smoke infiltrating her sinuses— not the cozy fireplace kind or the nostalgic scent of an autumn firepit, but acrid and nauseating and wrong. She watched the damp, trembling hands that were both hers and not hers twist the doorknob to her son's bedroom and throw the door open, nearly tearing it off its hinges.

Klare's eyes could not absorb the incomprehensible details of the scene laid out before her. Her invisible operator pulled the levers, controlling the limbs of her paralyzed body. She grabbed the boy—her boy? And in one perfectly choreographed motion, Klare flung him out into the hall behind her and whipped the comforter off the bed to smother the dangerous pile assembled on his floor.

She stomped and battered the blanket, all feet and fists, with a superhuman force that reverberated down to the foundation of the house. Her still-ringing ears were unable to hear the guttural noises coming from her throat, but the shrill, panicked screams coming from behind her broke through to arrest her fixation: "MOM! WHAT ARE YOU DOING? STOP IT! STOP IT!" As the voice she barely recognized shrieked at her, she slammed back into her body, finding herself on hands and knees, sweaty and panting. She looked behind her to see the tear-streaked, horrified face of her thirteen-year-old son begging her to stop.

5

Habitually the first one awake, Nic started a pot of coffee, peeked in on his softly snoring wife, and made for Finn's room.

This was a good idea—taking the day off. He wasn't necessarily looking forward to confronting his family's peculiar behavior from the day before, let alone the past few weeks, but he felt hopeful that it could be the start of getting things back to normal.

Stopping at Finn's door, he paused, reminding himself that Finn was a teenager now and would probably appreciate the respect of a knock first. The muscles in his neck tensed, sparking new life into the tinny aural whine when Finn didn't respond to the second knock. He took a steadying breath, knocked a third time, and let himself in. An invisible fist grabbed hold of his heart and squeezed.

Finn wasn't there.

He rushed in, leapt over the bed, and found Finn on the floor facing the wall, curled in the fetal position and bundled in the same gray sweatshirt from the day before. Nic's body moved before his mind would even let him consider the kind of thought associated with a parent's worst nightmare and roughly scooped Finn up from the floor.

Startled by such a violent grab, Finn let out a sharp shriek and flailed his arms wildly, as if pushing away a malicious perpetrator.

Startled himself by his son's outburst and at the same time overcome with relief, Nic stepped back, his arms up in surrender. "Hey, hey, hey," Nic stammered. "It's okay. It's just me. I'm sorry…"

As Finn's wild eyes met his father's concerned regard, he instantly softened and his chin began to tremble.

"Hey, now. Come here." Nic knelt and pulled his son toward him, sliding the hood back a few inches off Finn's forehead. His heart seized again at the close-up look of his son's swollen eyes and the plummy smears beneath them. Pushing the hood all the way back, he lifted Finn from the floor to the bed.

"Hey." Nic brushed sticky wisps of hair from his son's clammy forehead and kept his hand in place, checking for a fever. "Are you okay? I know you saw Dr. Hanada. What did he say? What happened?" Nic's nerves wavered in anticipation of his son's reply while at the same time wondering why, if Finn was this sick, Klare hadn't told him.

"Nothing." The flat tone of Finn's whisper was almost as dismal as his expression.

What the hell is going on here? Nic nervously thought back to his chat with Dennis.

Finn was naturally sensitive and cautious, but especially so lately, and Nic knew he needed to tread lightly. "It's clearly not 'nothing,'" he said softly. "Did you have a nightmare? Did something happen with you and Mom? I feel like the odd man out here. Tell me, what's going on?"

Finn remained silent, but his tired and sore eyes revealed the poorly patched cracks of an internal dam that he could no longer keep from leaking. Sensing the fragility of the moment, Nic slowed and deepened his breathing, intuitively inviting his son's breath to sync with his own. He scooted an inch closer and rested his hand reassuringly on his son's shoulder.

"We didn't go to Dr. Hanada's. We saw a different doctor," Finn whispered.

The faint flutter in Nic's chest became a noisy flapping, and the high-pitched peal in his left ear rose another octave. He stayed silent, consciously keeping his face curious. "Oh yeah?"

After a noble yet unsuccessful attempt to stay the flow, the cloudburst came. Tears of desperation and apologies poured forth, gushing with random, confusing words like *dangerous* and *sick*. Nic strained to listen through the deafening din within his inner ear, keeping his breath steady while his heart gasped and pinched. The intensity of Finn's remorse and ramblings about mistakes and misunderstandings was almost too much for Nic to bear.

What is happening here?! Why is he apologizing? Nic folded his son into his arms, pulling him close in a way Finn rarely allowed, and rocked him until the shudders stopped and his muscles relaxed enough to fully receive his father's support. Nic willed his love to envelop his son and take away his anguish as he whispered words of tender reassurance into Finn's ear.

When Finn dropped into the heavy aftermath of emotional release, Nic sat still and patient, waiting for his son to signal what he might need next. Moments later, Finn said he wanted to take a shower and rest, and Nic agreed that was a great idea.

"I'll check in on you in a bit, okay, buddy?" Nic rose to give Finn some space, and his son responded with a tiny nod.

Obviously, he's not going to the center today.

The sweet gratitude cushioned deep in his chest for this rare and tender moment with his son was not immune from the hot, fiery sparks of betrayal that peppered him from the inside out. With the shrill inner siren blaring and his chest afire, Nic closed his son's door and set out to find his wife, only half noticing that Finn's comforter wasn't on his bed.

He found her at the kitchen table, cradling a cup of coffee and rubbing the sleep from her eyes. Nic slipped into the chair opposite her, noticing the crumbs and dried spills smeared across the typically spotless tabletop. He focused on the lingering warmth of his moment with Finn to help tether him to what mattered most right now—the welfare of their son. The burning questions about his wife's unfathomable deceit would have to wait.

"Who is Dr. Myles?" His steely voice sounded like someone else's.

Nic watched the vertical lines between Klare's eyebrows deepen and her blinks become more rapid, as if trying to remember the name of some long-forgotten acquaintance. The klaxon continued its interior scream as an implausible thought occurred to him: *Is she trying to come up with another lie to cover this up? This is not my wife.*

"Klare, look at me. Who is Dr. Myles and why did you take Finn to see him?"

After a pause long enough to nearly snap Nic's already-fraying nerves, she spoke. "Well, the other night, uh, well, I smelled smoke and found Finn on the floor of his room. I think he was starting a fire, and—"

"We'll come back to that," Nic tersely interrupted. "Tell me about the appointment." The flicker in her eyes confirmed his suspicion that it hadn't occurred to her that he had also learned about what had transpired in Finn's room.

Staring into her mug, she continued. "He's a psychiatrist who works with adolescents. I found him online, and he could get us in right away. And I thought it would be best to talk to someone about Finn's symptoms. Get an opinion or something. Playing with fire is serious, Nic, and I just didn't—"

Nic interrupted again, unable to defer his ire about her deception, his words red-hot slashes of anger. "Symptoms? What are you talking about? And by the way, Finn didn't start a fire. But before we get to *that*, how in the hell did you think it was okay to go and talk to someone like that without telling me?"

"I don't know… I just…"

"You don't know how you thought it was okay not to talk to me about this, or you don't know why you would take him to a psychiatrist without telling me? I don't believe that you don't know, Klare. I think you know a lot and you've been keeping it from me." An invisible hand clamped around his throat, straining his voice and volume. When her head dropped, he leaned back in his seat, forcing himself to calm down. "Look. I just want to understand what happened yesterday. Let's start there."

Keep it together, Nic commanded himself. *This is about Finn right now, not you.*

Klare took a long, steadying breath and began again. "Between what happened after Finn's birthday and then what happened the other night, I don't know. I just got concerned they might be connected. Finn's been distant, staring off into space, isolating. I was already worried these were signs of something more serious, and when I smelled the smoke and saw him in his room, I just lost it. Nic, what if he had hurt himself?"

"Klare, I literally cannot believe what you're saying right now. Why haven't you told me about any of this?" He let out a heavy sigh. "What did this guy say?"

"He suggested we take Finn somewhere to have him formally evaluated. He said some of Finn's symptoms suggest he might be hearing voices. Voices telling him to do things. Like start a fire. He called them *command hallucinations* and said they can be very dangerous. It didn't help that Finn would not even look at the doctor, let alone answer a single question. The doctor said being that disengaged and nonresponsive could be a sign of psychosis. He called it *internal preoccupation*. He gave me some brochures to read over and…"

Is she seriously going to blame Finn for this? Trembling now, it took all Nic had not to unleash on his wife the tangle of fear, fury, and panic churning inside. He closed his eyes and imagined his feet glued to the floor—a strategy he'd mastered as a kid to help him stay present when painful emotions threatened to carry him away.

"Please tell me you did not make an appointment to take him in for some evaluation," Nic asked, as measured as he could muster.

"No! No… I don't know what to do, Nic. I'm afraid something is wrong with him, but I'm also afraid of what happens to people who are labeled and treated like mental patients. Like they're monsters and dangerous and—"

Nic yelled, "Klare! Stop it!" then lowered his volume, aware that voices carry. "Mental patients? Monsters? Honestly, I have no idea what to make of this. You can't seriously be thinking Finn is dangerous. And how could you not have told me about this? You just haul him in front of some shrink who says our son might be some unhinged psychotic kid? What the hell!"

"He didn't hear that part!" she yelled. "He was in another room when the doctor said all that. Then he gave me some brochures, and I just grabbed Finn and left. He didn't hear any of that, I swear."

Despair resounded in his wife's voice.

"Okay, I need a minute." Nic exhaled and tried to settle the tornado of thoughts and feelings and sounds wreaking havoc inside.

I knew something was going on, but this is unbelievable.

"Well, Finn heard a lot more than you think he did. What did you tell him about the reason for going to that appointment? He thought he was going to see Dr. Hanada."

A heavy cloak of shame enshrouded Klare, its weight causing her face to sag and her shoulders to slump forward, her elbows the only thing propping her upright at the table. Through the storm still raging inside, Nic felt a sliver of something soft break through. As angry as he was with her, he could also tell she was suffering. He recalled Dennis' words, "*ease the burden.*"

But what burden?

Klare's voice was now small and thin. "Not much. I just said we were going to see a new doctor. I'm sorry, Nic. Saying this out loud sounds ridiculous. I'm embarrassed."

"Klare, Finn was a mess up there just now. He was apologizing all over the place, as if he were the one who did something wrong. He told me about the other night, and he didn't start a fire. You totally misjudged that, and it sounds like you didn't even ask him what he was doing. Then you drag him in front of some shrink without even telling him why, making him think he's in trouble or that there's something wrong with him. This is not okay, Klare. Not at all."

Nic caught her by the wrists as she jumped up, obviously intending to go upstairs to see Finn. Taking a deep breath, he used the firmest, kindest tone he could find. "He's wiped out and said he wanted to rest. Leave him be. We obviously need to talk more about all of this. You need to hear from Finn what really happened the other night in his room. And he deserves an explanation from you. We both do. But honestly, I need some time to think." Exhaustion wafted through him, curbing his anger a notch or two.

Klare nodded her agreement, head heavy and eyes glued to the floor in shame. "Okay."

"I'm going to check in on Finn and then go for a run. I'll be back in a couple of hours. And seriously, Klare, *leave him be.*"

He had no confidence that a run would clear his head of the uncountable questions swirling through his brain, but he couldn't think of anything else to do.

6

What am I going to do? The smell of the stale, untouched coffee in front of her made her feel as though she might vomit. Leaving it on the kitchen table, she got up to grab some Tums from the bottle she kept in the pantry, ignoring the unwelcome awareness that she'd never needed so many antacids in her life.

Holding her breath to quash the acidic waves destroying her stomach, she ingested a half dozen chalky tabs and paused to appraise yesterday's arrangement of the canned goods: neatly spaced rows organized by content, then by size, with labels facing forward in perfect alignment. Proudly, she had resisted a neurotic urge to then arrange each row by expiration date, but the fact that she didn't do this seemed to irritate her.

This is ridiculous. She felt embarrassed by her sudden, irrational preoccupation with the state of the pantry.

Pangs of raw guilt inside the sour churning in her belly begged her to defy her husband's directive and check on Finn anyway.

You're already in enough trouble as it is. Leave him be, a stern voice inside chided.

"Ugh!" Klare sighed and turned to survey another untidy section of her typically neat pantry. Dozens of crumpled plastic grocery bags were shoved hastily into the slew of colorful reusable bags she never seemed to remember to bring to the store.

What's wrong with me? She tried to remember how long it had been since she had stopped caring about such things. Not long ago, all those bags would have been folded and neatly stacked inside the trunk of her car, ready for both planned and spontaneous grocery stops. Dismayed with herself, she began pulling the wads of bags from the shelf. *At least I can straighten this up.*

In the very back, she discovered one of the messy bundles was unusually heavy. *Did I seriously leave groceries in a bag?* She shook her head at the absentmindedness that had recently plagued her.

Unwrapping the plastic sack, cautiously expecting to find something rotten inside, Klare gasped and flung the weighted bag back onto the shelf, as if it were a snake that could've bitten her.

"Shit! What the hell?" she cried. Her mouth hung open in confusion as her already-overstrained brain tried to make sense of how long this benign yet tainted item had been tucked into the back of this dark cubby.

Years. At least three. No, more than that. What the hell?

A polluted memory rose from the depths of her mind, one that should have been clean and happy rather than soiled and spoiled. A birthday party. Her mother's unexpected offer to bring the "Groot" cake for her Guardians of the Galaxy-obsessed ten-year-old grandson. The *"healthier-for-them"* persimmon cookies that had shown up instead. Finn's courageous effort to hide his disappointment failing as he dissolved into tears. Bridget's hostile indignation at a gift not well-received. Klare's futile attempt to soothe both her son and her mother while Finn's few friends departed quietly. Nic's epic explosion at his mother-in-law for shouting at his son and ruining his party.

Bridget had stormed off in a furious huff, leaving behind the fancy glass container Klare remembered from her childhood home. Klare had angrily thrown the cookies in the trash and promised Finn a birthday party redo, which, no matter how much she pleaded and encouraged, he had declined.

That was the last of Finn's birthdays that Bridget had been invited to.

Klare picked up the glass dish and stared at it, unable to remember washing it, putting it in a bag, or storing it. In fact, she couldn't remember why she would have kept it at all. A fresh wave of nausea roiled through her, and she grabbed hold of a shelf as if it would keep her from drowning in it. *Oh, for heaven's sake, it's just a stupid dish!*

But she couldn't shake the *wrongness* of it. Like it wasn't supposed to be there, and she certainly shouldn't be touching it. A guilty shame ruptured open in her chest, causing little beads of sweat to break out across her brow and upper lip, as if she had just committed a terrible act and the glass dish was the evidence.

Gripped by an inexplicable compulsion to get rid of it, she rushed out to the side yard, threw open the lid of the outdoor trash bin, and hurled the corrupt container into it as if she couldn't be free of it fast enough.

It landed with a soft *thump* instead of the thunderous shatter she expected.

What?! Confused, she peered inside to see the dish, still very much intact, atop Finn's discarded comforter.

7

Nic didn't run for long, but he wasn't ready to go home. Instead, he grabbed a long lunch, wandered around Timken Lake for a while, then watched some local anglers cast their lines in hopes of catching a reservoir bass.

Glancing at his watch, he sighed. He'd been gone much longer than he said he would be and knew he needed to get back.

The house was eerily quiet. He popped in to check on Finn, who announced he was just reading, then rolled over on his bed, turning his back to Nic. Klare was dozing with a book still laid open on her lap. His heart ached at the expanse between the three of them, and he hoped tomorrow would bring some clarity and reconciliation.

Back downstairs, Nic paced between the kitchen, living room, and the small spare bedroom they had converted into a home office years ago. His tinnitus had been particularly bothersome all day, and he felt a headache coming on.

Aimless, he dragged his finger through a layer of dust atop the sideboard in the entryway, then stopped in front of the peace lily that had graced the table for years. It was wilted and drooping, the tips of the usually shiny lime-green leaves brown and crinkled.

Oh, man… A spark of painful awareness pierced his brain, momentarily pausing the high-pitched shrill. *Where have I been? How did I not notice this before?* Nic looked around and saw other signs of a neglected space—throw pillows tossed about indifferently, forgotten half-empty mugs that left crusty rings on glass tabletops, and a framed picture of the family that had apparently been carelessly knocked over and not righted. *What's happened to us?*

Confounded, Nic grabbed a bottle of water and made for the home office. Medical texts and reference books lined the higher shelves while the rest held hundreds of vintage LPs, pristine in their original covers, many of them dating back to Nic's teenage years when he first began to build his collection. One of Nic's hobbies, outside of running, was visiting antique shops in search of original records discarded in favor of the cassettes and CDs of the eighties and nineties. Even with vinyl making a comeback, Nic favored the hunt for the classics.

His preferred method was to choose an album at random and surprise himself. After his fingers selected *Déjà Vu* by Crosby, Stills, Nash & Young, he placed the album delicately on the turntable and sighed. Nic had a bittersweet relationship with this album as it was full of songs that reminded him of the mash-up of love and pain his heart always carried for his brother—when he was alive and long after. It was the same familiar feeling he'd just had when he looked in on Finn. Nic closed his eyes and let the lyrics from the first track cascade, evoking images of lost loves and going separate ways.

Nic knew. He didn't know what, but he knew something was not right; it hadn't been for a while. He considered it a wild stroke of luck that he had run into Dennis, quite literally, and the short conversation that at least got him on the path to finding out. *What would have happened if I hadn't run into him or stayed home from work today?* Anger bubbled as he thought about Klare's deception alongside the guilt for his failure to notice, and act, on what his gut had been trying to tell him.

"*Between what happened after Finn's birthday…*" His wife's words drifted back to him. That was the last time he could recall the three of them being together and being happy. The dehydration episode that sent Finn missing and then to the ER was certainly scary, but he ended up being okay. *But it's true. Things haven't been the same since then.* The headache he hoped would fade showed up in full force just then. He closed his eyes and rubbed his temples.

It had started out with such promise. Klare and Finn had been uncharacteristically excited about the invitation to the gardening event at Duncan Plaza, and the plan was to go out for Finn's birthday lunch afterward. That morning the three of them had set out together, the spring day buttery and warm. He'd enjoyed watching the attention his wife's quiet beauty and his son's elfin features received. The pair floated rather than walked, radiating an infectious serenity that left Nic grateful and proud. He'd consciously soaked in every detail and delicious moment of their perfect day. And it was perfect as he and Finn raced each other to the café. And then the day instantly changed.

Nic had always thought of his calm, reserved wife as the delicate balance to his more outdoorsy, spontaneous style. He adored his son, a miniature facsimile of Klare. Although he sometimes felt sad at how little he and Finn had in common, Nic was glad at least that they were so close.

But they haven't been like that since. Nic admonished himself, acknowledging how little attention he'd paid over the past several weeks. How had he not noticed his wife's typically easy disposition dissolve into this stiff, guarded woman he barely recognized? Or the state of the house? Or the dark circles under his son's eyes?

With his eyes still closed and his head sunk into the back of his recliner, Nic silently thanked the heavens for Dennis and let his mind drift to the events of the day before. He had left the house angry. Finn was sick in bed, or so he'd thought, and wouldn't talk to him. Klare had seemed remarkably unconcerned, drawing from Nic a sarcastic suggestion that she might consider taking their son to see a *doctor*, for which he had later chastised himself for sinking to that level of immaturity. But Klare had replied that she'd already made an appointment.

Did she ever. I know she knew I meant Dr. Hanada. He shook his head at how easy it was for Klare to lie to him. *It's like I don't even recognize her.*

Even the most familiar images, when turned upside-down, induce confusion—a disturbing uncertainty about that which, only moments before, we were well-acquainted and comfortable. Disoriented, we often fail to recognize the inversion as a prelude, a powerful harbinger of the gifts proffered by seeing through the lens of a new perspective.

8

Suspended in that fuzzy in-between where disorientation and confusion reign, Finn sluggishly sat up, stiff and sweaty from a deep and dreamless slumber that had begun before the sun set last night. Thin rays of sunshine peeked through the blinds, slowly vaporizing his brain fog enough to reveal the hollow pit in the center of his chest.

How much longer can this last? Despair and sadness circled in the void as Finn reflected on the last few days in his home. Mom kept to herself and Dad tiptoed around on eggshells. Awkward and uncomfortable, Finn felt like an intruder—a trespasser in his own home—and could not remember ever feeling so lonely. He spent much of the weekend trying to ignore the bottomless ache in his empty chest, but it persisted—a constant reminder that nothing was as it was supposed to be.

The emotional talk he'd had with his dad had brought a speck of relief. *At least I don't have to go back to that doctor.* But Finn also knew that the clandestine appointment with Dr. Myles was only a tiny drop in a very big bucket of secrets.

Finn dragged himself out of bed to make a quick dash downstairs for something to eat. Breakfasting with his mom had

55

all but stopped; granola bars had become his new staple. That is, *if* she remembered to go to the store and buy them. Otherwise, it was toast or sometimes nothing. Never one to complain, Finn had simply been grateful that at least he could count on having something to eat at the community center, but now that was gone too.

I don't know how much longer I can take this. With a heavy sigh, Finn made for the kitchen.

His dad's voice wafted up the stairs, sending an anxious ripple up from Finn's belly and into his throat. He froze midstep.

Why isn't he at work? Finn's fine-tuned antennae buzzed with alarm. His dad never stayed home from work this many days in a row.

He considered retreating back to his room, but he was famished and knew he'd have to come down for food at some point. Desperate, he made a split decision: pop into the pantry, grab whatever was closest, then head back upstairs. The thought of another day sequestered and alone in his bedroom was bad enough, but the idea of sitting in thorny tension with his parents in the kitchen was excruciating.

The hope that he might possibly be able to pull this off without being noticed was crushed the moment he turned the corner and ran smack into his dad.

"Oh, hey, Finn. Good morning. I was wondering when you might come down." Nic's easy and casual voice made Finn's stomach hurt; it didn't at all match his dad's recent vibe.

"Good morning," Finn returned, his face hot with discomfort. "I was just going to grab a bar or something."

Scooting around his dad to get to the pantry, Finn noticed his mom at the kitchen table with her head bent over her coffee. She didn't say anything, but the creases on her forehead and her marked avoidance of eye contact told Finn she was either scared or angry, or maybe both.

"Well, uh, I don't know what time you and your mom usually leave for the center, but I thought since I'm home today, I could take you this time. We can stop for breakfast on the way if you'd like."

Finn's head seemed to detonate, the scalding back draft swiftly sucking all his thoughts from his brain. He couldn't hear and wondered if he might collapse. He shot a pleading glance at his mom, desperate for a sign for how to best respond to his dad's casual offer. Devastated, Finn received no clear signal from her; he was on his own.

Rumbling deep, a thunderbolt let loose a flurry of questions too frightening to ask. *The center? I get to go back? Why isn't she saying anything? Why is he acting so casual?* Clashes and claps reverberated, unspoken words ricocheting about and sparring with each other. *Zeb. The center. But she said I wasn't going back. Zeb. Will he let me come back? I don't understand this.* The confusing incongruence of the moment terrified him.

Nic placed a reassuring hand on Finn's shoulder. "Hey, are you alright? If you don't want to go, that's okay. I just thought you—"

"No! No. I want to go," Finn insisted, much louder and more hurriedly than intended.

But no, I am not alright, Dad, he added silently.

Finn looked again at Klare, an automatic habit of late, for a sign, a signal, on what to do and say next. But she had gotten up from the table to wash her mug, her back turned to them both.

Seated in the passenger seat, Finn willed his body to be still while his insides vibrated and shook. Turning slightly away from his dad, he held one palm against his thrumming chest and rested the other against his belly. He took deep, slow breaths, like he'd learned to do at the center when they started the Friday wrap-up with a meditation. Terror pricked at the guarded excitement Finn was trying to contain. He had missed being at the center so much. It had only been a week, but it seemed like forever.

So much has happened.

Under his palm, beneath his T-shirt, Finn focused on the shape and substance of the small stone that rested there—a mysterious discovery found in the pocket of his cargo shorts when he got dressed to leave the emergency room.

He had never seen it before and had no idea how it got into his pocket. But both distracted by his peculiar experience that day and distressed by his mom's disturbing behavior, Finn returned the stone to his pocket and focused on getting home.

Later that evening, in the quiet privacy of his room, Finn had retrieved the stone and placed it on his desk to inspect it more closely under his lamp. It was about the size of a quarter but thicker, with a small hole that went through the middle, natural and not made with a drill or instrument. Matte and pale gray, it had hints of white variegations interrupting its primary color. He had never seen a stone like it and could not fathom how it had ended up in his pocket. But then again, he couldn't fathom most of what had transpired that day.

Picking it up again, Finn had found the stone warm to the touch, more than what would be expected even after being tucked away all day. The word *radiating* came to Finn's mind as something about the stone felt *active*. He wouldn't go so far as to say it was pulsating, but *alive* seemed to fit. He held it to his ear, the way people do when they come across a seashell and listen to the sound of the ocean resonating within its hollow cavity, then stared through the small hole, as if there were an answer to all of his questions on the other side. He had continued studying it from different angles, certain that he could feel the tiniest sensation, like a microscopic vibration.

Exhausted but vigilant from a day both fascinating and terrifying, Finn had lain down, hoping to recapture some of the comfort he had felt earlier. Trying to remember the sound of her voice, he had stared at the curious stone until he dozed off. Awash in the memory of wispy green softness, Finn's muscles relaxed, and the stone fell from his hands and landed with a muted thump on his chest. Immediately, a vibration rippled through him. The stone, the palpable origin of the buzz, activated a flutter deep beneath his heart. Finn jolted upright, clutching the humming rock in his fist. He wasn't imagining it. This stone was *alive*.

"Hey." His dad interrupted Finn's reverie with the same easy, casual tone as before. "I'm sorry it's taken me so long to see this place. You really like it there, don't you?"

Present tense. Oh no, does he not know? A shudder ripped through him. *But mom said "… we decided you aren't going back…"* His breath caught in his throat. *Oh my god, did she lie? Was this all her idea?* Afraid to say anything that might expose his mother's apparent dishonesty, Finn simply nodded.

Keeping his eyes trained outside, Finn rolled the worrisome questions through his mind: *If she lied about this, what else has she lied about? Did she lie to Zeb? Oh no! Do they think I just stopped coming? Are they mad? Will they even let me back?* The tension inside was almost too much. He concentrated on the feel of the stone against his chest, missing its rhythmic, calming pulses, and wondered if it would ever come back to life.

No, it's gone. Just like my bird. Just like her. She's gone too. I was too late.

Only a few minutes away from their destination, a hopeful thought sprang up. *Maybe he'll just drop me off! Not come in, not realize I've not been going!* The chance this could work filled his chest with cautious anticipation. *I don't know what I'll say to Cassie or Zeb about showing up again, but I guess I'll figure that out.*

As they approached the Okiciya Community Center, the pointed gold leaves of the peach trees came into view in vibrant contrast with the shamrock-green American sycamores shading the walkway. When Finn saw the familiar eagle with its massive wings stretched in midflight etched into the glass entry door, a tiny flutter moved from right to left inside his chest, alighting upon his heart. He exhaled a long breath he didn't know he'd been holding.

His dad turned into the circular parking lot, pulled into a spot facing the front of the rounded one-story building, and turned off the engine.

Oh no! Finn jumped out of the car, slammed the door, threw a quick wave back to his dad, and ran toward the center. *Maybe he'll just leave.*

"Whoa there! Wait for me!" Nic called as he leisurely exited the car.

Finn's stomach dropped. *He's coming in.*

Slowing his pace, he wondered again if he would be welcomed. Before they reached the entrance, the beautiful glass door opened and out sprinted a massive furry blur that nearly knocked Finn off his feet.

"Koko!" Finn buried his head in the blue-black lush of Koko's neck and was surprised at the lump that rose in his throat. He loved this furtive beast—a Groenendael, also known as a Belgian sheepdog. He had learned this was her breed back on his first day at the center. She was shadowy black with a shock of white on her chest and piercing glacial blue eyes that could seem menacing when she was in one of her more protective moods.

Finn heard an inner voice whisper, "*Don't worry. You're okay.*"

"Oh my lord! Finn!" Cassie cried from the door in her sugary southern twang. She walked straight to him and enfolded him in her arms.

Hugging her was easy. Cassie alternately smelled of flowers or cake, depending on what she brought into the center that day. Today she was all lavender and lemons.

"Please excuse me! I'm just so surprised to see you here!" She released Finn from her bear hug and looked square into his face. "Oh, it *is* good to see you." Her dark-lined espresso eyes shined with unapologetic tears.

The lump in his throat returned. *She doesn't seem mad. I hope Zeb isn't either,* Finn thought. Then he remembered his dad was standing right behind him, and a zing of fear shot through his chest.

"And you must be… Finn's dad?"

Finn thought he detected a hint of chilly wariness in Cassie's typically enthusiastic style of welcome.

"Hi there. Yes, I'm Nic." He extended his hand in introduction.

"Nice to meet you, Nic. I'm Cassie." She sounded more businessy than Finn had ever heard her before. "I don't recall Zeb saying y'all would be here this morning, so let me go find him. Come on in and make yourselves comfortable."

The pit flared in Finn's solar plexus again. His dad's face was blank, but his eyes were tense with incomprehension and something that looked to Finn like anger.

"She seems nice," Nic stated flatly. "What does she do here?"

Relieved to have something other than the obvious elephant in the room to talk about, Finn shared that Cassie was sort of the center's mother—she welcomed people, made sure they were fed and comfortable, and tended a huge rose garden out back.

"She's also a really good singer and leads the songs in some of the ceremonies," Finn added.

"Ceremonies?" His dad's word suggested curiosity, but his face and tone didn't match.

Finn observed his dad's forehead and eyebrows wrinkle, not quite a frown but something close. *I've never seen him look like that.* Another spear of anxiety poked at his belly.

Finn was grateful Koko remained beside him, as if communicating through the gentle lean against his legs, *"Don't worry. I am here."*

I love this dog, Finn thought as he watched his father wander around the half-moon lobby, impassively taking in the artwork and sculptures on the walls and shelves. *I wonder if he's actually looking. He seems far away.*

Starting to lose himself in a daydream of what Nic might possibly be thinking about, Finn snapped back into the present when he heard the rich, resonant voice of a man he'd grown to love.

Zebulon Paytah entered the lobby, the scent of sweet grass and sage wafting lightly behind him in feathery pale tendrils. His stately frame, broad shoulders, and thick, silver-streaked black hair held back by a strip of leather cast Zeb as a commanding figure who seemed much bigger than Finn's father, although when side by side, they were just about the same height. He wore his standard faded jeans and soft leather boots the color of the desert, and atop his mahogany-red T-shirt rested a small suede sac that Finn knew was Zeb's medicine pouch, the contents of which he had shared when Finn had asked him about it.

The flutter in Finn's chest returned, scurrying about like it wasn't sure where it wanted to go. The unmistakable quaver shot bursts of electricity through him. The divergent feelings inside—fear, excitement, worry, love—bounced from his throat to his heart to his belly and back again. He instinctively dropped his head to shield his face, hoping it wouldn't betray his struggle.

"Finn, I am so happy to see you," said Zeb, pausing until Finn looked up and met his ebony eyes. "And I am happy to finally meet your father." Finn's mentor extended a hand to Nic, who shook it silently. After a pause so long and charged that it threatened to send Finn over some invisible, precarious edge, Zeb finally continued. "Mr. Driscoll, it's nice to meet you. I would love to speak with you, that is, if you have the time."

Finn's stomach dropped as he watched Zeb lead his dad into his office. Not knowing what else to do, he turned in search of Cassie, Koko still glued to his side.

9

Shit! This just keeps getting worse. Klare watched Finn and Nic leave out the front door for the community center. *That you unenrolled your son from,* chastised her inner critic.

Klare's near-constant nausea instinctively nudged her toward the jumbo bottle of reflux relief on the top shelf of the pantry. As she mechanically turned toward the cabinet, she froze. An inexplicable dread smothered her, sending her to her knees right there on the kitchen floor as she frantically gasped for the oxygen that seemed to have been sucked from the room. Panic overwhelmed her senses, and terrifying images rose in her mind. *Am I dying?*

She managed to roll onto her side and closed her eyes, waiting—*hoping*—her breath would return. Within moments, she could feel her heart rate slow and her lungs fill, producing a welcome wave of relief that elicited hot and appreciative tears. Lying on the cool tile floor, she waited a couple of minutes until she was sure she could stand up and stay up.

Was that a panic attack? She'd never had one, but from what she'd read in stories or seen in movies, it seemed the most applicable conclusion.

On her feet and still confused about the sudden onset of this overpowering sense of dread, she took a step toward the pantry and froze again.

I can't go in there!

The pantry seemed absurdly ominous, as though something vicious waited for her in there. She shook her head in self-conscious frustration, but the sense of impending doom remained. Although the harmless white frosted glass door was wide open, showing only its neat and tidy rows of soups and sauces, she pulled it shut hard enough to hear the audible click, which somehow eased her nerves a little.

Upstairs, breathing, and safely away from the menacing food closet, Klare paced in her bedroom, trying to formulate a plan.

Maybe he'll just drop him off and be none the wiser? Yeah, right.

Then a shameful thought occurred to her. *What if they don't let Finn in? I unenrolled him… oh no. Would they really do that?* She rubbed her guilt-laden temples. *Probably not without talking to a parent first. Shit.*

Worrisome scenarios pummeled her brain: *What will they ask Nic? What will he tell them? What if Finn tells him on the way? No, he wouldn't do that. What if they say he's no longer welcome there? Because of me? Oh my god! What am I going to do?*

A cool voice drifted up and furtively offered a suggestion: *"You can say it was just all a misunderstanding."*

"A misunderstanding," Klare whispered as internal gears started rotating.

The nonchalant creature within expounded. *"Finn was sick. You needed to keep an eye on him. You didn't mean to keep him out so long; you just wanted to be sure he was okay…"*

Right! He was sick! Not himself. A tiny spot of relief opened in Klare's otherwise queasy belly. *Especially after the fire…*

"The fire," Klare muttered. *Yeah, the fire that Nic says wasn't really a fire. But he wasn't even there!*

Klare's lungs filled with an invigorating breath. *That's right! He wasn't even there!*

The little spot began to turn a dark and angry crimson, swelling in both size and force as if opening a portal through which anger's waiting brethren of resentment and blame could enter freely, infusing Klare with an electric righteousness.

Newly roused, the once abeyant fragments of truth begin to yawn and wake from their long slumber, unwittingly deploying the guardians of unwanted awareness. Obligatory lies and passable pretenses are delivered up in a valiant effort to keep hidden the splinters and slivers of reality that threaten our blissful oblivion, making it easy for us to believe we are fooling others when we are the ones being fooled. But do not fret. It is not the charge of our well-intended psychic protectors to guide us toward self-knowledge; that path requires a different kind of steward.

10

What the hell is going on here? Standing in the lobby of the community center, Nic felt embarrassed and awkward, like he was the last one to get the joke.

But this is no joke.

Nic had felt both warmed and mildly irritated by Cassie's enthusiastic welcoming of his son. She clearly cared for Finn, which was lovely, of course, but it seemed a tad excessive when Finn had only been out a couple of days. However, her obvious surprise at their arrival and then her comment about Zeb not expecting them to "be here this morning" had left a puzzling knot in Nic's stomach, which set off the high-pitched peal that he'd had only a short reprieve from that morning.

Entering the lobby felt more like walking into a home. Ochre walls accented with warm, earthy tones displayed prints of azure skies stretching out over vast golden plains, red rock mountains jutting into the night and bathed in the glow of a luminous harvest moon, and an eagle soaring over a stream bordered by towering cottonwood trees and untouched brush. A scent Nic could not immediately place hung lightly in the air—an amalgamation of something cooling and medicinal but also musky and herbaceous. He tried to focus on the artwork rather than the cacophony in his ear.

More confounding was the queasy disquiet slithering around inside like a furtive little garter snake. Watching Finn burrow into the fur of that massive hound who stuck to his side like a magnet had left Nic wondering, *Why have we not gotten this kid a dog of his own?* Nic also could not remember the last time he'd heard his son speak with such affection: "*The center's mother… rose garden… ceremonies…*" And there was nothing tenuous about the way Finn moved about the space, clearly comfortable and at home.

More than in our own home, a thought, green and prickly, inserted itself into Nic's private musings.

When Zebulon Paytah entered the foyer, carried in on that same pleasantly earthy fragrance, Nic felt the man's commanding presence strike deep in his chest, and his heart pulsed out a couple of extra-strong beats. Zeb was powerful and impressive, but not in an authoritarian way.

Spiritual, Nic thought. He watched the man attune to Finn, holding his son's look with his own until Finn responded to his greeting. Nic also caught his son's faint blush, and the shy grin that graced his typically stoic face. Another self-conscious nudge of jealousy roused within. Nic could tell in that moment how much Finn looked up to this man—revered him—and wondered if his own more laid-back approach had caused his son to seek a role model elsewhere. Someone other than him. A ruddy heat unfolded inside, a companion to a conjured-up image of Finn turning away from him and choosing the advice of another man, another father figure instead.

"Mr. Driscoll, it's nice to meet you," said this unexpected rival. "I would love to speak with you, that is, if you have the time."

Nic attempted to hide his grimace as he shook the man's hand and noticed a band of braided leather encircling his left wrist. "Yes, of course, thank you. And please, it's Nic." Insides twisted in knots, he accepted the offer to talk while he watched his son and the furry presence glued to his side hightail it toward a door that led elsewhere.

The inside of Zebulon Paytah's office was a concentrated version of the lobby, anchored by similar earthen images depicting people and animals enveloped by pure and untouched nature. A herd of bison, a kettle of hawks, a circle of people surrounding a fire pit. But the picture that caught Nic's attention most was an enormous panoramic of a vast mountain ridge. In the foreground was a pale statue of a bare-chested Native American warrior atop a horse, his left arm extended in grand authority and pointing to something outside the frame of view. The background showed the beginning stages of what looked to be a replica of the statue carved into the side of a massive mountain. With his giant resolute profile backdropped by deep blue skies and a white pile of clouds, the man appeared to be the somber custodian of the lands he overlooked.

Zeb opened a window and a cool breeze drifted in, a welcome relief from what had been an unusually humid stretch. He took one of the single leather chairs and Nic sat in one opposite. Never one who got called to the principal's office, Nic imagined this is what it might have felt like.

"I'm glad to finally meet you and that you have some time to talk. I must admit, I'm surprised to see you both here." While the man's warm, sonorous voice was candid and seemingly without reproach, another twinge slithered, and Nic pulled reflexively on his earlobe.

Having already deduced that he was not in possession of the full story, Nic continued to flounder, trying to figure out how to navigate what felt like hazardous ground. He obviously wanted to be brought up to speed, but the disquieting shame bubbling in his chest kept him from asking his burning question: *Why is everyone so surprised!?*

As if reading his mind, or perhaps the lines on his forehead, Zeb continued. "I'm glad to see Finn is feeling better. We were quite worried about him after being out for so long."

So long!? It was like two days! What is going on here? Nic steadied his breath so he wouldn't blurt out his thoughts and expose just how little he knew. Instead, he played a safe card and said, "Yes, he's much better."

"If I can be transparent," Zeb paused, waiting for permission. When Nic nodded in assent, he carried on. "We called to check on him, but after about the third call, your wife informed us that Finn would not be returning and asked that we not call again. I am curious, did something happen?"

You've got to be kidding me! Nic closed his eyes as his stomach bottomed out, sending him free-falling through space. He gripped the arms of his chair, needing something to tether his body to the earth. Countless thoughts and questions bombarded his brain, fizzing and popping like shots fired underwater. They zinged through his head, coasting on the piercing peal already on high volume, leaving him feeling exposed and in imminent danger. The volley eventually slowed, and words collided in his consciousness with a heavy thud… *"Fire," "Dr. Myles," " … informed us that Finn would not be returning."*

Nic took a long draw of air and mentally wiped the screen of his mind clean. When the vertiginous sway settled, he opened his eyes. Realizing he had no idea how long he'd been under, he was happy to see Zeb hadn't moved.

All Nic could summon up was, "I'm sorry. I…"

Offering a much-needed assist, Zeb finished for him. "You didn't know."

Nic blew out a frustrated puff of air, shook his head, and looked back at this implausibly patient man. "I'm sorry," he said again.

Anger swirled inside an eddy of nauseating shame as Nic wondered with whom he was more livid: Klare, for yet another lie, or himself, for how he had missed so much.

His wife had been keeping a noticeable distance, standing back, an apathetic observer. Sitting across from this gentle giant, Nic now began to wonder if his acquiescing to her repeated requests for "space" hadn't been the best response after all. Being raised by a "free-range" mother had shaped Nic into an adult who did not press or push, instead adopting a laissez-faire approach of giving others space to do what they wanted when they wanted. However, sitting here now, embarrassed that he had not asked Finn more about the center and regretful that perhaps he had given Klare *too* much space, he wondered if his permissive, hands-off style communicated an indifference or lack of concern.

That was never my intent, but maybe…

Zeb inhaled audibly enough to bring Nic back to the moment, and he sensed there was more the wise man had to say. Nic breathed in as well, as if Zeb's deep intake was contagious, forcing him to respond in kind. But that was all he could muster.

Still stuck in his embarrassment, he turned and looked out the window that faced the garden. There he saw Finn kneeling next to a girl about his same age, clearly teaching or demonstrating something to do with the plants in front of them. Koko was right beside him, lying in a pile of mulch and soaking up the day's warm rays. Nic felt his heart swell and his throat tighten. It was as if he were seeing his son for the first time after a long absence, which he supposed, sadly, was accurate.

"He is a special young man," Zeb said. "A natural leader. The younger ones, they flock to him—follow him. And the older ones, well, they defer and let him take the lead just as often."

The piercing pitch screamed in Nic's ear, and he remained silent.

"Finn doesn't use many words, as I am sure you know." Zeb grinned and resumed. "But he doesn't need to. He leads by example. He has a powerful energy inside that speaks for him. He doesn't seem to fully know that yet, but in time, I believe he will."

A wave of guilt pushed up against the budding pride Nic could feel forming inside. *How has Finn been coming here all this time and I had no idea what was happening? A leader? The kid everyone else follows? Is he talking about my kid?* The part of Nic that felt proud of Finn, surprised but also moved to hear his son described this way, pressed back against the flow of guilt in favor of respect.

He wanted to hear more and leaned forward. "This is… great to hear. Finn has always been such a loner. He prefers quiet, solitude, and struggles to make friends at school. It's surprising, to be honest, but in a good way." Nic stammered as he tried to digest this unfamiliar version of his child. "People following him, deferring to him. Frankly, I've never seen this side of him. It's good to hear that maybe he's finally coming out of himself a bit."

Zeb paused, again in apparent contemplation of how to proceed, nodding thoughtfully before responding. "I wonder if it may be more about Finn coming *into* himself, rather than out. He has a wisdom about him—a depth—like he's old in a young man's body. Trying to figure out who he is, who he wants to be."

Nic could tell Zeb was treading lightly, as if calculating how Nic might react to what he was being told. Taking a moment to gather his thoughts and uncertain what to say next, Nic opted for honesty despite the blushing discomfort of showing such vulnerability with a man he had just met.

"Finn keeps to himself for the most part, and I usually just give him the space to do that. But as I am sitting here now, I regret not having asked him more about his experience here, with you. I feel like you're talking about a side of my kid I don't know."

But one I'd like to know, he added silently.

Nic straightened his spine and turned to face the man who may know his son better than he. "Finn obviously is comfortable and seems to be getting so much from being here. And clearly, I need to have a conversation with my wife to better understand what happened. I'm embarrassed about that, and that I haven't been more involved in Finn's experience here. If it's an option, would Finn be able to return?"

Nic followed Zeb's line of vision back outside to Finn working assiduously, now alongside a younger boy who had joined Finn and the girl.

"I think it's safe to say that he's already back," Zeb offered in soft reassurance. "And in his element, as you can see."

Nic's face flared in shame. *I didn't even know he had an "element."*

"He is an important part of this community. It wouldn't be the same without him." Zeb looked out at the half-dozen people peacefully tending to the garden as one.

Community. The delicate touch of an old, wistful memory tickled at the back of Nic's brain—more felt than remembered at first—infusing his body with sensations both agonizing and comforting. *That's it. He's part of a community here. And it's part of him.* Nic yielded to the echoes of the past pressing against his awareness and remembered.

It was a struggle for Virginia Driscoll, affectionately known as Gigi, to keep her two young boys housed and fed after their father left. But when her youngest son, Elem, got sick, worry for the future of her little family eclipsed her usual sunniness.

It was a community—*their community*—that came together to help shoulder the emotional burden and ease the financial strain on this young mother. Food from the local co-op arrived at no charge, fellow struggling artist friends pooled their meager funds to help pay the family's bills, and home-cooked and hand-delivered meals kept bellies full even though appetites in the Driscoll household ran thin.

Nic did as much as any thirteen-year-old could have to distract his younger brother from his pain and ease his mother's burden. He became a little adult almost overnight. He ran errands, gave Elem his medications, kept the house clean, and still managed to keep up with schoolwork. While other kids may have felt resentful for these added responsibilities, Nic did not. To him, it was a noble obligation; he loved his little brother, and he loved his mom. His own needs and feelings became inconvenient trivialities he gladly tucked away.

When Elem's steady deterioration finally bound him to his bed, Nic's ability to ease his brother's pain eroded equally. The pall of the imminent end shrouded Nic in a darkness that banned all hope and light. Having become accustomed to not asking for help, the young man was at a loss for what to do about the despair that threatened to keep him in that desolate blackness forever.

It was a community—*their community*—that assembled and brought the needed light. Marshalled by Gigi's dearest friend Linda—a pixie with hair the color of milk chocolate, turquoise rings on her fingers, and fairy bells on her shoes—the artisan troupe filled the air with song, and the Driscoll home began to glow. Their cadence floated like a soft, metrical purr, communicating with sound and vibration in a nameless, breathtaking language. Tears cascaded down wan cheeks as the family was held in an embrace of profound peace seemingly incompatible with the sorrow felt by all. For days, they gathered, chanting and serenading in unison. And while their stirring intonations were not able to heal his body, Elem's soul was bathed in love, and it was within that soothing reservoir that the boy took his final breath.

It was a community—*their community*—that brought the beacon that rescued Nic from the dark, contained his mother's grief, and lovingly shepherded Elem to his next destination.

Community. Nic thought. *They came to us, surrounded us, took care of us. They leaned in, not out, when things got rough. How did I forget that? Where did I go wrong?* He held back the tears threatening to spill over and refocused on his son.

Suddenly aware that he had taken much of this astonishingly calm man's time this morning, Nic gathered himself internally in preparation to leave and to have the dreaded conversation with Klare. Wiping at his moist eyes, Nic took in the large abalone shell on the edge of Zeb's desk. The iridescent container held several small bundles of charred, dried, silvery leaves wrapped tightly around larger twigs of herbs and small flowers nestled between a few singed, rough-hewn wooden sticks. A fan woven from different colored and sized feathers held together by a length of leather leaned against the shell alongside a box of matches. An inexplicable sense of ease washed over him like a cooling balm.

"I'm sorry, I'm a little overwhelmed right now," Nic said softly. "Thank you for talking to me, and especially for sharing with me a part of my son that I would like to know better."

Zeb brought his tanned, earth-worn hands to his chest as if in supplication, dipped his head forward, and spoke softly. "Thank you for bringing him back. We have felt his absence."

Me too, Nic rued. *Me too. And I wonder if he's felt mine.*

11

That was embarrassing. Nic buckled himself in and started the ignition. The sharp corners of anger and humiliation elbowed his belly, clamoring for space against the hot indignity that filled the cavity of his body. The ringing in his ears had ebbed some while in the confines of Zeb's office, but it was ramping up again as he thought about driving home and the conversation that was waiting for him there.

She knew I'd be going in there blind. What was she thinking I was going to do—make it up as I went along? His chest burned at the idea that he had been set up by Klare, the last person on earth he would have expected to be so underhanded.

Pulling out of the center's lot, Nic decided to take a longer route home to give himself a chance to plan how he was going to approach his wife. Luckily, Zeb had suggested Finn stay for the rest of the day, acknowledging in not so many words that Nic would need the time.

And Finn? Why didn't he say anything on the way over? A pang of guilt sliced through the anger and gave Nic a moment of clarity. *That wasn't his responsibility. Poor kid, the drive over must have been excruciating.*

His friend Dennis' recent words floated back into Nic's memory "… *even take the stress on themselves. Anything to ease the burden and not make matters worse.*"

Like before, a nauseating surge ripped through him. *It's like she set him up too.* His heart hammered inside his hardened chest. *This is not my wife.*

Once home, Nic paused before going inside, forcing himself to take long, slow breaths to calm his trembling. Never had he felt this angry at his wife; in fact, he could not remember feeling this angry ever.

Except that one time with Bridget. Nic shook the loathsome memory from his mind. The residue of the role his own absenteeism had played in this current situation had been blown away like ashes in the wind.

He found Klare sitting on the kitchen floor in front of several emptied shelves and surrounded by stacks of decorative serveware. When he pulled out a kitchen chair and sat, he was immediately uncomfortable with the disparity in their physical positions.

As she continued her feverish rearranging of porcelain dishes and crystal platters without acknowledging his presence, Nic willed himself to speak as coolly as possible.

"Klare, can you please stop that and come up here? We need to talk about the meeting I just had at the community center." His heart knocked painfully against his ribcage.

"I'm fine down here." Klare's icy voice sent ripples through Nic's belly. "What do you want to talk about?"

The screaming in Nic's eardrums clicked up several notches, and he fought the impulse to storm from the kitchen.

I can't believe this.

"Klare. Stop it with the dishes. I need you to come up here and talk to me. And you know *exactly* what we need to talk about." Nic didn't like the sound of his authoritarian tone; it was not in his nature. But the insecure desperation building inside had impacted him, and seemingly Klare as well, as she promptly stopped her shuffling, stood up, and joined him at the table.

Her usually full lips made a tight line of her mouth, and the muscles in her jaw betrayed her grinding teeth.

I didn't think this would be easy, but I didn't expect this. Nic fretted at the sight of his unrecognizable wife. *I don't even know where to start.*

"So, obviously, you took Finn out of the center. What I'd like to know is why, and why you didn't tell me… and why you let me walk into that situation completely blind. That was beyond embarrassing, Klare."

"Embarrassing? Well, what do you think it's been like for me? Having to deal with all this on my own? I can't even imagine what they're saying about me over there. Nic, you have no idea what it's been like—"

"Klare!" Nic's hand landed heavily on the table, interrupting his wife's inconceivable tirade. "I don't know what you are talking about. Dealing with what? Between that ridiculous psychiatrist appointment and claiming Finn was starting fires, what the hell is happening around—"

"CLAIMING!" Klare shrieked. "Oh, so now I'm *claiming* he started a fire?" She stood, as if to give her lungs more fuel. "Nic, you don't know anything! You weren't even there, and now you're accusing me of making things up?! How dare you! You're never here, and I've had to deal with all this totally by myself!"

Nic flew up from his seat and grabbed her shaking fists by the wrists, his brain struggling to comprehend the image that passed through his mind of his wife striking him. They stared at each other, frozen, her eyes ablaze in unrecognizable fury and his filled with terror.

Oh my god, what's happened to her? Spots and flashes appeared at the edge of Nic's vision. Through the optical dappling, he felt more than he could see her as she pulled her arms away from him. He sat heavily back in his chair and heard her do the same. His vision began to clear, although the clamoring in his ears had reached deafening proportions. He wasn't sure how much more he could take.

When their eyes locked, Nic could see that her intensity had dimmed—barely—but it was far from gone.

This is not my wife. Who is she? He suddenly felt ill, as if something awful and revolting was squirming around inside his intestines.

"I need to get some air," Nic flatly informed his wife, his body simultaneously taut and numb. "I'm going for a walk before I pick up Finn. When we get back, we need to talk about whatever it is that's been happening around here."

"No, Nic, don't leave. I'm sorry. Just don't leave." Klare's *sorry* did not match her clipped, angry tone.

I can't bring Finn back to this, Nic thought protectively, and added, "Klare, I don't know what is going on with you, but you need to pull it together before we get back. I won't let Finn be talked to this way."

Klare stared blankly, and Nic turned to leave.

With a couple of hours to kill, Nic drove toward the community center and parked a few blocks away alongside a sheltered, wooded expanse. Ordinarily, he would opt for a run to decompress, but perhaps for the first time ever, a run sounded repulsive. He was shell-shocked from his alien encounter with his wife and had the sense that somehow his brain had stopped producing thoughts.

He sat in a frozen daze until the buzz on his cell phone reoriented him to the world he sat in.

> *Dad, can you come pick me up?*
> *The center is closing.*

"Shit!" Nic cursed himself. Looking at the clock, he saw he'd been sitting there for nearly three hours, but it seemed like a mere three minutes. Grateful he was so close to the center, he flipped the car around and headed for his son.

He knew he hadn't slept, but it seemed like he was waking from a dream.

Who is she? had bounced around in his anesthetized mental fog and his now-ticking brain spit out an unsolicited answer that reignited his nauseating dread.

Bridget.

12

Fiery adrenaline bitterly coursing through her veins, Klare abandoned her task and shoved the serveware back into the cupboard. *How dare he talk to me like that! Who does he think he is?*

Hands on hips, she surveyed the cluttered countertops and felt the sinister glare of disorder from the other side of the pantry door. "Oh, forget it!" she fumed and stomped out of the tormenting kitchen.

The living room offered no respite as discarded mugs and toppled pillows jeered from their forsaken spaces among the mess. She could see the layer of dust that covered every flat surface. An absurd image arose of a spiteful dust fairy traipsing around her house in the middle of the night, sprinkling her filthy wares.

I just cleaned all this! Klare grumbled and promptly left the room.

She stopped at the dust-covered mirror that hung above the entryway sideboard and tore her eyes from the sallow face that sneered back at her, severe and smoldering. The now-familiar wave of acidic nausea poached her esophagus, and the equally familiar urge to run for the closest bottle of Tums activated her muscles. But she didn't move. Frozen in place, she swallowed back the queasiness as her mind detached itself from her motionless body and watched from above, fixated on what had once been a beloved piece of her world.

On her fortieth birthday, Klare had had another painful row with her mother, who seemed especially skilled at burning celebratory occasions to ashes. After hearing the disappointing story, Dennis' wife, Lucy, had stopped by with a petite potted plantlet that, true to her style, held layers of significance and intention.

The peace lily, she had explained, was a symbol of peace and tranquility and a harbinger of hope. Whispering as though revealing a mysterious secret, she foretold of the flowers that would eventually sprout and unfold in creamy white spathes resembling the unfurling of a white flag of surrender. These, Lucy suggested, might serve as an invitation for Klare to surrender her perpetually unmet expectations of her mother and choose peace instead.

The poised and artful designer and feng shui specialist added that this plant would help eliminate negativity by converting it into positive energy and therefore recommended placing it near the front door to help transmute any deleterious vibes entering the house into something more favorable.

Never one to buy into the esoteric, Klare was nonetheless moved by her friend's thoughtfulness. She had placed the plant near the door, thinking, *I'll take all the help I can get,* and noticed the spot of shame that had flowered in her chest when an inner voice simultaneously rebuked, *It's just a plant.*

Klare had tended the young plant carefully, waiting patiently for it to bloom. The shiny dark-green leaves reminded her of feathers—beautifully long, narrowing to a point at the tip, and curving out and away. The first spear-like spike that arrived one overcast afternoon had stolen her breath and moistened her eyes.

For days, she had fervently monitored her leafy charge. She wept unabashedly when she woke to find that the stalk had unfurled a magnificent ivory spathe that protectively cupped around the yellow-green capsule flower inside, enveloping it in a delicate swath.

Like a mother protecting her tightly swaddled newborn, Klare had thought wondrously as she bore witness to this floral birth.

She had nurtured her cherished gift, talking to it lovingly and repotting as needed to give its roots room to grow. Within a couple of years, the tiny plantlet had become a thriving, glossy two-foot-tall centerpiece delivering an abundance of cocoon-like pearly spathes and capturing her delight.

"What happened to you?" she whispered to her once-flourishing treasure that now sat wilted and lifeless. Spent blossoms hung decaying among the dusty and drooping leaves. Klare poked at the bone-dry soil that seemed to have abandoned hope of ever having its thirst quenched. She stood confused in the face of obvious neglect.

A voice inside repeated back, "*What happened to YOU?*"

Drained of some of her righteous fury by the sad proof of her lack of presence, Klare gave her dehydrated plant a long drink and glanced at the clock. *Four-thirty! Oh my god! They should be home any minute!* Anxiety tore through her chest. *How long have I been standing here?*

Repulsed at the thought of returning to the kitchen, she hastily straightened some pillows and made for the couch.

Trembling, she slowed her breathing to settle her body, fearful of careening over some invisible edge into a black and bottomless abyss. The thinnest pane of glass separated her from what waited down there as pressurized pops and crackles threatened to shatter this perilous boundary. The cracks that had been forming over the past few weeks had allowed momentary glimpses of the murk: terror, confusion, shame—all floating in a restless ocean certain to swallow her whole if she were to fall in. It took everything she had to not tumble.

Thump… Thump. The consecutive muffled sounds of two car doors closing interrupted Klare's attempt to relax. She inhaled sharply and braced for her husband and son's arrival.

"Hey." Nic entered first with Finn trailing behind.

"Hey," Klare replied, trying to borrow her husband's low and flat voice.

Her heart thumped heavily as she watched Finn choose the seat furthest away from her on the L-shaped couch while Nic chose a spot in between. She pinched her lips tight to control her trembling mouth, remembering Nic's parting words from earlier, "… *you need to pull it together before we get back.*"

"Finn and I talked about a few things on our way back and agreed it would be best to start with what happened in his room."

He didn't say "the fire," Klare noted. A swell of defensiveness rose in her belly but cooled a bit when she also acknowledged, reluctantly, her husband's seemingly nonjudgmental tone.

"Okay." To her own ears, she sounded indifferent, although that was not her intention.

A pregnant pause hung in the air, and Klare watched her son rock slightly back and forth, his hand reflexively tapping at his chest. It was something he had done since he was a small child. Dr. Hanada called it *self-soothing* and said sometimes children come up with their own ways to calm themselves when they are anxious. It had bothered Klare back then when the doctor suggested Finn was anxious, but he'd reassured her that it was simply a nonverbal way Finn calmed himself down since he preferred not to use his words much.

He's always been more of a feeler than a talker, Klare thought while waiting for him to respond.

Assuming the role of intermediary, Nic stepped in to move the conversation along. "Finn, why don't you start with what you told me about what you were trying to do that night?"

Trying to do… He was trying to start a fire, Klare scoffed to herself. But when she saw Finn's typically smooth, placid features wrinkle and twitch, her heart unwound a bit. *Just listen,* a gentle inner voice encouraged.

"Um… okay," Finn sighed. "I was cleaning the air. Something I learned at the center." Finn delivered his sparse account in careful, wary words.

Cleaning the air? Her heart twitched.

Finn looked to his father, eyes pooled with uncertainty.

Nic nudged his son to continue. "Go on… it's okay."

Klare listened as intently as she could as her son described learning about a tradition in Zeb's culture of cleansing the energy in the air, sending prayers or wishes up and out on the smoke of sacred herbs, and preparing the space for something new to emerge. Finn spoke of visualizing the area free of anything old or unwanted so that the surrounding space was clear and ready. She kept her eyes trained on Finn while he drifted off to some faraway place as if daydreaming.

Cleansing the energy? Freeing the unwanted? She stole another glance at her wilted lily, baffled at how similar Finn's words were to Lucy's from years ago. *But sending out wishes on smoke? Clear and ready for what? What on earth has been going on over there at that center?! This is just too weird…*

STOP! she yelled at herself and cringed when her mind supplied a reminder of Nic's words from earlier. *Pull yourself together.*

She had never heard Finn speak in this way. His serene voice glowed reverently, and his nervousness from moments ago had been replaced with a calm confidence. Losing herself in her son's mesmeric account, she flinched when Nic asked Finn *why* he felt the need to clean the air.

Waves of fear started rolling again as she came back into her body. She looked at her son, who had also returned from his reverie, his face and delicate body bowed once more in burdensome doubt. She could tell he didn't want to answer his father's question.

"It needed cleaning," Finn responded without the elaboration his father had prompted.

Nic nodded and offered a supportive hint. "Okay, well, typically if something needs cleaning, it's because it's gotten dirty or messy or something like that, right? Is that how you were feeling about the air in your room?"

"The house. The air in the house," Finn clarified.

Aware this painstaking exchange could go on indefinitely, with Finn dispensing a few hesitant words at a time, Klare was desperate to get to the point. "Finn, okay, I don't fully understand, but I hear that you didn't feel good about the *energy* in the house and were trying to do something to make it better. But you could have hurt yourself, or even burned the house down by lighting something on fire in your room. That was really dangerous and not something—"

"Klare. Stop," Nic interrupted, restrained anger replacing the dispassionate neutrality from earlier. "You aren't listening."

Originating in her feet, a white-hot bolt of anger shot up through her body and seemed to explode out of the top of her head, taking her breath with it. Images flashed fast and furious: sparks and dark tendrils of acrid smoke wafting up toward the ceiling, her own hands grabbing a blanket to smother the burn, and from above, herself on her hands and knees violently beating the covering until she was sure it was out. "You. Weren't. There. Nic!" Hoarse words spewed from her throat.

Nic jumped at Klare's aggressiveness, eyes wide and mouth agape in shock.

"But I was," Finn interjected, firm and steady, stunning Klare and her already-stunned-silent husband. They turned to face their curiously assertive son. "Mom. There was nothing on fire. There was no fire. It was like the incense at Lucy's house. There wasn't even a flame." Finn remained clear and calm despite his trembling chin. "You stomped out something that wasn't there. And broke my shell and ruined my sage. And screamed at me. Whatever you thought was happening was *not* what happened."

Klare watched, speechless, as Finn closed his eyes and took several long, slow breaths, his hand held flat and firm against his chest. Her heart threatened to explode as the seconds ticked by before Finn opened his eyes, squared his shoulders, and lifted his chin. He remained sedate, as if he were channeling strength and resolve from some mysterious, hidden supply.

"You've been gone. Here but not here at the same time, and it didn't feel good to be here. I was happy at the center and then that was gone too. I didn't know what to do and just wanted it to feel better here, so I burned some sage." Finn held his mother's regard with a disquieting stare. Then the confident intensity seemed to bleed from his face as quickly as it had appeared, his features morphing back into shy uncertainty.

A sickly loathing threatened to erupt from Klare's stomach, and she pressed her palm to her mouth to block its escape. Thoughts vanished from her head as nausea highjacked her senses. She detected her husband's firm hand on her thigh.

"Finn," Nic mediated, gentle and cautious. "Your mom has been having a hard time, and I know a lot has happened, but we are—"

"We?" Finn asked, his tone implausibly sharp and prickly.

Klare watched her husband draw back, stung by Finn's question.

"You haven't been here either." Finn's regard was cold and flat. His challenging stare and her husband's dumbfounded expression were an utterly foreign sight. She wanted to bolt from the room, but some sliver of her awareness knew that would accomplish nothing.

Klare looked at Nic, who returned her glance in mutual disbelief, both still unable to manufacture a reply.

"I'm going to my room," Finn stated bluntly, and the distraught mother watched helplessly as her son walked away.

OH, THAT TINY murmur of caution from the depths of our soul, the fey warning to be wary. How easy it is to turn a blind eye or pretend we didn't hear its whispered portent. The intoxicating promise of fame and fortune, or perhaps simply the allure of sacred invisibility, can cause the most noble and fair to forget the high price of such clever covenants.

13

Finn flung himself onto his bed, tucking his old comforter around him and missing the one his mother had thrown out.

I can't believe I just did that. Finn couldn't recall if he'd ever corrected his parents, let alone confronted them. Shaken and alarmed by a boldness he had no idea existed within him, he half expected his parents to march into his room and reprimand him. Hearing no footsteps on the stairs, Finn slowly allowed his nerves to unwind.

I don't know what came over me, but it's the truth. He couldn't count the number of times over these past many weeks he'd thought he might explode from all he was holding inside. Most of it he'd wanted to talk about. In fact, he was desperate to tell, but there had been no one to talk to. His mom had become frightening and unapproachable, and his dad was almost never around. Then right when he was about to tell Zeb everything, he had lost that chance too.

There was, however, one thing he decidedly did not want to talk about or tell. Just thinking about it made his stomach hurt and his neck turn hot. It wasn't like him at all; it wasn't like her either. Nevertheless, an agreement was made—*a secret agreement*—one he felt obligated to keep, even though it seemed the terms of this duplicitous contract had changed.

How did everything get so messed up? Finn sighed and rolled himself tighter within the covers.

Never would he have imagined not being able to talk to his mom, especially about something so magical as his mysterious encounter that beautiful, sunny Saturday after his birthday. It was true, he didn't talk much. But he always knew that if he *wanted* to, she would be there to listen.

She always asked him how his day went, genuinely interested in whatever he wanted to share, even though most of the time he didn't say much. But she had always accepted his taciturn ways, and he'd never felt the need to appease her with idle chitchat. A quiet comfort had existed between them; they had a style of communication that didn't require dense vocabulary. They conversed in a lexicon of energy and feelings, exchanges of expressions, unstated resonance with one another.

She doesn't ask anymore. Doesn't even seem happy to see me. She looks... He searched for the right word. *Scared... she looks scared of me.* He gulped down the tightness filling his throat. *Well, I'm afraid of her too.*

Recalling the sequence of events of *that* day, he could come to only one conclusion: *It was as if the best thing that ever happened to me became the worst thing that ever happened to her.* This thought hurt his heart, and he agonized that this new, inhospitable version of his mother was all his fault. He didn't understand it but had decided the only thing he felt he could do to ease her burden, the suffering *he* was causing her, was to keep his distance, stay away, and hope that someday she would not be afraid of him.

Making matters worse, the climate at school had become even more unwelcoming and dismal than usual. Finn never shared the true nature of the unrelenting teasing and bullying, having no interest in making himself even more of a target by being the kid whose parents showed up at school to complain.

But the memory of the honey-voiced girl that had sung to him on that gloriously golden day filled his mind and his senses in all his waking hours. When he closed his eyes to better recall her voice, a teacher's reorienting nudge would embarrassingly break him from his reverie. Bony-elbow pokes and less-than-gentle shoves from his peers were humiliating reminders of his increasing obliviousness to those around him. The further Finn retreated into his private pursuit to relocate her voice and the hidden message it seemed to carry, the louder the juvenile snubs and adolescent slurs became.

It was miserable, but he wasn't about to talk to his mom about it. *Or Dad. He's never here anyway.* He wasn't sure how he would endure the few weeks left until school let out for summer, but he didn't see much of a choice. *Just keep your head down and wait it out.*

Yet, the next morning, an improbable solution presented itself. A sickly and squeamish proposal that lifted the tiny hairs on the back of his neck, soured his belly, and left his mouth dry and bitter. A terrible proposition to which he could not say no.

It was beautiful. No more troubled looks from teachers. No more ridicule from the peers-turned-bullies. A few quick hours completing the tedious assignments sent home. Then he was free.

There was just one condition.

"You can't tell your father, okay? This is just between us." His mom's voice had been soft, the way it used to be, but somehow it didn't leave him comforted.

Finn knew it was wrong—*very* wrong—but it was the first time in so long that he saw a tiny smile grace his mother's face, the first time she seemed pleased with him instead of suspect and evading. What she would be getting out of this secret pact, Finn was unsure; however, he felt like he had been given a gift almost too good to be true.

I should have known it was too good to be true. Turning over, Finn slipped his arm out of the comforter to take hold of the silent stone still hanging from his neck. *Still cold…* His heart ached as he pressed it hard to his chest, wishing for its warmth and presence to return.

The mysterious rock he'd found in his pocket *that* day didn't use words, of course, but its vibration and temperature—soft hums, a sleepy warmth, a random pulse—felt communicative. Sometimes when he placed the small stone just so against the bare skin on his chest, above where his inner companion nested, the girl's song would come to him clearer, closer, louder.

But even she is quiet now. She had arrived the same day as the song and the stone—a fluttery, flappy movement inside that Finn imagined as a little bird that had taken up residence inside his rib cage. She was a happy bird. He didn't know how he knew she was a *she*; he just knew. She purred and trilled and flitted from rib to rib, perching where she could best talk to him. She, too, did not use words but spoke in movement and motion. When Finn would settle his stone over his heart, she would nestle up right underneath it, and they would vibrate together—the stone warm and buzzy, she fluffy and purring. And with the memory of the girl's song resonating deep within his bones, he felt completely in sync, aligned, and in perfect balance. Understood and no longer alone.

But now they're gone… all of them… I should have told Zeb while I had the chance. And now that's gone too.

The Okiciya Community Center had been his mom's idea and part of the *agreement*. While he had enjoyed the escape from the harsh landscape of school, Finn had started to crumble under the severe and oppressive energy of his mother, unchecked by his dad's frequent absence. So he'd readily agreed when Klare brought up the idea at dinner one rare evening when his dad was there. It was a masterful piece of choreography that provided a seamless segue away from Nic asking probing, potentially exposing questions about school.

Finn had been surprised to find himself so warmly welcomed into the openhearted community center. A deep comfort had infused him along with a peculiar sense that he had been there before. The moment he met Zeb, a strange thought that initially didn't seem like his own arrived inside his mind, whispering, *"Yes, you can."* By the end of his very first day, the encouraging message had indeed become his own, and he knew what it meant.

"Here, you can tell. Yes, you can."

Finn had begun by scattering little bits and pieces of his story's details, testing the waters to see if it was safe to wade in deeper. The fear that Zeb might become afraid of him or begin treating him differently, like his mother had, was almost unbearable. But he had come to trust the consistent solidarity of the man and believed his new mentor would at least listen.

Of course, I felt the same way about Mom and look what happened there.

Finn's cautious toe-dips and vigilant temperature checks yielded no signs of reactivity or judgment. If anything, his tests were met with curiosity and interest. He had finally worked up the courage to show Zeb his stone, leaving out its remarkably expressive attributes for the moment. Zeb had taken a long pause to consider the stone before a knowing grin appeared on his tanned, lined face, deepening the crow's feet at the corners of his dark and shiny eyes. The story Zeb shared in response had made Finn's ribcage companion bustle wildly.

"In my tribe, there was once a great warrior chief, the most celebrated of them all. Even though he was brave and most skilled, he was shy. He would not often participate in dances or celebrations, even when they were in his honor, and preferred to stay on the periphery. But he was fierce in battle, and he defended the land and his people, and they looked up to him. A medicine man once gave him a small, sacred stone with a hole in the middle and said it would protect him and his horse *Inyan*—which means "stone"—from bullets. Some say he wore the stone, and others say his horse wore it. He was in many battles, but he was never wounded by a bullet. Many say it was because of the protection of the stone he kept."

Astonished by this unbelievable story, Finn had wondered if perhaps his own stone was enchanted, if it too held some sort of special power or magic. He mused quietly at the idea that maybe the warrior's stone spoke to him too through vibrations or heat or in song. It was overwhelming, but in a fascinating way.

"What was his name?" Finn asked.

"You may have heard of him. His name was Crazy Horse."

Curious, Finn had wanted to know more. "I'm not sure I have."

"As a young man, he went on a journey in search of guidance that would help him help his people. He spent two days alone on the prairies without sleep or food. And then he had a vision. A man on a horse appeared before him, and they floated and danced in the air as if they were spirits. The horse changed colors and seemed to be made of flowing shadows, which is in part how he received his name."

Finn could barely believe it. A sacred stone. Visions where things float and dance and change colors. Now he knew for certain. He was going to tell Zeb about the girl. The girl of *his* visions. It was time.

Speechless, Finn had reflexively clutched the stone beneath his thin shirt, wondering if he would also tell Zeb about the bird fluffing and flitting about beneath the stone as he spoke.

"Ready to go into Friday wrap-up?" Zeb had asked, interrupting Finn's trance.

"Yes."

In that moment, Finn decided he was going to tell Zeb on Monday. Everything.

But his chance never came. Instead of Monday being a day of beginnings, it became a day of endings. Painful, excruciating, heartbreaking endings wrapped in unbelievable betrayal.

Finn burrowed down deeper, pulling his blankets up around his chin. Time was strange these days. Some moments ticked away in slow motion while others sped by and left him behind, desperate to catch up.

So much has happened.

He held the unresponsive stone in his fist, sad at its lifelessness. The void where his avian companion had once nested remained in his silent chest.

And the girl. She's still dead. Dead and gone.

THE NIGHT WINDS down and a young man dozes off, longing for second chances. A stone held tightly begins to glow, reawakened by hope anew, covering the sleeper in a dazzling golden shimmer from the lively embers flickering within its core.

"**W**ow, what a punch to the gut." Nic straightened from his bent posture, using the back of the couch as leverage, and exhaled, trying to free the cramp stuck in his solar plexus.

Struck speechless by his son's charge and unable to formulate a response before Finn retreated upstairs, Nic brought himself back to the present with a few deep breaths, where the sobering truth resided.

It's true, I haven't been here. Looking at his wife's clouded face, he thought, *She looks as stunned as I feel.*

"But he's right, Klare. We've both been gone. You've been distant and preoccupied, and I've literally not been here." Dismayed, Nic shook his head. "I wanted to respect your request for space, but I didn't think about how it would affect him. Honestly, it never occurred to me that he would even notice." Guilt and regret pulsed alongside the ringing deep in his ears.

Klare's expression remained blank, but her knitted brow and twitching eye told Nic she was trying to sort something out. He reached over and pulled her hand into his, giving it a gentle squeeze to draw her attention. The anger he had experienced mere minutes before when she'd snapped at him had been eclipsed by Finn's surprising confrontation.

When she finally met his eyes, Nic inquired, as gently as possible to keep the somber calm of the moment, "What do you think he meant by '*Whatever you thought was happening was not what happened*'?"

Klare seemed to teeter on some invisible tightrope, her eyes wavering from side to side, as if trying to decide which fall would hurt the least. Finally picking a side, she did her best to describe the indescribable.

"I smelled smoke, and then suddenly I was flying down the hall, stomped out what was burning, threw his comforter away, and went back into the house. I have no idea if it was two minutes or twenty." She spoke of how she had watched herself, as if on a movie screen—both actor and audience at once—as a smoldering odor activated an internal alarm and triggered an involuntary sequence of actions that seemed to be controlled by something outside of herself. She had the strained, pained look of someone trying to recall a disturbing but important memory.

Nic gingerly advanced another step. "And he said there wasn't any fire. Not even a flame." The acoustic din rose and fell in concert with his tremulous worry as moments ticked by without a response from her.

"Klare?" Her eyes were glazed over, and Nic couldn't tell if she was even hearing him. "I know there's a lot we need to sift through, but it'll only work if we do this together. For Finn, for each other. Because we're all we've got."

It was true: they were all they had in terms of family. No grandparents. No siblings. Just them. Sure, lots of friends—well, Nic had plenty. Klare, not as much. And Finn, nearly none, except for the new folks at the center. If they were going to make it, they needed to do it together.

Nic's mother, Gigi, had passed years ago, just shy of her forty-seventh birthday. She was a sweet-natured painter and spent much of her time, especially after Elem died, out amongst the trees and in the restorative salty air of the sea. Nic always thought she and Klare would have loved each other, and Finn… well, he and Gigi were of the same cloth.

Her short life had been marked by painful losses, and in the end, Nic believed it was the grief that got her; she died—quite literally—from a broken heart. The rueful thought that he, in his departure for med school, had become just another person who left her behind had plagued him for years. But she had been so insistent.

Nic had breezed through undergrad, having channeled his own grief into academics. He'd received a full ride to Case Western in Cleveland, and when he had voiced his reservations over leaving, Gigi had been adamant he go and told him nothing would make her prouder. She would stay, of course, comfortable with her artisan community nestled in the coastal redwoods in Santa Cruz County. Nic was twenty-four and his mother a mere twenty years older; both had assumed they had a whole lifetime ahead of them.

But within three years, Gigi was gone. Nic had taken the time necessary to settle her affairs in California before he had returned to Cleveland, but without the same amount of heart needed to thrive in the intense, frenetic pace of med school. The gritty chafe of grief Nic had been able to tuck away since Elem got sick was no longer kept at bay by overzealous academic study.

Its abrasive press sent him running, literally, and he discovered his new diversion. He put in the necessary effort to pass his courses and spent the rest of his time on trails, streets, and tracks—anywhere he could lose himself in the run.

After meeting Klare, Nic was surprised to learn that she, too, had lost a brother and father at a young age. And like him, she had grown up alone with her mother, Bridget, who still lived in nearby Sugar Creek. Klare had told him that she and Bridget had never been close, and after the loss of her dad and brother, the chasm between them widened. Aware that sometimes loss splits people apart, Nic was grateful he and Gigi had remained bonded and close after Elem's death.

Klare had always been reluctant to visit her mother and didn't seem to enjoy talking about her, or their family's past. But once they found out Klare was pregnant, Nic pushed for them to build a connection with Bridget. After all, she would be the only grandparent their child would have.

Yet when Finn was four, Nic had seen a side to the woman who was lukewarm on the best of days, severe and icy on most others. He tried to forgive her—to extend her some grace after the incident where he almost lost his mind and very much did lose his temper. But after that day, Bridget became even frostier and more aloof. There were a few strained attempts to connect over a holiday or birthday, but they often ended in nasty, spiteful spats. In time, the visits ended altogether, and no one seemed heartbroken over it.

Nic studied Klare's frozen stare that seemed to look through him rather than at him, a precise portrayal of Finn's earlier comment about his mom being "*here but not here at the same time.*" Still holding her hand, he gave another squeeze to help usher her back when a dreadful thought erupted in his mind.

Oh my god. Her dad and her brother. Nic closed his eyes against the horrifying image his brain conjured of a smoldering house burned to the ground. *Dying in a house fire—that's what this is about.*

"Klare," Nic leaned in and whispered, controlling the intense urge to blurt out what felt like an answer that could immediately explain everything, but also one that needed to be offered up with caution. "Honey, I just had a thought that might shed some light on what happened the other night." He could hear the restraint in his words over the receding bout of tinnitus.

Seemingly startled by either his tone or words, or both, Klare's vision cleared, and her eyes locked on Nic's. "What do you mean?" she asked tentatively, slowly pulling her hand from his.

Sensing her guard raising, Nic reassured, "Just hear me out, okay? I think this could be important." His lungs pulled in a full load of oxygen to help him prepare for what he hoped would offer relief rather than pain.

"You said you smelled smoke and then it was like you were out of your body, watching yourself, and you even lost your sense of time, right?" Nic hoped the eggshells upon which he stood would hold up.

Klare nodded warily and he continued. "The smoke. Maybe it triggered an old memory. There wasn't a fire, and there was no danger, but you reacted like there was—like what Finn said about you thinking something was happening that really wasn't." Nic desperately hoped she would make the connection before he had to spell it out. The uncertainty resting heavily on her furrowed brow and in her squinting eyes made his stomach lurch.

Ugh, here it goes.

"Your dad and your brother. Maybe the smoky smell reminded you of losing them in the fire. So, you sprang into action, like you needed to save him, all of us. But it was from a memory. Not what was actually happening." Nic held, fearful that even the slightest breath might collapse the shaky foundation beneath them.

He watched her gaze, still locked onto his, fade and pull her back into some faraway part of herself while the shells underfoot slowly cracked and fractured into tiny, little pieces.

Klare rose from the couch, brushed imaginary wrinkles from her pants, and in a chilling voice that sounded nothing like her, said plainly, "I need some space. I'm going upstairs."

Nic shook away the sudden image of his mother-in-law stiffly walking across the landscape of his mind, an unwelcome guest in his internal home.

"No, Klare. Don't. We need to talk about this. Please. Come sit back down."

But his words held no substance. Within the clanging cacophony back in full orchestra, Nic watched helplessly as his wife turned her back and made for the stairs.

Alone, Nic wondered what to do next. He peeked in on Finn, who was fast asleep, and despite his reservations, gave Klare her "space." Back downstairs, he headed for his study and picked an album at random. *Mona Bone Jakon* by Cat Stevens.

That'll do.

He set the needle on side one, dimmed the lights, and collapsed heavily in his chair. A disagreeable soup of betrayal, shame, and worry sloshed, a nauseating concoction that reminded him of his final stretches of time with Elem—bitterness and resentment facing off against love and compassion in an incomprehensible battle that often left Nic defeated and desperate.

Stevens' soulful voice filled the room with poignant and passionate wisdom, forceful and gentle at the same time, pulling forward in Nic's mind the image of his childhood patron Linda, who embodied many of these same elements.

Linda had been a bit of a wanderer, a *nomad* she called herself, and loved to tell stories of her many travels. On the day that Elem died quietly in his bed, Linda had told Nic a story about how, in the beginning of time, there was no such thing as illness. But one day a man became unwell, and not knowing what to do, the people made a circle around the man and chanted prayers and sang songs of love… and the man got better. So the people started treating illness this way—by encircling ailing people and holding them in love and healing wishes until they got better.

When Nic had tearfully asked why it didn't work for Elem, Linda had folded her arms around him, pulled him in close, and whispered, *"Nic, the love and prayers that surrounded your brother helped him know that he was not alone. While his illness was too big to cure, I know in my heart that Elem could feel the love and care we all had for him, and I choose to believe that this brought him comfort and solace, knowing he wasn't alone, that we were right there with him, all the way to the end. Nic, when people are hurting, they need to be surrounded and held tight in love. It's important to move in close, not move away."*

A sorrowful tune, a woeful plea to be released from trouble's torment, alighted in Nic's ears, laying bare a reality he'd yet to acknowledge.

"I moved away," Nic muttered softly.

I didn't move in close when things got tough. I moved away. Shame spread through his chest, heavy and hot.

Just like my father.

Nic didn't remember much about his father. He had left when Elem arrived, a second child apparently too much to handle. Nic had vowed that he would never be like his absent father, would never dip out when things got tough.

But that's exactly what I did.

Nic closed his eyes against the burn of remorseful tears, took a deep breath, and reset his vow.

My family is hurting. It's time to move in closer.

He let the final track come to its close and set out to lean in with his wife.

15

Uncertain of what mysterious mechanism was making her body move, Klare allowed herself to be marched up the stairs, reflexively putting one foot in front of the other until she was safely on the other side of her bedroom door. As if the soft click of its close powered down the machine manipulating her movements, Klare collapsed onto the bed, a rag doll who'd lost her stuffing.

Her body was an empty shell, numb, and without thought, her awareness trimmed down only to the rhythmic *whoosh* of the blood making its circular journey through her system. Before long, other sounds and sensations began to permeate her consciousness: the coolness of her breath flowing through her nose, an irritating itch in the middle of her back, and then a swell of thick nausea as Nic's words surfaced, " … *your brother.*"

NO! She pressed her palms into her temples and clamped her eyes against the image of Scott. The face of her long-gone brother had been popping up unsolicited for weeks, each time bringing a painful stab of fear and guilt. She had worked hard to keep that part of her life in the past. That was another lifetime, one she had no interest in revisiting.

Nic was just trying to help, a kind voice inside offered.

From that simple assurance, her body flinched with a strong spasm of her stomach.

Oh my god. What is happening? The familiar question repeated its answerless probe, but this time, Klare supplied her own response: *The same thing that will keep happening if you don't…* She squeezed her eyes shut against words that came next:… *Talk to him.*

As if shocked back to life by these three simple words, Klare moaned and rolled herself up to sit on the edge of the bed, images volleying back and forth, knocking from one side of her brain to the other: herself on the phone with Dr. Myles' office, on the phone telling Cassie that Finn would not be returning to Okiciya, on the phone with the school—*twice.* Listening but not listening to their concerns and questions. And finally, herself in this very room, on the phone with the one person she never believed she'd reach out to for help.

How can I ever tell him? Just the thought of it hurt her brain. *How am I supposed to explain why I called, not just once, but twice?! I don't even understand it.* She rubbed her forehead, hoping it would help ease the pounding. *And taking Finn out of school? Telling him not to tell his dad? Ugh, I don't even know how to begin to explain that one.*

"Maybe you don't need to," a censorious voice inside tempted. *"What's done is done. And why make matters worse? Maybe…"*

The urge to ask her mother for parental guidance had vanished that long-ago day when Bridget had berated a four-year-old Finn and sent Nic into a fury. In truth, that impulse had slowly dwindled after Klare's brother and father died when she, too, was just a child and her mother had become a hardened shell of a person. So when the thought to call her mom for help had struck her after she received a "concerned" call from Finn's school, Klare was dumbfounded.

Itchy, that thought scratched and chafed at her for days despite her best efforts to dismiss it. She had considered calling Lucy, but for some reason that felt wrong, risky. But the compulsion to call her mother, despite how nonsensical it was, had been unrelenting. The more she'd attempted to ignore it, the stronger it had become, occupying her mind day and night, to the point where she was desperate for relief. By that time, Klare knew there was only one way to satisfy that itch.

"Hi, Mom. It's Klare."

"Oh. Hello, Klare."

Still icy as ever. Her gut retracted like a frightened turtle withdrawing into its protective shell.

"How are you?" she asked.

"I'm fine, Klare. What's wrong?"

"Nothing. Nothing's wrong. I just wanted to maybe get some advice from you is all."

Bridget scoffed. "Advice? From me? Hmpf."

I knew this was a bad idea. The muscles at the base of Klare's neck tensed.

"Yes, Mom. But if it is too much trouble, never mind. I just had a couple of questions about… Never mind, I—"

"Well, you already have me on the phone," Bridget interrupted with an irritated huff. "Might as well go ahead and ask."

Klare deliberated backing out of the call, annoyed and embarrassed that she had even considered this a reasonable idea. Her stomach concurred.

"You do *already have her on the phone… just ask,"* the impatient inner voice admonished.

"Um, Finn's school called with some concerns, and I wasn't sure the best way to handle it."

"What did they say? What kind of concerns?" Curiosity got the better of Bridget.

"Just some observations. They say he's been distracted, not participating in class, and there's some bullying going on it seems."

"He's bullying other kids?!" Bridget sounded indignant.

"No, Mom! He's not bullying anyone. He's *being* bullied."

"What does *Nic* say about it?"

Klare cringed at her mother's scornful emphasis on *Nic*.

"Uh, well, I haven't talked to him about it yet. He's busy, and I don't want to bother him…" More belly spasms. It was true she had not told Nic, but it wasn't because he was too busy. She couldn't actually pinpoint why; it felt like some sort of physical instinct not to, even though it didn't make sense to her brain.

"Good."

"Good?" Klare questioned. "Why good?"

"Because you know how these things get once everyone starts putting their opinions out there. Better to just handle it directly with the school. *Discreetly.*"

Klare's intestines twisted. "What do you mean '*discreetly*'?"

"I just said!" Her mother was becoming agitated. "Soon as people start sticking their noses into your business, it can get very ugly. Prying, accusations, then the targeting. You *know* this!"

"Mom, no one is sticking their nose in or accusing anybody of anything! And Nic is not just some random person. I just have never gotten a call like this before, and I wasn't sure how to handle it. I'm sorry to have bothered you with this. Maybe I…"

"Why now? Why are they concerned now?" her mother pressed.

Shit. She had chosen not to tell the school about Finn's *episode*, and she wasn't planning on mentioning it to her mother. The inner voice harped, *"You wanted advice. What are you waiting for?"*

Klare paused, feeling her mother's impatience pulsing through the airwaves. She didn't want to tell her about the incident, but the unremitting pressure from inside would not stop. She stared at the antacid bottle across the room but couldn't make herself walk over to get it.

"I don't know, Mom. Finn had a little episode a few weeks ago. The ER said it was just dehydration, and I didn't even tell the school about it. But I don't know, maybe they are related." Klare cringed as the words slipped from her lips.

"You took him to a *hospital?* Klare, you know what happens to people in those kinds of places. He probably got pumped full of medications, didn't he?" Bridget's tenor was taut and screechy.

"Mom! No, I just told you. It was dehydration and he was not put on any medications. What were we supposed to do—not get him checked out? He wasn't feeling well, and we had to make sure he was okay."

"Well, now you did it. Now they have a file on him. And they probably asked a bunch of personal questions, didn't they? I'm curious, what did you tell them?" Nothing about her mother's accusatory and angry voice was *curious.*

"This is ridiculous," Klare rebuked. "I didn't tell them anything except what they needed to know. Seriously, Mom, I just was hoping to get some advice on how to handle the school calling because I remember you went through this with Scott, and I thought you might be able to help. But obviously, I was—"

"DON'T YOU DARE bring your brother into this!" Bridget erupted with a blistering wrath Klare had not heard in years, but her body remembered it immediately as her insides withered and shrank. "Here you are dredging up the past and there is nothing good that will come from it. You've done enough damage already putting him under the noses of those doctors, and now the school's calling with *concerns*? You think that is a coincidence? You'd be wise to get him out of that school immediately, but it's probably too late now."

Deflated and defeated, Klare felt angry that she'd listened to the irrational part of herself that had somehow convinced her that making this call was a good idea.

"I'm sorry I called, Mom. I didn't mean to upset you. I just thought…"

"You just thought, you just thought," Bridget mocked. "No, your problem, Klare, is that you *weren't* thinking. If you were, you would *not* have put your son at risk, and you would have told the school to mind its own business. Now everyone's gonna start talking, and you know how *that* goes."

"I didn't put Finn at risk, Mom." Even to herself, she sounded unconvincing.

"Yes, you did. And you should have known better." Her voice was steel.

"Mom…" Klare's stomach turned over with enough force to snap an already-thin internal thread, detaching a part of herself from her body and sending it drifting up and away from the rest of her.

"I don't want to hear any more of this. You have ruined my perfectly good day."

Click.

For days, Klare had been filled with self-reproach, stunned at what she eventually decided must have been some bizarre slip of judgment—a momentary lapse in reason related to her recent lack of sleep. She certainly would not be heeding her mother's advice and definitely would not be telling Nic about her embarrassing break in common sense.

Then the second call had come. It was Mrs. Boyle, Finn's principal. Klare knew it wouldn't be good, and she was right; it wasn't just a follow-up on the "concerns" expressed by Finn's teacher earlier that week. This call included questions, the kind that sent Klare cascading down the very path her mother had warned her about.

"Finn looks so tired. Is he getting enough sleep?"

Prying.

"We're curious if there might be anything going on at home that might be bothering Finn?"

Accusations.

"He's caught the attention of a number of teachers on campus who have expressed worry about him."

Targeting.

Klare's attempt to stay grounded during the call had been thwarted by her mind's stretching and pulling itself apart, establishing two separate camps inside her brain.

One faction sat in fear, and its leader asked, *What is happening to my son?*

The other faction sat in judgment, its leader challenging, *"Are you going to let them do this to your son?"*

Paralyzed, Klare had felt suspended between two divergent hemispheres and powerless to move in either direction. She'd had just enough awareness to recognize that she was not responding to their questions and how easy it would be for them to see *that* as a problem, but she could not find any words or make her mouth say them.

Then the blow had come—the one she hadn't been aware she was bracing for: "We'd like Finn to meet with the school counselor. To perhaps get some insight into Finn's recent presentation?" Mrs. Boyle's statements—her *accusations*—came out more like questions.

But Klare knew what Mrs. Boyle was getting at.

And Klare knew then what she needed to do.

Klare stood, stretched, and made her way to the bathroom. After brushing her teeth, she stepped into what she hoped would be the kind of shower that would wash away the loathing and disgust that seemed to have made its way through her pores to her very soul.

This isn't how it's supposed to be. Nic's right about needing to work together, but…

Tolerating as much heat as her skin could handle, Klare closed her eyes, letting the near-scorching deluge cascade over her, imagining it sucking the shame, pain, and disgrace out of her body and sending it down the drain. She let the swirling steam envelop her and imagined it expunging the fear and loathing that clung to her skin. When the shower cooled enough to bring her back to her senses, she was well-pruned and exhausted.

Wrapped in her thin terrycloth robe, Klare wiped the fog from the bathroom mirror. The flush in her cheeks mildly obscured the purple half-moons that hung beneath her eyes. She stared back, focusing on the gold haloes that encircled her bottle-green eyes.

Together.

It was bizarre how a word—one that spoke to unity, closeness, partnership—left her at such odds. Part of her longed to be free of her private burden—the secrets and the tremendous fears behind her inexplicable actions—but another part recoiled at the thought of telling.

I don't know if I can.

As if her worrisome thoughts had telepathically drifted downstairs, Nic was suddenly there behind her, his soft sable eyes meeting her reflection. He wrapped his arms around her and whispered, "We're going to get through this. Together."

16

Two more days, then Zeb will be back! A dull stitch of disappointment had pinched Finn's insides when he'd learned that Zeb was going to be out for a couple of days. He knew he had no real option other than to be patient, so he focused on his happiness about being back at his beloved center.

The past few days had been a roller coaster of slow, anxious climbs toward fleeting peaks of hope, rapid descents into valleys of sadness and worry, and stomach-dropping twists of fear and anticipation in between. He was glad his parents were semi-talking again but found himself bracing when he'd walk by their bedroom, as if he could feel the tendrils of friction and strain unfurling from under their closed door.

But he hasn't said anything yet. Finn fretted each time he thought about his dad. He wondered just how long it would be before his own complicity in the early-withdrawal-from-school plan would be discovered, and the thought made his stomach sore.

When not sequestered behind closed doors, Finn had painfully watched his mom struggle to engage during meals and with conversations. He could tell she was elsewhere, preoccupied with something painful and weighty that caused her face to pinch and twitch.

Like something wicked has a hold of her. The sticky edges of a familiar remorseful thought had emerged. *Because of me.*

A tender bruise inside sorrowed over the shadowy something that persisted in tormenting his mother, over the loss of the girl and her song, over the continued absence of the uplifting company of the stone that had hummed in harmony with the flit and flutter within his ribcage. But the edges of that purply sore spot singed red with the sharp reminder of his mother's betrayal.

Well, at least I'm back at the center now.

To help soothe the burn, Finn had spent his week reacclimating to his dear community and rehearsing his plan for telling Zeb, finally, about his special secret.

I'm not going to lose my chance this time, Finn silently avowed.

Finn had desperately wanted to talk about the girl with the mysterious message and how her song had first arrived and enveloped him in a shimmery cocoon. He ached to share the discovery of the mystical stone in his pocket, and the new and feathery fluttering presence in his chest. All of it. But both of his parents had been quickly rendered unavailable the very day the girl arrived in his world.

He had no words to explain how he knew—he just *knew*— that she'd come to him on purpose and that there was something he was supposed to do. Over those first few days, curiosity and intrigue had reigned, deferring sleep for hours while he pondered, certain that if he thought enough about it, the answer would come to him.

Sleep-deprived and desperate, Finn had continued inspecting his stone, driven by an unyielding sense that it was some sort of clue or key in this mysterious puzzle. Turning it over and back and looking through the small hole in its middle, without thought, he brought the stone up to his lips and blew softly through its center cavity.

Whoosh. An infinitesimal puff answered back, lifting the fine hairs from his forehead.

Oh my god! Heart hammering and ribcage full of excitable flutter, Finn brought the stone to his lips once more.

"Hello? Can you hear me?"

A silvery, ethereal chord sprinkled forth, quiet as the predawn mist.

"Oh! I can hear you! I can hear you!" his trembling voice whispered urgently.

Terrified to lose the thread of connection, Finn gently pressed the stone to his right ear and felt his hearing reach out through the aperture.

Tears sprang to his eyes as he listened to the same sweet, wordless melody that had first called him to her. His heart thrummed in concert with his breastbone dweller as a weightless energy whistled through his bones.

Finn carefully lowered himself onto his pillow and rolled onto his right side to keep the connection between the stone's opening and his ear unbroken. He'd closed his eyes to heighten his aural sense and was instantly captured inside her lyrical hymn. Awash in happy relief, Finn surrendered to the cottony warmth that seemed to reach through the small eyehole and envelop him while taps and raps ricocheted softly within.

I hear you. I'm listening.

Finn had given himself over to what felt like an invitation. Images of rolling emerald hills materialized against the backdrop of a glittering azure ocean, and the sweet notes of her delicate refrain drifted faintly upon the breeze. Not dreaming and not fully awake, he was somewhere in between—suspended.

By virtue of the collusive deal with his mother, Finn relished the days at home, alone in the privacy of his room. With the stone's amplifying aid, he could enter the pristine realm of grassy greens and sapphire blues undisturbed. There, he would search and seek, fervently trying to catch a glimpse of her, but she remained elusive.

When he had to break contact with that magical place to make a brief appearance at dinner or to not draw too much attention to himself, it was excruciating. But he'd quickly mastered a strategy to ensure he put in just enough face time to evade parental scrutiny and had taken to wearing the stone on a thin cord around his neck, beneath his shirt, to keep it close to his heart.

Essentially unrestricted, Finn dove deeper into his majestic world. New details began to emerge—undulating meadows, a sinuous coastline, tiny vessels with billowing white sails swaying gracefully on the tides. He could see the faint traces of smoke wafting up from distant chimneys, and what he thought were either wagons or carts making their way along paths and trails, led by miniature people. He strained for a closer view, but his towering bird's-eye vantage did not allow it.

Then one day, as though catching hold of the tail of a windswept kite, Finn grabbed onto her voice. Vibrant and crystalline pure, it filled the entirety of his being. He pulled himself closer on the invisible tether of her song and nearly lost his breath when he finally, after all this time, saw her.

He wasn't close enough to make out precise details but he was near enough to see that her hair was coppery-gold, as if each amber, honey, and poppy shade of an autumn sunset had been delicately woven into her locks. She seemed to be about his age—not quite a girl but not yet a woman. Even so, a wise and clever aura surrounded her, leaving Finn with the sense that she was brave and used to being on her own.

As if the glowing center of the stone had linked them, Finn watched from a distance. The girl with the sunset hair sang by the indigo seaside, ran through the hills, picked wildflowers in the open countryside, and walked through tiny portside towns. She sang to him, and he asked her questions.

What is your name?

Where are you?

What am I supposed to do?

Although she never responded—at least not with words— he felt in the core of his being that she had come to him for a reason. His head had not quite figured out what exactly that was, but his heart swelled and fluttered and buzzed with a *knowing* that there was a reason and that, in time, he would understand. He loved her, and although he could not explain how, he knew she loved him too.

When Finn had finally decided he was going to tell Zeb everything, he'd spent all weekend rehearsing how he would share his story. But on Monday morning, his world had caved in. He couldn't imagine anything worse happening. But it did.

He had hurriedly dressed and rushed down the stairs, hoping his mom would be finished with her morning coffee so she could take him to the center early. As he stood in the doorway, he had wondered if the vibrancy rippling under his skin and setting his bones ashimmer would be as evident on the outside as it felt on the inside. He'd stifled an excited giggle, laughing at the image of himself sparkling and aglow with electric glitter.

But when Finn had entered the kitchen and saw his mother sitting at the table, steam from the hot mug in front of her masking the deep hollows beneath her eyes, he had felt the twinkling inside and around him sputter and go out, extinguished in an instant by his mom's static, foreboding look.

Halted by her demeanor, he stood still, wondering if she even noticed him enter.

"Finn, we decided you aren't going back to the center."

He remained frozen, his brain unable to comprehend his mother's words, while the rumble inside his chest gasped in understanding.

"You've been spending so much time there, and I think it'd be good for you to stay at home for a little while."

Why?! I love it there! Stay home? With you?! Finn's internal voice shouted at his mother.

What she was saying was incomprehensible.

Finn had stood for what felt like an eternity, staring in disbelief at this woman he did not recognize. Her pale, haunted face remained fixed on her untouched cup, her eyes never once connecting with his.

Without a word, Finn had turned his back on his mother and dragged his deflated body and broken heart back upstairs.

After the crushing blow delivered by the woman masquerading as his mother, Finn had spent the rest of the day secluded in his room and at a loss for what to do. He briefly considered calling the center, but the distraught and devastated jumble inside overwhelmed his brain's ability to produce what he could possibly say.

He stared bitterly at the shelf of fantasy books he and his mom had read together. Lofty quests and treasure hunts stood alongside brave journeys and the discoveries of secret worlds. They had almost finished a novel set in the gardens of mid-twentieth-century England, where they learned about the *pharmacopoeia*—sacred texts of the apothecaries that contained botanical and herbal recipes to remedy all range of ailments. Hours reading up on the history of the Society of Apothecaries that began in the 1600s had led to curious conversations about what it would be like to visit the famous Chelsea Physic Garden, which still stands, nearly 350 years later, on the edge of the Thames in London.

That once-warmhearted memory now seemed fake, like it hadn't really happened. The memory simply couldn't coexist with his life with his mother—*that woman*—right now.

"*… we decided you aren't going back to the center.*" As his mother's words reverberated in his head, Finn had dug his fingernails into his palms, trying to fight back the tears burning his eyes and blurring his vision.

When his father had peeked in on him late that evening, Finn had already pulled the covers up over his head and feigned sleep.

How could they? It was his mother's words that ruined him, but she had said "*we.*"

He'd squeezed and clutched the stone hanging around his neck, beseeching whomever or whatever might be listening to help him. *Please. Please. What should I do?* His tight fists had shaken with desperation and fatigue.

But the inside of his ribcage was unusually still and quiet, and the stone remained flat and cold within his fist. He could not hear the girl, no matter how hard he listened. It was as though his mother's fateful message had caused them to dwindle and die a little on the inside, just like he had.

After hours of fruitless attempts to locate her voice or receive some sign as to what to do next, Finn had concluded the only real option left was to go to sleep and hope she would visit him in his dreams.

And she did. But it was not the sort of dream he had hoped for. It was an awful, terrible nightmare wherein he watched helplessly from his great distance as she ran to escape her hunter. She was strong and brave, all the way up to the end.

Finn had not been able to turn away from the horrific nightmare that forced him to witness her murder at the hands of a most improbable assailant.

The girl without a name who had come to him on a breeze and enveloped him with her songs. She, who had stirred a sense of rightness, a belonging he had never known. The copper-and-sunshine-haired girl who wrapped him in effervescence and brought him the mystery of hope and the promise of something more. The girl he loved and who he was certain loved him… was gone.

Swaying between the wistful sorrow of loss and the buoyant prospect of second chances, Finn lay his head on his pillow, closed his eyes, and waited for the pendulum to slow. A solitary reminder emerged just as the weighty plumb settled in perfect balance.

"You know what to do…"

THAT WHICH IS hidden always seeks to be found. Surreptitious scraps swept under invisible rugs or messy morsels tucked into dark pantry corners are left with a mark—a trace signature that beckons, a continuous and relentless plea to the captor to be released from its prison, causing us to wonder: Is it we who are the keepers of secrets, or are they the keepers of us?

17

Bleary-eyed and drowsy after a heavy and dreamless sleep, Klare reached over to find her husband gone and the indentation on his pillow cool to the touch.

What time is it? What day… ? She stretched her sore muscles and rolled her neck from side to side to get her bearings, squinting at the bright sunlight streaming in from the edges of the blinds. *Ah, yes. Wednesday. Still morning, I hope.*

With her body waking up quicker than her groggy mind, Klare tried to anchor herself to Nic's assuring message—*together*—a lone buoy of a word floating in a restless, anxious sea as she pulled her robe on and shuffled down the stairs.

On the kitchen table, she found a note pinned under a lukewarm cup of black tea: "Taking Finn for breakfast then to the center… will be back around 11 ~ N."

She dumped the cooled liquid and brewed a new mug of herbal tea. *No caffeine for me this morning.* Anticipating the conversation she knew was coming once Nic returned, little jitters began a swirling dance in her belly.

How am I going to explain all of this when I don't even understand it myself? Klare hoped Nic's typically unruffled character—one of his strongest qualities—would help pave the way for all she needed to tell him.

"Do you really need to tell him everything?" a reedy, surreptitious voice asked from somewhere inside her.

Klare sighed. She was scared and knew that she had backed herself into a corner where stories and excuses would no longer help her.

Or lies, her conscience added.

She poured her tea over ice and made her way outside to the small table on the backyard deck. Fluffy heaps of cumulus clouds to the west were already lifting, forecasting another hot and clear day. She watched the russet and gray song sparrows flit from tree to tree, slightly jealous of their chirps and chatter, their cheerfulness an injustice against her tense, apprehensive mood.

Closing her eyes, she tried to imagine that the carefree birds weren't mocking her on purpose.

"Hey." Nic's mellow voice arrived from behind.

"Hey," Klare offered back as he settled into the seat next to her. A reassuring breeze moved through her in response to his proximity; she was happy he hadn't chosen the chair directly across from her.

The two sat in silence as each readied themselves for another inevitably difficult talk.

Quiet, contemplative sitting typically existed within the comfortable nest of their shared security, neither ever feeling a need to fill the space with words or meaningless commentary. But startling deceptions and harsh, unaccustomed retorts had seared the edges of the nest, leaving both its occupants guarded and careful.

Within the wary silence, Klare's chest strained against the swollen balloon of her heart, verging on exceeding the limit of what it could hold. Beneath, her stomach roiled and pressed. She breathed slowly to limit any additional air from coming in and impinging on the little space available inside. She needed relief, something to release the buildup so that she could breathe.

Say something. Anything.

She wasn't sure if those thoughts were directed toward Nic or herself, and she began a familiar tumble down the rabbit hole of trying to decide if it would be better for her to start, or to wait for Nic to begin, or if she should…

"So. Where should we pick up?" Nic's question pulled her up and out of her heady labyrinth.

Klare could hear the thinly veiled hurt in his voice. Or perhaps it was anger? Fear and worry collided in her belly, making it difficult to think.

"I'm not really sure." Klare didn't want to think about Nic's suggestion that the loss of her brother and father had anything to do with what was happening in the present, let alone talk about it. If she were being honest, she didn't want to discuss any of it.

Nic expelled a discouraged sigh. "Why don't we try to start from the beginning? Before the doctor's appointment or the incident in Finn's room. You took him out of the community center. Maybe we should start there."

Oh, no. I don't know if I can do this. The tip of this colossal iceberg was overwhelming enough, and she could hardly fathom dipping below the icy waters. She felt Nic's hand take hold of hers, a sturdy anchor that warmed the chill rattling her bones, and she breathed in a lungful of the summery air.

"Nic, I don't know how to explain it all…" *I can't believe I'm going to say this,* "but there were some things that happened before I took him out of the center."

Inside, two distinct sides were locked in a tussle, one that felt a loyalty to her husband and a desire to be honest and *together*, and the other side that rippled with guilt, reproach, and wrongdoing. It was a confusing mess.

Nic's face was unreadable, but his fingers remained interlaced with hers. She could tell he was consciously pacing his breath and could see a vein in his neck pulsing.

Together. Just start.

"Just bear with me, okay? This is really embarrassing…" Another deep breath, girding herself for his response. " … but I called my mom."

"Okay?" Nic's question carried the weight of anticipation. "So how is Bridget nowadays?" Klare could hear the bitterness in his voice and knew he was not truly interested.

"She is the same old Bridget. Angry. Cranky. Totally put out by life… By me…" Her words sounded distant and disembodied within her ears.

Nic nodded in that *"Of course, were you expecting anything different?"* way.

Klare knew she needed to take advantage of his question. If she clammed up now, he may not offer her another.

"It's embarrassing. Honestly, I have no idea why I would have expected anything else from her." She braved a quick glance at her husband's face, and her heart issued an extra-strong thump when she saw his jaw clenching.

"So, you called her for a reason, I assume?" He was clearly measuring his words and his tone.

Klare inhaled fully, her chest painfully expanding by just an inch.

Together, Klare reminded herself of her husband's reassurance, a grace she wasn't sure he'd continue to offer after this conversation.

"I think I need to back up a little bit first, okay?" She glanced at him again and saw the set jaw and flat stare—his arduous attempt at patience.

He's so pissed. Klare's stomach clenched to squeeze the words from her throat. "I called her after I got a call from Finn's teacher. She said he looked tired and seemed preoccupied. Was having trouble paying attention and that some of his peers were picking on him a little."

She drew in another thin stream of air and continued. "I remembered when I was a kid that the school sometimes called my mom about my brother, and I just thought maybe she would have some advice for me about how to handle it. I don't know, Nic. Even saying it out loud right now sounds ridiculous."

Why isn't he saying anything? Now the pulse in her neck throbbed. *Just keep going.*

"And of course, it was a terrible conversation. Full of her typical rhetoric about people being nosy troublemakers and needing to mind their own business and all that. Honestly, a couple of minutes into the conversation—if you could even call it that—it was obvious she wasn't going to have anything helpful to say, so I just let her finish and got off the phone. I felt stupid for even calling."

"Okay, a lapse in judgment. That can happen to the best of us, I suppose." He finally looked in her direction, his features softened just a bit. He raised his eyebrows as if to say, *and…*

Klare exhaled and emptied her lungs of the air she hadn't realized she was hoarding. *It's now or never.*

"There is more. A lot more. I'm so sorry, Nic." Klare's belly was in full topsy-turvy mode now, flipping and flopping as if it had a mind of its own.

It was Nic's turn to expel the air his lungs had been holding onto, his exhalation rushing out with an audible *whoosh.*

"Well, let's hear it then."

Klare tried to slow her intestinal roller coaster so she could focus. She needed her wits about her to talk about what came next. And next after that. And after that.

He might never forgive me...

"So, I didn't do anything—at that point. The school had never called before, and I figured I was just overreacting. But... then they called again. They asked questions about how things were going at home—had Finn been sick, had he been sleeping, eating—things like that. I wasn't sure what they were getting at. It just seemed like they were insinuating something."

"What did you say?" Nic's strained voice rang hard and hollow.

"Nothing. I got upset. I felt like they were accusing me of something but wouldn't say what. I told them there was nothing going on, and then they said maybe Finn should see the school counselor. I don't know how to explain it, but I just had this overwhelming sense that I needed to protect him. From the teacher, the kids who were teasing him. There wasn't much left of the school year at that point, so I pulled him out early." Her pace picked up the more she talked.

"You what?" A crack in Nic's façade caused her to lean away an inch.

"I pulled him out early. I called the school back the next morning and told them he wasn't feeling well. They said they could send the rest of his schoolwork home, and since his grades were good enough..."

"I can't believe this." Nic dropped his head into his hands.

And this isn't even the half of it. Numb and disconnected from her body, Klare hadn't felt Nic pull his hand from hers, but she noticed the several extra inches he'd scooted away.

When he lifted his face, his eyes glowed with anger and betrayal. "Klare, how could you have done this without talking to me? How on earth did you think that was okay?!" His volume had gone up a notch, and the tautness in his tone followed accordingly. He tugged roughly on his right ear lobe as he shifted his eyes away from her and onto the ground.

"Nic, I don't know how to explain it. I just had this terrible feeling that he wasn't safe. That if I didn't get him out of there, something bad would happen. I couldn't shake it, and I don't know… it seemed like the best solution in that moment. And then I found the community center and it seemed like… I don't know… like a *safer* place for him to be."

Klare reached over to grasp Nic's hands and thought for a moment he might pull them away. "Nic, I am so sorry. Honestly. It seems like so long ago, and I felt confused and scared. I'm sorry."

He stretched his neck side to side, clearly trying to steady himself. "The school called not just once, but *twice*, with concerns about *our* son and you didn't think to talk to me about that? Instead, you thought you would call *your mother* for advice." Nic's unveiled, sarcastic tenor betrayed his furious disbelief.

"I don't know. I was overwhelmed. It was like a part of me knew I should tell you about the calls and we'd figure it out together, but then some other part of me just sort of took over. I can't explain it, but it felt like some sort of threat, and I just needed to take control. I wasn't thinking. I was just doing."

Nic's face was pinched in focused concentration, and he nodded slowly. "Klare, this is not like you at all. What is this really about?"

"I don't know." Klare was exasperated. She desperately wanted to go back inside and crawl into her bed, but she knew that was not an option. She'd already spent so much time under the covers, and it hadn't helped.

"Nic, I don't have a good explanation, but I'm really trying to understand it myself. But there is more I need to tell you…"

Nic raised his head, restacked his posture, and took another deep breath. "Okay, what else?"

Klare's stomach gurgled, and she fought back a wave of nausea.

"I called her again. A couple of weeks ago."

Klare shook her head. She knew Nic's incredulity was justified. Her memory fell back to that one afternoon, nine years ago, when Bridget had hammered the wedge that had splintered the already tenuous connection between her and her daughter's family.

Finn was four at the time, and Bridget had agreed to watch her grandson for a couple of hours so Klare and Nic could have a day out. Finn was Bridget's only grandchild, and Klare knew she loved him, even though her stiff guardedness made it hard to see that sometimes. Bridget would often comment that Finn was like no other four-year-old boy she had ever seen and very much unlike Klare's brother, Scott, who she said had been "all bruises and scrapes, dirt and tangles, and moved around this world like a miniature whirling dervish."

They had pulled into Bridget's driveway, still absorbed in the contented glow of a beautiful summer afternoon alone. Klare opened the door on her side of the car and froze midmotion. Upon exiting his side, Nic caught his wife's bizarre halt and stopped short. It took only a split second to hear the screaming voice coming from the house, but Nic was in motion before Bridget's violent shrill reached Klare's consciousness.

He flew through the front entrance, nearly taking the flimsy screen door off its hinges and letting it slam back against its frame with an audible *crack!*

Klare's legs forced her to follow her husband through the door, across the living room, and around the sharp left-hand turn into the small, narrow kitchen, even though her mind could not grasp what could possibly be happening.

Finn was backed up against the wall just to the right of the fridge, and Bridget was towering over him, shrieking accusations and shaking her closed fist in his tiny, terrified face.

"What the fuck, Bridget?!" Nic shouted as he threw himself in front of Finn and faced his mother-in-law. The fury of his physical form forced her to take a step back.

From her frozen post at the doorway, Klare watched the exchange in disbelief.

"Look at this!" Bridget screamed, cheeks contorted in purplish-red rage. "He could have set this whole place on fire!" She leaned to the side to try and meet Finn's face again. "What were you thinking?! How dare you!"

Nic moved toward his mother-in-law, physically pressing her back and away from his son with the full presence of his body.

"BRIDGET! STOP IT!" Nic's thunderous rumble shocked Bridget into silence.

Klare was stunned to see her mother gasp and sputter while her own body shook and trembled.

Just then, Nic grabbed the wrist of Bridget's right hand, and her proffered clenched fist reflexively popped open, revealing a small fluorescent-yellow Bic lighter, barely two inches in length.

Klare's stomach lurched, and she felt her knees buckle.

Nic's voice decreased by several octaves, and he spoke to his mother-in-law in clipped constraint. "Bridget, he is a child. He wouldn't even know how to work this thing. What has gotten into you?"

Bridget was a picture of bruised ire, the image of Faye Dunaway in *Mommy Dearest* in true form.

Keeping a grip on his mother-in-law's wrist, he turned toward Finn, who was stock-still pressed to the wall behind him with eyes wide open in tearful terror.

"Klare!" Nic called to her.

Her body did not move, but her eyes slowly locked onto Nic's.

"Klare!" he repeated with a little more force this time, successfully breaking the spell that had bound her and triggering a sharp intake of breath.

Turning her face toward Finn, Klare dropped to her knees to catch her boy as he ran and collapsed into her arms. She picked him up and looked back at her husband for direction.

"Take him to the car. I'll be right out."

Just remembering that fateful afternoon sent flurries of shame, guilt, and nausea through Klare's system. She knew it had taken everything in Nic's power not to shove Bridget, and she could not convince him that there was no way her mother would have struck Finn.

She could not remember much about the event other than small, insignificant details—a thin crack on the countertop in her mother's kitchen that she hadn't noticed before, a place where the linoleum was starting to peel up in one corner near the sink, the caustic smell of bleach.

She always uses too much bleach.

Klare knew she had frozen, but only because Nic had told her as much. She chalked it up to being shocked and surprised at her mother's behavior, and to seeing Nic so angry.

Maybe it was more than that. The disembodied voice offered, and Klare swiftly pushed that idea aside.

THEN THERE ARE the other kind of secrets—the ones we keep even from ourselves. Guarded by the wardens of unwanted awareness, those painful truths simply too difficult to acknowledge appear to us in the outside world, recast and reassigned to the character of another, freeing ourselves from that terrible, unknown burden.

18

Swinging open the impressive eagle-etched glass door, notes of cinnamon and apple greeted Finn's nose. Cassie said Zeb would be back sometime later in the afternoon, so he set out to channel his mentor's patient authority while he waited.

When he'd returned to the center earlier in the week, Finn had been touched to discover that his peers had stepped in to maintain the sector of the community garden he had volunteered to oversee. He was proud of his plot—Guardian strawberries encircled by white coneflowers, all backed by a row of tall Russian sage—free of weeds and spent blooms, lovingly manicured, and looked after with noticeable care. Shared responsibility was a value highly regarded by Zeb, who talked about its virtues often.

With his section immaculate and freshly watered, Finn moved to another sector, one less tended to than his own, and sunk to his knees to get to work. The cool, moist soil welcomed his hands and grounded him to the earth. Valerie, a girl a few years older than he, joined him, and they worked in comfortable communion, in harmony with the vibrant morning birdsong.

"Hey, Finn?" Cassie's call brought the young man back to the present. Absorbed in the loamy smells and verdant textures of the earth's offerings, Finn had been transported to a place that transcended time. When he stood, he noticed Valerie was gone, and the shade's shadow had wandered across the yard. A bolt of anxiety shot through his chest, reorienting his mind to his current time zone.

How long have I been out here? What time is it? Did I miss Zeb? What if I'm too late… again?

Cassie, reading the worry that flashed across his face, tendered a broad, compassionate smile that radiated a reassurance that put Finn's fear to rest.

"Zeb's back. Figured you'd want to see him before the end of the day," she said with a knowing wink.

Feeling he might fall over with relief, Finn got to his feet and made haste for the lobby.

As promised, Zeb was there, carefully hanging a large colorful print on the east-facing wall. Just seeing his mentor was a salve to the burn of eagerness Finn had felt most of the week as he had waited for his second chance.

The print was radiant, an abstract portrait against a backdrop of electrifying swirls and swaths of brilliant color. Finn first noticed the obscure features of a man's face and quickly discerned the outline of an elaborate feathered headdress. An image of a horse was subtly embedded into the background, along with shapes of other animals and birds suspended in splashes of yellow-blue and purply red. The picture seemed to shift and dance as if it were alive, emitting a powerful visual energy.

Words from Zeb's story about Crazy Horse swam up into Finn's mind, " *…floated and danced in the air… the horse… changed colors… made of flowing shadows…*" The stone that had hung flat and cold around Finn's neck for almost two weeks suddenly felt warm and tingly against his skin. Reflexively, Finn gripped the stone and felt a stirring charge pulse through his body. The inside of his ribcage awoke with flits and flutters, sparking a sharp gasp as oxygen rushed into his lungs.

It's time.

"Hello, Finn," Zeb greeted in his low, resonant way. "Are you alright?"

Finn hadn't realized that he'd made his way up to his mentor's side, staring wide-eyed at the print before them, nor the audible inhalation that must have alerted Zeb to his presence.

"Uh, yes. Yes." Finn could not feel his feet touching the ground. He stammered through the kaleidoscope of excitement and wonder in his belly, "Is that… that… Crazy Horse?"

Zeb smiled. "No, it isn't, but it is a relative." Sighing wistfully, Zeb began his story. "This is a portrait of my great-great-uncle, Nicholas Black Elk, who was also a warrior before he became a powerful medicine man. Many say he was the greatest spiritual leader of his time. His gifts came to him as a child, but he was young and didn't understand. He told no one, afraid people would not believe him or think him a fool. He kept everything inside for many years."

Gifts? What gifts?

A voice within urged, *"Listen!"* and stopped the flurry of questions blowing through Finn's mind.

"When he was seventeen, he finally told an elder medicine man what he had been experiencing since childhood. And the man laughed—not to mock or make fun, like Black Elk had feared, but because he was so astonished by what he heard. He told him that he had been given a rare and mighty gift, and he therefore had an obligation to carry out his divine calling."

But what gifts?! Curious and confused, Finn strained to keep his focus.

Zeb continued while he made final adjustments to center the print. "Black Elk lived a long, adventurous life, imparting his gifts and helping bring healing and unity to many people. When he was a very old man, he said that his one great mistake was having delayed telling anyone for so long. He was remorseful that he had spent so many years hiding rather than embracing what had been gifted to him."

I get it. This was not one of Zeb's stories that made one search for the meaning or moral. *It was my great mistake too—not telling and keeping everything inside.* Finn resonated with the great man's fear of not being believed or being thought a fool. *Or worse, a dangerous monster.*

But gifts? Although he liked what he had been experiencing and the feelings that came with the girl's presence, her voice, and her song, he didn't see them as *gifts.* Something that suggested a meaning, yes. Perhaps even a purpose? Maybe. But gifts?

"What was his gift?" Finn asked.

"He was a visionary. He started having visions as a small child—visits from the great ancestors who foretold of the future and what he needed to do to bring the people together in unity and peace."

Visions?! Visits?! Now! Tell him now! Finn's heart became a big bass drum, booming through his body. He could hardly believe what he was hearing but knew deep down in his core that none of this—his own intention for being here, the painting, the story—was a coincidence. He was meant to hear it.

He exhaled all his air and slowly filled his lungs to prepare, finally, to share the story of his visions—his *gifts*, if that's what they were—his chest aflutter and his stone pulsating in dazzling vibrato.

"Zeb? Um, I'm not really sure, but, uh, I think…"

"Hey, Finn! Hello, Zeb," a familiar voice called out.

A sentiment clearly meant to be cheerful and welcoming sliced through Finn, snatching the rest of his words before they could leave his mouth. He turned and saw his father walking toward them, his arm mid-wave in greeting.

Oh no! No! Everything around began to collapse, disintegrating into dust and powder, and Finn wondered if he, too, was dissolving.

"Hello, Nic. How are you?" Zeb kindly returned Nic's salutation and extended his hand for a shake. "Finn here was helping me get this print up on the wall."

This can't be happening. Why is he so calm?! Finn looked up at Zeb, certain the panic inside him was shooting out through his eyes in fiery red laser beams.

Zeb smiled, placed a strong hand on Finn's shoulder, and gave it a firm squeeze. "We'll pick up our talk on Monday, okay?"

This can't be happening. The panic exploded, extinguishing his breath and setting his body aflame. *I can't move.*

"Yes, you can. You must." The reassuring voice that lived deep inside spoke.

Finn barely felt the weight of his father's arm draped across his shoulders, and his feet seemed to move without his command, walking his body away from his second chance, the chance to fix *his* great mistake. He tried to wring comfort from the reassurance of Zeb's words and those of the quiet inner voice that continued to whisper, *"It's okay."*

Aching with disappointment of another lost chance, he wanted to believe… He *needed* to believe it was true. Finn focused on the warm pulse of the stone beneath his shirt and the spirited twitch within his ribcage that seemed to echo, *"It's okay."*

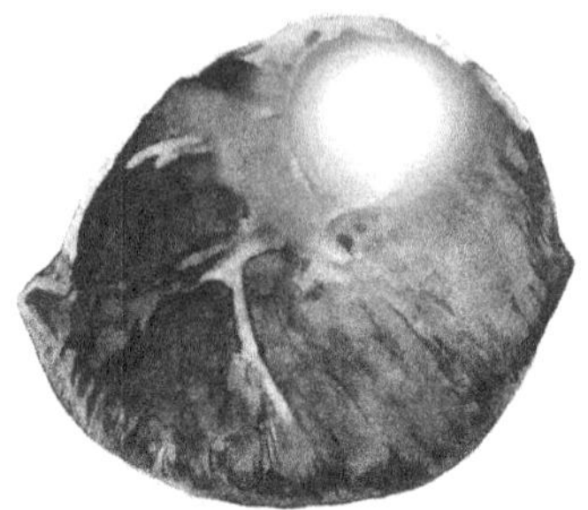

Successors of an eternal lineage, we each carry the cargo of those who came before us: the residue of an ancestral memory, the longing for a place never seen, a bit of ancient wisdom bequeathed from beyond. Dead or distant, known or not, their ghostly fingerprints wield their legacy until we are graced with the awareness of lineal choice.

19

It had been a struggle *leaning in* while Klare shared her string of deceptions. But after acknowledging the dreadfulness of her call with Bridget and the frightful lapse in judgment that led to making that call in the first place, to hear that she had called her mother *again* was simply too much. Nic had disconnected himself in that moment. Ironically, now it was he who *needed space*.

Shamefully aware he was not making good on his "*we're in this together*" pledge, Nic had gone to work the next day and busied himself with needless tasks in a badly failed attempt to sort himself out. By the time he'd come home, both Klare and Finn were asleep, so he sought out his downstairs recliner again. As he sat, remorse overwhelmed him. He had *moved away* when the going got tough.

Just like my father, he admitted with sour disgrace. He swallowed the max dose of Tylenol to help ease the clanging in his eardrums, although that remedy never seemed to help much, and leaned himself back into the broken-in chair.

When sleep finally found him, the riotous ringing had transformed into something more like the tinkle of fairy bells jingling sweetly upon the shoes of a fawn-haired pixie donned in silver and turquoise.

He rose, stiff and sore, followed the scent of coffee to the kitchen, poured himself a giant mug, and noticed Klare was sitting out on the patio instead of at her usual spot at the table.

"Hey." Nic took the seat next to hers. "Thanks for making coffee."

"I already took Finn over to the center," Klare said flatly without looking at him.

Oh boy, Nic moaned. *This isn't going to be pretty.*

"I'm sorry for not being here yesterday. And I'll apologize to Finn too. I just needed some time to… never mind. That's no excuse. I'm sorry and I'll do better." Nic felt like a heel, angry with himself for making what was bound to be another difficult conversation even harder.

"Well, I get it," she offered, her voice a touch softer this time.

After stalling as long as he allowed himself, Nic took a deep breath and jumped into the inevitable waiting waters. "So, what happened when you called your mom the second time?"

Klare scoffed. "As you can imagine, it was even worse than the first. I didn't even tell her about taking Finn out of school. I just wanted to ask her about what my brother was like when he was thirteen. I thought maybe it would help explain some of the changes I've seen in Finn."

"What do you mean, changes?" Nic's heart skipped a beat.

Klare paused and sighed, brows furrowed upon her tired face. "Isolating. Distant. Secretive, like he was hiding something. I don't know… edgy. He just seemed off, like something wasn't quite right."

Nic rubbed at his temples and shook his head, unable to fathom how Klare kept her concerns from him.

"Well? What did she say?" He clenched his jaw, bracing himself for the next disclosure.

"She was pissed. Yelled a lot. '*Why are you dredging up the past? Why are you trying to cause trouble? Why can't you just let things be?*' And so on. She basically said to knock it off and stop trying to create a problem out of nothing. You think I would have learned my lesson after the first call."

Nic stared at her, trying to choose his words carefully. "After everything that has happened with your mom, it's hard to believe you asked her for an opinion, about our son, of all things."

"I know, I know. It sounds insane." Klare's neck flushed dark and splotchy.

"No, Klare, it doesn't sound insane. It *is* insane. Honestly, after what she did to Finn, the things she said to him, why would you even think of going to her for anything regarding his well-being?"

Or not come to me? his wounded self wondered.

"I know, Nic. Again, I can't explain it, but I can tell you—it won't happen again."

Nic's eyes narrowed with skepticism. "How do you know? It happened twice already. What's going to keep you from calling her again next time?"

"I promise you. I won't. And if the thought even enters my head, I promise I will talk to you first," she pleaded, although breaking eye contact weakened her sincerity.

Nic shrugged and checked his watch. He itched to go for a run but knew he needed to stay.

"So, what about the community center? Did your mom have anything to do with that?"

Klare cringed, her sheepish countenance suggesting she knew this question would come up eventually.

"No. Not directly. I didn't even tell her about him going to the center. But I think all her talk about nosy people and the trouble they cause and needing to be careful who you talk to… all that paranoid ranting she does, I think it just got under my skin and I got scared."

"Scared." Nic could feel his patience wearing thin. "Scared of what, Klare? Honestly, what could possibly scare you so much that you thought the best thing to do would be to yank Finn out of there?" He turned to face her again and held her stare.

And hide it from me? Anger and hurt tussled in his chest.

Klare pressed the palms of her hands into her eyes, hard.

What does she not want to say… or see? Nic's pulse sped up, thready and anxious.

After a long, weighty pause, Klare removed her hands from her face but did not turn toward him. "It's like I said before. I had this overwhelming sense of dread or doom, that I needed to keep an eye on him, keep him close, protect him. I know it sounds ridiculous and doesn't even make sense. I knew it was irrational, but I just couldn't shake the feeling that he was in danger."

"In danger of what?" Nic pressed, eyes still trying to get hers to connect while panic crept into the edges of his vision. "Klare, look at me!"

Unable to behold his intensity, she settled her sight closer to his chin. "I don't know. Like something might happen to him. What if he gets lost again? Gets disoriented and wanders off? But rather than being found by some nice ladies in a church, he gets picked up by someone and taken away? What if he gets hurt or… hurts someone accidentally? I just got scared he…"

"Hurts someone?! Klare, what are you talking about? Finn? Hurting someone? Where are you getting these ideas?"

Klare didn't answer but lifted her fatigued eyes and looked back at him.

"Wait, is that what this is about?" Nic exhaled hard, a wave of empathy suddenly washing over him. "That day at the café and the ER? I mean, that was scary, and it could have been worse, but it wasn't. Is that what you've been worried about?"

"No, no." Klare brushed the question away like a bothersome gnat.

Genuine confusion bled in from Nic's periphery. "Are you sure? You don't sound very certain."

"I said no! What else do you want me to say?" Klare snapped.

Recoiling as though his wife's snap had landed like a slap, Nic was stunned silent.

Oh no, here she goes again. Nic stared at this distorted version of his wife, and an image of his mother-in-law surfaced repulsively in his mind.

Bridget.

As if some invisible hand had reached into her head and flipped a switch, *his* Klare was gone, replaced by this terrible imposter. The other invisible hand, or perhaps the same one, had also reached into him and flicked off the light, plunging Nic into darkness. His belly went cold with the severed connection, the swell of compassion was gone, and he could only think of one thing to do.

I gotta get out of here.

In the spiky, barbed silence that followed, Nic mentally sifted through his preferred running spots, absorbed in deciding which one would be best for a day like this. A series of short buzzes emanated from his pocket, pulling his attention back to the present.

> *Hey. You guys up for BBQ*
> *tonight at the house?*

Nic stared at the text from Dennis; he couldn't fathom going anywhere with Klare right now.

> *Would love to, but not a*
> *good day for us.*

> *Not a good day like in other*
> *plans... or not a good day?*

> *Not a good day.*

> *We could come over there if*
> *that would be easier... we'll*
> *bring everything.*

> *Sorry. Not sure if 'easier' is*
> *possible today.*

> *Hey, when the going gets*
> *tough...*

> *The tough get going?*

> *Seriously? No, you circle*
> *up, man.*

> *Haven't heard of that one.*

> *Well, you should. Bill Withers,*
> *dude. Keep it in mind.*

Bill Wi… Ahh… Nic rolled his eyes. *I get it. Lean on me…*

The lyrics to one of the greatest songs of all time poured forward with its iconic melody.

Nic placed his phone back in his pocket, sticky embarrassment reminding him that it wasn't all about him. Dennis was leaning in, as good friends do.

Grateful for his clever friend, who may or may not have intentionally oriented Nic back to his childhood champion's sage words, Nic thought of Linda.

"Nic, when people are hurting, they need to be surrounded and held tight in love; it's important to move in close, not move away."

Nic sighed. All thoughts of a run wiped clear from his mind, he turned to Klare, intentionally keeping his voice calm, "Okay, look. No more calls, okay? Not to your mother, not to doctors, to the center—anywhere—without talking to me first."

Klare nodded in agreement.

"He's my son too, and it is not okay that you kept these things from me. Not just your decisions but your concerns and worries too." Bolstered by his friend's reminder, Nic sank back into compassion and kept his voice soft and sincere.

"I know. I'm sorry," Klare replied, accepting Nic's bid for connection.

"I am glad you're telling me these things, and I'm sure there is more to it. Coming clean is the first step, but you need to clean this up with Finn. Tell him the truth about school, the center, why you took him to that appointment with Dr. Myles. You need to make this right."

"I know. I will." Klare winced in agreement. "And with you too."

Nic stood up from his chair and leaned over to plant a gentle kiss on Klare's forehead.

"I'm gonna go pick up Finn a bit early. Oh, and Dennis and Lucy invited us over tonight. Think about it, okay?"

20

Am I taller? I feel taller. Finn wondered as he strode up the pathway to the center, a newfound energy in his step. The beautiful sunlit morning reflected the sunny glow of his hopeful heart.

He had spent the weekend poring over a most remarkable story, one that seemed to breathe precious life into his stone and his bird and, therefore, his soul. The stirring support he felt inside fueled his plan of action.

Today is the day.

Entering the lobby, Finn was greeted by the thick perfume of roses and the sight of Cassie juggling several fragile containers. Quickly, he rescued one of the more precariously balanced vases and placed it gently on the edge of her desk.

"Thank you, dear! My rose bushes are on fire right now! They just love all this heat!" Cassie's sweet drawl and effervescent disposition mirrored Finn's golden mood.

He followed her into the kitchen where more vases waited to be filled with the scarlet, pink, and apricot bundles of cut stems strewn across the countertops. Turning to face him, Cassie answered the question Finn hadn't yet asked. "He's out back at the circle. Said y'all have a meeting this morning, so go ahead on out there. Koko's out there too."

"Thank you!" he exclaimed, and hastily made for the door.

The warmth of Cassie's kindness lifted the corners of Finn's mouth as he went in search of Zeb. The narrow gravel footpath that curved toward the circle at the back of the property was flanked by galvanized steel garden tubs to the left and Cassie's abundant rose bushes, bursting with bright colors and heady fragrance, to the right. The tubs were filled with leafy lettuces, curly purple kale, tomatoes, and all sorts of summer herbs, ripe and ready for picking.

I hope our garden at home will look like this, Finn wished, thinking about a conversation he and his dad had over the weekend about planting a garden in the backyard.

He walked quickly, aware of the tingling anticipation that had settled in his bones the night before. He was still stunned by what he had read and beyond eager to talk to Zeb about it.

The faint return of the familiar hum and purr encouraged him, even though a lonely void remained inside for the girl who had yet to return.

Because she's dead. That painful memory was still sharp.

"I know. It's okay," reassured the quiet, private voice.

Finn sighed. He was determined to make good on what now felt like an obligation—a special contract he had made with himself and with the man whose story he'd read. It was no longer an option *not* to tell.

A sacred obligation.

He found Zeb exactly where Cassie said he would be. A few of Finn's peers were there as well—Valerie, Reuben, Jed, and Angela—helping to take round, flat stepping stones from pallets and placing them around the perimeter of a cleared circular space. The order and intended shape evident, Finn silently joined the assembly-line process.

Not interested in interrupting the coordinated harmony of the group, and bolstered by his sense of *obligation*, Finn surrendered to the flow, and time slipped away like it always seemed to when he was in the zone. The kinetic rhythm of simply moving rocks from here to there generated that same secure feeling of doing exactly what you are supposed to be doing, as he often felt when working in the garden. Koko, the center's resolute sentry, supervised the crew from her spot in the shade.

He had no idea how much time had passed when he paused and noticed that his peers had vacated their posts, likely in search of a break from the labor and some of Cassie's snacks, of course. He was surprised and admittedly relieved.

"Okay, it's time."

"Zeb?" Finn asked politely. "Can we talk?"

"Of course." Zeb straightened, stretched his back, and made for one of the benches in the shade next to Koko, who lay down as if she could finally relax into a well-earned nap now that those under her watch were on break.

Finn followed. A soft honeydew shimmer danced around the edges of his vision. Amused by the fleeting thought that perhaps he needed some water, he knew the peripheral sparkle had nothing to do with dehydration. What exactly it meant, he was not sure, yet. But he welcomed it freely whenever it decided to arrive.

His mentor waited patiently while Finn reviewed his mental notes about what he'd read so he could make the proper connections.

Finn's initial distress at his father's early arrival on Friday had slowly dissipated on the ride home when he decided to do some research about Zeb's distinguished relative. It was an act of strength to be patient during the Fulton's barbeque that evening. Dennis and Lucy's kids were all much older than he, but he enjoyed their company, especially after the unusually long stretch without seeing them. Sadly, his mom remained preoccupied and appeared disinterested, while his dad struggled to socialize, with most of his attention focused on her.

Once home and in bed for the night, Finn had found an e-book available for instant download through his library and had dived headlong into the story of Nicholas Black Elk, the revered Oglala Lakota holy man. Snippets of Black Elk's life, told by him to a man named John Niedhart, glowed like sparks of kindled flames and embers lifting off the page and dancing in front of his eyes to light up the very air he breathed.

"… when I first heard the voices…"

"… like somebody calling me…"

"… happened more than once…"

"… a strange power glowing in my body…"

The synchronicities between his and the illustrious leader's experiences buzzed bright with magic. The avian flutter near his heart and the subtle pulsing of the stone against his chest felt it too, resuscitated by this man's story.

"… but what they wanted me to do, I did not know…"

"I liked to think about it, but I was afraid to tell it…"

Finn had no words to describe the kinship he felt with a man dead more than fifty years before he was born, but it was there.

Colors and light and heat and energy had flowed unobstructed in the channels of his body, humming through his bones as if they were hollow. The same shimmery azure green pulsed and vibrated around him like an electrostatic field. Finn didn't know what it meant, but he was certain it meant something, and he knew in that moment *how* he would tell Zeb his story.

"I read about Black Elk," Finn began, his eyes locked on Koko's leisurely swishing tail. Zeb did not respond, but Finn was well-accustomed to his mentor's clever use of silence to encourage people to keep talking. "His visions were not just dreams. He had them when awake." Finn looked over to see Zeb's affirming nod. "And he also heard voices."

"Yes, they were part of his gifts," Zeb clarified, speaking as if this were the most natural of conversations.

Gifts. Finn could not wrap his head around *his* experiences being *gifts*, but the flutter around his heart seemed to understand just fine.

"Zeb, did you ever have visions?" Finn bit his bottom lip nervously. His eyes remained trained on Koko's comforting presence while his ears waited in anticipation for Zeb's reply.

His mentor nodded, and a sentimental smile appeared on his bronze, deeply lined face. "Much later in life. Few are blessed to receive visions unbidden, like Black Elk. Most go on a quest in hopes of having a vision that will offer direction. It took me a long time before I was ready to go on my own journey, and I was lucky that my request for guidance was answered. But like my great-great-uncle, it wasn't until I shared my vision with my people that I was able to understand what it meant, and the path it was directing me to follow."

I can't believe this. The fuzzy, cocooning sensation dancing joyfully in Finn's periphery seemed as excited as he was.

"What kind of vision did you have?" he asked, hungry to hear more, and stole a sideways glance at Zeb's face.

Just as the man began to answer, a piercing screech cut through the air above them, calling their attention skyward. A majestic bird with a body the color of alabaster marble and a vibrantly fanned auburn tail drifted gracefully against the backdrop of blue on outstretched black-and-white-striped wings. She floated aloft on the invisible wafts and then settled near the top of a nearby white pine.

A deep and hearty chuckle broke free from Zeb's typically tranquil demeanor, snapping the spell that bound Finn to the noble bird above. He was taken aback by his mentor's animated reaction and the laughter that continued while he shook his head, amused by some unspoken joke.

"Well," Zeb dabbed at the corners of his eyes and continued, "our beautiful friend here just offered me a not-so-subtle reminder. This is a time for me to listen rather than talk. Please, tell me more."

Finn didn't understand the private exchange that seemed to have happened between Zeb and their aviary visitor but decided he would ask about that later.

It's time.

Finn's heart thrummed in sync with the ripple within his ribcage and the warm murmur of his stone. He did not have a word to adequately describe the sense of connectedness that traveled through his entire body, but it sizzled with life. He took a steadying breath.

Obligation.

"I think I had a vision." His most precious secret floated free from his mouth.

"Visions," an inner voice pressed.

"Visions," Finn corrected and turned his vulnerable face toward Zeb.

Zeb bobbed his head with slow, pensive nods, and Finn's emerald aura shivered in delight. His mentor looked up at the beautiful lady hawk still perched on her lofty branch. "I'm listening."

Finn mirrored his nod, lifted his chin to the sky, closed his eyes, and inhaled long through his nose. Energizing, magical words swirled and swelled inside, an effervescence pushing them forward until they tumbled from his lips, plump and full of spirited strength.

He began with the first day the girl's honeyed melody called to him—a beautiful song tucked inside a breeze that wafted its way to his ears through the branches of the trees' rustling leaves. The beckoning lilt he blindly followed, only to find himself blocks away without knowing how he got there.

Lovingly patting his chest with his right hand, Finn then told of the stone he mysteriously found in his pocket and its powers of amplification that seemed to connect him to the girl's song. And the stone's feathery counterpart, a lively presence living inside his chest that Finn pictures as a tiny bird the color of sand and snow.

With eyes misted in fond remembrance, the young man revealed the girl's visits to his dreams and the times he could sometimes hear her, even while awake. How he could see her from a distance, but never so close that he could touch her or talk with her. That when she was near, he felt special and important, that his body would fill with liquid sunshine, and that for the first time ever, he didn't feel alone.

Tears trickled from the corners of Finn's eyes and ran freely down his face. The relief he felt was almost overwhelming, and yet, an ache remained.

I miss her so much, he thought.

He took a full breath to dissolve the lump in his throat and opened his eyes. What he saw both surprised and comforted him.

His stalwart role model held his palms to his chest, one over his heart and the other grasping his medicine bag. He swayed lightly from side to side, and a soft smile graced his serene face.

He's listening! Finn noted with wonder. He could feel the weight of Zeb's ebony eyes upon him. The man sparkled with…

Excitement? Fascination?

After a long, reverential moment, Zeb straightened his spine, expelled his held breath, and spoke slowly. "Finn, this sounds like a very special experience. I'm curious what you believe it means."

Finn's shoulders fell in sync with the drooping of his mouth. His head rolled forward, and a choked sob escaped from his throat.

"Finn?" Zeb leaned in closer, his concern palpable.

"I don't know, and I'm afraid I'll never know." Sorrow enshrouded him, leaden and gray, threatening to wash away the comfort of the bottle-green glow. "I always had the feeling that she was trying to tell me something. That I was supposed to *do something*, but I couldn't figure it out."

Finn released a tiny, wounded moan.

"But then she died. In my dream, I watched her die." Tears seeped steadily down his cheeks. "And when I woke up, everything was cold and quiet inside. I should have told before. I wanted to. And now it's too late. She's gone." The jagged skip inside made Finn wonder if his bird was crying too.

"Okay, hang on there," Zeb responded softly. "Our dreams, our *visions*, the images that come to us, are not necessarily…

literal. Often, they are symbolic, and thinking about them that way can sometimes help us discover their meaning."

Another strong flutter ricocheted off his heart. *Is it possible she could still be alive?*

"One thing that is important to know is that making meaning and discovering purpose cannot be done in isolation or by keeping it all inside. Black Elk's visions came to him when he was alone, but it wasn't until he started talking about them that he understood what they meant and then what he was supposed to do. My vision came to me when I was alone, but I could not fully understand what it meant for me and my purpose until I talked to others who could help me."

"Can you help me?" Finn asked in shaky desperation.

"I will absolutely help you."

A most welcome release in Finn's body sparked the return of new tears—tears that held promise and hope, of possibility and potential—and the noticeable absence of the fear that had imprisoned his words for so long.

Finn could barely comprehend the next question the man he had just revealed his most sacred secret to asked: "What do your parents say about it?"

Noooo! Terror sliced through him, leaving his sight dotted with black spots and his hearing muffled, his words trapped in the darkness of his throat.

Still sequestered behind a choke, Finn was incapable of vocalizing what screamed in his mind. *I can't tell them! I won't!*

Zeb's astute keenness, written all over his face, assured Finn that he was still listening.

A thread of safety arose inside and pressed forward a reminder. *Obligation.* Despite his misgivings, he somehow knew this was true. He drew a steadying breath to relax his throat enough for his words to connect with his voice.

"It's my mom. She can't right now. I can't… I haven't told them."

Zeb contemplated Finn's response, his brow revealing concern. "What's happening with your mom?"

Finn looked skyward and noticed the lady hawk was still perched high in the pine. Part of him felt like talking about his mom was some sort of ugly betrayal, like telling someone else's secret. But another part of him urged forward. *"Zeb's listening. He's listening to you."*

Trusting, Finn spoke about his mother: her distressing reaction in the ER, the furtive side-glances of suspicion and mistrust, the withdrawal from him and his father behind an impenetrable wall of distance and unapproachability. Guilt throbbed in his belly, detesting the picture he was presenting of his mother.

But it's true.

"She's never been like this before. It's like something snapped in her." Sour, disloyal words sat heavily on Finn's tongue, pressing against the inside of his lips. True words. Words that needed to be said. "Then she took me to this doctor, after she told me I wasn't coming back here, and it was awful."

Finn recounted the heart-shattering visit to Dr. Myles. The stark, depressing office of the sweaty, puffy doctor who assured Finn's mother that the mirror between his office and the room where Finn waited was completely soundproof.

"But it wasn't. I could hear almost everything. My mom thinks I'm hallucinating and starting fires. The doctor talked about schizophrenia and danger. He gave my mom papers about sending me for a mental evaluation…" His voice quivered. "She thinks I'm a monster." The bleak despondency he felt that day returned in memory, thankfully not as intense, but enough to bring a thick lump back to his throat.

"I am sorry, Finn. That sounds terrible." The pinch in Zeb's brow was back, and he shook his head in what looked to Finn like disappointment. "Finn, you are no monster." He placed his hand on Finn's shoulder. "And your mom…" His mentor's voice trailed off and concerned confusion rose on his typically unwearied face.

"My dad told me I would not be going back to that doctor or be sent away." Finn relayed how his father had also apologized, both for not being aware of all that was happening and because his mother was not herself right now.

"She hasn't been herself. It's like something happened to her, and she hasn't been the same since. And I'm afraid it's…" He paused, afraid to speak it out loud, to make real a thought he had long-hoped was not true. " … because of me. That's why I haven't told them." Relief at releasing these truths was dampened by the guilt of talking about his mother.

"I'm sorry she is suffering, and that you have been suffering too. And I'm glad your dad stepped in. Is he helping your mom right now?"

"He's trying."

"Do you think your dad is someone who can help us with this?" Zeb's voice was gentle.

"Yes." Through his fear, Finn also felt a glimmer of hope spring from the thought of not carrying all this alone anymore.

"Good. Here's what I suggest. We ask your parents to come in. I will support you in telling them what you shared with me, and we will talk about a plan for helping everyone get the support they need. Would that be alright with you?"

Inside, a battle brewed. Fear and the urge to run away and hide squared off against the longing for more relief—to be free from the binds of secrets and distrust that had overtaken his family, and to not go back to feeling alone in his own home.

Finn paused to consider Zeb's suggestion, and a throng of butterflies found his stomach and began their frenzied dance.

"Finn, experiences such as yours are complex, rarely clear, but full of infinite possibilities—like a giant jigsaw puzzle. We cannot know what picture the puzzle will reveal until we've sorted through and figured out where all the pieces go. And for a puzzle this big, we can't do it alone. We need others' help."

Finn looked at his mentor with gratitude, his eyes pleading for more.

"Your mom has her own puzzle, and so does your dad. But they are all connected. There is a lot to figure out, but it'll work best if it's done with guidance."

The sparkly aura revved up again, dissolving the hesitancy that had been lurking around the edges. Taking in the visible care that shone in his mentor's eyes, Finn squared his shoulders, stacked his spine, and nodded his head.

"Okay."

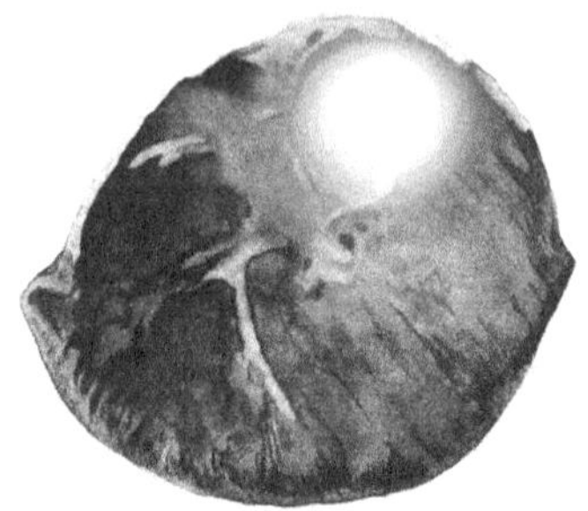

IN OUR ANGUISH-DRIVEN misdirection, we relish the dark, yet long for the light. And while the reason for our concealment may be unknown, its consequence is visible to all. A wise man once said there are three things that cannot remain hidden long: the sun, the moon, and the truth. And the truth must be seen to reveal what comes next.

21

Klare woke with the familiar feeling of a boulder resting hard and heavy in the pit of her stomach, keeping her lungs from taking a full breath. She curled onto her left side and folded her right arm over her middle to help quell her nausea.

"This is a good thing!" Nic had reassured her last night. *"You've been concerned about his distance. Maybe he's ready to open up."*

Try as she might to squeeze even a drop of cool comfort from her husband's optimism, her insides remained an arid and desolate void.

Nic had talked about the importance of showing up for their son, especially considering his confrontation regarding their respective absences of late, but Klare was still feeling the sting of her son's words when Zebulon Paytah had called and asked that she and Nic come to Okiciya for a meeting the following afternoon. His vagueness about the purpose of this meeting sent cascades of queasy wariness through her system.

By morning, her guarded mistrust had swelled into dreadful paranoia.

Why wouldn't he just say it over the phone? What is he holding back? Who else has he talked to? Did he ask other parents to come in, or just us?

The only thing that helped keep the onslaught of dubious theories from overwhelming her was the fact that she knew there was no way she could avoid this meeting. She wasn't exactly sure how she was going to pull it off, but she had to be there.

Klare closed her eyes and gave herself five more minutes to rest before she forced herself to get up and face the day. A few chalky tabs and a cup of herbal tea should do the trick. But it didn't. Neither did the deafening solitude at the kitchen table while she watched the clock count down the time until she and Nic needed to leave.

Ugh, this is gonna be a disaster. I can feel it.

On the way to the meeting, Klare concentrated on the pressure of Nic's hand on her knee, imagining it holding her in place so she wouldn't float away.

I can do this. If he wants to talk, fine. It doesn't mean I have to. Even to herself, she sounded like a bratty teen. *Just show up and listen. Just listen.*

Klare glanced over at her husband, whose light and carefree countenance contested her own. Rather than feel reassured by his easy presence, she felt even more scared inside, as if he knew something she didn't. She popped a few more Tums.

Upon entering the lobby, the strong perfume of roses sent another woozy wave through her. She quickly accepted the cold bottle of water Cassie offered and held it to her forehead.

"It's pretty hot out there, isn't it? I have more if you need any. Just go ahead and have a seat and make yourselves comfortable. Zeb and Finn should be in any minute."

Why is she so cheerful? Her nerves set on edge, she looked at Nic. *How is he so calm?* Irritated, she sipped at her water and tried to settle herself.

Finn and Zeb arrived a few minutes later, and by the looks of them, they'd been busy with some sort of outdoor activity—faces aglow with the sheen of sweat and a layer of dirt or dust, or both, on their clothes. They had apparently stopped by the kitchen to wash their hands and were attempting to tamp some of the earth from their sun-kissed arms.

Klare felt a sliver of relief at what she instantly read as Zeb's collected calmness and Finn's quiet contentedness in whatever laborious task he had been engaged in.

Maybe it's not so bad? she wondered cautiously.

"Thank you for coming." Zeb greeted Klare and Nic with firm, friendly handshakes and motioned them toward his office. Inside, the pair took the couch by the window while Finn opted for one of the solo chairs. Zeb promptly took the remaining single chair next to Finn.

"Thank you for asking us in," Nic replied in a tone that, to Klare, came off a little overenthusiastic.

Resolute in keeping herself composed and steady, Klare turned toward her son. "You look like you've been working hard out there! Are you having a good day?" Her voice sounded awkwardly reedy and far more anxious than she intended, and she stifled an embarrassed groan.

"Yes," Finn affirmed and kept his eyes trained on Zeb rather than meeting his mother's.

He's nervous. A pang of fear darted through her chest, and with it, a stab of wary suspicion. *I hope they don't turn this on me.* She flashed on the memory of calling Cassie to inform her that Finn would not be returning, and of her fingers tapping *decline* on her cell phone when the center's number showed up later as an incoming call.

"Sorry for the mess," Zeb continued to dust off his T-shirt. "We're building a medicine wheel out back. A lot of lifting and moving, and Finn has been a great help. We plan to have it completed in time for the autumn equinox ceremony. I hope you will both attend."

"We'd love to." Nic's reply was casual and relaxed.

What is wrong with everybody? Klare took a deep breath and looked out the window. *I wonder how long we're going to sit here and beat around the bush.*

"Again, thank you for coming in. As I mentioned on the phone, Finn and I had a long talk yesterday. He agreed with my suggestion that he share with the two of you what he shared with me. And we both thought it might be helpful to do this all together."

Share what? Klare's stomach lurched, and she crossed a protective arm across her middle. *Breathe, Klare.*

She looked to Finn and willed her face to adopt a soft, inviting expression. "Okay," was the only word that came to her mind in that moment. "What is it?"

Nic, apparently not nervous at all, chimed in. "Hey, buddy." Nic physically adjusted his body to face their son directly and leaned forward. "We're here for you, and we want to hear anything you want to share with us, okay? We love you. You can tell us anything."

To Klare, Nic sounded his usual, unruffled self, which prompted a stab of jealousy that she was not able to feel that way right now. Hoping that copying him would help her relax, she deliberately relaxed her posture and tilted her head inquisitively. She watched Finn look from his father, to her, then back to Zeb, as if he were trying to decide what to do next.

"Finn," Zeb encouraged with a solid, resonant timbre. "Why don't you start with the dreams?"

Dreams? A knot cinched in Klare's belly.

"Okay," her son muttered softly.

Time must have stopped at some point, as Klare could not gauge if ten minutes or a hundred had passed since her son had started speaking. She did her best to stay focused, relying on the strength of Nic's hand gripping hers and the compassionate disposition of Zeb to keep her anchored in the room. Despite her efforts to hang on to it, her mantra from earlier—*just listen*—had vanished like a weightless feather swept away with the wind.

Stop. Please. Don't do this.

It was not an abrupt *snap!* like she had experienced before, but instead, a gradual unraveling, as if something inside was slowly unfurling and trying to extricate itself from a mass of tangled and twisted threads. Once sufficiently loosened, this ethereal part slipped out of the knotty mess, no longer bound to her physical form, free to drift up and out of range.

The part of her that remained stuck inside her body heard Finn's words:

"A girl who sung to me…"

"She visited me in my dreams…"

"I felt like I was supposed to do something…"

"I asked her all the time, but she never answered me…"

"Then she died. She was killed by a man with a sword…"

But the other, incorporeal part, the part that watched and listened from the ceiling, heard different words. Bits of phrases and strange terms that did not fit in the lexicon of Klare's physical form. A dark and antiquated dialect:

"Delusions of grandeur…"

"Visual, auditory hallucinations…"

"Ideas of reference…"

"Command hallucinations…"

"Dangerous…"

And that was not the worst of it for Klare. These bizarre snippets and the confusing jargon brought images with them. Disturbing flashes of her brother Scott's bedroom, swaths of red smeared over hastily painted jet-black walls. Brief clips like from an old movie reel flipped through her mind: Scott yelling at someone who wasn't there, Scott demanding that this invisible creature answer him, hushed conversations behind closed doors of her parents arguing, her mother crying, her father leaving.

Klare's head swam with incomprehensible words and the barrage of uninvited and terrifying visual intrusions. Peripherally aware that what she was experiencing inside was not necessarily obvious to the others in the room, she willed herself to stay still and kept her eyes trained on her son's face.

Breathe. In and out. Breathe. In and out.

It was all she could do to stay upright on the sofa.

Then the smoldering smell arrived in her nostrils. Faint at first, almost imperceptible, something familiar, yet a scent that did not belong here. The odorous tendrils licked at the fringes of her mind, her brain stretching to identify what this elusive, caustic aroma was. And then, she had it.

Smoke.

Klare bolted up from her seat, startling everyone, even the unflappable Zeb, spilling Tums from her toppling purse and sending her bottled water rolling across the floor. She was not aware of her body's movements and felt nothing other than a disembodied sense of urgency. Her wild eyes darted around the room and out the window all at once, searching for the source of the acrid smell.

It took a couple of beats before Nic's sharp voice slammed against her eardrums, the reverberation jolting her back into her rigid body. "Klare! Stop! Stop!" Nic shouted at his wife. "Stop it!"

Her vision slowly refocused, and she looked down to see Nic's hands gripping her upper arms before she felt the firm pressure of his grasp. Her eyes then moved up to meet his, and she was taken aback by his face, frozen in fright.

Pulling back from Nic's clutches, she noticed Zeb was also standing, with Finn peeking out fearfully from behind the man's stately, authoritative stature.

She recognized the look on her son's face.

The emergency room.

"Oh my god, I'm so sorry. I don't know… I don't…" Klare stammered as she took in the expressions on each of their faces and realized, with horror, that she had completely lost it.

"Klare." Nic's voice was now calm and hushed. "Please sit down."

She let him guide her back into her seat and felt the flush of shame and humiliation begin its slow and sticky descent over her body. Dropping her head into her hands, she focused on slowing her heart down with her breath.

"Are you okay?" Nic asked and prompted her to sit up and take some sips from the retrieved water bottle.

She nodded and complied, noticing the still-cold water making its way through her dry mouth and down her overheated esophagus.

The strain that remained hanging in the air was interrupted by a tiny knock and the door to Zeb's office opening just wide enough to see Cassie's concerned face.

"Is everyone alright in here?" she asked in a slow, drawn- out tempo.

Zeb's answer was directed at Cassie, but his regard remained fixed on Klare. "Yes. Thank you, Cass. We just had a little moment here, but I think we are all okay now, right?"

Klare inhaled deeply, squared her shoulders, and nodded her assent with an embarrassed smile.

"Okay, then. Well, y'all just holler if you need anything. You good on water? Need anything else?"

"No, we're okay. Thank you," Zeb assured, and Cassie closed the door with a quiet click.

Klare, having regained a hairsbreadth of her footing, apologized again. "I am so sorry." She rubbed the back of her neck and looked down at the floor, unable to meet anyone's eyes just yet. "I don't have an explanation. I thought I smelled something for a second and, um, just lost myself for a minute. I'm so sorry."

"Mom?" Finn asked delicately. "What did you smell?"

Zeb and Nic had returned to their respective seats, but Finn still stood, a tentative expression gracing his golden-brown eyes.

"Don't say it!" A private voice admonished Klare.

Together. A different voice, one that sounded more like her own, offered another suggestion.

She sighed. The thought of telling yet another lie seemed exhausting.

Without the energy to produce a reasonable sounding explanation, she opted for the truth, despite how wrong it felt. "I thought I smelled smoke for a second. It must have been my imagination playing tricks on me because there's obviously no fire." She chuckled sheepishly as her eyes flickered over to the shell on Zeb's desk filled with dried leaves and other items she could not discern.

"… broke my shell…"

"… ruined my sage…"

Klare felt herself slipping away again as she recalled Finn's words. She swiftly affixed her hand to Nic's.

"Was it like that other time?" Finn continued. "In my room?"

Klare was speechless. But Finn was right. It was exactly the same. There was no sense in denying it, but the thickness in her throat silenced her from speaking. With a trembling chin and pleading eyes, she looked at her son and bobbed her head in confirmation.

She watched Finn nod in response while he made his way back to his chair. His eyes were sad, and she thought she saw his chin tremble, not unlike her own.

"I'm really sorry, honey." Shame loosened its grip on her throat just enough to let her use her desperate voice. "I know I scared you that night, and I, uh… I imagine I scared you again just now. I'm really sorry. I didn't mean it. And…"

Nic squeezed her hand and leaned in closer, but his words were aimed at Zeb. "Klare has mentioned this has happened a few times. Where she doesn't feel like herself or like she gets lost in a thought that doesn't totally fit with whatever is going on."

Klare met her husband's worried and troubled eyes and felt the heaviness of his burden weighing on her heart, and despite the protests issuing from deep in her body, she decided to take over. "I don't know how to explain it, but I've been struggling, and I know I've made some big mistakes and I am truly very sorry. I just… I'm not sure what to do."

She looked at Zeb, apologetic and embarrassed, noticing Finn's and Nic's eyes were also on the man who somehow still held an air of calm despite what had just transpired in his office. His face was pensive, like he was contemplating something profound and serious. Klare ordinarily would have fretted over what grim thing about her he must be thinking, but she no longer had the energy. She was drained, depleted, and felt like giving up.

When he finally spoke, his voice was thick with care. "Seems like a lot has been happening in your family. Finn has been having some experiences that have been confusing to him, and it sounds like you, Mrs. Driscoll, have been too."

Klare puzzled at her reaction: an incompatible mash-up of terror with something that felt like possibly… *hope?* She wasn't sure, but it certainly felt confusing.

Turning to Nic, Zeb continued. "And my guess is you, as well, noticing both your son and your wife struggling."

"Yes," Nic added and exchanged apologetic looks with his family.

"Well, it's a good start that everyone seems to agree. And things have not been getting better on their own, right?"

Headshakes all around.

"I know a therapist who works across town. She has been helping families for a very long time. With your permission, I'd like to give her a call and see if she's available to meet with you. She is a very special person, and I think you will all like her a lot."

A cramp seized Klare's abdomen, recoiling in reaction to this suggestion. Her brain knew that Mr. Paytah's proposal was meant to be helpful, but everything in her body wanted to scream in objection and flee from the room, another instance of her body and her mind not being on the same page.

Nic asked his family, "Is that okay with you guys?"

Finn replied with a rapid yes, which Klare found noteworthy, considering Finn's generally more thoughtful pace. She held Nic's look with eyes wide and body frozen, and Nic turned to Zeb and nodded his head in assent.

The three listened as Zeb called his colleague, Dr. Isabeau Hirsch, who agreed without hesitation to meet with the Driscolls on Friday—just two days later.

When he hung up the phone, Zeb confirmed, "Okay then, Friday it is. I'm happy you'll be meeting with her. I am certain you will like her."

Led through the lobby by her husband's strong hand on her lower back, Klare allowed herself to be steered toward the car and buckled in. Unable to bear meeting their eyes, she closed hers and rested the side of her face against the passenger-side window. Mortified in more ways than one, Klare's one specific indignity took center stage in her muddled mind.

No way I'm going to see that therapist.

22

Nic piloted into the final turn on their route home, his hands vice-gripped around the steering wheel. *What in the world am I supposed to do now?*

Stealing another peek at his wife, he saw she had not moved the whole ride home; her head was tilted back and away as though craning to see something from her passenger-side window that they had already passed. Her reflection, however, revealed that her eyes were closed, not in a restful, napping way, but glued tight as if to make sure nothing got in.

What had started as confused concern about Klare's state had slowly grown into a tight anxiety during the drive back from the center. *This is so much bigger than I thought.* His anger about her recent concealments was quickly absorbed by apprehension. *Yeah, but how much bigger?* Nic remembered her words from the other night, *"It was me, of course, but it also wasn't."*

Now I get it. The Klare he experienced in Zeb's office this afternoon was unrecognizable. Her, but not her. *But where did my wife go?* The throb of his heartbeat knocked urgently against his chest.

And what about him? Nic sought out his son's face in the rearview mirror and found Finn's countenance startlingly untroubled.

"How ya doing back there?" he asked quietly.

Finn nodded and offered a subtle grin as Nic pulled into their driveway. Still puzzled by his son's calm disposition, he handed his keys to Finn and asked him to open the door for them while he helped Klare from the car. Her laborious movements confirmed that she was both emotionally and physically wiped.

"Thank you," she whispered, and noticeably did not meet Nic's eyes.

Once inside, she softy declared that she'd like to rest and robotically made her way upstairs, waving off Nic's offer to walk her up.

I feel so helpless. Worry and sadness dominated.

Finn stood silently next to Nic while Klare reached the top of the stairs and entered the bedroom. For several moments, neither moved.

Nic hadn't felt this powerlessness since he was a teenager, impotently watching his younger brother dissolve until he disappeared altogether. That fleeting memory sent a stab of remembered pain through Nic's chest.

What am I going to do?

"You know what to do," Linda's voice rose out of the past. *"Move in."*

Without another thought, Nic wrapped his arm around his son's shoulder and pulled him in tight, warmed by Finn's receptive lean in.

When Nic's cell phone chirped, he ignored it until a second, then a third buzz prompted Finn to pull back. Nic stared at the device, contemplating turning it off.

"It's Dennis."

"You should see what he wants, Dad." Finn's relaxed manner contrasted sharply with Nic's shaky uncertainty, and his ambivalent hesitation garnered another nudge from his son. "Go ahead, Dad. See what he wants."

He smiled at his son. *Who is this kid?* Delicate threads of gratitude wrapped themselves around his worrisome heart.

> *Hey. Everything okay? You keep popping into my mind today. Are you guys good? In your neck of the woods. Want some company?*

The threads offered an extra squeeze. *Dennis always shows up at just the right time. Kinda spooky, actually.*

"He's in the neighborhood and just checking in. I'll give him a call later."

"He should come over," Finn countered, his voice that of a confident guide.

"Uh, after today, I don't think it's the best time. I have a bit of a headache and—"

"Dad, tell him to come over." Authority infused his son's directive.

Wow. Who's the parent here now? Nic silently teased himself and studied his son's poised face.

"Uh, alright then."

"Good." The issue settled, Finn made for the backyard.

Nic returned Dennis' text and went outside to find Finn on the west-facing side of the house where they had discussed planting their garden. The yellow sketchpad depicting the rough draft plans laid on the ground next to a kneeling Finn, who had already retrieved a small shovel and hand trowel from the shed.

From his vantage point on the deck, Nic marveled at his son's serene and fluid movements as he removed clumps of weeds and crabgrass, then sank his ungloved hands into the dirt up to his wrists and began kneading the soil as though preparing bread dough from scratch. "*His element.*" He remembered Zeb's praises from the first time they met, unbelievably barely a week ago. The residual shame Nic felt at his original "*I didn't even know he had an 'element'*" thought was replaced by the warm glow of love and pride.

An hour before, Nic had watched his son stand, frozen in fright, as an invisible terror temporarily seized his mother. Yet here he was, seemingly content with the weightless gaze of someone without a care in the world.

How is this possible? Maybe he's in shock? I don't want to interrupt him, but…

"*Move in,*" Linda's remembered words chimed, and so he did.

"Hey, Dennis is bringing dinner and he'll be here in a little while, but, um, do you want to talk about what happened today?" he asked, surprised by how nervous he felt.

"No, I'm okay, Dad." It didn't sound like a brush-off, but he wondered how that could be true. He himself was still reeling from his wife's *episode*. A tiny streak of worry zipped through him.

"Well, that's good, but your mom… um, that was…" Jumbled words sputtered from Nic's mouth.

"I feel sad for Mom. She's in a lot of pain." Again Finn's composed and sympathetic tone took Nic by surprise and he blew out a long puff of air.

"Yes. A lot more than I was aware." While Finn tended to his earthy aeration, Nic continued. "I'm sorry about today, Son. We were there to hear what you had to say, and then, well, it took a big turn there with your mom, and I just want you to know that…"

Finn stopped, sat back on his knees, and looked up to meet his father's eyes.

A lump formed in Nic's throat as he looked into Finn's numinous golden-amber eyes that shone with a brilliance Nic had never seen. His son's face was a picture of vibrant serenity, and for a moment, Nic thought his son's skin seemed to *glow*. A shiver tickled down from the top of his head and wrapped him in a momentary cocoon of peace, silencing the buzzing in his ears.

What's happening?

"Dad, I'm okay. Honest. Mom needs to talk to someone. I'm glad we're going to see Zeb's friend. And maybe you need to talk to someone too."

"Me?" Nic was beyond confused.

"Yes. When will Dennis be here?"

As if politely dismissed, Nic left Finn to his elemental work and went inside to check on Klare. The door to their bedroom was ajar, and peeking in, he saw that she was fast asleep atop the covers. He eased the door closed and left her to continue her recovery nap.

A faint knock on the front door alerted Nic to Dennis' arrival. He came in overloaded with Styrofoam containers wafting the aromatic, mouthwatering flavors from their favorite Chinese food restaurant. Until that moment, Nic hadn't realized how hungry he was.

Finn joined, lured inside by the delicious smells before Nic had to retrieve him. Nic made and set aside a plate for Klare before sitting down with two of his favorite people.

As they ate, Nic was nervous—about what exactly, he wasn't sure. Some of it was about filling Dennis in on all that had transpired. It was overwhelming. But his son was right; he did need to talk, and Dennis was as sound and reliable as they come.

Bellies sufficiently filled, Nic busied himself rinsing dishes, the spray of the faucet drowning out the conversation continuing at the table.

"Your dad says you've been over at Okiciya. How do you like it?" Dennis asked Finn.

"I like it a lot," Finn offered with an agreeable nod.

"You know, one of my guys volunteers over there from time to time. His name's Bran. Have you met him?"

Finn's head shot up and his face beamed. "Yes. I like him. Very much."

"Yeah, he's a great guy. I hear they do really great work over there."

Finn grinned and offered another nod, seemingly pleased with the connection between Okiciya and his dad's best friend.

When Nic finished the dishes and made to take the waiting plate upstairs to Klare, Finn interceded and asked if he could take it up instead.

"Sure, if you'd like." Nic was surprised, not realizing he had assumed Finn wouldn't be ready to see his mother yet. But much about this day had been a surprise. "Then you want to join Dennis and me in the backyard? Show him the garden?

"That's okay, I have some reading to do. Can I be excused?"

"Of course, but are you sure you don't want to come hang out with us?" Nic needed to talk to Dennis alone but didn't want his son to feel left out.

"No, I'm okay. Can I go?" Finn asked sincerely, a touch of eagerness embedded in his pitch.

"Sure. Let us know if you need anything," Nic offered.

"I will. Bye, Dennis." Finn smiled and turned to leave with Klare's plate of food in hand.

"See ya, kid." Dennis smiled back.

Nic offered his friend a beer and motioned for him to follow him out to the small table on the deck just off the kitchen. He grabbed another bottle to take with them.

I'm going to need at least one more of these.

It was hard for Nic to believe only a couple of weeks had passed since the conversation with Dennis that spurred him to cancel the rest of his patients for the day and head home to intervene on his wife's suspicious behavior. He had called Dennis a few days afterward and filled him in on all he had learned—the clandestine appointment with a psychiatrist, the "fire" that was not really a fire, Klare's surreptitiously pulling Finn from the community center, but also from school last May, and the mind-boggling calls to her mother.

Dennis had been his usual supportive self and agreed none of what Nic had shared sounded like the Klare he and Lucy knew. He had also added that Klare hadn't returned any of Lucy's calls or texts lately. Klare was by reputation reserved and introverted, but it did seem out of character for her not to reply at all. When they had ended their call, Dennis had assured Nic that he was there to talk if anything more came up, and Nic had scoffed and stated that, sadly, he was certain there would be more.

The pair took long pulls from their icy ales as they settled into the cooling late-July evening. It had been in the high eighties earlier in the week, but today had dropped nearly twenty degrees and offered a welcome reprieve from the heat.

"Well," Nic began. "There has definitely been more since we talked." He held a moan inside and shook his head as if to clear his thoughts.

Dennis replied with a sympathetic sigh, "Yeah, well, you've all been on my mind for sure. I figured there was some reason."

"Oh, I'll give you a reason," Nic interjected dryly.

"That bad, huh?" Dennis shifted in his chair to face his friend.

"Remember how I told you that Klare's been saying she hasn't been herself lately?"

"Yeah."

"I saw it in its full unadulterated form today." Nic paused for another long pull to finish his first beer and popped open the second. "It's bad. Worse than I could have imagined."

"Oh man. What happened?" Dennis took a sip and sat back to listen.

Nic told of Zeb's call asking him and Klare to come in and how the first part of the meeting had gone this afternoon—Finn's recurrent dreams about a girl with a song or a message, but then she died and how Finn now feels sad because he never figured out what she was trying to tell him.

The familiar peal pinpricked inside his ears.

Oh no, please not now.

"She died?" Dennis broke in.

"Well, yes. In his dream, she apparently died and then he hasn't dreamt of her since, and he's really upset about it." Another sip and Nic continued. "So we're in the director's office, listening to Finn tell us about his dreams, and all of a sudden Klare just flipped."

Dennis looked confused. "About what?"

"Well, that's the thing. I don't think it had anything to do with what Finn was saying. She *seemed* to be listening, but then she just bolted up out of her seat. She was in a panic, looking all around the room and out the window, like she was in danger or something. She looked terrified. I can't even describe how bizarre, and frightening, it was to see her like that."

"Shit. Is she okay?" Dennis cocked his head in curious sympathy.

"I think so. It's like she went into a trance. I grabbed her arms and sort of shook her and then she came back. Her eyes cleared and then she realized where she was. She was super embarrassed and just kept apologizing."

"What do you think happened?" Dennis asked.

"The only thing I can think of is that she was caught up in some sort of old memory. She said she thought she smelled smoke and then brushed it off as her imagination playing tricks on her. But Dennis, I have got to tell you, this was not a little trick of the mind. It's like she wasn't even there—her mind, her whole body, was somewhere else. The director there referred us to a therapist he knows across town. We have an appointment on Friday."

The pair sat in contemplative silence for a few moments. Nic peeled the label from his bottle while Dennis opened his second and stared off toward the sun, just starting its slow descent to its golden bed in the west.

"She thought she smelled smoke, but there wasn't any smoke or fire, I assume?" Dennis asked.

"Nope."

"You said there was a night not that long ago where she thought Finn had a fire in his room and she flipped out then too, right?"

Nic turned toward his friend. "Yeah?"

"Something to do with how her brother and dad died?" A perplexed expression rested on Dennis' face.

"Yeah, I thought about that. It would make sense that she'd be overreactive to smoke or fire. But, Dennis, there was no smoke. No fire. And she wasn't just jumpy or reactive. This was like pure terror. Finn said it was what she looked like that night when she freaked out when he had lit some sage in his room."

Dennis' pensive eyes were distant, as if arduously contemplating the arc of the setting sun.

Either that, or he's solving some complicated calculus problem in his head, Nic thought while he pulled on his earlobes and watched his friend.

"What are you thinking?" he asked eventually, his voice belying his exhaustion.

Dennis drew in a big breath and swallowed the air in an audible gulp. "You said she pulled him from school and the community center because she was worried about what people were thinking about him?"

"Yeah."

"That people would think he was mental or a monster or something like that?"

"Yes… ?"

"And then secretly took him to a shrink to find out if he was dangerous?"

"Dude!" Veins pulsed in Nic's temples, pumping in time with the clanging in his ears. "What are you getting at?!"

Dennis pulled in another long breath and released it in a whoosh through his puffed-out cheeks. "Losing her brother and dad in that fire was awful. I can't even imagine. But I don't know, Nic. I wonder if this is less about the fire and more about all the stuff that happened afterward."

"What do you mean all the stuff afterward?" Nic's neck muscles squeezed a new pressure into his head.

"You know. All the rumors. And then everything that happened with her mom. I remember my mom used to say how she always felt so bad for Mrs. Martin."

Nic pitched himself back against his chair and tossed his head up toward the purpling sky. The sting in his eyes was irritating, a counterpart to the burning twinge spreading across his chest, and nothing compared to the high-pitched scream in his middle ear. He took a steadying breath and, without looking at his friend, spoke in as calm a voice as he could muster.

"I have no idea what you are talking about. I know about her brother and dad and the fire. And that she was young. And I'm sure nothing was ever the same again for Klare or her mother. But I don't know anything about any rumors or what you mean when you say 'what happened with her mom.' But I gotta tell you, I feel a little crazy right now."

"Shit."

Nic beheld Dennis' troubled grimace, his black eyebrows squeezed so tight that it looked like a long caterpillar had stopped to rest on his forehead. He shook his head from side to side.

"Shit," Dennis said again with another whoosh of exhaled air. "I don't think I should be the one telling you all of this, but it seems Klare isn't in any shape to, and I don't think going to Bridget is a good idea."

Nic didn't say anything, but his piercing eyes pleaded, *Tell me.*

"Okay, you're gonna need another beer first." Dennis took up Nic's warm, undrunk second bottle and headed inside to return with a fresh, cold one.

The sun had firmly tucked itself in for the night, leaving behind a bruised and mottled nighttime sky. Nic sat stunned, his body fused to the chair as if he had become part of it—heavy, wooden, and hard. His stare was distant and flat, although his eyes still burned and stung.

At first, Dennis' words had swirled so frenetically inside Nic's head that he had trouble following along. Then one by one, like pin tumblers aligning within a tamperproof cylinder lock in just the perfect combination to release the catch and grant access, a channel inside Nic's brain opened and the once-blocked flow rushed through.

So many things made sense all at once while Nic's body remained paralyzed and fixed to his chair. When he finally could get his neck to move, he stiffly turned to Dennis, overcome and wordless.

"I'm so sorry, man. I can't believe you didn't know any of this stuff. It was a long time ago, and I just assumed you would have known." Dennis rubbed his hands together, and his face remained a blend of pity and sympathy.

Nic rolled his neck from side to side and back and forward, his blood beginning to circulate enough for more than just basic movements. Then, with a sudden burst of adrenaline, he jumped to his feet.

"I need to go talk to her. Right now. I cannot believe she didn't tell me any of this."

Dennis rose with just slightly less haste and placed a supportive but also firm hand on his friend's arm. "Dude, I don't think that's a good idea right now. Seems like she's barely hanging on as it is. You guys have that therapy appointment on Friday… maybe wait 'til then?"

"I don't know. This is almost too much. I mean, it might explain some things but… I just can't… I can't believe this. And I *cannot* believe she never told me any of this."

"Yeah, this is a lot. But I don't know if it's a good idea to bring it up while she's in this state. Having some professional help is probably the best idea."

Ugh, he's right. Nic collapsed back into his chair and dropped his head into his hands, nodding in agreement with Dennis' often-wise and always-reliable counsel.

"I'm sorry, man," Dennis muttered again and lowered himself to sit quietly with his friend.

What am I going to do? Nic thought for the hundredth time today.

As if his closest friend could hear his thoughts, Dennis added, "You're not alone, Nic. There are people here to help. We're here for you too."

23

The lump in her throat and the tears anxiously awaiting enough privacy to release themselves rounded out the overwhelming cacophony reverberating through Klare's tattered body. She felt raw, like an exposed nerve that would singe and recoil against the slightest breeze.

Before she had the chance to close the bedroom door behind her, her cell phone buzzed.

Lucy. I can't right now.

Klare tapped the decline button, flung herself onto the bed, and curled her body around one of the larger pillows, pulling it against her belly and holding it tight, as if shielding a small child from a vicious windstorm. She squeezed her eyes closed and made no effort to stem their leaking. Flashes of pictures from the day bounded through her alongside snippets of words and phrases.

"Delusions. Dangerous."

"Klare! Stop it!"

"I smelled something…"

"… like the other night?"

"I'm so sorry."

"I know a woman. She's a therapist."

And somehow, amidst the ocean of shame and fear, bobbed something little and light. Something foreign. A tiny kernel, golden and implausibly calm. A seed resting within, untouched by the chaos that swirled around it.

Together, the gilded pebble whispered.

I can't! she countered.

With another tight squeeze of her eyes, and despite her best efforts to shut her mind off, Klare's attention was pulled toward the small glowing globe. Impossibly strong for its diminutive size, the marble seemed to reach out and capture her in its field of energy and hold her there, immobile, keeping her from being swept up by the whirlwind of dread and despair threatening to drown her.

Together. This time from the outside edge of her mind. *Together*.

"I'm trying," she whimpered. *But we can't go to that therapist. I can't.* The thought was petrifying, and she was far too tired to let herself go down that terrifying rabbit hole. She wasn't sure why the idea was so aversive, it just was.

Together. The luminosity of the peculiar tiny pearl inside seemed to beat back in objection to her thoughts.

I can't! she silently screamed out in frustration.

Together, pulsed the yellow touchstone held afloat within in a murky sea.

Too exhausted to continue to volley, she surrendered to sleep.

A quiet flapping sound stirred her from the depths of slumber. Still curled around her pillow, she opened her eyes. The daylight that had filled the room had faded purple; she estimated it was close to dusk. She unfurled herself and sat up to stretch the kinks from her back and neck.

The fading memory of a huge but graceful white bird hung in her mind, high above, backdropped against an endless azure sky. She sighed in peaceful gratitude for experiencing such a comforting dream amid her mental chaos.

A soft tapping echoed from the other side of her bedroom door, and she recognized it as the gentle sound that had roused her.

Why doesn't he just come in? She felt confused and still a touch groggy as she eased herself from the bed and toward the door. It took her brain a moment to answer her own question.

Because it's not Nic.

She opened the door to find Finn standing patiently, a foil-covered plate in one hand, a napkin and silverware grasped in the other. Her heart fluttered at the sight of him; she hadn't expected he would want to see her.

"Are you hungry? Dennis brought over Chinese." Her son's tone was light, and his face shone with heartfelt invitation.

Klare hoped her surprise didn't register on her face to the degree she felt it in her body. She could not remember the last time Finn had come to her door.

Or the last time he talked to me.

"Hi, honey," Klare replied, embarrassed at the slurry of butterflies that darted through her middle. "This is very sweet of you. Uh… yeah, I could eat a little."

She reached for the plate, and Finn stepped into the room.

He wants to come in? She was seriously confused at this point.

Sitting on the cushioned bench at the foot of the California king, she motioned for her son to take a spot on the bed. With the proffered plate resting on her lap, she lifted the foil and inhaled the sweet and spicy smells.

"Mmmm." She met Finn's eyes for a brief moment, then turned back to her meal. "Thank you."

Finn sat silently while she nibbled at her dinner. Another flitter of nerves wiggled through her.

He looks different. She took another few bites and found herself increasingly apprehensive at the silence.

When she finished all she was going to eat, she set her plate aside and looked at her son. *Why isn't he saying anything?* The belly butterflies were in a feverish flutter now, hundreds of gauzy wings grazing her insides. *Maybe he's waiting for me?*

She took a breath and began. "I'm sorry about today. I wish I had a better explanation for what happened. I just don't know…"

That's not good enough. Shame flushed warm from her head to her toes. *He deserves more than you not having a "better explanation."*

She took another breath and continued. "But I don't know if we need to go see a *therapist*. I think I just need a little time to…" Her voice trailed off in response to Finn's solemn and penetrating expression. "What?" she asked timidly.

Finn's visage began to unnerve her. He didn't look angry or stern, but something more like *calm*. Inexplicably *tranquil*, not the disposition she would have expected in her son, in anyone, after the events of the day.

"The events of the past couple of months, you mean," the familiar inner critic reproached.

"Honey, are you okay?" In a move that felt both vulnerable and bold, she leaned forward to position her face directly in front of her son's, locking their eyes together. "You aren't saying anything."

Finn paused before responding. "Yes, I'm okay. I just wanted you to know that I'm sorry too." His voice swelled with sincerity.

A bolt of self-loathing stabbed through her. "I'm not sure what you mean. Sorry about what?"

"I'm just sorry…" Her son's voice remained unruffled, his countenance placid. " … that you're having such a hard time.

That something happened to you. To make you so afraid…
of me."

Klare felt a sharp snap inside, followed by a tumble of broken
shards and jagged fragments raining down like a decaying
building caving in on itself, leaving behind nothing but plumes
of dust and piles of debris. She brought a protective hand up to
her chest, as if to keep any remaining bits from falling out. Her
throat, choked with the caustic residue of her heart's collapse,
could only issue a painful moan. She closed her eyes in hopes of
locating her breath through the grainy fog. When she found it,
she drew in a thin stream of air and opened her watery eyes.

Finn had not moved, nor had his expression changed. His
patience and equable repose lingered. It was quite unsettling.

"Finn." Her voice shook with blazing conviction. "I am *not*
afraid of you. I could never be afraid of you. I cannot believe…"

"But, Mom, yes, you have been. You *have* been afraid of
me. Or, whoever you think I am." Not an ounce of hesitation or
doubt marked his words. He held her eyes with his own in clear,
unflappable confidence.

She leaned in close and took her son's face into her trembling
hands. "Honey, what are you talking about? I don't think you are
someone else. I don't understand what you're saying."

"I know, Mom. But it's okay. You will." Fluorescent flecks of
golden sureness danced and bounced in Finn's amber eyes, their
luster adding a touch of radiance to the dusk-shadowed room.

Klare leaned back and ran her hands through her sleep-
tangled hair. She could not understand Finn's words or fathom
his uncanny, benevolent composure, but she had an inkling that
she was not going to, at least not right this moment.

"Okay. Okay." She sighed in a frustrated surrender. "I don't
understand. But I hear you."

Finn added, "I'm glad we're seeing the doctor on Friday. We need to go. Dad is outside right now talking to Dennis. I get to talk to Zeb almost every day. It will be good for you to have someone to talk to too."

She dropped her head and flashed on a memory, one far less distant than she wished, and marveled at her son's eerie perceptiveness.

Weeks before, when she was still convinced that she could manage what was happening with Finn without telling Nic, Klare had found herself sitting at the kitchen table scrolling through the contacts in her phone, looking for the name of someone, anyone, she might be able to call and talk to. Dennis, the dentist, Dr. Hanada, Lucy, the mechanic, Nic's cell and his clinic number, the pharmacy, and a handful of professional contacts came and went as she made her way through the alphabet. A couple of former coworkers, several names of people she had no memory of, and her mother.

My mother. Is that seriously my only option? No one else? This is pathetic. I'm pathetic.

That was a miserable day. She did not call her mother; she'd done that twice already, and both had ended in what should have been predictable disaster. She had stared blankly at her phone until it went black and, with a heavy sigh, put it back on the charger and left the room.

"I'm happy Dad has Dennis and that you have Zeb. I can always call Lucy." She offered an embarrassed smile to her son and guiltily thought about how many of Lucy's calls she'd declined of late.

I can only imagine what my mother would say about us going to a therapist. Klare shivered inside.

Finn offered the kind of coy smile that suggested her reply was being entertained but not believed. "Friday, Mom. It'll be alright." Finn rose from the bed, gently planted a kiss on her cheek, and started toward the door. "Goodnight."

"Goodnight."

Stunned, she watched her son leave and waited a few moments to let the touch of his soft kiss linger while she tried to make sense of what had just happened.

What am I supposed to do now?

She sighed, rose, and took her plate down to the kitchen, where through the sliding glass door she saw Nic and Dennis sitting on the patio drinking beers and talking.

Finn's words floated back to her. " … *be good for you to have someone to talk to…*"

She thought for a split second about going out to say hello but decided to leave the two alone when she saw her husband's serious expression. Usually it would be the four of them out on the patio—she and Nic, Lucy and Dennis—with Finn off somewhere reading or exploring.

She flushed again with prickly embarrassment as she thought about her behavior in Zeb's office. *I wonder what they're saying about me now.*

Deep down, a part of her wanted to talk to someone, but she was clear she didn't want it to be a *professional.* Even though she didn't believe her mother *now*, the years of listening to Bridget's tirades about *professional* swindlers and quacks had left a mark.

She watched her husband and his friend for another moment and turned to make her way back upstairs, reflecting on Finn's words, "*Friday, Mom. It'll be alright.*"

She wanted to believe him.

Together, the little golden orb vibrated.

FINN CLOSES HIS mother's bedroom door with a soft snick. The satisfying sound of the latch seamlessly clicking into its mortise echoes the quiet alignment occurring inside Finn's body. The vibration at the top of his chest syncs with the feathery pulse deep within his ribcage, and their harmony sends signals to the rest of his system that all is in position.

In position for what?

Finn has no idea, yet. But he will soon.

And as the afternoon makes her lazy transition into eve, the once loose and loopy threads inside begin snugly pulling together as an invisible tailor works her magic to fashion a tight and guiding seam.

24

It had begun in Zeb's office, midway through telling his parents about the girl. When he had gotten to the part about his hunch that she had something important to tell him, the sublime sea-green shimmer returned. As if detecting the glittering emerald aura, his stone and his bird began speaking in their own phantom dialect of vibration and winged effervescence. A sense Finn could only later describe as a *knowing* slowly bubbled up inside like sweet honey warmed by the summer sun.

He hadn't shared this with Zeb the day before—his private viridescent encounters. He wanted to preserve it, protect it. To hold it close. *Later*, he had thought. He had wanted to finish telling his story first, to keep the commitment he had made to Zeb, and to himself; he would not mismanage another chance.

With that, Finn had chosen to do both. While one part of him held the vibrant, resonant rightness of the *knowing* precious and close, another part continued with his account of the girl all the way through to her death.

But before he'd had the opportunity to consider whether he was going to share about the rest of his ethereal experience, his mother had bolted up from her seat, the mask of terror he had seen before once again painted on her face. It was scary at first just like the other times, but the soft shimmery glow he felt surrounding him moved in and held him close.

The first time was in the emergency room. An unrecognizable version of his mother, a stunt double who was rude and interrupted and accused with a pinched, suspicious look on what was usually a calm, kind face. He didn't know *that* mom.

Then there was the night of what she called "the fire." That was not *his* mother either. That was a doppelgänger, a terrifying collaborator, an alien twin who screamed and threw and stomped and lied. *His* mother would never act like that.

His *real* mother would never have pulled him from school in a deceitful proposal too tempting to decline, or told him to keep it from his father, or taken him from his much-loved Okiciya, or to that awful doctor who spoke of schizophrenia, danger, and psychological evaluations. His *real* mother would not have done any of these things, let alone lie about them and keep them secret from his father. From him.

What happened to her? Finn had asked himself a hundred times. *Where did she go?*

The mother that jumped up from the sofa in Zeb's office earlier that day was decidedly not *his* mother.

His *real* mother had been listening, leaning forward with her eyes trained upon him. Then Finn had noticed, although he could not recall at exactly what point in his story, that her eyes had changed. And he knew she was gone. It was as if, in that split second, a tear had mysteriously ripped open the universal fabric. A shadowy, invisible hand from another dimension had grabbed hold of and extricated his mother, replacing her, temporarily, with some feral imposter from another time and place.

Another time and place. Those words had landed in Finn's mind with a resonant *boom!* as he had watched, from within his protective cocoon, his father seize his mother's arms and effectively send the imposter mom back to where she came from.

I don't know that other mom.

The hair on the nape of Finn's neck had raised while his skin had prickled with the shivery spookiness of presque vu.

Which means… she doesn't know me.

His mind reached and craned for the bit of *knowing* that he knew was within reach, its whisper breathing faintly upon his cheek like a silent hint. He stretched and strained, widening the net inside, feeling himself closing in, almost there…

Which means… all this can't be because of me.

The reservoir of guilty remorse that he was indeed the cause and, therefore, to blame for his mother's agony drained from his body in an instant rush. And by capturing that elusive prize, the needle was threaded and the stitching commenced—mending, repairing, and beginning to make whole the tapestry of Finn's soul that had been torn asunder by this woman pretender.

What had started in Zeb's office as a familiar fright had morphed into a fuzzy awareness that offered a reassuring consolation, an ally to the soothing sea-green and golden murmur radiating through his bones. While his father and his mentor had attuned to his mother, Finn had directed his focus to the sensational surge inside, and in turn, it supplied him with a comfort and security unavailable to him in the room at that moment.

Held by this mysterious, invisible presence that seemed to at once come from inside and outside of him, Finn curiously watched his father guide his mother back to the sofa, Zeb return to his chair, and Cassie's not-so-subtle welfare check. By the time Finn had returned to his seat, the fear had dissolved, leaving a deep compassion for his mother in its place.

As Finn sat, a soft but clear message emerged from within. *"You know."*

He remained in quiet contemplation on the drive home, watching his father minister to his mother and hoping the comfort of the *knowing* wouldn't disappear as the shimmery aura melted away bit by bit. Once home, he floated rather than moved—gracefully plunging his hands into the dirt of the future garden, mindfully feeding himself dinner with Dad and Dennis, and gliding up the stairs to bring Mom her meal.

He knew she needed to rest but had felt compelled to talk to her, in the best way that he could, about his nascent awareness of the source of her struggle. It was not him. In some ways, it was not even her. Finn had chosen not to share his *"an invisible hand from elsewhere kidnapped you and replaced you with an imposter"* hypothesis but simply wanted her to know that he *understood* and believed, in time, she would too.

A gossamer shawl of drowsy contentment wrapped itself lightly around Finn's shoulders as he looked out at the plummy sky from his upstairs west-facing window. Slate-gray clouds sat splotchy against the horizon, rimmed in ruby and violet.

I wonder if it will rain.

He was tired, and his bed called to him, but he was eager to read more about the courageous men from Zeb's stories and their visionary voyages, and that thirst overcame the desire to sleep.

Last weekend, Finn had felt an intense connection with Zeb's great-great-uncle Black Elk. The synchronicities between Finn's own and this eminent leader's experiences buzzed with magic.

"… like somebody calling me…"

"… happened more than once…"

"I liked to think about it, but I was afraid to tell it…"

Finn had then recalled the story Zeb had shared about the powerful Lakota warrior, Crazy Horse, who it was said carried for protection a small stone with a hole in it.

Just like mine, Finn mused, while a tiny flutter glowed in his chest.

Hungry for more, Finn propped himself up on his pillows, pulled his laptop from his desk onto his lap, and dove into a search about visions and the quest to understand their meanings. Links to articles on the *vision quest* appeared, and cursory scans revealed it as a special rite of passage practiced by many tribes, each with their own unique ritual for undertaking the deeply spiritual endeavor.

He bit his lip and forced himself to slow down as he pored over accounts of individuals, typically boys on the brink of manhood, venturing out alone into nature in hopes of having a vision to help them discover their true path and purpose.

"This is amazing," he murmured. "Amazing."

He pressed his hand against his hammering heart and let out a long, steadying breath, captivated by the notion that some individuals initiate a vision quest, as Zeb did, to ask for guidance on fulfilling one's life purpose, but sometimes, people experience visions unbidden, like Black Elk.

Like me. Finn's skin tingled in resonant kinship with these two ageless men.

A few more clicks and suddenly Finn's heart released a pulse that rattled his stone and sent his bird scattering for another rib on which to perch. He bolted upright as a single word floated forward from the page, alive and candescent. He cocked his head as primordial recognition sent sparkling shivers rippling under his skin.

"Hanbleceya."

He stared at this term, foreign to his eyes but understood by his soul. The deep-rooted rumble in his heart told him he had known it since the beginning of time.

He carefully sounded out the morphemes as noted on the page, "hahn-bleh-chay-yah." The sounds rolled from his mouth like the whisper of a long-forgotten language, an original tongue.

A vision quest was called a *hanbleceya* in the Lakota Sioux dialect, which translated into "crying for a vision." The word stem *hanble* meant "vision or dream" and *ceya* was "cry."

He whispered it again, his voice thick with wonder, *"hahn-bleh-chay-yah."* Warm and grateful tears slid from his eyes as the stitching seam inside tightened even more, fusing him to an ancient and known truth.

I bet Zeb knows more about it. He could not wait to ask his friend to shed more light on this magical word, although new to his eyes, known from some other place and time.

Deliciously enthralled by all he was learning, Finn still felt the heaviness of exhaustion creeping in, spent from the energy being used on the renovations happening to his internal landscape. He let his eyes close to ponder the notion of his own *hanbleceya*—if that was truly what was happening for him—more closely.

His visions had come through his ears by way of her honeyed song and to his body through the shimmering green-blue aura and the sight of the girl on the distant edges of his dreams. Even his bones felt the visions—the vibrations and flutters that were undeniably real and very much alive, even though nobody else could see or hear or feel these corporeal sensations.

… even though nobody else could see or hear or feel…

A surge of *knowing* jolted Finn upright in his bed again, and with a sharp intake of breath, his eyes opened wide.

… nobody else could see or hear…

"Or smell," he muttered aloud.

Finn's heart knocked loudly against the inside of his ribs, momentarily hijacking the calmative flutter that had been purring in that space since the afternoon. He covered his gaping mouth with one hand while the other moved instinctively to grasp the stone that hung from his neck, its texture smooth and warm.

Mom.

His golden-auburn eyes sparkled and danced in the twilight of his bedroom while his brain scanned and searched for a thought-thread he could catch and follow. Words bounded against the inside of his skull, springing back to collide with other bouncing words. Slowly, the volley decelerated enough for Finn to capture one here and there, and the flow of his thoughts began to take shape.

She has been having visions. Not good ones. But still, visions. Seeing a fire when there wasn't one. Smelling smoke when there was no fire. Seeing me as somebody else—someone I am not. Could she be on a vision quest? Is there such a thing as a nightmare vision quest? It does mean "crying for a vision."

Possibilities leapt through his mind, his system electrified by their sheer volume.

If she's on her own kind of vision quest, then she's on a journey to find purpose. But the visions she's getting are scary and awful and confusing.

He remembered what Zeb had said about the elders or medicine men in his tribe helping interpret visions to reveal the purpose within and reading about the role of guides, both during the vision quest and after.

She needs a guide.

Finn thought about the appointment they had scheduled for Friday with the doctor Zeb recommended.

The doctor! Maybe she can be Mom's guide.

Consoled by the hopeful thought of his mother having someone to help her, Finn's heart slowed its steady pounding. He floated back against his pillows, held alight by an overwhelming faith that things were going to be alright. His heart thrummed softly in unison with the purr of his bird, and his eyes filled with the warm tears of relief.

Huh. A faint smile graced Finn's lips as he thought of this remarkable coincidence. *We are both on a vision quest. A hanbleceya.*

A whisper drifted in from his periphery.

Maybe it is not a coincidence.

As Finn begins his release into slumber, another truth, muttered on the wisp of a blue-green breeze by a girl with golden hair, will wake him with the brilliance of a thousand suns.

Trailing several paces behind Nic and Finn, Klare looked dubiously at the pale-yellow cottage framed with white plantation shutters and baskets spilling over with pink and purple flowers. The cheery charm of this tiny house set her nerves on edge.

Are we in the right place?

There was no visible shingle to confirm they were at the office of Dr. Isabeau Hirsch, but when she saw the *Welcome, please come in!* sign that hung from the doorknob, Klare glumly admitted defeat. She had hoped, as unrealistic as it was, that they wouldn't be able to find the doctor's place of work.

Reluctantly heeding the invitation, she startled at the tinkly chime that seemed to broadcast to the entire neighborhood that they had arrived at the psychologist's office. Multi-paneled double French doors on the opposite side of the foyer stood slightly ajar, beckoning them to enter. Filmy ivory fabric offered privacy but allowed the filtered glow to stream in from the other side.

This is a doctor's office?

Fresh flowers let loose from colorful vases and softly lit floor lamps contrasted with the sterile, withered mood of Dr. Myles' office, which she had assumed all shrinks' offices embodied.

"*Dangerous… symptom of schizophrenia… formal evaluation…*" Dr. Myles' bleakly concerned voice rang in her ears. *Ugh.* She had been so nervous about exposing her son to such judgment, and now here they were, just weeks later, back in front of another professional *judge*.

I wonder what this one's going to say about him? Her stomach rolled with reservation, and she tightened her grip on the purse she had stocked with chalky antacids before they left the house.

This isn't just about him, a calmer part of herself reminded. She was loath to acknowledge that they were sent to this doctor after *her* episode at the community center, not Finn's.

As Klare reached in for the bottle that never quite delivered on its promise of intestinal relief, a willowy woman with curly silver hair and lucent cornflower-blue eyes pulled the French doors inward and stepped gracefully forward. The shift and sway of her kimono—pale-gray silk dotted with bright yellow flowers—offered a peek at the woman's bare toes. Klare quickly reset her left eyebrow, which had involuntarily raised in disapproval.

"Hello!" the woman, who had to be at least in her seventies, sang warmly and cheerfully, as if she'd known them for ages.

Klare looked at Nic, who stammered as if caught unawares by this playful, barefooted woman. "Uh, hello. We're here to see Dr. Hirsch?"

"You found her! Please, come in." Her smile was as merry as her voice.

Through the creamy, delicate drapes, Klare, Nic, and Finn stepped down into the doctor's office, their footfalls received silently by the plush carpet. Overstuffed grey and blue armchairs, a plump lilac loveseat, and a variety of rounded ottomans and poufs were arranged in a semicircle, velveteen and cottony blankets draped across the edges of each. A variety of mismatched pillows in all shades and textures were strewn about, yet somehow managed to give the appearance of being perfectly coordinated.

Klare watched Nic and Finn scan the room, just like she was, their faces aglow with what seemed to be wonder and awe. There was no desk, file cabinet, or anything else that one would expect in a professional office, and though the sharp edges of skepticism still rubbed against her attention, a tiny pinprick of something soft emerged to momentarily soothe her belly.

"Please, have a seat wherever you wish," Dr. Hirsch requested.

Klare unenthusiastically followed Nic as he relaxed into the loveseat and watched Finn and the doctor each choose one of the armchairs.

Gee, make yourselves at home, guys. Her neck flared with embarrassment at the bitterness of her internal voice.

As if joining a casual tea party, Nic complimented the doctor on her space and asked her where she was from.

"Oh, I've lived lots of places." She chuckled. "But mostly here. I have been in town for many, many years. How about you?"

Nic shared his journey from California to Cleveland, then on to Stark County fifteen years ago. Disinclined to look the part of the unwilling participant, Klare added that she was a local native with Finn, of course, the same.

The doctor's eyes sparkled as she spoke. "I am so happy to meet you all, and so glad you came in. I would love to hear about how you all have been doing, and how I might be able to be of help."

Klare tried to dispel the suspicious apprehension she held toward this woman whom she'd just met and who seemed to be nothing but kind. She knew she was being irrational, yet her stomach clenched, bracing for the proverbial other shoe to drop. Nic repetitively pulled on his left earlobe while looking around, seemingly distracted by something she couldn't see. Finn, on the other hand, was a picture of serenity, hands clasped lightly in his lap and looking eagerly at the doctor.

Are they waiting for me to start? Anxiety pulsed up from her belly into her chest. *No way.*

She lightly elbowed Nic to bring him back to the present in hopes he would begin.

"Well, I can start." Nic refocused and stopped tugging on his ear. "We've had a rough go recently, especially over the last couple of weeks. My wife…" Nic put a reassuring hand on Klare's thigh. "She has been pretty overwhelmed, and I have not been great at supporting her, or my son. And things seem to be far more, uh… *complicated* than I think any of us were aware. Right?" He ended his summation with an inquisitive glance at Klare and Finn.

Boy, is he walking on eggshells. She knew her husband's synopsis was a severely watered-down version of what had been happening of late, but she wasn't going to argue.

"Mmmm. Complicated." Dr. Hirsch nodded slowly and thoughtfully. "Please, say more."

Glancing at Finn, Klare noticed his calm countenance didn't waver. Nic stayed quiet, his eyes inviting her to elaborate.

Shit. She had hoped to keep her talking to a minimum, but a wiser part of her knew that was unrealistic. While she wanted to protect Finn from another doctor's appraisal, she also didn't want to look like a mother who didn't care.

The knot in her stomach tightened as she thought about Finn's disclosures at the community center, confessions that nobody seemed to be all that alarmed about.

A singing girl with a message who visits him in his dreams and then gets killed by a man with a sword… yeah, nothing to be concerned about here.

She also didn't want to put herself in the hot seat.

Sure, and you smelling smoke that isn't there and completely losing your shit in front of your family and a complete stranger… yep, nothing to be concerned about here either.

"Honey, you have anything you want to add?" Nic nudged.

Certain *not really* wouldn't go over well, Klare went with what first came to mind.

"I'm not really sure what to say. I've, um, had a couple of incidents where I guess I've overreacted to situations that maybe weren't as big of a deal as I thought at the time." She looked at her husband's patient, imploring face. "I don't know how to describe it. It's like my feelings got the better of me, and I just did what I thought I needed to do in the moment."

Dr. Hirsch, an embodiment of care and curiosity, leaned in slightly and asked, "What you needed to do?"

Klare's *whoosh* of a sigh was audible.

"*Careful*," an inside voice warned.

She thought about what she had already shared with Nic and reluctantly added, "I've had some moments of feeling like I need to protect my son, to protect myself. It doesn't really make sense. It's not like he, or we, are in any danger or anything like that."

"How long have you been feeling this way?" Dr. Hirsch asked gently.

The muscle in Klare's leg tightened under Nic's steady hand, and she squirmed in discomfort.

"I'm not exactly sure," she replied and looked to Nic for assistance. When all he tendered was a smile, she continued. "Um, a couple of months, I guess. I, uh…" With all eyes on her, she knew she needed to offer more than what she wanted, so she went with the next thing that came to her mind. "I overreacted to a couple of calls I had gotten from Finn's school and pulled him out early for summer. So, it had to be around that time, I guess."

You didn't just pull him out early. You made him a deal. On the condition he kept it secret. Klare twitched in response to this inner voice, prompting an extra-supportive squeeze from Nic's hand.

"It was before that." Finn's calm, matter-of-factness struck her chest, forcing the breath from her lungs. She sat immobile and, from the periphery, watched Nic and the doctor turn their heads toward her son.

Her hearing as thin as her breathing, Klare barely caught her son's curtailed account of that Saturday afternoon in May, right after his birthday: the community gardening event, the sprint to the café, his going to the bathroom then wandering off, and the trip from the church to the emergency room. Through the muffled sounds, Klare did take note of Finn's omission of *the girl* he talked about in Zeb's office.

"That sounds awfully frightening. Were you okay?" the doctor asked.

Nic interjected, "It was ruled acute dehydration. It was warm, and we hadn't eaten and apparently hadn't had enough water. Finn ended up getting disoriented and a bit lost, but when we found him, we took him in just to make sure he was alright." As the rush of words left Nic's mouth, Klare wondered why he was so quick to interrupt.

As though he were thinking the same thing, Nic sat back in his seat, turned his attention back to Finn, and nodded for him to continue.

"It was in the emergency room." Finn shifted his focus from the doctor to his mother. "That was the first time I saw you not like yourself."

The color drained from Klare's face, pooling thick and viscous in her belly. She couldn't move.

Finn, in patient repose, spoke gently to his mother rather than the doctor. "It was like it was you but not you at the same time. Your voice was different. Angry. And your face. It was different too." Klare watched a thin fracture crackle through his calm countenance, letting loose a quiver in his chin that beheld the sadness in his tawny eyes.

She fished for words to explain, but Nic squeezed her sweaty hand in a silent prompt to let their son finish.

Before her eyes, their son drew in a slow breath that eased the tremor in his face and transmuted the sadness into compassion. He restacked his posture and continued.

"I never saw you like that before. Then it happened again. The night you thought I started a fire. And then when you told me I wasn't going back to the center. At that doctor's appointment. It's happened a bunch of times."

Klare's grip on Nic's hand tightened to the point of strain. He reached over with his other hand to pry her fingers from his and folded her hands into his own. He leaned in close and whispered, "It's okay. It's okay."

She looked back at him and nodded, although she did not believe him.

Nothing about this is okay.

Klare closed her eyes and swallowed, knowing deep down that she had to respond to Finn's report. Unsure where the words would come from, she simply began speaking. "Yes. Those were some of the incidents. One night, I could have sworn I smelled smoke. I ran into Finn's room and thought he had started a fire on the floor. I ruined his comforter 'putting out' the fire." Klare gestured with air quotes. "He told me later that he was just using some sage to clear the air." She paused to collect herself. "And then in Mr. Paytah's office. I thought I smelled smoke again and had this overwhelming sense of us being in danger. But there was no smoke. There was no fire." Klare's chin dropped heavily to her chest, and she pulled her hands from Nic's grasp. "I just don't understand, I'm sorry." Defeated, Klare had no more words to offer.

"But I do." Finn's calm assurance drew all three faces back to him.

"It is because of me. It started with me."

So often are the enticing paths of evasion and surefire routes of escape revealed as exquisite collaborators in a divine conspiracy, one that ensures we return to face that which we seek to avoid and receive our elysian invitation to affect our destiny.

26

Caught between empathy and anger, Nic stifled a sigh and stole another sidelong glance at his wife's flat and distant visage, hoping that perhaps her stance would have shifted on the drive to Dr. Hirsch's office.

Nope. She definitely does not want to be here.

Looking at his son in the rearview mirror, he marveled; Finn sat as content as could be with a soft smile resting easily on his untroubled face.

Nic was eager for this appointment, even more so after Klare had *forgotten* about their scheduled follow-up earlier in the week, forcing an embarrassing last-minute cancelation. Luckily, the understanding Dr. Hirsch was able to squeeze them in as her final Friday appointment.

He could appreciate Klare's reluctance, especially with how their first session had ended with Finn's near-nonchalant proclamation of his belief that his mother's struggles started with and were because of him.

The doctor had surprisingly suggested that they *not* talk about Finn's hypothesis when they got home but that they would pick up where they left off when they returned on Tuesday.

The appointment Klare forgot about.

Nic wasn't convinced she actually *forgot* about the appointment, but somehow it didn't surprise him. She'd spent the days following their first meeting withdrawn and preoccupied, and even after his efforts to engage, he ultimately gave her the "space" she asked for.

Well, here we are again. He pulled the car to the curb and set the brake. *Let's hope this time goes better than the last.*

The same peculiar, buzzy sensation from their first visit nipped at the edges of Nic's mind as he entered the doctor's lobby. The elegant two-toned parquet flooring presented a teak mosaic that immediately drew his eye to the magnificent compass medallion inlaid in the very center of the space. Thin strips of metallic gold marked the arrowed points of the four cardinal directions.

The vase containing white and blue hydrangeas that had graced the antique sideboard last week now held mounds of white, salmon, and burgundy sweet peas that released a sweet, summery fragrance through their delicate butterfly-wing petals. Nic smiled and took an extra-long inhale through his nose.

A large baroque mirror hanging above the cabinet reflected a dazzling violet-gold amethyst geode that sat atop a heavy marble pedestal to the right of the lobby. Easily two feet tall, Nic figured it would have taken a small crew to lift this breathtaking gem into its place of honor. Staring at the glittering purple facets, he noticed the shrill peal in his ears transform into a low, deep timbre.

There's something about this place, Nic mused. *"Enchanting"* sprang forth in his mind.

"Hello!" Dr. Hirsch emerged from the other side of the French doors, as if materializing from a wispy fog. "Please, come in!"

"Hi." Nic smiled and led his family into the recessed inner office. Like last time, his sight was immediately drawn to the beams of natural light streaming in through a massive, opaque sliding shoji screen that made up the entire north-facing wall. Sheer batik curtain panels hung in front of the windows, their cottony folds puddling in luxurious pools on the carpet below.

I really want to see what's out there.

A faint scent of vanilla hung in the air, wafting from candles set in clear glass hurricane vases in the center of a squat coffee table. Instinctively, Nic took in another full breath as if infusing himself with the pleasant and comforting fragrance. His worrisome thoughts and troubling feelings about how the meeting might go seemed to evaporate on his exhale.

After reclaiming their original seats, Nic turned to Dr. Hirsch, whose casual aura radiated patience. Finn modeled himself after the doctor, sitting relaxed in his chair. In stark contrast, Klare sat stiff and straight on the edge of the loveseat, her hands tightly wrapped around the purse held on her lap.

Oh boy, I hope she can settle a little. Hoping the physical contact might assist, Nic scooched closer until their legs touched.

"It's nice to see you all this afternoon," the doctor started. "I'm glad you could make it in."

"Yeah, we're really sorry about Tuesday," Nic apologized.

Directing her care toward Klare, Dr. Hirsch asked, "Is everything okay?"

Klare looked at Nic, her eyes suddenly worried.

She's so nervous. His heart ached for his wife, so much more fragile than he had ever believed her to be in their nearly fifteen years of marriage. He offered an encouraging smile that said, *It's okay, go ahead.*

"Um, yes, I'm sorry. I left to run some errands and time completely got away from me. I didn't have my ringer on, so I didn't hear Nic's calls, and by the time I looked, it was well after our appointment time. I'm sorry, it was an honest oversight and I…"

"Klare, it's alright. Sometimes time does tricky things when it encounters our emotional worlds. And where we left off last week was certainly emotional. How have you been doing?"

A hint of a smile twitched at the corners of Klare's mouth, and Nic felt the chilly energy wafting from her body warm by a couple degrees. She softened the death grip she had on her purse, and Nic breathed a quiet sigh of hope.

"About the same," Klare offered. "I feel confused and can't seem to sort any of this out."

"Well, luckily, that is why we are all here. To help sort things out. Why don't we pick up where we left off and take it from there?" she suggested tenderly.

While Nic felt comforted by the doctor's easygoing confidence, he knew what he had to say couldn't wait.

Last week after Finn had recounted his experience of when he first saw his mother *not being herself* in the emergency room, Nic had tried to recapture his sense of their time in the ER. Scanning his memory, he hit upon the image of Klare's atypically snappish manner with the attending staff. He had replayed the scene in slow motion, going frame by frame in search of a clue that might explain her conduct that day, having previously chalked it up to the stress of that eventful afternoon.

Dr. Andor's mental status exam. Shit. Nic then recalled his talk with Dennis, the conversation he had yet to broach with Klare. *Now it makes sense.*

Nic had followed Dr. Hirsch's suggestion they not talk about Finn's "*it started with me*" theory, but was eager to now that they were back in session. He wasn't sure if he knew exactly what

Finn meant, but he had an inkling, and he knew they would need the doctor's support to determine if what he suspected was true.

"I'm sorry." Nic exhaled and squared his shoulders. He couldn't tell if he was imagining another slight ease in the tinnitus or if it was a legitimate lessening. Either way, he embraced the tiny reprieve and stepped in. "This is very difficult, but there's some information you should know that I think will help clarify some of this."

Klare shot up and away from Nic's reassuring hand, putting a noticeable distance between them. For a flash, he thought she was angry, but her eyes said something else entirely.

She is terrified.

"Honey, it's okay. Please." He reached out his hand. She looked at it for a moment before accepting his invitation. He scooted over to close the space she had created.

"Klare's father and brother died in a fire when she was young." He turned to face his wife. "You were nine or ten?"

A perplexed nod was all she could muster.

"When Dennis was over last week, he shared some of what he remembers from back then. A lot of things I had never heard about. And now that I know, I think it might relate." The eggshells on which Nic lightly treaded creaked.

He stole a glance at Finn, who remained poised and still. Knowing it was time, he then turned to Dr. Hirsch to explain.

"Dennis is my best friend. He grew up here in town and was about Klare's brother's age—maybe seventeen or so—when all this happened."

Turning back to face his wife, Nic continued. "He said there were rumors that went around after your dad and Scott died. And that your mom had a lot of trouble and sort of withdrew from everyone."

Oh my god. Nic was stunned by Klare's flat stare. *Could she possibly not remember any of this? Is this why she never told me? Shit.*

He leaned in closer. "Honey? Do you know what I'm talking about?"

Her eyes blinked in plain effort while her forehead creased in concentration.

She doesn't remember. Oh my god.

"Klare?" Nic heard the anxious tremble in his voice.

"Uh, a little, I think." Klare pinched the bridge of her nose. "I was young. Um, I know my mom sort of fell apart. I mean, of course she did. I don't think we left the house very often after that. I remember people stopped coming over." She shook her head in confusion. "What does this have to do with anything?" The sharp edges had returned.

"Klare, if I can interrupt for a moment." Dr. Hirsch's voice was a salve. "I am so sorry to hear about your dad and your brother. That is tragic and heartbreaking."

Nic was thankful for the doctor's intercession and found his breath again.

She continued. "This would be traumatic at any age, but certainly, at the tender age of nine or ten, it would be completely normal not to remember it all."

A speck of relief fluttered in Nic's belly as he watched Klare lock eyes with the doctor and nod her head cautiously.

"Are you in a place where Nic can continue?" the doctor inquired gently.

"Sure." Klare's unblinking eyes remained fastened to the doctor's as if they were an invisible lifeline.

"Excellent, you are doing just fine," Dr. Hirsch assured.

Nic watched Finn while the doctor held Klare's eyes and thought with no small measure of awe, *He looks just like her. A mini well-seasoned therapist.*

Looking to the doctor, he saw her incline her curly silver-gray head, prompting him to continue. Nic shifted his body to face Klare and started again, hoping the eggshells would not turn into land mines. "Dennis said some of the rumors were about your brother having been troubled, or sick, and that maybe *he* had something to do with the fire."

He watched Klare's eyes begin to blink rapidly, her brain clearly scanning for something to help her remember what another part wouldn't, or couldn't. He knew all of this needed to be out in the open, but he ached, knowing how much distress his words were causing his wife.

After an impossibly long pause, Klare straightened, and that all-too-familiar indifference returned to her face.

Oh no. Please, not again. Nic had no idea what was on the other side of the giant shoji screen but imagined for a moment being out there rather than in the room with this Bridgetesque version of his wife.

"I don't remember any of this," Klare stated in the voice that wasn't hers. "But I'm not surprised. People make up all kinds of stories about things that are none of their business." She fixed her stony stare on Nic. "*Again*, what does this have to do with anything?"

Nic stifled a shiver in response to his wife's rancor. In an invisible tug-of-war, he strained to balance his attention between Finn and Klare through the rising aural racket. It was clear the puzzle pieces were not yet fitting together for his wife—pieces that would set in motion a painful recognition of the puzzle's picture.

What must he be thinking right now? he wondered, worried that Finn had already deciphered this mystery before Klare did.

Nic looked to Dr. Hirsch again for some assistance, the tension almost too heavy to bear.

The doctor's compassionate, knowing smile spoke volumes. *She gets it.*

The volume inside dropped an inch.

"I know I'm hearing this for the very first time," Dr. Hirsch remarked. "And I get the sense that you might be too, Klare. May I offer a perspective?" Her voice was barely above a whisper.

Klare offered a small, tight-lipped nod.

"Okay, thank you." She paused to organize her thoughts. "So, what I am hearing is that you lost your father *and* your brother in a fire when you were a child. And then your mom, already overwhelmed with loss, starts hearing rumors that people are talking about your brother being troubled and that the fire might have been at his hand. I can only imagine what that must have been like to hear that people—her friends—were talking about your brother like that. So, she withdraws, avoids people so she doesn't have to talk to them—people who she believed were judging and accusing her son, or even her, by proxy, as his mother."

Klare's face melted during Dr. Hirsch's summation; her eyes drooped with a burden of sadness, and the corners of her mouth sagged, pulled downward by gravity's weighty hand. The hardness held in her features a moment before had turned to sorrow.

Nic gently reached over to rub Klare's shoulder, encouraging her cautious acceptance of the doctor's premise. But he knew the deeper connection between her past and her present had not yet been stitched together.

"Mom?"

Finn's gentle utterance drew the other three faces in the room to his like a magnet.

Shit. Nic's stomach plummeted. *He got there first.*

Klare turned toward their son.

"You were worried I was like Uncle Scott."

"Finn, no!" Klare shouted. "Come on. There is no way…"

"Klare," Dr. Hirsch gracefully interrupted. "Let's hold on here for a moment. We are still just trying to figure out some of the pieces to this very complex picture, so any ideas and perspectives only serve to help us. Finn, please, continue."

As if channeling some sagacious ancestral guide, Finn spoke with confident, comfortable ease. "Mom, it makes sense. You were trying to protect me. You didn't want people to think bad things about me. Or us."

"Finn…"

"Mom, it's okay," Finn reassured with a soft smile. "You don't have to be afraid."

Nic watched in wonder as this astonishing young man, his son, spoke with a wise self-possession he usually associated with sages and old souls. He remembered Zeb's words, "… *a natural leader… a powerful energy inside that speaks for him.*"

"Klare," Nic stepped in. "It does make sense. Why you took him to that doctor. Took him out of school and the center. Even why you called your mom. You were trying to protect him. You said that, Klare. That you've had this overwhelming urge to protect him."

Klare's expression morphed back into confusion and fear. "I don't understand. I wasn't thinking Finn was like Scott. Yes, I was worried about him. And just wanted to make sure he was safe and okay… I don't understand." Frustrated tears threatened to spill from her troubled eyes.

She's so close. Nic turned to the doctor in worried supplication.

"I would like to give you some information that I believe will bring some clarity. But first, let's begin with a couple of deep breaths to help get settled."

The family followed the doctor's mindful demonstration, and then she began sharing some of her wisdom.

"With trauma, the mind has this way of grabbing up painful memories and tucking them away into a separate compartment. Once safely out of awareness, the person can then go on functioning and managing in their daily life. You can think of it as an internal protection system. Those sequestered memories can stay hidden for a very long time, possibly forever, like an old forgotten box stuck way back in a closet. That is, until something happens that awakens them. Then they become active. But because these little fragments have been so well-concealed, they are not really known to the person. So, the body remembers without the brain fully understanding what is happening. These memories are *felt* rather than *understood*. They can show up as emotions that don't make sense, intrusive thoughts and images, physical symptoms that don't have any medical basis, even seeing or smelling things that aren't actually there."

Like fire, like smoke. Nic looked at Klare. *Is she getting this?*

"It is like the memories of the past hijack the present so that events in the now are experienced through the filter of the past. But the person is not aware this is happening. So, reactions to ordinary events can be big and not fit with what is truly going on. It's like the person is split into two selves: the one experiencing things through the lens of the past, and the other who is in the here and now… feeling out of control and confused about what is going on."

Nic shuddered in anticipation, his thoughts volleying between fear that Klare would angrily reject the doctor's explanation and hope that it would land softly enough to give his wife some much-needed assurance.

He nudged her with caution. "Klare?"

Eyes wild with the disquiet of dawning awareness, all Klare could do was nod.

The doctor continued, "Klare, I believe you've been in the throes of a sustained trauma response. A long-sequestered part of you, stored away in one of your mind's hidden cupboards, to protect the rest of you from painful truths, was activated—called up from the past—that day in the hospital. And since then, it has been transposing memories, scenes, images from the past into the now—distorting the view of the present to the point that it has become hard to tell what is real, what isn't, what is now, what is then."

Giddiness rippled through Nic's chest, and he suppressed an impulse to laugh. *Hold yourself together here, pal.* His eyes rolled heavenward in silent thanks for this wise woman's salvific words.

"I'm having a hard time following this." Klare stood and slung her purse over her shoulder, as if making to leave. "I'm sorry, I don't think I can do this."

"Klare, please! Please sit down. We need to talk about this," Nic pleaded. The shrill pitch was back, in concert with the alarm ripping through his body.

When Klare stood in frozen limbo, the doctor gently stepped in.

"I think we should stop for right now. This is a lot, and the brain can only take in so much at a time," Dr. Hirsch reassured. "Klare, if you are willing, I suggest you and Nic take some time outside here in the courtyard to give your brains and bodies some time to digest and rest. And I can stay back here and chat with Finn for a while. How does that sound?"

The doctor winked at Finn, and Nic noticed a sparkle move across his son's face.

"That sounds good," Nic said with great relief and stood to join his wife.

Dr. Hirsch rose and crossed the room to the shoji screen. The panels slid silently apart to reveal what looked to Nic like an alternative dimension. A charming courtyard encircled by age-old trees whose branches intertwined overhead to create a dappled, shaded canopy. Cushioned wicker chairs and stone benches faced a bubbling pond that popped with pink and yellow lotus flowers amid emerald lily pads. Birdsong filled the air and intermingled with the whiz and zips of hummingbirds and dragonflies.

Nic's mouth hung in awe as he guided Klare into the enchanting quad while visions of fairy tales and Thomas Kinkade paintings sprung to mind. He almost laughed out loud again, light-headed with wonder and suddenly free of the clanging that filled his ears mere seconds ago.

Having turned back with a grateful nod to the doctor as she slid the screens closed again, a contented sigh escaped his lips when he felt Klare fold herself into his side within the comfort of his waiting arms.

27

Finn watched his parents vanish into a courtyard haven, swallowed up by trailing vines and outstretched branches that proffered shade and sanctuary. The unexpected outdoor oasis beckoned with its natural song.

A lightness contracted and expanded within his body—a slow, rhythmic pulse with a breath of its own, the same sense he had felt in Zeb's office, before his mom had her *episode*. The young man had stopped searching for words to define this indescribable experience, opting to simply let it be and enjoy its pleasant vibration.

From his contented vantage point, he watched the doctor pull the screens closed and refold herself into the plush sky-blue chair.

"How are you doing, Finn?" she asked coolly.

"Well. Thank you." His tempo was as slow as his restful heartbeat.

His eyes followed the path of an impossibly long Golden Pothos vine that spilled from an earthen pot atop a corner bookcase. It snaked across the top shelf toward one of the windows as if reaching for the sun, where it then wrapped its verdant lime tentacles around the curtain rod before trailing down toward the floor.

I can feel your energy. Finn silently acknowledged, envisioning oxygen molecules radiating from the variegated green-and-white leaves and feeding the light inside of him. *Thank you.*

"How do you think our meeting is going so far?" the doctor asked in an equally unhurried tone.

Finn drew more nourishing oxygen into his lungs and nodded in thoughtful contemplation. "Good. I knew it would."

"Oh, yeah?" She chuckled. "I'm not sure your parents are so sure."

"No." His smile mirrored hers as he glanced between her and the bookshelf behind her.

Rather than books, the shelves beneath the crawling plant held an array of tchotchkes—ceramic animals painted in lively shades of red and purple, pieces of aquamarine sea glass polished smooth by years of ocean tumbling, and a variety of miniature clay saucers and bowls lovingly molded by hand. The only non-earthy bauble was a Daliesque clock dripping from a ledge as if it were melting.

I wonder where all these things came from. Finn was thoroughly charmed by the medley that hinted of gifts both given and received.

The doctor eased back into the supportive arms of her cozy chair. "Can I ask you something?"

He met her gaze with a silence that said, *Go ahead.*

"How did you know? That today would go well?"

A faint flicker traveled through the muscles in Finn's stomach, and he responded with a benevolent smile. He found the reflexive warning amusing—residue from the fear and worry that had troubled him before the *knowing* took hold.

"Inside. I knew… I know." The lightness inside beamed.

"You knew on the inside that today's appointment would go well?" One of Dr. Hirsch's eyebrows lifted above the other with an air of riveted curiosity.

"Not just the appointment. But her. That she would be okay." The oxygen wafting from the breathing plant permeated Finn's pores, shooting tiny sparks of energetic life into the growing light inside. "I don't know how to describe it. I just feel it."

"Hmmmm. Some people might call that intuition—a sense of knowing something in their bones even though they have no idea how they know it. Something like that?" The doctor's voice carried notes of crisp awe and eager intrigue that danced in the sparkle of her clear, sapphire eyes.

A smile spread across Finn's face. *Exactly.*

The reason he had been amused by his stomach's cautious flicker was because he already *knew* he was going to tell her. He knew it when he and his parents entered the circular foyer, when they crossed the threshold into her office the very first time, when he *knew* his mother was exactly where she needed to be, and when he glimpsed the magic that waited outside in the courtyard garden. The *knowing* had been with him the entire time.

Excited as he was to tell her about the girl's arrival and her sweet song, about the bird in his chest and the amplifying stone that hung beneath his shirt and over his heart, and about the emerald blue-green *visions* that danced around him, Finn knew that was for another day. Today, he wanted to tell her about his dream and the mystical confirmative message the girl had finally brought to him.

Finn closed his eyes and pulled more oxygenated sustenance into his lungs. He liked the image of nourishing himself with nature's life breath. Once filled, he opened his eyes to the doctor's expectant face and shared what had transpired in his dream the night of their family meeting with Zeb.

Finn had drifted off with visions of protective stones, quests for answers, and sage guides. He hadn't wanted to sleep, enthralled as he was with the stories of Nicholas Black Elk and his second cousin, Crazy Horse, but slumber pulled him under and into the land of dreams.

He found himself atop a vast plateau, looking out over a dazzling cerulean sea where the echoing, rhythmic splash of the waves was the only sound he could hear. There was a tiny glimmer far off in the distance. The reflection from the sun? Perhaps a solitary sailboat? He was captivated and strained in concentration in hopes of figuring it out.

Absorbed in the mystery, Finn had failed to notice the presence that had taken up a seat on the grassland beside him. It wasn't until the *whoosh* of a great shearwater flying low overhead broke Finn's oceanic trance that he noticed a beautiful girl about his age sitting next to him, her strawberry-flaxen hair blowing gently in the salty breeze.

"It's you. It's you!" Finn could barely contain his shock as he stared, finally, into the face of the girl he knew was the one who had been singing to him.

Her only response was a breathtaking smile.

From his mouth poured dozens of questions, strung together like a string of blinking lights, each bulb bursting into brilliance before the one next to it had yet to extinguish. Finn paused his excited inquisition to take a breath when he realized he'd not given her as much as a second to reply. She simply sat and listened, her divine face patient and kind.

Clear she wasn't planning to respond to his quizzical litany, Finn held back the other dozen questions waiting in the queue and took another breath. A becoming-familiar, reassuring phrase drifted up silently from within, coating his urgency with a balm of comfort: *You know.*

Outside, but somehow also inside of him, listening to his thoughts, the girl finally spoke, her voice the same sweet honey as in her songs: "Yes, you know."

"But I *don't* know!" Finn pleaded. "I mean, I *do*, but I also *don't*. And I don't know what to do!" Even in this dreamland, Finn blushed at how senseless he sounded.

"Yes, you do." Her lovely lilt calm and certain, she continued. "You've always known, as have so many before you, as it will be for many who have yet to come."

"But I don't understand. What am I supposed to do?" Finn believed her and knew her words were true, but he still felt unsure about what it all meant for him, and his family.

Another kindhearted smile graced her face, radiating a shimmery blush that felt warm and tingly upon Finn's own. "You mustn't turn away from that which speaks inside you. Listen. And then, follow."

Finn closed his eyes as if to help his brain—no, his heart— soak in her wisdom. Her words glowed golden in his mind's eye, like the trails of Fourth of July sparklers. Once certain they had been sufficiently emblazed so that he would not forget them, he opened his eyes. She was gone.

"But I was not sad she was gone." With a contented sigh, Finn concluded his dream story with the doctor. "At least not this time."

Dr. Hirsch sat stock-still on the edge of the chair, her mouth slightly open and her eyes ablaze with wonder. With a tiny but sharp inhalation, she leaned back and released her bated breath.

"Well. Finn, I must say, that sounds like quite the dream. I'm curious what you think about…. wait, wait. I'm sorry, what do you mean by 'not this time'?"

Before he could answer, a diminutive whisper echoed up from his chest—the familiar buzz from his stone, felt rather than heard. It pulled his attention over to the bookcase. There was something there, beyond the meandering plant and the host of gems and adornments.

His body tilted forward, and he wondered, *What is it?*

"Would you like to take a closer look?" invited the doctor, noticing Finn's preoccupation.

Finn stood and crossed partway to the case before suddenly freezing midstride. He cocked his head to aim his right ear toward the shelf, then closed his eyes, turning off one sense to amplify the other. It only took a few seconds.

There it is. I hear it.

Eyes back open, he completed his trek across the room and came face-to-face with the origin of his fixation.

The shimmer vision was back. It swam into the edges of his senses, enveloping him with a warm vibration that at first muffled, then removed all sound, leaving Finn suspended in a silent, weightless space.

He could not tell if the airy voice whispered from inside his head or if it arose from elsewhere within this emerald aura, but its message was clear: "*Listen. And then follow.*"

The ocean-jade iridescence began to recede from Finn's periphery, enough for him to sense Dr. Hirsch's presence to his left. Small sounds returned to his ears—the wispy hum of the fan, the thin ticks from the melting clock. He was pleased that a tender afterglow continued to embrace him.

Directly in front of him was a plum-colored bottle vase that contained a myriad of long, elegant feathers—white goose plumes, brown-and-tan hawk quills, and blue-black spikes from crows and ravens.

But it was the luminous object hanging from the neck of the urn that had drawn Finn's attention.

"Ah, the eye stone," Dr. Hirsch proclaimed, tendrils of fond remembrance wrapping around her words. "I found that right after I arrived here. Or I should say, *it found me.*"

A thin strip of leather threaded through the small hole that tunneled through a flat gray stone about the size of a half-dollar. About the same size as his. Finn's heart thudded with a force that rebounded in his skull.

An eye stone?

As if she'd heard his question, she answered, "They are sometimes called hag stones, adder stones, or even witches' stones. There are lots of names. They are thought to be sacred because they hold a lot of power. To protect, to heal, to bring luck to whomever the stone finds."

"Who the stone finds?" The earthquake quivering within set Finn's lips trembling and his voice shaking.

"It is said that the stone finds the person instead of the other way around."

Frozen—not in fear, but in astonishment—Finn leaned closer to study it.

How can this be?

A reminder floated up and landed softly in his mind: "*Listen.*"

"I had just arrived in town." The doctor continued, her voice low and shaded with memory. "I was a bit lost, trying to figure out why I was here. One day I took a long walk along the Tuscarawas, wishing for a sign that would help me understand what I was supposed to do."

The shimmering aura dappled through Finn's vision as he hummed and buzzed inside with the *knowing*.

She was on a quest. For a vision. She was on a kind of hanbleceya.

He felt a tad light-headed and placed a hand on one of the shelves to keep himself steady as the doctor, with whom he already felt a comfortable kinship, continued her story.

"And I looked down and there it was. Just sitting there all by itself with no other stones or pebbles around. It was like it was waiting for me. So, I bent down to pick it up, and the most calming feeling came over me. I didn't know exactly what it meant, but I knew for certain that it was important that I stay here." Her voice was thick with the tender touch of memory.

Gripped by the paradox of external immobility and internal seismic activity, Finn remembered the plant's oxygen support and visualized using his lungs to drink from its proffered fount. He began to feel less faint.

"You know," the doctor went on with a renewed enthusiasm, "another quality the eye stones are purported to have is that the little hole is actually a portal. A special gateway to another world." She whispered these last words as if sharing a marvelous secret.

Dr. Hirsch carefully lifted the stone from the vase and held it up to the diffuse light coming in from the courtyard on the other side of the shoji screen.

"What do you think, Finn? What might be on the other side?" she asked playfully.

He leaned over and stared through the small tunnel and thought about his parents sitting in the enchanted garden mere feet away. He thought about his mother. About helping her. About helping people. He didn't know what was through the portal of Dr. Hirsch's stone, but he was beginning to sense that whatever was on the other side of *his* stone was about to get clearer.

All I have to do is listen and follow.

With a grateful sigh, the doctor returned the stone amulet to its place of honor and turned to face Finn.

Finn stifled a small smile when he saw the doctor's cheeks flood pink and vibrant. Her hand shot up to cover her open mouth.

Dr. Hirsch was no longer looking at Finn's face. She was looking at the small stone atop his T-shirt, hanging from a thin piece of leather, resting in the center of his chest right next to his heart.

28

Passing over a freshly dried dish, Nic stiffened when Klare turned and halted midmotion as her hand touched the pantry doorknob. It was as if an invisible finger had pressed pause, freezing her in place and space.

Behind him, Finn continued his sudsy postdinner work. Nic slowly dropped the drying towel on the counter and moved cautiously toward his wife.

Mindful to not startle her, or Finn, he whispered in her ear, "Hey, are you okay?" His heartbeat quickened, setting off a shrill internal pulse.

When she didn't immediately respond, he placed a tender hand on her shoulder, his physical touch breaking the momentary trance that had seized her, the same one he saw take hold of her earlier during breakfast.

That's strange. She was in front of the pantry then too, he pondered.

"Oh, sorry," Klare replied, shaking away her heady fog. "Um, would you guys mind finishing up?" Her eyes had taken on that faraway, drowsy look Nic was becoming familiar with.

"Of course. I'll bring up some tea later?" He bit on his lower lip, concerned about her increasing distractibility. He thought about Dr. Hirsch's description of *dissociative symptoms* and her reassurance that these types of freezing responses are not unusual when the brain and body are working so hard to process strong and often confusing feelings. Taking a deep breath, he joined Finn at the sink to finish what they had started.

Chores complete, Finn said goodnight and made his way toward the stairs.

Reluctant to bring the weekend to a close, Nic called out, "Hey, you want to listen to some music?" An amusing anticipation of his son's answer fluttered in his chest.

"Yes!" Finn's brightness showered Nic's heart like a refreshing spring rain.

Following Finn to the study, he replied with equal cheer, "Alright then, how about you pick the album?"

Their Friday afternoon session with Dr. Hirsch had been emotionally draining, especially for Klare. Nic remembered the way her face looked as awareness poked and prodded, trying to help her stitch together the connections he, Finn, and the doctor had already made—her eyes wild with uncertainty, her forehead clenched in confusion.

God, I'm glad the doctor was there. Despite the worry he felt about his wife's reaction to what would certainly be a painful enlightenment, he also felt the reassuring presence of hope. Hope that the family, especially Klare, had someone to help shepherd them through this unfolding process.

Outside in the doctor's courtyard oasis, she had remained quiet, her words held captive by her overbusy brain. But she had leaned in and allowed him to hold her in his supportive embrace, and for that, he was grateful.

"Today was exceptionally promising. I know it was a lot, and there is certainly more to come, but this was a really important step." Nic had taken great solace in the doctor's assurances as they had said their goodbyes and set their next appointment.

They had spent the rest of the weekend together at home as a family. The edgy vigilance of recent weekends had softened into a respectful mindfulness of the vulnerability of Klare's mood shifting in response to the slightest whisper of the wind.

Nic had felt nourished and renewed by his time spent with Finn as they toiled and sweat in the August sun, digging borders and building raised beds for the garden. Klare had stayed close by, quiet but present, a refreshing change from her physical distance of late. With a warmth greater than what the sun offered, Nic had watched Finn radiate serenity, in fluid harmony with nature.

Sheathing his most recent listen—*Eat a Peach* by The Allman Brothers Band, a classic rock staple compiled of live and studio recordings—and returning it to the shelf, Nic watched Finn stop and pull his selection.

Immediately recognizing the image of a vintage San Francisco building backdropped against an abstract extraterrestrial terrain, a grin spread across Nic's face, and he shook his head in wonder at Finn's unconventional choice.

This kid is something else, Nic mused. "Impressive pick there, Son."

Finn beamed while Nic placed the vinyl—the Grateful Dead's 1974 *From the Mars Hotel*—on the turntable. Using the cue lever to position the arm and needle to begin with side one, track one, Nic lowered the lever then jumped when a THUMP! rained down from above.

Reflexively, Nic reset the arm back to its original place and looked at Finn, whose eyes were fixed on the ceiling. Seconds ticked by with no further disturbance, but the thud had triggered both his and Finn's antennae.

"I'm gonna go check on your mom," Nic said, already in motion.

Finn followed, his brow creased in concern.

"Nooooooo." A ghostly, tormented moan issued forth before they had reached the top of the stairs, followed by another whimper, louder and more insistent.

"Scott! Please!" Klare's anguished cry seeped out from under the crack of their closed bedroom door, sucking the air out of Nic's lungs and standing the hair on the back of his neck on end.

"Shit!" He flung open the door to find her writhing in a tangle of sheets that coiled around her limbs, a linen snake constricting its prey. Her face was a sweaty, choked crimson, and her eyes were squeezed shut against whatever it was her mind was seeing. Sorrowful sobs escaped her clenched mouth.

Nic scooped his wife into an embrace, holding her tight against his body with his left arm, while his right hand sought to free her from the clutches of the serpentine sheets.

Watching instinct and adrenaline guide his father, Finn waited at the door.

"Shhh… shhh… shhh…" Nic rocked her and shushed into her ear. She seemed to calm immediately, and he brushed long damp strands of her auburn hair from her forehead. Slowing the sway of his body and the tempo of his breathing, he held his wife tight against his chest as if to compel her respiratory rhythm to match his own.

"It's okay. You're okay. I'm here. We're both here…" Nic continued his gentle ministrations until he felt her body relax into his and her breath return to normal.

Shit. Like she hasn't had it hard enough already. His heart ached for her.

"Klare. Honey. Wake up, okay? I'm here. Please, wake up. It's okay." Nic raised the volume of his voice slowly until it broke through his wife's unsettled slumber, at the same time mindful of Finn's presence.

With a muffled sigh, Klare opened her eyes, her blinks long and slack, reminding Nic of patients he had seen waking from anesthesia. He sat her upright and reached to pick up the full water bottle from the floor, the obvious cause of the startling *thump!*

After a few sips, the haze began to clear, and her eyes regained their ability to focus and track. Nic rubbed her back while she nearly finished off the bottle and let out a long sigh. Finn kept his sentinel position at the door.

"Hey." Nic's voice was cautious and tender. "Are you okay?"

Klare closed her eyes and nodded. Then finally, "Yeah. Ugh, that was awful. Thank you for waking me up."

"Do you want to talk about it?"

She closed her eyes again, her brow furrowed as if contemplating how, or if, she wanted to answer that question.

Nic waited, his hands still caressing her back.

"I don't really remember it. It's sort of a jumble."

"Mom?" Finn took a couple of tentative steps into the room. "You were dreaming of Uncle Scott. And it sounded like a really bad dream."

Klare frowned as she regarded her son. "I don't really remember." She paused. "Maybe you guys bringing him up got under my skin somehow."

Her features morphed slightly, confusion becoming something more irritated and annoyed. Nic's stomach dropped, and he shot a cautious look at Finn, who remained still.

"I'll be right back." And with that, Klare excused herself to the bathroom. After a moment, the water came on, and they could hear her splashing her face. Nic straightened the bedding and fluffed the pillows, trying to bring some order to their chaos, while Finn took a seat on the bench at the foot of the bed.

Klare, her hair bundled back in a loose ponytail and her face damp from a fresh wash, stopped and seemed almost surprised to find Nic and Finn waiting for her.

"Are you feeling better?" Finn asked.

"Yeah," she replied offhandedly. "I'm fine."

The disingenuousness of her outward indifference set Nic's nerves on edge, and he kept his eyes trained on his son, wondering if Finn felt the same way. His calm repose suggested not.

Or he's really good at hiding it. Nic hoped that wasn't the case.

"Mom, I think we should call Dr. Hirsch."

"What?" she scoffed and shook her head in dismissal. "No, that isn't necessary. It was just a dream."

"Klare, remember the doctor said this could happen and that she'd be happy to take our call," Nic encouraged.

Dr. Hirsch, at the end of the appointment, had shared how sometimes when forgotten experiences that have been tucked into the back cubbies of the psyche begin to see the light of day, memories, feelings, and images can bubble up to the surface, both while awake and asleep. She had cautioned Klare to not be surprised if this happened and invited them to call her if it did. That she was there to help. That *they*, while looking directly at Klare, were not alone.

We're not alone. A wave of comfort rolled through Nic's chest as he thought about the doctor's reassurances and wished his wife would accept the offer.

When Klare didn't respond, he tried again, adopting a more laid-back approach this time in hopes of forging an alliance with her. "Let's just give her a quick call in the morning. No big deal. Just to let her know."

Nic could tell her wheels were spinning, and he visualized crossing his fingers for luck that the little white roulette ball would land on the winning color.

"Mom," Finn reassured. "It'll be okay. She's here for you. For us."

Heartfelt pride bloomed as Nic regarded his kind and soothing son.

Klare's eyes fluttered up toward the ceiling and then back to meet Finn's face.

"Fine. Okay." She acquiesced with a resigned sigh.

Annoyance jabbed at Nic's insides until he looked over and saw a broad smile stretch across Finn's face.

Watching his son look at his mother with such love and acceptance dampened some of the prickling, but not all of it.

I wish I could see what he sees.

29

Returning to the study, Nic reset the needle to begin where he and Finn had left off.

As the peppy "U.S. Blues" transitioned into the mournfully haunting "China Doll" in the background, Nic and Finn debriefed on the evening's unexpected turn of events. Ultimately, they agreed that while they wished Klare were more eager to call Dr. Hirsch, the fact that she agreed, albeit hesitantly, was a win.

Finn politely excused himself and went up to his room but the infusion of adrenaline kept Nic alert. Trying to relax, he softened his gaze while the third track—"Unbroken Chain"— rolled tenderly into its spellbinding lilt. He had almost dozed off when the word "brother" seemed to whisper in his ear.

Brother. Nic's heart rang with the softly tapped cymbal of remembrance. *Brothers. Look at us… we each lose a brother while still too young to fully understand.* Thoughts of Elem always led to thoughts of his mother and the extra bite of heartache of losing her to the deadly weight of her grief.

Bridget. Her name tumbled forth, a lonely domino tripped by its neighbor, Gigi, followed by the oddly unprecedented thought, *Well, I suppose Klare lost a mother to grief too.*

Nic's stomach churned with habitual aversion dotted with blots of cold pity as he thought about Klare's mother. Over the years, he had tried to be forgiving and lenient with her, calling upon his inner empath to offer grace to a mother who lost a son and a husband in one fell swoop. Even after the "lighter incident" where she screamed at Finn, he tried, but…

Shit. A sharp spark interrupted Nic's stream of thinking. *The lighter.*

A painful groan bellowed up from Nic's belly. *The fucking lighter.*

"Oh my god," he said, the words slipping hoarsely from his throat, his eyes squeezed shut with sudden understanding.

Like Klare. Bridget thought something was happening that wasn't. Like Klare. Her trauma playing tricks on her.

Compassion rose inside his sternum, more than he had ever been able to cultivate for his mother-in-law. He concentrated on its gleam, willing it to expand.

I can give her that. It doesn't make up for how she abandoned Klare, but… His forehead scrunched as another insight dropped. *Maybe she didn't know what was happening to her either. And had nobody there to help her see.*

Dr. Hirsch's kind and reassuring face was the next domino to tumble, igniting a surge of affection for the woman helping them find their way. It was astonishing how their time with her had already provided enough balm to begin unsticking the rusty cogs of this traumatic tangle. Klare's nightmare was proof of the momentum.

Everything about her and that place is comforting—the foyer, her inner office, and most of all, that amazing courtyard.

When he had entered the canopied enclosure with his arms wrapped protectively around Klare's shoulders, a peculiar familiarity had descended upon him. He had taken in the awning of the sturdy, interwoven branches with wonder while honeysuckle and jasmine released their heady scents and bees, in apiary heaven, drank from an endless supply of sweet nectar.

Though his first time in the courtyard, it felt *known*. His ears had filled with the harmony of nature's music, echoes of nostalgia and melancholy held in the orchestra of birdsong, trickling water, and rustling leaves.

It's like I've been here before, Nic had thought wistfully as he held Klare tight.

A memory nipped and danced at the edges of Nic's mind, a watery mirage waiting to come into view, invoked by the mesmerizing melody that sang of endless nights, winter days, and floating feathers.

He closed his eyes, and a boy's memory stepped from the periphery into the crystal clear open.

Thirteen-year-old Nic sat outside in a sheltered courtyard while too many people to count amassed inside the tiny church, waiting for the funeral to begin. His feet dangled from the concrete ledge, his back to a bubbling fountain. Nic counted the faded bricks below, pavers of dark red and earthen clay inlaid at perpendicular angles with mottled ashen gray blocks. Tufts of Irish moss squeezed up from in between the uneven slabs that pushed up at odd and crooked angles from the massive tree roots protesting beneath their concrete ceiling.

A wispy brush upon his arm alerted him to his mother's presence. How long she'd been sitting there, he had no idea. Despite the winter chill, she wore a flowy kaftan of chestnut and ivory layers trimmed in black, and he thought she looked like a beautiful bird… a fragile bird.

Sympathetic pain had caused Gigi to lose much of her appetite during Elem's fateful journey, leaving her limbs thin and long. But she hadn't lost any of her grace. She enfolded Nic in a swath of chiffon folds and gave him a long squeeze. "It's time to start, baby."

Nic drifted through Elem's funeral upon snippets of sound. The bells that signaled the top of the hour and the commencement of the one o'clock service clanged inside his sore and hollow body. The stifled sniffles mixed with the rustle of tissues pulled from purses and pockets, quickly turning as tattered and soggy as he felt.

However, when they started singing, a trace humming unfurled in Nic's empty chest, its vibration thawing the stark numbness that had taken up residence in his body and his mind when Elem's spark departed.

The harmony of a hundred voices, young and old, high and deep, rippled through his heart with reverence. He didn't know the words to these heavenly songs, but the choral vibrato lifted him into invisible arms and cradled him while he wept. The radiant chants pulsed deep in his bones, reminding him that he was solid and real, broken and unbroken at the same time. He longed for his brother with a cavernous ache, yet also felt a comfort in the celestial songs embracing him. He remembered Linda's soothing advice—*"move in, not away"*—and with that reminder, Nic had let himself surrender to the ethereal limbs that held him complete.

Silence roused Nic from his meditative reminiscence, the record having reached side one's final track. He sat for a moment as the at-once sorrowful and soothing memory of the day he said goodbye to his only brother slowly dissolved and transmuted into another awareness.

The church!

Nic bolted up from his recliner as some slippery notion poked in and out of his consciousness with earsplitting volume. He squeezed his eyes shut and tried to remember what Dr. Hirsch had said while they were saying their goodbyes.

Something about a church?

With his attention split between supporting Klare, keeping an eye on Finn, and thanking the doctor for her time, he must not have been fully tracking everything she was saying.

What church?

With his brain locked in tight concentration, Nic pulled his earlobes as if to release the noisy tension enough to let his memory remember.

What did she say? Something about coming "back to the church next time"? What church?

An inner voice spoke from beyond the ball of strain building in his head. *"You know what church."*

"Wait a minute. The church where we found Finn?" Nic whispered.

With that question, the binds clamping and clenching in his brain relaxed, sending a reminder to his lungs to breathe and quieting the deafening peal. He inhaled a full breath, and his eyes fluttered open as a new awareness dawned.

The church!

When they had found Finn, it was all about getting him to the emergency room to make sure he was okay. Once they were told it seemed to be a simple case of overexertion and dehydration, and not something more medically serious, Nic's relief had all but wiped from his memory everything that had transpired prior.

I don't remember the church coming up in the meeting. Maybe Finn said something when we were in the courtyard?

A pang of guilt twitched in Nic's belly as he wondered if he had missed yet another piece in this unfolding story that had thrust Klare into the spotlight while Finn stood in the shadow of side stage.

If he brought it up, it must be important.

Infused anew with the pull of free-floating threads desperate to be linked, Nic tapped open his phone's search engine to find the church on Cherry Street where they had found Finn.

St. Mary's Parish—on the north side between First and Third in downtown Massillon. It was an impressive and towering structure that Nic had passed by dozens of times; a beautiful building for certain, but not one he had ever paid much attention.

The church's website listed the expected, basic information— hours, Mass times, an events calendar. The history tab offered a detailed timeline of the parish: founded in 1839, first church built in 1842, rebuilt in 1853 after a fire, torn down in 1875 for the construction of a new building, completed in 1880. More facts and figures about rectory, convent, and school buildings, the church's formal consecration in 1926, and its designation in the National Registry of Historic Places in 1979.

Interesting. But nothing that stood out as to what would make this place so significant to Finn, other than it was where he was found.

An unexpected image surfaced in his mind's eye—a still frame of Finn standing in front of that grand church. A shiver rattled up from the base of Nic's spine. *Oh my god. Maybe he went there on purpose?*

Further down the page, the church proudly announced that it was the home of the national shrine for the patron saint of those afflicted with mental or nervous disorders.

He shook his head. *Mental or nervous disorders, huh? How ironic. That pretty much sums me up right about now.*

A link directed him to the webpage of the National Shrine of St. Dymphna.

St. Dymphna. Never heard of her.

It was getting late. Nic's body was too tired to get up and flip the album over, but his brain remained jumpy. Knowing sleep was far off, he continued his research on this unknown saint.

What the heck? Nic's breath caught in his throat when he saw the photo of the statue of the church's honored patron against a sweeping backdrop of a vaulted stained-glass window. The fawn-haired, golden-crowned saint was draped in copper and gold robes and held a down-pointed sword in her right hand while her left extended, palm up in offering. Her head dipped forward, slightly downcast.

He had barely noticed her, consumed by the motionless form of his son collapsed on the floor below her statue.

The visceral memories of that moment when he had first glimpsed Finn's slumped body came back to Nic in a rush of jumbled fragments and snapshots—on his knees pulling Finn into his arms, checking the pulse of his son's carotid artery while simultaneously scanning his head and body for signs of injury. Holding Finn's face by the chin and watching his son's eyes open in glassy confusion, then transform into near-panic as he shot glances around the room as if looking for a familiar face, unable in that moment to see the one right in front of him.

Finn's eyes had eventually slowed before locking onto his father's. Nic hadn't registered the anguish swimming in his son's hazel orbs until this moment. The only thing he had felt was a surge of relief.

"I've got you… I've got you… I've got you…" Nic had repeated over and over into the side of Finn's face, holding him close to his chest while he rose to his feet, his brain already mapping the quickest route to the nearest emergency room.

Cousin to the twitching pang of guilt felt mere minutes ago, a stab of doubt pierced sharp in his chest.

How did I miss so much? What else have I forgotten?

Now troubled by the notion that he had overlooked or entirely missed some critical details related to Finn's experience that day in town, Nic continued to read about the unknown saint held in such honor by this church.

He learned that the original shrine had been constructed in 1938 for the state psychiatric hospital in Massillon, established there to bring comfort to the patients in residence, and that the shrine was relocated in 2012 from the hospital to St. Mary's Parish. A fire had destroyed the shrine just two years earlier in August of 2015, and the building reopened on Christmas Eve last year after a sixteen-month renovation. Every year a celebration is held on the saint's feast day, May 15.

You've got to be kidding me. Another internal flare flushed the air from his lungs in a heavy *whoosh,* and Nic rolled his eyes skyward. *May fifteenth. Finn's birthday.*

"This is ridiculous," Nic quietly scolded himself and set the phone down on the side table.

Nic considered himself relatively open-minded, but in truth, he was much more comfortable drawing conclusions based on verifiable facts. His medical training only served to further anchor him in relying on observable, tested data rather than making assumptions. For the most part, he considered coincidences as random—chance occurrences or flukes of happenstance.

"But is it?" the other voice from within challenged.

The skin on Nic's arms prickled with gooseflesh, and a chill wrapped itself around his spine.

A part of him was tempted to abandon the rabbit hole and be done with this nonsense, but another part, the one with the questioning voice, could not turn away now.

"Who is she?" the curious voice wondered.

Nic picked up his phone and tapped the link to read the history of the unfamiliar St. Dymphna. He didn't realize until he was finished reading her story that he had been speaking aloud.

"A beautiful Irish princess, just fourteen when her mother died…"

"Her father, the king, mad from grief, pursued his daughter…"

"Escaped across the sea to the little village of Geel (formerly Gheel) near Antwerp…"

"But he found her and begged her to…"

"Unwilling to listen to her protests, he drew his sword…"

"And killed her…"

Nic's heart slammed inside his ribcage, beating so hard he could hear the thumps both inside and outside his body.

Wait! Bells as loud as sirens clanged and wailed within. *Wait!* He drew in as much air as his lungs could possibly hold, held it for as long as he could, then released the breath in a long, slow stream until there was not an ounce of oxygen remaining. Then did it again. And again. Until his heart rate calmed and the cacophony in his ears lowered its discord.

Finn's dreams.

He recalled the words his son had used in Zeb's office, a day that seemed so long ago, when Finn tried so bravely to share with his parents the dreams he'd been having.

"Then she died. She was killed by a man with a sword…"

Nic had been so concerned with Klare's outburst that he had completely forgotten to go back and ask Finn more about it.

Has he been dreaming about this saint?

The pangs and stabs returned in force, and Nic resumed using his breath to soothe the painful blows.

Nearing midnight and depleted, Nic wasn't sure what to make of all that he had read and remembered tonight, but he knew one thing: he needed to talk to Finn.

He closed his eyes for a moment, hoping to gather enough strength to make his way upstairs to bed. But he slipped instantly down the slope to sleep, with one final thought.

Is this really all coincidence?

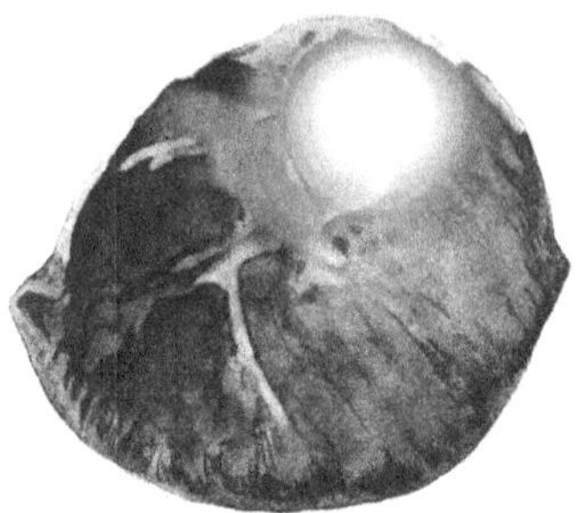

To HEAR THE song of synchrony's native tongue, one must listen closely for the subtle accent that whispers of a mysterious plan and the cadence of the clever unmasking of truths disguised as happenchance. Often delivered up as a dull, washed-out sea bottle, unbefitting of a second glance, one must be willing to turn back and uncork the ancient vessel to release the message within—a treasure not sought, but one seeking to be found. Because in the devices of destiny, there is no such thing as chance.

30

Corralling the tiny bits of her eviscerated napkin into a neat pile, Klare literally bit her tongue to refrain from giving voice to the critical thoughts bounding through her brain.

I'm fully capable of making my own phone call, Nic.

This is so ridiculous.

I should have never agreed to this.

I'm not a child!

At the kitchen table, Klare listened to Nic leave a voicemail for Dr. Hirsch and was taken aback when he left her cell phone number instead of his.

"Why'd you do that?" she snapped. "She can just as easily call *you* back." She cringed at the harshness in her voice. She didn't like this side of herself.

"Well, because *I* need to take Finn to the center, and I think it would be better if she heard from you directly." Nic's nonchalance grated on her nerves.

She suppressed an eye roll, regrettably aware of how immature and petulant she sounded.

You do *kind of sound like a child right now,* the less juvenile part of her rebuked.

"Make sure you pick up her call!" Nic called out as he exited the kitchen into the garage, Finn close on his heels.

Klare hoped there would be no return call, but the hollow pit in her stomach told her that was quite unlikely.

She cleaned up her heap of shreds and stared at her phone on the counter, its black screen taunting her. With a heavy sigh, she picked it up, tapped the screen to make sure it was on, and checked the volume. She didn't want to talk to the doctor, but she wanted even less to have to try and explain to Nic how she missed the call.

And as if that very thought pinged the airwaves, the call arrived.

Ugh. Nervous flutters irritated her belly.

She waited a couple of rings, then picked up.

"Hello?"

"Hello, Klare, how are you?" The doctor was her usual cheerful self.

"Uh, I'm fine. Thanks for calling back." She tried not to sound too discontent. "Um, Nic and Finn thought it would be good for me to call you. I had a nightmare, and I don't think it's really that big of a deal, but they wanted me to let you know." She rolled her eyes, thankful there were no witnesses.

"Oh, my. Well, I'm certainly glad you did. What was your nightmare about?" Curiosity came through loud and clear, sending a guilty ripple through Klare's middle.

She's so nice and I'm being so rude.

"I don't remember much, but Nic and Finn were worried." In truth, she remembered much more than she had admitted to her family. "I mean, it didn't even really make sense."

But it was so real, she added silently. *Too real.* A new wave of nausea rolled in.

"Yes, dreams and nightmares often don't make sense on the surface, but they can offer hints as to what it is we are struggling with underneath… feelings, conflicts, worries. Are you willing to share some of what your nightmare was about?"

Not really. Klare winced at her unspoken insolence. "Um, yeah, okay," she tendered instead.

Looking at her phone, Klare could hardly believe they'd been on the phone for thirty-five minutes. It seemed like only moments, and the details of what she had shared were already fading from memory.

What she could recall, however, was Dr. Hirsch's suggestion that she come in for an individual meeting, an unexpected proposal that had caused Klare's heart to drop.

Oh my god. This just keeps getting better and better.

Klare said she would talk to Nic about it, thanked the doctor, and ended the call, her brain already crafting ways to avoid another session.

Shit. She ran her fingers through her hair, the internal war stirring once again between how much to tell and how much to hold back.

Shaking a few alkalescent tabs into her hand, she went outside for some fresh air and to wait for her husband's return.

"Oh, yeah?" Nic seemed genuinely surprised. "I think that's a really good idea, actually. What did you say?"

Klare's noncommittal response earned her a questioning eyebrow raise from her husband; her defensive hackles rose.

"I don't think it's necessary. Honestly, I think you all might be overreacting a bit. I mean, it was just a nightmare." Her unpersuasive minimization caused Nic's already-raised brows to reach up into his hairline.

"*We're* overreacting?" he scoffed. "You've got to be kidding me, Klare. You know, I've been trying to be patient and supportive, give you *space* when you ask for it, but you know what? This isn't just about you. This is about Finn. And me. This is about all of us."

Internal walls ground slow and coarse into their garrisoned position. She could feel the peculiar *separating* and the threat of a part of herself detaching to float and observe from above. Klare tried to contend with its superhuman force, but her own strength waned, and all she could muster was a feeble, "I'll think about it."

She held Nic's flat stare, knowing she should say more, but her brain would not supply any words.

"No. That's not good enough, Klare. I mean—" the buzz of his cell phone interrupted Nic's inbound lecture. "It's Finn. I'll be right back."

A torrent of thoughts broke through the barrier that had only moments ago sequestered them from her.

Why is Finn calling him?

Why is he walking away from me?

What doesn't he want me to hear?

Frozen and suspicious, Klare surveyed her husband from across the yard as his expression bounced from confusion to head-nodding curiosity, then to an amused smile, and finally an affable laugh. Obviously, it wasn't an emergency; a conclusion that drew a sharp pang of guilt that her initial response to Finn's call wasn't about him, but about her.

"This isn't just about you." Nic's words echoed.

He ended the call and sauntered back toward her, all previous irritation wiped from his face, replaced by an easy lightness that left her more suspicious than relieved.

"Hey, I need to drop by the office to check in, then I have a few errands to run. Would you mind picking up Finn later?" The abrupt change in his demeanor set her nerves abuzz.

"Uh, sure."

"Great, thanks. See you in a bit." He planted a quick kiss on her forehead and made for the garage, leaving Klare alone with her bewilderment.

"Huh?" Klare pulled into the driveway, next to the SUV she recognized immediately. Brows stitched, she looked at Finn, whose placid eyes revealed none of the clarification she sought.

"That's weird. Well, let's go see what's going on." Uncertainty bubbled in her belly as she exited the car and followed Finn into the house.

As Klare tossed her keys into their usual valet on the entryway sideboard, her stomach issued an extra-strong lurch when she noticed the peace lily she'd been rehabbing was not there.

What is going on?! Trepidation hummed through her veins.

With uncharacteristic speed, Finn beelined to the kitchen and out the door into the backyard. Hesitantly, she followed.

"Hey, there you are!" Lucy peeled off a pair of gardening gloves, clapped her hands to release some loose dirt, and walked toward Klare, arms outstretched to pull her in for one of her famous hugs. "It's so nice to see you. Thank you so much for having us over. I've missed you!"

Klare haphazardly hugged her friend back while scanning around for clues to make sense of this baffling scene.

She forced a smile and took in Nic and Dennis busy at the barbecue while Finn had stepped up to observe from his father's left. Behind Lucy sat the lily, freshly repotted in a container Klare had never seen, with its spent leaves and brown tips trimmed, already looking perkier than it had in weeks.

Heart hammering at what felt like walking into a performance midscene without having rehearsed her script, Klare struggled to find her lines. "Hey. Wow, thanks for tending to my plant here. I guess it needed a little TLC, huh?"

"Of course—he'd gotten so rootbound, poor guy wasn't getting what he needed to live. So, I gave him a pretty new home with lots of extra space to grow into. He should be fine now that he can breathe a little better. But speaking of fine, how are you doing? You haven't been taking my calls." Lucy asked with a raised eyebrow, but her concern felt genuine.

"Ugh, I know. I'm sorry. A lot going on. You know." Splotchy heat traveled from beneath Klare's T-shirt up over her chest, neck, and into her cheeks. She looked at the ground rather than at her friend, ashamed over her dismissive nonresponse.

"Well, missy, I don't believe that for one second." Glancing over at the evening's chefs, Lucy then turned back to her and said, "I think they're going to be awhile. Let's go inside."

Shit. Lucy's diminutive, five-foot-three nature-loving airiness was the real deal, but so was her fierce and stubborn side when she set her mind. Klare knew there was zero chance of evading Lucy's decree and followed her friend, already halfway through the kitchen door.

Bracing herself for the inevitable conversation her friend was certainly not going to let her out of, Klare took a deep breath, entered the kitchen, and found Lucy pulling plates out of the cupboard.

"Silverware is already outside. Where do you keep your sheet pans again? They'll need them for the steaks." Lucy's sometimes frenetic, multitasking energy was an amusing contrast to her otherwise docile, intentional way of moving about her spaces.

"Uh, I'll get them." Klare crossed the kitchen and stiffened when she grabbed the doorknob to the pantry. Anxiety ripped from her chest down her arm and into the hand that had yet to turn it. She stifled a reflexive gasp, instantly irritated at her ridiculous reaction.

What the hell is wrong with me? Once again, she thought of something malicious lurking on the other side, hiding in a dark corner waiting for her. *Oh my god! Stop it! This is ridiculous. There's nothing in there!*

Immobilized longer than she was aware, Lucy had materialized at her side and softy asked if Klare was alright.

She released her hand from the door, stepped back, and squared her shoulders before turning to face her friend's compassionate face.

"No. I'm not alright." Her quiet voice freed a truth she both knew and didn't know at the same time, taking with it a weight she hadn't realized had been sitting like a stone atop her solar plexus, pressing heavily against her diaphragm and making it hard to breathe.

"Hmmmmm…" Soothing noises emanated from Lucy's nodding presence.

To her surprise, she didn't resist letting Lucy's unspoken embrace wrap around her like a comforting blanket. Tears of relief welled in her eyes.

"What can I do?" Lucy whispered.

These four little words seemed to carry a power as overwhelming as it was irresistible. That same kernel, golden and calm. A tiny seed nestled within, protected by a glowing aura that swelled, pushing back the bindings of fear and expanding to create a quiet and untouched space in which she could, finally, take a full breath.

I know you.

"Together," the gilded pebble whispered. *"Together."*

She held her friend's regard for a moment, took another deep breath, and found her voice again. "Are you free on Friday?"

31

After buckling himself in, Finn rolled down his window for one more wave to his mother. Cinching her robe tighter as if chilled on the already warm August morning, she yawned and waved back.

They expected to be gone much of the day, having mapped out a five-mile trail hike in Cuyahoga Valley National Park. With travel time, plus breaks and lunch, Finn and his father estimated they'd be back around dinnertime.

"Hey, I'm looking forward to today," his dad said as he took the ramp to merge onto northbound I-77. "I hope you won't miss too much at the center." His voice was bright and teemed with gratitude.

"I won't. I'm glad we're doing this," Finn assured him and noticed a giant grin beam across his dad's face.

He's happy. I am too. The flutter in Finn's chest tickled. *I really want to talk.*

Finn had been eager to share about his experience with Dr. Hirsch. The profound and unexpected bond he and the doctor had discovered between them last week still held Finn in its vibrant grip. Gazing out the passenger-side window into the baby-blue morning sky, Finn savored the sense of wonder.

I still can't believe it, he thought, reflecting on their mystical shared experience.

"Yes, you can," a voice within chimed.

He smiled, content in the *knowing* that rested securely in his heart.

But there is so much more. The girl's return, her message, the vibrating golden emerald-blue aura that had been present more often than not of late. So many things.

He felt eager, but not rushed. Perhaps it was the *knowing*, but he was no longer worried about missing his chance. He knew, when the timing was right, he would tell.

"I'm glad Mom is seeing Dr. Hirsch today," he added, keeping his eyes on his father's expression.

A wily smirk raised the corner of his father's mouth. "Yes, that was a very clever plan you came up with—Dennis and Lucy coming over to the house—and it obviously worked beautifully. Nice job, Son." Nic winked and reached over to pat Finn's knee.

Warm energy pulsed forward from his stone, sending a rippling purr through his chest, where his bird happily chirped.

Forty-five comfortable minutes later, they pulled into the parking lot near the Octagon Shelter close to the Pine Grove Trailhead. As they transferred their lunches from the cooler into their day packs, Nic recapped the plan to walk the Pine Grove Trail loop first, break for lunch, then head over to hike the Ledges, where there were several notable spots he wanted to show Finn.

"There's only about a hundred-foot elevation change and lots of places to stop and rest, so we can just take our time," he added as he shrugged on his pack.

He's worried I'm going to get worn out. Amused, Finn grinned. *That explains the extra water he brought.*

The loop was lined by soaring oak and hickory trees that framed the clear, open sky. The flat, well-worn, all-dirt trail with wooden bridges that spanned the rockier areas made the pathway easy to traverse. After Finn reassured his father for the second time in fifteen minutes that he was fine and didn't need a break, Nic settled into an easy pace alongside his son.

His dad had allotted two hours for the first leg of their journey, so when they completed the loop in less than an hour, Finn, having not even broken a sweat, refrained from teasing him a bit.

He must have thought I'd need to stop every few steps to rest! he laughed to himself.

Nic checked his watch and furrowed his brow. Seeing his father seemingly at a loss over his miscalculation, Finn jumped in to ease the moment.

"Dad, that was great. I'm okay waiting on lunch if you are. Do you want to keep going?"

"Yeah! Let's do it!" As if bolstered by his son's enthusiasm, Nic pulled out his water bottle and oriented to the connector trail that would take them over to the Ledges.

Finn smiled and took a drink of water to wet his throat, and to ease his father's veiled worry.

Entering the Ledges was altogether different from what Finn experienced on the first loop. At the junction where the gravel road transitioned to the trail, they stopped and opted to start the loop to the right.

Maple and beech trees interspersed with towering oaks and sycamores created a shady and sun-speckled canopy under which yellow wingstem and goldenrod trailed densely and in abundance. Rounding their first curve, Finn drew in an inspired breath, taken by the massive walls of moss-covered sandstone with roughhewn alcoves and rocky overhangs.

His skin buzzed against the clean air, pores absorbing the oxygen pumped out through the billions of leaves that hung from the thousands of trees, plants, and bushes that made up this protected preserve. Looking out into the lush woodland that framed the trail, he could almost see the conversion process in action—flora capturing the sunlight and pulling the carbon dioxide out of the atmosphere, mixing it with the water held inside each leaf, big and tiny alike, filtering out the oxygen, and releasing it back out into the atmosphere. Nature's filtration system operating at full steam. He took a deeper breath and imagined every molecule in his system being washed and cleansed. It reminded him of his experience in Dr. Hirsch's office, which reminded him of his mom.

She'll be in good hands today.

As if the image of the doctor in Finn's mind had leapt into his dad's, Nic broke the silence. "Hey, Finn? Can I ask you a question about something Dr. Hirsch said?"

"Sure." An eager flicker pulsed in his chest.

"She said something about 'coming back to the church next time,' but I wasn't sure what she meant. Did you guys talk about church?"

"Yes." Another flick.

They slowed to duck under an outcrop, then turned sideways to shimmy through a narrow slot between two giant boulders before picking up their steady pace and conversation.

"What about church did she think we should come back to?" Nic asked tentatively.

Finn's heart skipped a beat and then knocked hard against his ribs, sending feathery flutters throughout as his bird moved and then resettled herself.

The church! He's asking about the church!

Finn had briefly mentioned the church when Dr. Hirsch had asked about where his stone had *found him*. He still didn't remember how the stone got into his pocket, but the *knowing* told him it had to have been around the church.

"Not church. *The* church. You know, from before the emergency room," he answered plainly, although his heart maintained a faster pace than usual.

His dad moved a step or two in front of him when the inclining trail had become too narrow to walk side-by-side. Finn couldn't see his face, but imagined it was puzzled.

Several beats passed before Nic continued. "I wasn't sure you remembered the church. When we found you there, you were really out of it—like you weren't sure where you were. It took a minute or so for you to come around, and then we just rushed you out of there to the ER. But you remember it, huh?"

How could I forget?! His bird was wide awake now, flitting from rib to rib, and he was certain his stone was literally bouncing under his T-shirt in unison with the cadence of his heart.

Finn took a deep breath of the filtered oxygen proffered from the surrounding vegetation. At the top of his inhalation, a voice both inside and outside his head whispered, *"It's time."*

"Yes. I, um… when I heard the singing, I followed it, and it led me to the church."

The steep path had broadened as they neared the peak, so Finn had a clear view of the side of his father's face, his fast-blinking eyes, and the minute up-and-down bob of his head.

I wonder what he's thinking. Finn wasn't so much anxious about *what* he had shared; it was true, and he had made the decision that he was going to start being honest no matter what.

He was, however, a touch nervous about what his dad was thinking of *him.*

Maybe I can be like Zeb. He thought about his mentor's eternally patient manner. Most people Finn knew used all means of superficial or irrelevant chitchat to avoid the discomfort often triggered by unfilled silence. But not Zeb. Silence, to him, was an ally—a faithful companion that conveyed without words, "*We have all the time in the world for you to say what you need to say.*"

Holding Zeb in his mind's eye, Finn borrowed a steady resolve from his mentor and waited.

"*Trust,*" the inside-outside voice reminded him.

And he did.

The summit revealed a vast and breathtaking overlook of Cuyahoga Valley. A few hikers had stopped to take in the view, and one young woman stood behind her artist's easel, capturing the magnificent perspective in watercolor. The vibrant cerulean sky, as seen through the thick woods of towering sycamore maples and the understory of hornbeams and sassafras, made Finn feel like he was looking through a tunnel, some magical doorway to the heavens.

Nic walked to a flat spot atop the range of gigantic boulders, took a seat, and dipped his head in invitation for Finn to join him. Lowering himself to his dad's left, Finn glanced at his father and found neither judgment nor fear. In fact, his wide eyes and soft smile communicated genuine curiosity. He waited, silence at his side.

"You were *led* to the church?" Nic asked calmly.

"Yes. I heard the singing first at the café. When I went outside, it's like it was calling to me. I followed it to the church, and when I went inside, it was all I could hear. I closed my eyes so I could listen better, and it's like I drifted off. Then you and Mom were there. And, you know the rest." Finn held his father's gaze, wrapped in the relief of sharing what he had so ached to talk about.

"Why didn't you mention any of this? In the ER or later?"

A spot of sympathy pulsed high in Finn's chest as he caught the sadness in his father's voice.

"Everything happened so fast. I was confused and then Mom… Well, you know. I didn't want to scare her even more. Then you were gone a lot. I was going to tell Zeb, but then… I was worried about Mom. I just didn't want to make things any worse."

As good as it felt to talk openly about this, Finn couldn't help but hurt for his dad. His father looked crestfallen, and Finn could only imagine what was going through his mind at that moment. He didn't have to wait long.

Nic adjusted to face Finn in full and put his strong, tanned hands upon his son's shoulders. "Finn, I am truly sorry. Sincerely. For not being there for you. For not asking you more questions. For not being there for your mom. For missing so much since that day. I feel awful, and I want you to know that I want to hear all of it. About that day and your dreams and everything that happened with Mom, and what you do at the center, and… well, everything. I am just so sorry."

Finn soaked in his father's words while his chest expanded in love and admiration, tears tingling behind his eyes. His throat filled with gratitude, restraining his words, so he nodded his consent instead.

His father's eyes were equally moist, and Finn wondered if perhaps his father was feeling the same way.

After a few moments of silent communication, they rose and followed a connecting trail about a half mile to a picnic area to stop for lunch. Near a sheltered structure, they chose a table with some privacy from other picnickers.

Unpacking their well-wrapped sandwiches and pieces of fruit, they settled in to replenish. Finn smiled and accepted the extra bottle of water his dad offered from his pack, even though he had plenty of his own.

He was eager to talk more but waited for his dad to open the door. Like before, he didn't need to wait long.

"The singing you heard that day. Do you want to talk about it?"

"Yes!" the inside-outside voice shouted. Finn tempered his enthusiasm before he replied, not to suppress his eagerness, but because he wanted to savor the telling. He had waited so long.

Finn thoughtfully recounted what happened at the café—how he first heard a bit of a whisper, then a girl's voice, which became a melodious singing so sweet he could not turn away. He described being so swept up by her enchanting tune that he could hear nothing else, and his overwhelming compulsion to follow, as if her voice were calling to *him*.

As he spoke, his bird fluffed and fluttered, as if joyfully playing in her private birdbath behind his breastbone. And beneath his T-shirt, his stone emitted the tiniest of warm and vibrational pulses, communicating in its own mineral language that it, too, was happy.

When he got to the part about what happened in the church, a faint quiver of caution echoed from his belly.

Quickly, Finn imagined that feeling floating away with the breeze. *I am done being cautious. This is what happened. I am not going to hide it anymore.* The strong voice of his true self reassured him, and he continued.

"When I went inside, everything seemed fuzzy, sort of foggy. I could hear her singing, but everything else was muffled. I just wanted to close my eyes and listen. Then next thing, you and Mom were there and . . ." Finn sighed at the memory of being wrested from such a splendid experience and finding that he could no longer hear her.

He wondered what his dad might be thinking.

"Were you scared?"

Scared? No! Finn's head shouted.

"Not at all. It was… nice. Comforting," he offered with a nostalgic smile.

"Hmmm."

Finn watched the features of his dad's face twitch in what looked like careful deliberation, although he thought he saw a flash of recognition pass over him.

"Yes, well, things being fuzzy and muffled… that would have been the dehydration."

A chuckle bubbled up, and Finn shook his head. "Dad, I wasn't dehydrated."

His father stared back in bewilderment.

"It wasn't dehydration. Or overexertion, or heat stroke, or the other things they talked about in the emergency room. I don't know exactly what it was, but it wasn't any of those things."

Finn both heard and felt the puff of air his father expelled from his lungs. He could tell he was trying to digest the unsettling possibility of some other explanation for what occurred that day—one that didn't fit cleanly into a medically diagnostic box.

When Nic let out another heavy sigh and cast his vision skyward, Finn followed his father's stare and smiled as a great blue heron sailed silently above.

"I read something online. About the church we found you at… I mean, where you went. It was interesting, and I was wondering if you know anything about it." The space between his dad's eyes remained pinched in calculation.

A frisky wing tip brushed against Finn's ribs as he waited for his father to continue.

Nic reiterated what he had learned about the church's patroness. The young princess losing her mother, and her father's grief-stricken descent into madness. Her escape, and his finding her to demand she be his new bride. Her bold refusal and, because of that defiance, her death.

Finn listened intently until a series of increasingly adamant pecks from inside his ribcage demanded his attention. Confused and slightly startled, he looked down to see his hand wrapped tightly around the stone beneath his shirt, unusually hot to the touch and emanating tenacious little pulses. *That's strange*, Finn thought. But he had never heard this story.

"Well, it wasn't just that she died. He killed her. With his sword." His dad paused in strained anticipation of Finn's reaction.

The abundance of free-flowing air instantly ceased, and Finn's muscles froze. A resounding chime rang inside his ears, like a hard-struck tuning fork, but not shrill or harsh; it was an even, pleasant peal that seemed to go on forever. He closed his eyes and focused on that single, lengthening note, as if it might offer a path for the infinite sensations exploding in his mind and body.

He waited, without any awareness of time passing, listening until the slowly fading tone extinguished its final breath and decided it was complete. Then, silence. Pure, crisp, clean silence. He welcomed it, a calm reprieve, and waited.

There it is. Finn breathed in a thin stream of oxygen, time and the foliage having resumed its atmospheric purification. Another deep inhalation, and the sound of his heartbeat returned. Yet another and the aviary flutter was back, along with the minute hum of the stone. Air fully flowing now, he relocated his voice, opened his eyes, and stared into his father's.

"That's her. That's the girl, Dad." Tears of wonder pooled and threatened to spill as belief and disbelief swished and splashed equally in his belly. "I don't understand," Finn whispered wistfully. "But wait! What's her name?"

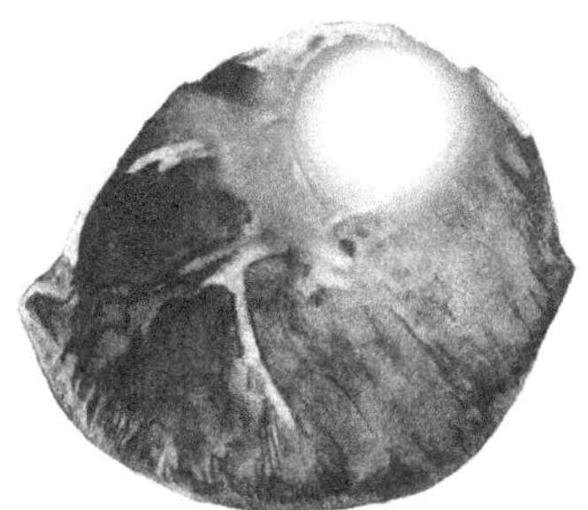

ONCE LIBERATED, TRUTHS pour forward on a rushing river, wild and swept forth on the momentum of unbridled yearning. Overcome, we cower and close our eyes against their frenzied flight from captivity, uncertain of the messages they carry and wishing for their swift retreat. However, upon their first taste of freedom, they expand and swell, fortified by the light, and are now far too big to be put back into that dark repository.

32

"**O**kay," Finn said after a full breath in and out. "I'm ready."

Nic exhaled just as fully when the invisible stranglehold on his heart released its grip. *Oh, thank god, he's back.*

Nic had shared the girl's name—Dymphna—and watched his son smile and nod while the tears balancing on the brim finally gave way and trickled down his cheeks. Nothing about his son's face was sad; it was quite the opposite—the visage of pure and blissful relief.

With his hand pressed firmly to his chest and his mouth slightly open, Finn had seemed to hang enchantedly on Nic's every word as he shared the rest of what he could remember.

After escaping at fourteen to what is now Belgium, Dymphna built a hospice for the sick and needy before her father found her. Almost 800 years later, a church was built in her honor, and pilgrims from all over came looking for help with mental ailments, starting a revolutionary kind of mental health care that still exists there today.

Heartened in his son's delight, Nic had continued.

"Because of what she stood for, she was canonized *Saint* Dymphna, becoming the patron saint of those with nervous disorders and mental illness…" Nic's voice had trailed off as he had watched his son's just-radiant face fall, melting into a heaviness that made the corners of his eyes and mouth sag.

"Finn? What is it? What's wrong?!" Panic had shot up from his chest, filling his ears with a shrill parasitic buzz as he watched Finn shut his eyes and slowly extend his arm, palm facing outward, stopping inches from Nic's face.

He sat across from his son at the picnic table, the thunderous beating of his eardrums agitating the jumble of thoughts reverberating inside his skull. *What did I say? What's wrong with him? Shit! Should I do something?*

He craned his neck one way and then the other, as if seeking some direction from the trees and foliage that surrounded them.

"You know what to do," the soothing voice from his childhood echoed from inside and outside at the same time. *"Move in."*

Emboldened by the reassuring reminder, Nic rose and carefully moved to the other side of the table. Honoring Finn's *stop*, he resisted a paternal urge to pull him into his arms. Instead he quietly sat down, close enough for Finn to know he was there.

Nic held his supportive presence and visualized love radiating from his body and wrapping itself around his son like a soft cocoon, remembering how Linda talked about surrounding Elem with their love, holding him tightly so he knew he wasn't alone. Within moments, Nic watched Finn slowly lower his arm to his lap while his opposite hand remained pressed against his chest.

Wow. That worked… so… fast.

Focused on the encircling love, Nic slowed his thoughts and, one by one, they emancipated themselves from the anxious cascade inside, becoming detached and disembodied, distant, flat words that *suggested* worry and fear but strangely brought none.

"… *internal preoccupation…*"

"… *troubled…*"

"*… symptoms…*"

Wait! Nic's heart quickened, and he thought back to Dr. Hirsch's explanation of dissociative *symptoms*—responses she said can be common when the brain and body are working hard to process strong and confusing emotions.

Finn remained stock-still, but Nic noticed his eyes were anything but. REM-like, his eyeballs darted back and forth and up and down under his lids. *Ah, he's working something out.* The hopeful thought brought his aural ringing down to a barely perceptible hum.

Reluctant to take his eyes off Finn, Nic kept watch while continuing to mentally infuse his son with love and care, repeating a silent mantra, *"I'm here for you. Whenever you're ready. I'm here for you. Whenever you're ready."*

Chilly shivers moved across Nic's sun-warmed skin as he watched Finn's eyes flutter to a stop, his features soften back into a cool, contented countenance, and his breathing return to a steady, even pace.

His son took a full inhale and opened his eyes.

"Okay. I'm ready."

Startled and unprepared for his son to answer as though he had heard his thoughts, Nic momentarily lost his words. Finn patiently waited while Nic took a breath and found some.

"Um, okay, then. Excellent. Uh, how are you feeling?" he sputtered, a bit embarrassed over his bumbling reply.

"I'm fine, Dad. Thank you." Finn's calm self-possession had returned.

Relieved Finn was *back* from his voyage inside that had lasted only a few minutes but seemed like hours, Nic still felt compelled to tread lightly. "Do you want to talk about what just happened? I mean, did I say something that…"

"Um, maybe in a little bit," Finn asserted. "Can we just walk a little more for now?"

Walking south along Ledges Road, they picked up the main trail again and curved left to loop back northbound. On the wide path, Nic walked side by side and stole frequent glances at Finn, who seemed charmed by nature's surrounding abundance. He wondered if he should be more concerned about his son's strong and peculiar reaction to the St. Dymphna story, but the lightness in his chest and the noticeably absent clanging in his ears assuaged his doubts.

Interesting. Must be all this fresh air, he wondered. *Or not.*

They crossed over the second of two wooden bridges, then through a rocky gully created by towering boulders that plunged them into shadow. Nic interrupted their silence. "Finn, you feel that?"

Eyes wide in wonder, he wrapped his arms around himself and squeezed. "Yes!" he whispered in surprise.

The temperature had plummeted as they passed the Ice Box Cave—a deep, yawning cavern set back into the ledges, home to a population of hibernating little brown bats, its entry now safeguarded by a large metal gate to protect the near-endangered species.

Around the corner, and the temperature back to normal, they shot each other sideways glances and smiles. They passed other hikers who'd stopped to take pictures of one of the park's most popular and spooky sites and continued north. Nic intentionally slowed his pace to oblige Finn's frequent stops to run his hands over the exposed and twisted roots of ancient trees that seemed to climb out of the ground and plunge back in like arboreal tentacles.

His element. There it is again. Now I see what Zeb meant. Cherishing the awareness, Nic took a mental snapshot to keep the image of his son at his most serene fresh in his memory.

The start of a long stone staircase winding up through a craggy crevasse appeared, its terminus out of sight where only sun-dappled leafy branches backdropped by the bright blue sky waited.

A stairway to heaven, Nic mused. *I wonder how many other people have thought the very same thing standing here.*

"You up for it?" Nic asked Finn. "We can backtrack and cut over where it's flatter if you want."

Nic laughed at his son's *"Are you kidding me?"* grin, and the two set off.

Even as an experienced runner, Nic was sufficiently winded by the time they reached the top and needed a break to catch his breath. He noticed Finn had a thin sheen of sweat on his forehead and was taking a few steps to the right, where a weathered wooden bench sat atop the cliff.

"Are you out of breath? Are you okay? Do you need some water?" Nic's questions came in rapid succession.

Finn chuckled. "No, Dad. I'm fine."

"Sorry. That's right, it wasn't *dehydration*." Nic rolled his eyes at himself in jest.

"Nope." Finn smiled back.

Recovered, they sat beneath the shade of the verdant canopy and looked out over the valley. Nic watched Finn in apparent meditation, his eyes half-closed with a soft, contemplative expression.

I wonder what he's thinking. He looks so peaceful, but thirty minutes ago, he was completely frozen.

Taking a cue from Finn, he lowered his eyes and sighed, savoring the experience. Gratitude for this time together and for the openness expanding between them sat lightly upon Nic's heart. He continued breathing into the light until a tiny, tinny noise began to rise inside his ears, bringing with it unsolicited and unwelcome memories of Klare's words, words he angrily dismissed at the time.

"*… command hallucinations…*"

"*… could be a sign of psychosis…*"

Eyes now squeezed shut in agony against the shrieking acoustic clamor, snippets from his psychiatric hospital rotation joined the fray and hatched a vignette that stole his breath and threated to explode his brain.

A parent brings her kid to the unit, says he's hearing the voice of a long-dead saint, followed her singing to a church, thinks she has a special message for him… oh my god, I'd absolutely be thinking psychosis, schizophrenia, maybe even drugs… my first thought definitely would have been mental illness.

"Dad, are you alright?" Finn's voice quietly emerged, breaking the spell of this dreadful, dreamy realization. "Dad?"

Nic shook the images and ideas from his head while attempting to relocate his body and remember where he was.

"Whew! Sorry!" he exhaled and wiggled his arms and hands. "I must have fallen asleep for a second. That was really weird." He grabbed his water, hoping it would help relieve his splitting headache.

After a quick swig, Nic's stomach dropped when he saw Finn continuing to stare at him, his brows knitted together and his bottom lip faintly trembling.

"What? What's wrong?" His nervous belly flipped and twisted. No way he was going to tell Finn what his half-asleep, half-awake *dream* was about.

"Do you think I'm sick?" his son's voice shook.

"What?! Finn, why would you say that?" It wasn't just his head that threatened to explode, but now his heart too.

Finn's only response was a sustained, expectant stare.

He returned the look with equal measure, studying the golden rings encircling Finn's hazel eyes and calling up from recent memory the image of Finn in his *element*—serene, self-assured, secure. He thought about Finn as a young child—inquisitive, sensitive, and… *intuitive*—a child who somehow knew the answer to questions that hadn't yet been asked, a child who seemed to just *know*. Zeb's words drifted in, landing like a soothing balm in both his head and his heart.

"He has a wisdom about him—a depth…"

"Son…" Nic's voice was quiet and slow, his heart rate restored, and the ringing suddenly gone. He took hold of his son's shoulders and leaned in. "You are a lot of things. Wonderful things. Special things. But one thing you are *not* is sick."

Finn slowly nodded and dropped his gaze, apparently working to digest the words and trying to decide if he believed him or not.

"Are *you* worried?" Nic asked.

After a few more contemplative nods, Finn straightened his posture and lifted his chin. "No. I never thought anything was wrong with me, but I was worried everyone else would. Like Mom. Like what that doctor said. Even you sometimes."

The shadowy stranglehold returned, grabbed Nic's heart with its massive fist, and squeezed. Flashes of Finn's return from the Dr. Myles appointment, of Klare's episode in Zeb's office, even his own daydream acknowledgment of how easy it would be for anyone, even himself, to jump to that conclusion. He shuddered internally at the disastrous implications of such quick and hasty assumptions.

"I'm so sorry, Finn. That must have been really hard, keeping everything inside because you were worried about what other people would think. I'm sorry I didn't ask you more… didn't ask you sooner." Nic wondered if his aching heart was actually bleeding.

"Zeb says that you can't figure things out by keeping it all inside. That you have to tell. You have to share your thoughts and feelings and dreams and…" Finn paused to take a deep breath. " … and your visions. It's the only way to understand. The only way to then know what you're supposed to do."

"Zeb sounds like a very wise man. I'm glad you felt comfortable enough to tell him, and I'm glad you're telling me today. I hope you'll keep telling me." The fist rewarded Nic by releasing its grip.

"I hope Mom will talk to Dr. Hirsch today. I think she has a lot of things inside that she needs to share too."

Nic's freed heart warmed and fluttered at his son's thoughtfulness. "Me too, Son."

Checking his watch, he realized Klare would be in her appointment right now. *If she went,* he thought with a touch of worry. "We should probably start heading back."

"Okay. Today was good, Dad."

"Yes, it was."

And with a tousle of Finn's soft auburn hair, they set off for the car.

On the drive home, Nic suggested they bring Finn's *"it was never dehydration"* account to their next appointment with Dr. Hirsch, along with the story of St. Dymphna. Since the doctor had lived locally for so long, perhaps she had more insights to share about this little-known saint and the church she is represented by. Finn agreed, eager to hear Dr. Hirsch's take and certain she would have an interesting perspective.

"And I think it will be easier for your mom to hear all of this with Dr—"

Finn finished his sentence. "Yeah, she's already stretched to her max."

Nic glanced at his wise son and shot him an agreeable smile before turning his eyes back to the road.

In the pockets of comfortable silence en route, Nic thought about his wife and hoped she was experiencing with Dr. Hirsch the kind of burgeoning understanding he had today.

Now I get it. Her knee-jerk reactions. Her attempts to protect our son. Even those phone calls to her mom.

Trying to anchor to the calm confidence sprouting in the core of his being, he took a long inhale and settled into the growing knowing that in time, all of this would make sense.

33

"Wow. Just wow. So beautiful!" Lucy slowly spun in a circle to take in the panoramic of Dr. Hirsch's foyer. Klare knew Lucy would appreciate the pleasingly spiritual décor.

"Hello, Klare. Nice to see you." Dr. Hirsch materialized through the wispy drapes into the lobby as if from some other dimension.

"And you must be Lucy." She extended her hand in greeting. "Isabeau Hirsch, pleasure meeting you."

"Likewise. Thank you for letting me come along today. I brought a book to keep myself company." Lucy gently tapped the bag hanging from her shoulder.

"Well then, I have just the place for you." Turning gracefully, she led them through the inner office and slid open the shoji screen on the far wall.

Amused, Klare watched her friend extend her neck to peek into the vibrant courtyard, then glance back, lips grinning and eyes sparkling. Lucy stepped over the threshold one careful step at a time, as though tiptoeing into a sacred temple. Looking back once more, she giggled, then vanished into the waiting wonderland.

"I knew she'd love it. Thank you again for letting her come today." Klare watched while the doctor slid the screen closed. *Because it might have been the only way I would've gotten here*, she added silently.

"Of course, of course. I'm glad you called, and I'm glad you brought some support with you." Dr. Hirsch smiled sweetly and motioned for her to take a seat.

I can't believe I'm here.

Klare's heart raced, and she felt a sliver of herself detach to observe from its lofty place above. Settling in, she willed the rest of her to stay present against this unnerving splitting experience with which she was becoming all too familiar.

I can do this. I have to do this.

"I'm glad you came in," the doctor began. "I'm curious to hear more about your dream."

You mean nightmare. "Um, yeah." Klare was having trouble finding words. Her mind felt both blank and chaotic at the same time, and she couldn't seem to pull her eyes from the floor.

Dr. Hirsch leaned in and, in a soft voice, offered, "Klare, why don't we take a minute and get ourselves settled before we dive in, okay?"

Klare felt a small release in her belly, her body responding less to the words and more to the warm resonance of the doctor's voice. Her eyes automatically drifted up to meet the woman's. Another tiny release. Klare nodded.

Dr. Hirsch stacked her spine, elongated her neck like a graceful swan, and gently uncrossed her ankles so that both feet rested flat on the floor. She folded her hands in her lap and drew in a slow, full breath.

Klare mirrored the doctor in both movement and posture, her eyes never breaking contact.

"Lovely. Just follow me for a moment. Excellent."

Her mind settling, Klare's ears picked up the whispery whir of the small fan on the bookshelf, and her nose noted the bright, cleansing scent of rain-washed linen wafting from the candle on a little table just to her left, objects she hadn't noticed when she first sat down. As the skin of her right elbow detected the plush of the velvety green blanket beneath her arm, Klare rolled her shoulders and felt the shadow of her hovering self reenter her body.

As if she could sense her return, Dr. Hirsch said, "Hello again," with a kind, benevolent smile, welcoming her back from a momentary vacation.

Klare exhaled. "Thank you."

The doctor offered a humble nod where no words were needed. Her eyes remained inviting and ready.

Okay, I can do this, Klare told herself.

"Well, it was more of a nightmare than a dream. Kind of awful, actually. And I know it rattled Nic and Finn. Me too, I suppose."

The doctor's patient face wordlessly suggested Klare continue.

She swallowed. *Ugh, why didn't I take some Tums before I came?* Taking a steadying breath, she repositioned her body and limbs to match the composed doctor's, hoping to calm her protesting stomach.

"Why don't we just start from the beginning and then take it from there, okay?"

"Don't do it," Klare's belly seemed to say. But then she thought about Lucy, here solely to support her, and the commitment she had made to Nic and Finn.

I can do this, Klare repeated to herself again and began.

"It was so strange. Like I was in the dream but also watching it. But in the dream, I was little. I was with my mom, outside somewhere, and we were being chased by birds—like in that scene from *The Birds*—flapping, pecking, screeching at us. I was terrified and trying to run but my mom kept hold of my arm, and she just walked through them, batting them aside as if they were nothing."

Klare paused, her nerves buzzing with the memory of the crazed and flailing fowl, talons outstretched, ready to rip into her tiny face.

"Then we got to this building, like a warehouse, but everything inside was lavender, like the color of my room when I was that age. There were all these hallways and corridors, like a maze, but we had to pass through these loud buzzer gates in between each one. It went on forever, and I couldn't tell if we were going up or down. I was crying, and so scared, but my mom just kept hold of me and marched right through like she knew the place."

Her chest tightened, and her stomach squeezed in the way it did even now when her mother's demeanor didn't match what was really going on. For a moment, she could feel the hot impress of her mother's fingers digging into her upper arm.

Another steadying breath. *Just keep going.*

"We finally got to this one room and my brother was there. Just sitting there, but laughing, as casual as could be. The birds were pecking at windows that were up near the ceiling, trying to get in. It felt dangerous, but he just sat there and laughed. My mom started ranting and yelling. Then these workers showed up, like in a lab—white coats, formal—and they started shouting and running around like something was happening."

Klare shook her head, shooing out the raving racket, and looked at Dr. Hirsch, who simply nodded in gentle invitation for her to continue.

"Then I was outside. I saw something in the distance and ran toward it to get away from the birds. I think it was a lady—a very tall lady. I couldn't see her clearly, but I followed her to this little glass cabin-type place in the woods and went inside to hide. But my mom was there. I ran out and there was a car, not our car but someone else's, and I tried to get in, but Scott was inside and had locked all the doors. My mom and the birds were right behind me, and I just kept pounding on the windows, screaming for Scott to let me in."

Heart racing in recollection of this final dream-scene, palms red and sweaty, Klare reached for the water bottle in her purse and took a few long sips.

"And that's when I woke up, er… when Nic woke me up."

Dr. Hirsch nodded, a pensive look on her face.

Yeah, it's overwhelming, isn't it? Klare thought, assuming the doctor was trying to digest it all. Taking a deep breath, she noticed with some surprise that her stomach felt better.

She wasn't exactly looking forward to the doctor's interpretation. *Isn't that what shrinks do? Too late to take it back now.*

"That sounds frightful." The doctor's voice and eyes conveyed her sympathy. "Do you remember how you felt when Nic woke you up?"

"Scared. Then relieved." Klare sighed and remembered, with no small measure of remorse, how quickly she'd rejected his asking if she wanted to talk about it. "It felt so real. It doesn't make any sense, but…" she shivered against the pleasantly cool temperature.

"Seems you were trying to get away—*run* away—the birds, your mom's grip, the shouting. What about Scott?"

"That part was weird. It didn't make sense, all the laughing. But strangely, that didn't bother me. It was my mom …" Klare's stomach released a fresh woozy wave. "The way she ignored those awful birds, how she walked through the halls like she owned the place. I was so scared, and she acted like nothing was happening."

"And in the room, with your brother?" Dr. Hirsch queried.

"That was the worst part. You know, she was like those birds! Flapping, screeching, totally out of control. That's not my mom. I mean, I've seen her lose her cool a couple of times, but she typically keeps herself well buttoned-up… *tight*." Klare's muscles tensed and constricted, her instinctual defense against Bridget's frosty edges.

"What about the lady?" The doctor leaned forward.

"I don't know. It was vague. But she was very tall, like I had to look up to see her, like she was above or over me in some way. But I just followed, like it was what I was supposed to do." Klare closed her eyes. A tiny flutter released in her belly as she thought about that single, brief moment in the middle of her frantic, feverish nightmare, where she felt something other than fear… something like… *hope?*

The therapist nodded, a small smile forming on her benevolent face. "Anything else stand out about—"

"Oh! I remember!" Klare interrupted. "In the room where Scott was, he was sitting on this round, high-back bench-type thing, kind of like what you might see in the middle of a big hotel lobby. It was really out of place."

"The room where the workers were—the ones in the coats?"

"Yes, white coats, like you see in a lab, or in a…" Klare stopped. A shudder that quickly became a tremor tore up from the depths of her core, slicing up through her chest and lodging in her throat, separating her from her words and leaving her staring blankly, mouth agape, at Dr. Hirsch.

"Klare? Just take a breath," the doctor gently urged. "It's okay. Whenever you're ready."

"Uh, I was about to say… or in a *hospital*. But I don't know why I would say that. It didn't seem like a hospital." Tiny beads of sweat broke out on her upper lip, and she swiped them away with the back of her hand.

"A hospital," Dr. Hirsch echoed softly.

Klare's eyes darted back and forth as her brain flipped through fragments of images left over from her all-too-real dream. Some small part of her didn't want to think anymore about this terrible dream-scene, but the rest of her was already searching for an elucidatory clue.

A pleading voice from deep within offered up a feeble *Noooooo. No.*

But the revelatory piece had already shown itself, somehow immune from objection, and Klare's brain stopped scanning.

"Oh no." Her desperate eyes met the doctor's.

"How old do you think you were in your dream?" the doctor cautiously inquired.

"I don't know. Maybe eight or so?" An apprehensive flutter danced across her middle.

"So, early eighties…" Dr. Hirsch nodded her head, her face suggesting she was making some calculations before she continued.

"Klare, I believe I know where you were. It is a real place, although it looks much different now."

Klare's heart picked up its pace.

"You don't want to hear this! Just get up and leave," the watchful voice urged.

But then she thought about Lucy out in the courtyard, having cleared her entire afternoon to support her. *I'm not leaving.*

She stared back at Dr. Hirsch nervously.

"I believe you were at the Massillon State Hospital over on the south side of town. It has a different name now. But I worked there, in the late seventies. The lilac walls were painted that color on purpose. They thought it would be soothing for the patients. All the doors back then, at least on the locked unit, were operated by buzzers to keep the patients contained and to control the flow of visitors. In the lobby, we had this giant circular bench, just like the one you described. And it really *did* look out of place."

Klare's hand rose to her chest, unconsciously pressing to contain her pounding heart. Her eyes blinked rapidly. It was her turn now to digest what Dr. Hirsch had just said, made difficult by her thoughts jumping and vaulting over each other, looking for a place to land.

Inside her body, an incongruous sense of relief swam alongside a dread so deep she could not bring herself to acknowledge its full existence. But she felt it.

I feel totally crazy right now.

"A psychiatric hospital? Are you sure? It must be some strange coincidence… Right? You even said that was a long time ago," her voice trembled.

"And the windows in that room were up high on purpose, for safety." The doctor tiptoed.

"So, you're saying that my brother might have been in the psych hospital, and that my mom took me there with her?" She could hardly believe the words coming out of her mouth.

Dr. Hirsch's face was a mix of compassion and something else.

Sympathy?

Klare continued to stare, her eyes imploring the doctor to say something, anything, that might make this make sense.

"And you said she seemed to know her way around, like she'd been there before, so I wonder…"

"She'd been there before. Maybe more than once." Klare finished the doctor's sentence.

The pair sat in contemplative silence for a moment, Dr. Hirsch holding the laden space secure while Klare processed this unbelievable tale.

"She never talked about Scott being in a hospital. But she never talked about anything, so it's possible I wouldn't have known." Klare scoffed as dawning clarity melted away some of the haze of confusion.

Dr. Hirsch leaned forward. "Sometimes our dreams sort of stitch together detached pieces of our experiences that we weren't able to make fit while awake. Especially if those pieces have been sitting dusty on some old, forgotten shelf inside the mind and therefore outside of our conscious awareness. You were very young, Klare. And although your mom, your parents, might not have *told* you much about your brother, you likely would have *sensed* it. Children are very perceptive, even if, especially if, words are not being used."

She bobbed her head, allowing the doctor's counsel to sink in. Both her bouncing brain and her hammering heart calmed into a slower, steadier pace.

"Klare, sometimes the mind will repress or push out of awareness some of the details of an event, or even the whole memory of it, when the event is particularly stressful or traumatic. It's like part of the mind steps in to protect the rest of the emotional system from the overwhelming intensity of the feelings that went with the event."

"Sort of like denial?"

"Sort of, but different. Denial is more of an external process, like refusing to believe or admit something for which evidence exists. Repression is *internal*—the blocking out of memories and emotions that are too overwhelming, but done unconsciously, without awareness. It's not excessively common, but it can happen, especially with regard to childhood experiences when the brain is not yet fully developed and simply can't process the event without significant emotional overwhelm."

Klare leaned forward, elbows to knees and hands clasped.

"Let's assume for a moment that part of your dream was actually a piece of memory. What about it do you think would have been so distressing that your child brain would have protectively pressed it out of awareness?"

Klare's stomach bottomed out. She held her belly tight with one arm and pressed her free hand tight against her mouth.

I know, but I don't want to know.

She took a breath, dropped her hand, and dove in. "I don't think it was about my brother being in the hospital, if that's where he was."

She looked back into Dr. Hirsch's ashen-blue eyes, an emerging awareness of what a separate part of her did not want to acknowledge washing over her.

"It was my mother. Her behavior. Her actions didn't match what was happening—ignoring the birds like they were nothing, not paying attention to how scared I was. And she was out of control, yelling and acting totally inappropriately. It was so confusing and super scary… like she was someone else entirely."

Someone else entirely…

Klare's body fell back, her head colliding hard against the back of the sofa. Her throat filled with a painful lump, and her tightly closed eyes began leaking, with hot tears cascading down the sides of her face, unbidden. She didn't even try to stifle the sob that choked forward, a painful moan escaping through her mouth to hang sorrowfully in the space between her and the doctor.

"Oh my god," Klare moaned. "Oh my god." She lifted her head and looked at the woman's attentive, caring expression. She needed an anchor, something that would keep her tethered to her body, to the room, so she wouldn't float away.

Her insides burned, ignited by the kindling of dawning comprehension that needed only a hairsbreadth of wind to set the fiery flames ablaze.

Me, in the emergency room, causing a scene.

Me, yelling at the school and yanking Finn out of there.

Me, acting like a maniac and stomping out a fire that wasn't even a fire.

"Oh my god. What have I done?"

34

Fluffy steel-blue-lined clouds decorated the periwinkle sky, so bright Finn had to shade his eyes on the short trek between the car and Okiciya's lobby. He waved back at his dad with his free arm and hustled for the entrance.

His bird and his stone pelted each other with balls of energetic excitement in an invisible game that sent bubbling ripples through Finn's body. He could not wait to tell Zeb about the magical hike with his father and the discovery of a mysterious puzzle piece—one he had no idea where it went but knew it belonged.

He's so right, Finn mused about his mentor's message about sharing and not going it alone. Since talking to his dad, he had been feeling more connected and more confident, even if the puzzle didn't make sense… yet.

And it seems to be working for Mom too. He grinned, picturing her face when they drove up the week before to find Dennis and Lucy at the house. He had told Zeb of his mom's reluctance to call Dr. Hirsch after her nightmare and his worry that she might not continue with their therapy sessions. Zeb had shared another story about guides and allies and asked about Klare's allies—anyone in her life who could be called upon to help—and with a simple phone call to his dad, the *Project Ally* plan had been hatched.

As he swung open the wide etched-glass door, Cassie's pretty laugh, mixed in with giggles of a voice he didn't recognize, landed musically in his ears. Following the melodious mirth to the kitchen, he found Cassie and an unfamiliar woman engaged in some sort of culinary contest, it seemed. Armed with long wooden spoons, both women hovered over a clear, barrel-shaped cistern, frantically stirring its liquid contents into a swirling eddy, splashing themselves with sweetness. Dozens of hollowed-out lemon halves littered the countertop next to a big bag of sugar that had been knocked over in the melee. It was a beautiful mess.

"Oh, Finn! Hi there!" Cassie greeted, slowing her stirring but not her laughter. "This is my friend Mary," she introduced through her chuckles. "We're just whipping up some lemonade for the troops today!"

"Mmmmm, I'll definitely be back!" Finn hollered behind him as he left through the back door, leaving the two to their refreshing antics while smiling at their camaraderie.

Cassie's roses were aflame with reds, fuchsias, pinks, and oranges that fluoresced on the verge of artificial, but their floral perfume wafted true, and Finn paused to drink in their scent. The galvanized drums on the opposite side of the path spilled over with plump bulbs of heirloom tomatoes—plum, ruby, and golden—causing instant salivation and begging to be picked. Bees darted about in their pollinating dance while a few dotted ladybugs took care of any errant aphids that may have been looking for a snack.

Everything has a purpose, Finn thought. *Working together for the good of all.*

Continuing down the path, he waved to his peers who were tending to different sections of the communal garden. As if choreographed, hands passed tools, joined to tackle a stubborn weed, and shared in the tilling. Koko, the ever-present sentry, stood watch, her glacier-blue orbs ablaze, while her tail swished in maternal pride of her flock.

Everyone working together, for the greater good.

Rounding the bend, Finn slowed to a stop and lifted his face to the radiant sun. He took in the temperate air, his chest expanding in depth and breadth. His bird trilled while his stone hummed in flinty vibration. He could feel each individual pebble of gravel beneath the soles of his shoes, connecting him to the earth below. Unmoving, he basked in the energy rippling and flowing in and all around him. Words from where he did not know emerged in his consciousness. *I'm part of this place as much as it's a part of me.*

Sated, Finn resumed his journey until he arrived at the medicine wheel. Zeb and Bran were on the far side of the circle with their backs turned, looking out across the grassy clearing bordered by a long thicket of trees. Craning his head to the right, he saw the focus of their attention. A beautiful doe with her little white-spotted fawn nibbled casually at the lush foliage. Sweet and gentle, Finn marveled, sensing himself in the presence of something vast. The familiar shimmery blue-green aura that dotted the edges of his vision seemed to whisper, *"You are."*

The tribe of two trotted back into the woodland, and Zeb and Bran turned.

"Heya, Finn! Come, join us!"

35

"Ugh, it's so humid in here!" Klare fanned her face with her hands and followed Lucy deeper into her treasured greenhouse. "How do you stand it?!"

"I find it refreshing, actually," Lucy answered. "They love it," she said, sweeping her arm in showcase. "It keeps everything so healthy and happy."

Klare had dropped by with an iced tea from Lucy's favorite teahouse, a simple gift to thank her for supporting her in getting to the appointment with Dr. Hirsch.

Seedling trays were lined up on the worktable. Rows of fresh shoots of mint, basil, and thyme poked out, ready to be transplanted into slightly larger containers and ushered toward their transition to their own personal pots.

Lucy flicked on a tall oscillating fan to circulate the air, obviously for Klare's comfort.

I'm so grateful for her. Guilt still lingered around her heart as she thought about the dozen calls she'd rejected over the past couple of months. *I feel like such a fool.*

On the drive home from the revealing session, Klare had told Lucy about the doctor's memory-tucked-inside-a-dream theory as well as her own horrifying realization of just how much she'd been acting like Bridget; not just acting, almost *channeling* her. With Lucy's gentle questions, she had shared about her peculiar splitting experiences—feeling like two people: her physical body and then another part that floats above and pulls the strings. Lucy had been her usual kind and compassionate self.

"I had another appointment yesterday." Klare could feel the familiar chastising pull that warned her to keep quiet. But she'd committed to the doctor, and to herself, that she'd try to do something different than what she had been doing. "*Opposite action*," the doctor had called it.

"Oh yeah. How'd it go?" Lucy balanced her attention between Klare and the new, roomier homes she was prepping for the waiting seedlings.

Klare recapped the doctor's discourse on *trauma responses*, finding herself better able to comprehend now than when she first had heard about the confounding notion of how the body can remember memories of which the person has no conscious recollection. That these memories can bring forward emotions, thoughts, and images that make no sense. The sensations are *real*; they just belong to old memories rather than the present. And if a person doesn't know any better, it's easy to believe it is because of something happening in the current moment.

"Ahhh, I get it. Like me and water. Used to be if I couldn't see the bottom, no thank you. Instant panic. Never made any logical sense because I learned how to swim when I was a kid. But my mom told me later that I almost drowned when I was an infant. Of course, I don't remember, but the rest of me certainly did."

Klare knew this about Lucy; she'd gone on to become an expert swimmer in part to treat her fears, but more so to make sure her own children were strong and capable in the water.

"See, that makes perfect sense to me. I just don't get it for me though. What is my body remembering that I have *no knowledge* of?" A tiny cramp from her stomach shot a little bolt of burn up to Klare's solar plexus. She flashed on the bottle of antacids in her purse back in the car but let the thought go. It was an unusually mild bolt.

"Something about losing your dad and your brother? Or maybe finding out that Scott might have been hospitalized?" Lucy asked curiously as she reached over to pull the seedling trays closer.

Klare fluffed her shirt and repositioned herself closer to the fan.

"I really don't think so. It just doesn't seem to fit, as weird as that sounds. They never really talked to me about Scott, but I knew he struggled. I think it has more to do with my mom. Her outrageous behavior—the part that was in my dream. I've seen it before, like with Finn when he was a kid, and a few other times. But I feel like it must be something else, something I've yet to remember or piece together."

"Okay, but why now?" One by one, Lucy lifted each delicate plantlet, gently separating the tangled tendrils of roots and lovingly nestling each into its new home, leaving plenty of space between for room to grow.

"I don't know," Klare said with a frustrated huff. "Dr. Hirsch thinks being in the ER that day with Finn triggered something related to fears about illness and loss. Actually, it was Finn of all people who suggested I was somehow thinking he was like Scott, and that it set off this instinct to protect him from people thinking bad things about him… about us."

"He is one intuitive kid, that one. So wise for his age," Lucy remarked.

Yes, he is. Klare smiled as she pictured her son's docile face.

"But I didn't think of him like that," she stressed, but then remembered the night of the fire-that-wasn't-a-fire. Images of her brother's face coming from nowhere, internet searches on fire-setting and behavioral problems, setting up that dreadful appointment with the equally dreadful Dr. Myles.

Her belly issued another squeeze, more sizzling than the one before.

"At least, I didn't think I was, but I guess I did at some point. Maybe that's what Dr. Hirsch meant when she talked about how we can sometimes take memories from the past and project them onto the present."

Klare's head swam in unison with her intestinal waves, the muddled ocean inside kicking up a storm.

"But with Scott," she continued, "these aren't *my* memories. I knew he had some issues, but this is a whole different level. She said kids are perceptive, even if things aren't being talked about. Maybe I knew but didn't know at the same time? Or I was feeling what my parents… my mom… was feeling, and I just didn't know it?"

Klare paused, brow stitched in strained concentration, until a gasp flew from her mouth, causing Lucy's head to snap up in attention.

"Maybe they aren't my memories but my *mom's* memories?"

Ahhh. There it was again, the little golden kernel. The tiny glowing seed that brought a slight release with it. The unfurling of something tightly wound that made space for the oxygen to better flow and the waves of nausea to settle. She didn't understand it but welcomed it.

"That sounds weird, doesn't it?" she asked her friend, intently and thankfully, aware of the cool air upon her face from the refreshing fan.

"Not really. I mean, values, styles of speech, habits… they get passed down through families all the time. Why not memories?"

"That's a scary thought." A trembling energy traveled through Klare's veins, but the lustrous pearl inside remained solid.

"Sorry, friend, but I think you might be on to something here."

"I don't know. Maybe I was too young. Maybe it wouldn't have been appropriate for my parents to talk to me about mental illness or whatever. But what about after? When I was older? My mom could have told me about him, what it was like, what happened."

Lucy had set aside her task to turn her full empathy to Klare. "Yes, I imagine that would have made things different." Lucy continued. "And you know, maybe secrets are passed down too. Not necessarily the secrets themselves, but what happens when secrets are kept hidden."

Ugh. My head hurts.

"Okay, so, I've got all these things inside me—fears, memories, even secrets, which might not even be all mine—and they're taking up all this space, and honestly, I can't even breathe half the time. How am I going to sort all of this out? How does anybody?"

"Taking up all the space… so much you can't even breathe…" Lucy raised a knowing, amused eyebrow.

Rootbound. Klare didn't have to say it. She could tell from Lucy's savvy expression that she knew that she was getting it.

"Well, we can't just lift you out of your current pot and plant you in another one, can we? So, how do people make space when all they have is the container they came in?"

You get rid of things, clear things out, let go of what you no longer need. Klare resisted rolling her eyes; it was an easy answer, but one she didn't like.

"Alright," Klare replied. "But how can I let go of things that I don't even know are in there?"

Lucy raised her eyebrow again.

"No. No, Lucy, I know what you're thinking."

Her friend stayed silent.

"No. I can't."

"Klare, you can protest all you want. But I think you know the answer to your own question."

The tides in her stomach continued their swish and sway, but the little beacon stayed afloat, a tiny but bright buoy, a light in the middle of a turbulent ocean.

36

Entering Dr. Hirsch's foyer seemed to Nic like he was stepping back into a realm at once foreign and familiar.

What is it about this place? He wondered while his eyes drank in pieces of sparkling and colorful décor. Some he remembered and some seemed new since the last time they'd been there.

The doors opened with a flourish and there stood Dr. Hirsch, aglow with fairylike radiance in her flowy dusty-rose and silver ensemble.

"Hello, hello!" she sang. "So nice to see you all. Please, come in."

The family stepped down into the sunken circle of the doctor's inner office and habitually took up their same seats. Soothing floral fragrances infused the air, reminding Nic of the luxury day spa Klare had talked him into going to a few years before.

"How are you?" the doctor asked to no one in particular once they had all settled into their respective spots.

"Quite well, actually." Nic smiled and exchanged agreeable glances with his family. "It's been an eventful couple of weeks."

Cautious hope had recently taken root inside Nic's body, edging out some of the more worrisome feelings as pieces of the mystery of his wife's recent behavior had begun to make themselves known.

We're not out of the woods yet, but at least we seem to be on the right path.

Klare's budding awareness of the similarities between her conduct and her mother's, although a painful and mortifying acknowledgment, had prompted profuse apologies and promises of increased cognizance.

The prospect of Scott being hospitalized, and the seeming confirmation that the old rumors might have held some truth, had brought a measure of relief, even in the face of the sadness of that truth. Following her second solo appointment with Dr. Hirsch, Klare had shared with Nic and Finn that it wasn't so much the truth that she found distressing; it was its concealment.

"I can understand not telling," Finn had said. The pale-blue melancholy that had tinged his empathic declaration had achingly reminded Nic of his son's dilemma with candidness and sparked a renewed compassion for Klare's struggles with honesty. It had also reminded him of his and Finn's united decision to wait until they were with the supportive Dr. Hirsch to reveal the interesting discoveries they'd made while on their hike.

"That's exciting," the doctor affirmed. "Tell me, what has been going well?"

Klare cleared her throat, signaling that she would start. "I don't know if I'd call it *going well*, but I had a curious conversation with Lucy that I thought we could talk about today."

The ever-present ringing in his ears thinned, and Nic took an extra-deep inhalation, relieved at Klare's initiative.

She recounted Lucy's notion that, just like values and beliefs, perhaps memories can be passed down in families, as well as secrets. "I don't really understand it, but it's like she was saying that I've somehow *inherited* from my mother some of *her* feelings about my brother. But it's confusing because my mom didn't talk much about anything, and we're just now starting to figure out how much she kept hidden."

I'm so glad she's talking about this, Nic thought with relief. He didn't fully understand it either but trusted that they would figure it out as long as they kept talking.

Looking at Finn, his heart warmed at his son's calm and peaceful air. Last weekend in the garden, he had seen the contented aura come over his son and asked about it. "It's a knowing," Finn had answered, and described a sensation of his inside feelings being in sync with the outside world around him.

"*He has a wisdom about him—a depth…*" He was so grateful to be experiencing what Zeb had talked about.

"Ah, yes. Your friend is quite right," the doctor validated. "Memories, experiences, secrets, even trauma can absolutely be passed down in families, even across multiple generations."

"Even when you don't know what the secrets or traumas were?" Klare's voice was uncertain.

"Yes, especially then." To explain her point, Dr. Hirsch shared the classic fable of *The Emperor's New Clothes* and the story of the town that had collectively agreed to uphold the illusion of the emperor's fine garments rather than expose the truth that their leader was, in fact, naked. "Why would everyone go to such lengths to hide the truth?" she asked rhetorically. "To escape the emperor's displeasure? To dodge the ridicule of being the one to call out the uncomfortable obvious? To avoid being shamed and run out of town for being the one who disrupted the peace of pretense? Sure. But, it was much safer to play along and uphold the façade in the service of keeping everything nice and stable."

I know where this is going. Nic looked at Finn, who seemed to be thinking the same thing.

Eyes focused on Klare, the doctor inquired, "So, what happens to people who put all their energy into denying the truth in favor of maintaining a safer and more favorable image?"

"Well, I guess they start to believe their own lies. The lies become the truth."

"Precisely. It wasn't so much about the secret itself—that wasn't the issue. It was about all the energy that went into maintaining the façade—the lies and deceptions, the desperate attempts to uphold a fragile house of cards." Dr. Hirsch paused as if to give Klare a moment to digest before she continued. "Because what would happen if an unsuspecting person came along and pulled back the curtain?"

Nic leaned back as Klare leaned forward, ensnared in the doctor's Socratic lead and ready with her answer. "*They'd* be called the liar, made out to be crazy…" Klare sighed, and her face drooped, " … *accused of making things up.*"

Nic ached for his wife as another hurtful awareness of Bridget's legacy dawned.

"Right, so it's not about the secret, it's about *the fear of telling the truth*. The sense that naming the obvious is dangerous, that terrible things happen when the truth is spoken. And *that*, Klare—*that* is what gets passed down." Dr. Hirsch concluded her summation definitively.

Nic draped his arm across his wife's shoulder as she collapsed against the back of the couch. While relieved with the progress being made, he remained aware that the process was a particularly painful one for her. He made eye contact with Dr.

Hirsch, grateful for her support, and then with Finn, appreciative of his patience.

Brow cinched in contemplation, Klare sought more information. "This is hard to get my head around. So, I've been carrying around this fear, that isn't so much mine, but sort of a mindset passed down to me, by my mother?"

"Who likely inherited it from her parents, and those before her. Keep in mind that we aren't just talking about the seventies and eighties, but *generations* that grew up in the fifties, in the twenties. Think about how mental illness was thought about back then, how most people were treated."

The doctor's voice was heavy with sadness and sympathy.

"Like monsters. Locked away, banished." Klare closed her eyes and shook her head solemnly. "It's so sad. No wonder people wouldn't want to talk about it. They probably were afraid to even admit there was an illness at all."

A somber silence filled the room in collective acknowledgment of the tragic reality of how mental illness has been viewed throughout history.

Breaking the humble reverie, Nic added, "Society has come a long way since then, but we still have a long way to go."

"Very true, Nic," Dr. Hirsch validated. "But what we are doing right here, right now, is part of changing that paradigm. Learning how to liberate yourself from the emotional binds of the past, and instead determine your own opinions and perspectives, not necessarily about *illness* per se, but about speaking the truth. Freely and without fear."

A warm, knowing smile spread across Klare's face, a sweet and tender visage Nic hadn't seen in so long, one that set aflame the deep love and respect he carried for his wife.

Eyes bright with a new and different dawning, Klare looked at Nic and then set her sight upon Finn. "If I can release the inherited mindset, then maybe…" she smiled even broader, "it won't get passed along to Finn."

"Precisely!" Dr. Hirsch exuberantly grasped her hands together. "Your liberation from the old narrative in essence breaks the hereditary chain of fear so that Finn, and his children, and their children don't have to carry it."

"This is mind-blowing. And I must admit, a little scary. I feel like this is just the tip of the iceberg. I have no idea what other secrets and hidden realities are lurking around in here." Klare tapped at her belly.

"Well, I believe it's safe to say that we are officially on a journey—for truth and, therefore, freedom. We've unearthed some clues, and there are certainly more discoveries to be made so long as we stay the course." Dr. Hirsch's eyes sparkled with the intrigue of a mystery waiting to be solved.

"Like a quest!"

All faces turned to Finn's enthusiastic exclamation. For the second time in this very office, Nic could swear his son's face was glowing—literally glowing—with radiant beams of shimmering gold tinted a brilliant blue green.

What is it about this place?! Nic marveled at Finn's optimistic reframing of what most might find an intimidating and arduous undertaking.

The doctor chuckled. "That is a lovely way to put it, Finn. So, we must keep our eyes and ears open for clues, heed the signs, and possibly even solve some riddles along our way to finding the treasure." She paused long enough to make eye contact with each person intentionally. "And I'd be remiss if I didn't remind us," Dr. Hirsch added, "that sometimes quests can be treacherous. Pitfalls, traps, dead ends. It will be very important to make sure that we stay together and work together to make our way through."

Clues… signs… riddles.

"Speaking of clues," Nic ventured in. "I think Finn and I came across some big ones while on our hike."

Noticing a tiny twitch at the corner of Klare's mouth, he inched closer so that the sides of their thighs touched.

Oh, I hope she can hear this.

He started with the church and opened with owning that, in the commotion of that day, he had forgotten all about it. Embarrassment lined his face as he admitted to assuming the church held no special significance other than it was where they had found Finn.

"But it wasn't really where Finn was found. It was where he went. Right, Son?"

With a silent *You're up,* Nic passed the proverbial talking baton to Finn and registered another tiny twitch discharge from Klare's body.

Finn, happy to take the cue, recapped what he had shared with his father on the hike: the singing that called him to the church and the sublimely fuzzy hush that came over him when he went inside.

"Is that when you passed out?" Klare asked with a slight tremor.

Finn looked at Nic, who responded with an easygoing nod. "Go ahead. Tell them."

He nodded, lifted his head in confidence, and spoke with clarity. "I didn't pass out. I wasn't dehydrated. I'm not sure exactly what it was, but it felt good… and I was sad when it ended."

"Honey," Klare extracted herself from the nook of Nic's arm and sat forward. "I don't understand. You were disoriented, and the doctors said it was acute dehydration… How come you didn't tell us any of this? Why didn't you…" her voice trailed off as the shadow of awareness came over her. "Oh no. Oh, honey." Klare's shoulders dropped, and her posture folded. "Because of me? At the emergency room?" Shame pulled tightly at the corners of her mouth and creased her forehead.

"Not just that," Finn assured her before sharing that although the unusual experience was wonderful, it was also confusing, and he wasn't sure how to bring it up without sounding *crazy*. "It felt… important somehow. I didn't want the feelings to go away."

Nic watched as Klare looked into Finn's eyes, over to Dr. Hirsch, then back to Finn. Not finding any evidence of alarm anywhere in the room, she leaned forward and sighed. Nic could tell she was grappling with her son's story.

"I'm sorry I scared you," Finn offered softly, "by walking away and not telling you what really happened."

Nervous about the return of the piercing peal, Nic took a deep breath and glanced at the Dali-inspired clock melting down from one of the shelves across the room.

"There are a couple of other things that came up during our hike, one in particular that I'd like to get to if we have the time."

Without looking at a timepiece, Dr. Hirsch responded in an easy tone, "We have all the time we need."

Nic's belly clenched, momentarily gripped with anticipation about the tale he was about to tell, and Finn's connection to it.

"I read up on the church and came across the story of the saint held in honor there. It was fascinating and gave us a few additional surprises, right, Finn?"

Finn's face held a light, knowing smile as he nodded back at his dad.

Nic offered an abbreviated account of what he had discovered about St. Dymphna and the fateful story behind her canonization as the patron saint of nervous disorders and mental illness.

"But the most astonishing part about this was how she died."
Nic tipped his head toward Finn and asked, "Would you like to
take it from here?"

Barely bridled eagerness rippled over Finn's face as he pursed
his lips together and took a deep breath. His dazzling golden
eyes darted between Dr. Hirsch and Klare.

"Mom, remember at Okiciya when I told you and dad about
the dreams I was having? About the girl? And how she had died
before I understood what she was saying to me?"

On Klare's face, Nic saw flashes of fear competing with her
valiant attempt to stay present and open to Finn's disclosures. He
took her hand in his and gave it a reassuring squeeze. *Hang in
there.*

In contrast, Dr. Hirsch was alight with interest, nearly
matching the sparkle in Finn's eyes.

He continued, his voice brimming with excitement. "Well,
she died the same way as the girl in my dream. Mom, she's the
one I dreamed about. It was her singing that called me to the
church that day. It was her all along."

Klare stuttered, "I don't… I don't understand." She looked
around the room imploringly, clearly desperate for help.

"If I may?" Dr. Hirsch asked softly.

Nic intertwined his fingers with Klare's while she nodded her
consent.

"I have another piece of information about our saint here that
may hold some significance to this story."

Feeling his wife's tension, Nic leaned in closer and offered
her a reassuring smile.

Hang in there, babe. Hang in there.

The doctor took a moment to gather her thoughts while
Nic's heart flipped under his breastbone. He suppressed a snort
as an absurd image flashed in his mind: his heart, having become

detached, was ricocheting around the inside of his chest cavity like a pinball. It was as if his heart cheered the prospect that all these details and bits of information were connected in some mysterious way, but he could literally feel his brain trying to shut down that excitement. It was a strange battle between childlike wonder and adult decorum.

"You're being ridiculous. We aren't on some wild treasure hunt. This is serious," a deep, distant voice scorned.

But as strong as that disparaging pull was, it only took Nic one look at Finn's face, and he was back in the game, intrigued by the possibility that all these seemingly random coincidences could be part of some intricate tapestry woven together by a force just waiting to be discovered.

When Dr. Hirsch began, Nic assumed it was simply more interesting, semi-fascinating information about this saint's place in the local history. He glanced at Klare, noticing her face remained locked in wary confusion while Finn, on the other hand, seemed to be drinking in the details, quenching a part of himself that had been thirsty for a very long time.

I wish I could be hearing all this through his ears, Nic thought longingly, and when he glanced over at Klare, he thought, *Her too.*

Dr. Hirsch shared how in the 1930s, a shrine to St. Dymphna had been commissioned for the local psychiatric hospital's chapel to serve as a source of comfort for the patients. In the 1950s, the shrine was moved to an elegant rosewood and glass enclosure that had been built in a grove of fir trees on the hospital grounds. The doctor recounted how the superintendent at that time had taken great pride in keeping the hospital estate so lovely and well-maintained that people from all over would come to see the grounds, picnic onsite with their families, and visit the breathtaking arboreal shrine of St. Dymphna.

"And there it stayed, nestled in the woods, for over fifty years, until it was relocated, just a few years ago, over to the very church you are talking about. It was a beautiful sanctuary."

Fascinating. Nic felt the weighty press of connection as he remembered scooping Finn from the floor underneath the saint's statue at St. Mary's.

Three sets of eyes glimmered and glowed with the spark of intrigue and the thrill of an unspoken invitation to throw caution to the wind and dive in feetfirst.

However, the fourth set was dubious and suspicious. Microspasms flicked randomly across Klare's face. Her typically honeyed amber eyes had turned dull and muddy. Absorbed in the wonder shared by him, Finn, and Dr. Hirsch, Nic hadn't noticed that she had pulled away and was sitting as far as she could from him on the lavender loveseat they shared.

Finn was the first to notice. "Mom?" he asked. "What's wrong?"

She didn't respond.

"Babe?" Nic scooched over to close the gap she had put between them. "What is it?" His free-floating heart had stopped its lively rejoicing when he saw his wife staring at an invisible spot on the plush carpet between her feet, her jaw clenched. His desire to be patient vied against a simmering fear that she was slipping away, back to that walled-off, sequestered place inside.

As if the thump within Nic's chest reached over and prodded her, Klare suddenly broke her fixation with the floor and returned to the present moment. "I'm sorry," she offered self-consciously. "I just lost focus for a second. Sorry."

Dr. Hirsch leaned forward, her cornflower blue-gray eyes intently tracking Klare's face, body, and breath rate. "Something important?"

"I don't know."

Nic was confused, but he trusted things would make sense eventually. His wife's face was more perplexed than his, while his son teetered expectantly on the edge of his chair.

"The shrine. It was at the hospital where my brother would have been?" Klare's forehead creased in concentration.

"Yes."

"In a wooden and glass structure, surrounded by trees…"

"Mmmhmm," the doctor affirmed knowingly.

Flutters danced in Nic's stomach in odd symmetry with the noise in his ears. Dr. Hirsch's face remained benevolent, while Finn's knowing countenance brimmed with wisdom.

Oh my god, does he know where this is going? I'm totally lost.

"Mom. Were you there?" Finn sat riveted with his eyes alight in dazzling ambers and golds.

"I don't know." With a subtle, invitational nod from Dr. Hirsch, Klare relayed the rest of her dream, admitting she'd not thought it relevant when she had originally told them of her memory-tucked-inside-a-dream about being at the hospital: the birds, running from her mother, and finding refuge in a *glass cabin in the woods.*

"Wow. Mom, I can't believe you were there. When you were just a kid!" Finn seemed thrilled with this magical bit of synchronicity, if indeed it were true.

Suspended somewhere between awe and disbelief, Nic wasn't sure what to make of this newest clue. *I mean, seriously, what are the chances?*

"And…" the doctor nudged Klare, almost playfully.

"I don't want to say. It sounds totally ridiculous." Klare's words said one thing, but the glint in her eye and quiver in her voice suggested otherwise.

"Mom, remember. The *truth.*" Finn was glowing again.

Klare held her son's intensity for several beats, took a deep breath, reached for Nic's hand, and spoke her truth. "I didn't just go to that cabin. I thought I saw a lady—a tall lady—and I followed her there."

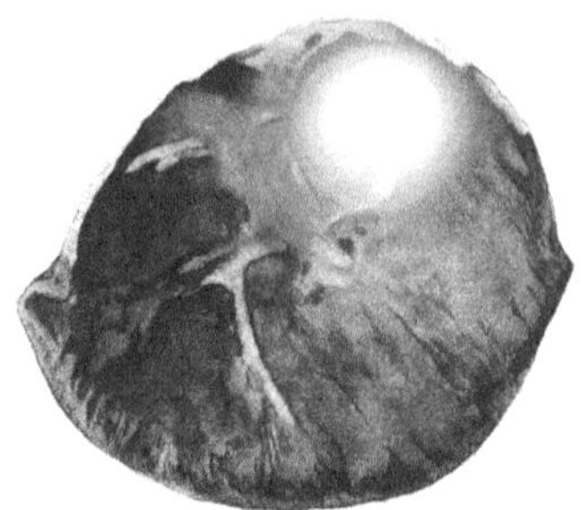

FINN FOLLOWS THE aroma of cinnamon and melted butter and finds his father putting a fresh stack of French toast in the warmer. The table is already set with jars of maple syrup, marmalade, and a bowl of powdered sugar.

"Good morning! Hungry?" Nic greets his son and hands him two glasses of freshly squeezed orange juice. In a cheery mood, he is enjoying sharing his culinary specialty with his loved ones.

"Mmmhmm," Finn hums eagerly and takes a seat while his dad serves up thick slabs of the perfectly browned bread. He is a butter and sugar person, while Nic prefers preserves and Klare, the syrup.

This is the first morning Finn is wearing his stone on the outside of his shirt. It was a carefully deliberated decision, and when his father notices, they exchange a warm smile.

"Where's Mom?" he asks before taking his first bite of savory deliciousness.

"Still sleeping. I didn't want to wake her," he answers as he sits down across from his son.

Klare has been slumbering longer and harder than usual over the past couple of weeks, ever since their *quest for the truth* started heating up in their work with the esteemed Dr. Isabeau Hirsch. Recovering memories and discovering a hidden past while trying to figure out how it all fits together in this unfolding story is exhausting work.

"How are things going over at the center?" Nic's voice is sunny. He, too, has been sleeping well, not due to the fatigue of arduous internal excavation but because he's relieved his wife is getting better. They all are.

Finn finishes his mouthful before eagerly sharing about helping to complete the medicine wheel in time for the autumn equinox ceremony due to take place near the end of September.

"Would you and Mom want to go? All the families are invited."

"We wouldn't miss it for the world. Of course, we'll be there," he says, and refills his son's OJ.

"Mmm. Good morning, you two," Klare mumbles as she enters the kitchen, groggy and still waking up. "It smells incredible. Is there coffee?" She is normally a tea person, but lately, she has required something stronger.

Nic stands and guides his wife into an empty chair before retrieving her favorite mug and the French press. Finn fills her juice glass and slides the syrup in front of her.

"Thank you, honey. But coffee first." Her eyes are still half closed.

Nic returns with the steaming brew, and she inhales the intense aroma before taking her first sip.

"Oh, this is amazing. Thank you."

As she slowly gains wakefulness and attunes to her breakfast, her two men continue chatting about Nic's plans to resume his regular running routine with Dennis and Finn's new ideas about what to plant in the garden.

"Speaking of the garden," Nic says to Finn, "you won't believe what I found out there this morning."

The young man looks at his father with a sly smile that says, *Try me.*

Nic puts his fork down and walks over to the windowsill to collect his curious find.

When he offers it to Finn, his son blooms all shades of rose, vermilion, and honey. Rather than accept the proffered treasure, he reflexively wraps his hand around his stone and shivers in the warm late-summer morning air.

He stares as Nic twirls a black-tan-and-white-striped red-tailed hawk feather, its thick quill pinched delicately between his fingers.

"It wasn't there when I went out early this morning. Then I came back inside to grab my coffee, and when I went back out, I found it just sitting there. Right in the center of the garden plot, like it had just been dropped." Nic's wonderment makes him glow.

"Dad. You didn't find it. *It found you.*" Finn is nearly breathless. He begins to impart bits of stories shared by the eminent Lakota leader at the Okiciya Community Center, Zebulon Paytah, recounting how feathers are a sacred gift—a nudge from the universe to stop, pay attention, and listen for the message.

"Okay..." Nic smiles, humoring his son. "What am I supposed to be listening for?"

"I don't know. But it came to *you.* Whatever it means, it's a sign." Finn's eyes radiate golden in the magic of pure certainty.

Nic laughs. "A *gift*. A *sign*. Ooh, maybe it's part of our *quest*."

"Well, Dr. Hirsch said we have to keep our eyes and ears open." Finn is clearly enjoying himself.

Suddenly, Klare mechanically rises and makes for the pantry. Opening the door, she steps in and eases the door closed behind her.

Nic and Finn stop laughing and exchange a concerned look.

"Uh, Klare?" Nic calls out and walks toward the pantry.

She opens the door, eyes bright and smiling.

"I have an idea."

But before she shares her idea, she talks about how her dreams of late have been less like regular dreams and more like her mind filling in the gaps with unknown memories and forgotten details. She explains how sometimes it's difficult to separate out what is just a dream from what might be a memory of something that really happened.

"But the dream I had last night..." Her eyebrows squish together, and she rubs the back of her neck. "I'm pretty sure it was a memory kind of dream."

Nic and Finn sit quietly, their respective gazes fix on her face in either nervousness or curiosity, or perhaps a bit of both.

"Remember at Dr. Hirsch's, when I talked about seeing a tall lady and following her?"

Her husband and son nod but don't make a sound.

"She was in my dream last night, but this time it was different... clearer. She wasn't tall; she was *in the air*. Floating, in all these golden robes, like a ghost. But I wasn't scared."

"Like an angel," Finn offers an alternative idea.

"You *were* there," her husband whispers.

"You *followed* her," her son adds.

Klare takes a big breath in and lets it out with a soft "*hummmm*" before finally sharing her idea.

"I think we should go pay her a visit."

THE CLASPING AND linking together of seemingly unrelated affairs vibrate with a certain resonance very few can hear, and Klare's idea turns up the volume of this already-beating rhythmic pulse.

37

Klare bit her lip and fidgeted with the strap of her purse as they pulled into the parking lot across the street from St. Mary's Parish. She thought the towering gothic building with its dark, weather-stained façade and two soaring spired towers looked like something out of mediaeval Europe. Intuitively, she knew they had to make this visit, but she was tentative about her expectations.

I hope this helps. Her chest ached in anticipatory disappointment at the prospect of leaving today without the clarity she hoped for.

"Don't get your hopes up," a familiar voice inside reproached. *"You know this is just a fool's errand."*

Stop it. She'd been practicing talking back to *that* voice that was both hers and not hers at the same time.

They entered the looming church through the middle of three arched doorways and walked into the vestibule where an elegant statue of Joseph, Mary, and baby Jesus stood in reception.

The morning weekday Mass had ended a couple of hours earlier, so the church was empty, for which Klare was grateful. She wasn't sure how she would feel returning to a site where her only memory was of the distress of finding her boy crumpled on the floor after a terrifying and frantic search.

So far, so good. They entered the nave, flanked by rows of glossy wooden pews. Immediately, her senses were overwhelmed. The faint smell of lemon wood polish and musky incense hung in the air, and she found herself captivated by the stunning stained-glass windows that lined the walls and led to the semicircular, domed recess at the northern end—the focal point of the church's altar and sanctuary. The apse was painted a rich, vibrant blue and stenciled with gold filigree.

"It's very beautiful," Klare whispered and saw, by the looks on her husband's and son's faces, that they fully agreed.

It's okay, she reassured herself. *Not bad at all. Just a little hot in here.* She hoped their reason for coming—*clarity*—would eclipse any residual adverse association with the place.

He seems so happy to be here, she mused with gratitude, even though she hadn't been particularly worried about Finn's reaction to the idea of returning. He had been enthusiastic from the moment she suggested it.

Klare glanced at her husband, who, in that moment, looked so much like Finn; his wondrous eyes conveyed a boyish joy that made her heart swell in youthful love.

But ugh, the air. Why don't they have the air conditioning on? She pulled her hair up to cool the back of her neck as they ambled up the aisle, taking in the ornate adornments—crosses and candles, lanterns and stations. Not having grown up in the church, she didn't know the names of the saints who stood in peaceful repose as marble custodians of the space. *But I do feel calmed by their presence. And I do know her name.* Looking to her left, she saw her.

St. Dymphna, in her gold and copper robes, hovered at least six feet above the ground. Tawny brown curls fell to her shoulders, and a decorative golden crown rested atop her head. Her peaceful face seemed to look out over the pews, her left hand extended in open invitation, while her right held a sword, pointed downward. A kaleidoscope of brilliance rained down from the thousands of colorful mosaic pieces that comprised the thirty-foot-tall stained-glass windows behind her.

Another flash of heat bloomed, causing Klare to feel light-headed.

How did I miss her?

But she knew how. Finding Finn, first missing, then collapsed in a motionless heap on this very floor, had filled her entire being with a horror that left no room to notice anything else.

Finn was the first to approach the statue. Lifting his arm, he reached out his hand as if to touch the base on which she stood. Suddenly, he stopped, his outstretched arm frozen in place.

Klare's heart quickened as she wondered what was going through her son's mind. She coached herself to not react. *Give him his space. He's fine.*

Keeping her feet planted firmly, she wiped the droplets from her forehead. *Why is it so hot in here?! I should have brought my water with me.* Another wave of light-headedness washed over her as Nic took a couple of steps forward and quietly stood next to Finn.

They both watched, he from right beside him and she from a few feet back, as their son pulled his arm back and placed his hand over his heart. He lifted his head, and she could tell his eyes were closed. Elation emanated from his face.

Rapture?

At this thought, her stomach clenched, and *the* voice rang out, shrill and scolding inside her head, *"Are you just going to stand there while your thirteen-year-old son acts like he's in the throes of some spiritual fervor? This is absolutely embarrassing! I mean, thank god no one's here to see this display."*

STOP IT! Her *own* voice, her *real* voice, snapped back. *Ugh. This is really irritating. When is this voice going to stop?* she wondered for the thousandth time.

She moved forward and stood just behind them, noticing Finn's position hadn't changed. *He looks like someone fully engrossed in some symphonic crescendo.* He looked serene, and she tried to quiet the internal protests by reminding herself of both Lucy's and Dr. Hirsch's feedback about passed-down attitudes.

Glancing toward her husband, she noticed his eyes were also closed, and tears were sliding quietly down his cheeks. Yet, his face didn't look sad. It looked…

Peaceful? What is going on here?!

Although Nic and Finn both *appeared* okay, happy even, Klare felt a shiver radiate up through her feet and legs, move through her torso and arms, and finally reach her head, where it seemed to expand and fill the whole of her being with a droning buzz. The hum even reached into her ears, leaving her hearing slightly muffled.

I need some water. She didn't want to walk away from her family, nor interrupt their experience, so she focused on taking some deep breaths—the kind she had practiced with Dr. Hirsch—to steady herself.

Responding to her stabilizing breaths, the vibration eased a little, enabling her to focus on the statue of the saint they had come to see and the hundreds of multicolored electric votive candles nestled at her feet.

I wonder why I was there. She had asked herself this question many times since the theory of her possible childhood visit to the shrine had emerged. *Possible,* she thought, and remembered she'd yet to call her mother, as had been proposed during her recent conversation with Lucy.

Klare looked up at the saint, afloat upon her riser, elevated in the air.

From a child's height, she would have appeared even taller, like she was in the sky.

With this image of herself as a child materializing in her mind's eye, she drifted back in time on the wings of the memory-dream she'd had a few nights before. A warm, sleepy fog seemed to envelop her, dampening the outside sounds.

From within this bubble of memory-dream, Klare watched her eight-year-old self sit on the floor of a beautiful little outbuilding made of dark wood and tall glass windows through which she could see lush evergreen trees. Little Klare stared up at the tall lady draped in robes the color of a golden sunset with candles all around her feet. She was completely alone. Yet, she didn't *feel* alone. The lady, standing in a shaft of bright light, seemed to watch over her—*like an angel*.

Noticing that just a few candles were lit, Little Klare scanned the space until she saw an empty votive jar with long matches sticking out the top, the kind her parents kept way up on the fireplace mantel. She knew she wasn't supposed to touch the matches at home, but this wasn't home. Compelled to act, she carefully selected a single long match and looked around for the box to scrape it against, just like her father did. But there was no box here. Improvising, she moved to touch the end of her matchstick to the flame of an already-burning candle, when suddenly a hand came out of nowhere, clenched her wrist, and slapped it so hard the unlit matchstick went flying from her tiny fingers.

"What are you doing!?" a shrill voice shrieked. Startled by her sudden appearance, it took Little Klare a moment to realize it was her mother. "What is wrong with you!?" Mother wouldn't stop screaming.

Little Klare's wrist throbbed and stung as her mother dragged her away from the angel and shoved her out the door so hard she fell to her knees. Before she could get up from the ground, Bridget yanked her up, this time by the arm, and pulled her toward the parking lot. She yelled that her arm was hurting, but Mother paid no attention.

When they arrived at the car, Little Klare was forcefully shoved inside and landed in the backseat next to her brother, who laughed and rolled his eyes at her. Once in the driver's seat, Mother slammed the door and turned back toward her children, her face crimson with rage. "Not a word to your father. Or anybody else. About any of this. Either one of you." The clipped and precise delivery of her command froze Klare in place.

"Klare!" An urgent whisper connected with her eardrums and her eyes snapped open. She hadn't realized she'd closed them.

"Mom?" Finn asked in a voice just as quiet but far less urgent than her husband's. "Mom, is everything okay?" He had slipped his hand into hers and squeezed it tightly.

"Babe?" Nic's voice was calmer now, and his hand rested firmly on her shoulder.

"Oh my gosh. I didn't even realize I'd closed my eyes." She let out a nervous laugh. "I was about to go get some water. I just got really tired suddenly." When her words echoed shallow and silly, even to her own ears, embarrassment blossomed pink on her cheeks. "Uh… can we sit down?" Her body still vibrated with the rest of the memory just now revealed inside her waking dream.

Klare and Finn, still holding hands, took a seat on a nearby pew while Nic went to get a water bottle from the car. While her face still held the residual blush of awkwardness, her son's had that same serene, self-possessed expression she had seen once in

Dr. Hirsch's office and another time when he had come to her bedroom to talk.

"*The knowing*," she remembered him calling it.

Klare slid over to open a space for Nic when he returned with the water, sandwiching herself between the two men she cared most about. She took a long drink of the still-cold water. "Thank you."

"Are you okay?" Nic asked.

"Yes, I'm fine… I, uh, I'm not sure what to say." Pink rebloomed in her cheeks. "I feel super embarrassed right now."

"Mom, no. Why are you embarrassed?"

"Uh, I don't know. I just… how long were my eyes closed?" Her heart released a few extra-strong thumps, anxious about the answer.

"I don't know, not very long. Both you and Dad had your eyes closed." Finn's voice was lighthearted, amused even. "Dad opened his first, then you a little bit after, when Dad said your name a few times."

Oh boy. I can't imagine someone walking in and finding a whole family standing here with their eyes closed, locked in a dream. Klare's face blazed. *What do they call that—a folie* à *famille?*

"I noticed both of you had your eyes shut." She turned to her husband and said tenderly, "You had tears on your face."

"Yeah, I did. I was remembering my brother's funeral, which I have been thinking about recently. You know, it was probably the saddest day of my life. Before the funeral started, I felt so alone. But once I was inside and surrounded by all these people who loved him and loved me, I felt better. There was a lot of singing, and it was like all those voices just wrapped around me and I didn't feel alone anymore. My only brother was gone, my best friend, but somehow, I didn't feel alone." Sentimental tears misted Nic's eyes.

Klare reached over and squeezed his hand. "That's beautiful."

He smiled and sighed. "Yeah. It was." Nic looked at Finn. "How are you feeling?"

Finn smiled and simply nodded. After a few contemplative moments, he shared all he apparently needed to: "When I came here that day, I was by myself, but I didn't feel like I was alone either. I felt that again today."

I guess it's my turn. The throb of an oncoming stomachache thumped in Klare's belly as the twisting and roiling returned. This time though, she knew why. *My body is remembering the memory*, she recalled Dr. Hirsch's words. *No Tums for that.*

Looking at their expectant faces, she took a breath and began recounting the first part of her memory: being inside the structure that held the statue and not feeling alone, even though she was by herself—like she was being watched over, possibly by the towering woman in the golden robes.

That was the nice part. Klare tried to keep hold of that safe feeling while she prepared to tell her family the rest of what she remembered from that day.

She took another sip from her water bottle and noticed her hands were still trembling. *"Maybe you should just stop there,"* a faint voice cautioned.

Klare considered it, but only for a moment. *No more secrets.*

As if hearing her thoughts, Finn asked, "What else?"

"Ugh. Yeah, there's more," she sighed heavily. "Well, I think I just remembered some more of that dream—memory—when I was at the hospital with Scott and my mom. It's not very nice."

She felt her husband's supportive touch upon her leg and studied her son's kind and compassionate face. *I'm so lucky.* Love bloomed warm in her middle, chasing away some of the turmoil that had just been there.

Feeling more settled, she detailed the rest of it, from her wish to light a candle all the way through to Bridget's aggressive interruption, her screams and slap, and finally, Bridget forcefully removing her from the shrine and dragging her to the car. She ended her summary with the part about her mother's hostile demand for keeping it all a secret.

"I'm sorry, Mom," Finn soothed, squeezing her hand again. "You didn't do anything wrong. I'm sad that happened to you."

"Thank you, honey. And you know what? You didn't do anything wrong either. I am so sorry for the times I misjudged you and reacted poorly. I am so sorry."

His reassuring smile melted a little more of the turmoil inside, leaving a cozy pool of gratitude in its place.

"I'm sorry too, Klare," Nic added, "but I'm also really angry. That was a terrible and inappropriate way to treat you. You didn't deserve that. No one does."

Klare nodded, digesting her husband's supportive words.

"And Finn didn't either," he continued. "How she treated you was exactly how she treated Finn that day at her house with the lighter."

Her husband's voice was tight, and Klare could hear his effort to stay calm. She let out a long exhalation as the clash and rumble of conflicting emotions continued their chaotic dance inside—the sweetness of love and gratitude contending with the bitterness of anger and shame.

Bittersweet. She supposed that was an accurate way to describe what she was going through.

"It's true—that was the exact same response. And all the secrets. There were so many. I know in her own misguided way, she thought it was helping. Protecting us, keeping us safe, but really, from what? All the secrets did was hurt and harm and ruin. There's no way we were better off keeping everything secret.

It destroyed us. It didn't protect anything." Sadness seeped and oozed, draining out in painful but healing purification.

After several quiet seconds of respecting the intimacy of the moment, the family clearly having achieved something very important on this visit, Nic suggested they go grab lunch.

As they rose, Finn stopped them. "Mom, you never got to light your candle, did you? Do you want to do that now?"

Another burst of love blossomed in her chest. "How did we get so lucky to have a son like you?" She tucked a lock of his sandy auburn hair behind his ear. "That's a lovely idea. Thanks, honey."

The votives were now electric, surely a modernized safety measure. With no matches needed, Klare paused and then picked an aqua-blue jar and pressed the button to ignite the faux, symbolic flame. She smiled as it clicked alive and took a beat to honor this full-circle moment.

"Mmmmm…" her contented sigh brought them all back to the present. When they opened their eyes and turned to leave, all three halted in their tracks, steps frozen in midstride, breath suspended when they saw it. A shaft of glittering, brilliant light enveloped them, casting everything around them in shadow. Instinctually, they all looked up, expecting to see a giant spotlight that had somehow been clicked on to capture them in its bright beam.

But there was no such light bulb or theater lamp above. The ray of light was coming in through a smaller, round stained-glass window at the peak of the window montage that backdropped St. Dymphna. Just as their scanning eyes located the origin of this resplendent illumination, it flickered and then winked out, returning the church to its natural light.

What was—?

"Mom…" Finn interrupted her thought as he found her hand and Nic's arm, communicating the answer to the question written on both of their faces through his knowing glance.

Could it be?

She searched Nic's face, whose eyes were wide with wonder.

No, that would be crazy.

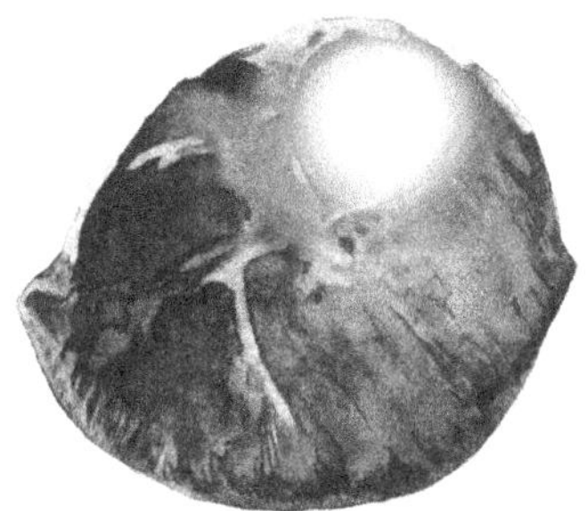

It's astonishing how much stamina is lost after taking a break from regular training, even for an established runner such as Nic. Astonishing, and also quite irritating.

"Dude," Nic is panting and calls feebly out to Dennis, who is an easy several strides ahead. "I need to stop... for a second."

"Alright, alright," his best friend ribs him. "We gotta get you back in running shape."

"Well, I've been doing a different kind of running lately, if you know what I mean." Nic bends over, plants his hands on his knees, and breathes in through his nose and out through his mouth. Fat drops of sweat drip off his face and spatter on the concrete below.

Not winded in the slightest, Dennis walks back to join his puffing friend. These two have been diligent exercise partners for years, and this is the first time they've gone this long without their near-daily running sessions.

"Excuses, excuses," his friend teases, then adds, "Seriously though, how are things going at home?"

Nic huffs out a thin laugh. He's glad to be back in his routine, and even happier being back to spending regular time with Dennis. Standing up straight, having slowed his breath sufficiently enough to do so, he pauses to remember where he'd left off with his friend.

"She's had a rough go," he says. "Lots of details have come out about her childhood. I never knew how bad it was, and honestly, she didn't either. By the way, I'm glad you told me about those old rumors. Having that information helped me help her."

"Yeah, man, no worries. Sorry you had to learn it that way." Dennis motions him over to sit on the edge of a retaining wall that borders the street.

"Thanks," replies Nic as he takes a seat, appreciating the longer rest. "So much has come out. Not just all the stuff about Klare and her mother, but all sorts of things Finn's been going through." He pauses and looks hesitant to say any more, but then continues. "And, I've had some interesting experiences myself lately." He shoots a side-look at Dennis, as if worried about what he is thinking.

"Oh yeah? Like what?" Dennis' voice rings with clean curiosity.

"Uh, I don't know... sort of like déjà vu but a little different. Like things happening that shouldn't be connected but seem like they might be. Coincidences that maybe aren't coincidences? That sort of thing." Nic pauses and glances self-consciously at his friend.

"Like synchronicity?" Dennis' voice is confident, and he shifts his body to face Nic.

Nic is clearly eased by this response as his shoulders drop a few inches. "Yeah, I guess that's a good word for it..." he starts and then dives into sharing about the numerous points of connection with a certain saint—from Finn's dreams to Klare's childhood encounter to the ethereal illumination he and his family shared at the church just days before.

When Dennis doesn't immediately respond, Nic nervously offers, "This sounds crazy, right? I mean, if you look hard enough, you can see patterns or connections in just about anything, right?" Nic's backpedaling sounds like an unconvincing attempt to save face, although he simultaneously sounds disappointed.

"Well, I suppose that's true," Dennis states with the kind of tone that tells you a "but" is coming, and it is. "But... haven't you ever had those spooky kinds of experiences, like when you think about someone you haven't talked to in forever and then the phone rings and it's them? Or sitting next to someone on a plane and noticing they're reading the same book you are? Those kinds of random encounters that make your hair stand on end?"

Despite knowing Dennis for over fifteen years, Nic looks utterly surprised at his friend's philosophical take on this. "I guess that's part of what I... we... are dealing with. So many things that seem like coincidences but somehow turn out to be connected. We're still looking for the meaning behind it all."

"Well, that *does* sound interesting. I suppose if you're open to the possibility of alternative explanations to the random, or signs that seem to point you in a certain direction, then the meaning will eventually come."

Nic leans forward, enamored by Dennis' near-metaphysical musings, and takes the plunge.

"Well, speaking of signs, I found a feather the other morning, or, according to Finn, it found me..." He relays the story and finishes it with Finn's comment about the feather being a sign, an invitation to listen and pay attention.

"Well, there you go then," Dennis says matter-of-factly.

"Dude, you'd tell me if this sounded crazy, right?" he asks, searching for a bit more reassurance.

"Listen." Dennis smiles broadly. "If you think it's crazy, then it's crazy. If you think you're on to something meaningful, then maybe just follow that idea for a while and see where it leads. I mean, everyone thought Einstein was off his rocker, but where would we be if he just believed them and gave up? Or what about that guy from Pink Floyd? Certifiable and also a phenomenal musician, so you choose how you want to see it."

Nic scoffs and jabs back at his friend. "Dude, I don't think we're going for a new world-changing theory here or releasing a blockbuster album, but I get your point."

Goose bumps sweep up Nic's arms as he hears the familiar serenade of black holes and shining diamonds from the ballad written in tribute to the man whose name Dennis had just *randomly* spoken, floating out of the open window of a passing car.

His eyes widen, and he looks at Dennis, whose raised eyebrows and twinkling eyes tell Nic that he heard it too.

"Well, there you have it, dude. I don't think it matters what you call it. What matters is what you're going to do with it. Give up so no one thinks you're crazy, or see where all of this takes you."

JUST AS DECISIONS come quick and clear when one's heart is open, the whispers of the universe become impossible to ignore once one is ready to listen. And Nic appears to be listening.

NEARLY FORTY PEOPLE stroll through the Okiciya lobby, infused by the bright, herbaceous scent of white sage and the vanilla of sweetgrass. Cassie had taken great care creating a path lined by luminarias and giant pillar candles to guide guests to the outdoor ceremonial circle.

The love and care she poured into these details are felt by all, even those who have no idea it stems from her deep gratitude for finding a place to call home. The young woman had found herself in Massillon after a series of stops that had failed to support her search for safety and belonging. Although she loved her family, and still does, she knew from a young age that she needed to leave her tiny East Texas town along the Neches River if she were to ever stand a chance of escaping the violence and swampy turmoil that had claimed so many of her kin. A woman of deep faith, she had sought comfort at St. Mary's Parish and had made a good friend, aptly named Mary, who had introduced her to Zebulon Paytah. A sense of déjà vu had come over Cassie that day, leaving her with a feeling that she had met the tanned and towering man before. Intrigued by the profound spirit at the heart of the center he had built, with its philosophy of *helping others help themselves*, she had asked if he needed any help, and he'd offered her a job on the spot. Her every interaction demonstrates the love that flows between this beloved young woman and the place and people she now calls home.

As the final few arrive, the sun is nearly asleep in his western bed, and the moon is peeking out, her waning crescent face grinning in the east.

Cassie's path, wrapped in magical, ambient-gold light, leads each guest to an assortment of wooden benches surrounding the circle, forming a second perimeter to the one inlaid with stones. Some take seats at the first available bench while others wander around, searching for the perfect place to sit. The Driscolls sit on the far side of the circle, noticing quickly that Dr. Isabeau Hirsch is seated opposite them. The four exchange affectionate smiles and waves.

A hush descends as Zeb and a wiry man with long black braids and a scar running from his forehead, over his right eye, and down half of his cheek emerge from the path. The man raises a thick bushel of sage, herbs, and lavender to the sky for a moment before setting it alight with the flame from a nearby candle. Once ablaze, he blows out the fire, leaving the bundle smoldering with crimson and orange embers. Mindfully, he begins his walk outside the ring of benches, swinging his bouquet back and forth. With a long feather, he wafts plumes of earthy smoke toward the middle of the circle, resembling a priest or deacon swinging the ageless thurible, sending prayers heavenward on the tendrils from the burning incense inside.

His focus is mesmerizing to those watching this man who, as a teen, had exchanged one dangerous environment for another. His absence had barely been noticed when he'd left his home on a small South Dakota reservation at fifteen to escape the violence and addiction that had infiltrated much of his community. The next two years were a blur of homeless shelters and dilapidated projects that brought just as much hardship as the home from which he'd fled. Somehow, after traveling through dozens—maybe even hundreds—of cities and towns, he had ended up in Massillon. Badly beaten and left for dead in a vacant apartment complex, Bran never discovered who found him, or how he'd ended up at an emergency clinic on the outskirts of this town, or the name of the young intern who'd saved his eye and tended to him with such kindness. A few days later, stitched and patched, and in awe that the hospital had forgiveness for those who could not pay, he had left, determined to change his life. Walking along the streets, struggling to see, he'd noticed the black, orange, and white signs in nearly every storefront window. *Go Tigers!* and *Tiger Pride!* and one that read, *We're Hiring!* Barely eighteen, Bran had landed a maintenance job at the Paul Brown Tiger Stadium working for their new facilities manager, Dennis Fulton. Many years later, he'd been astonished to learn about the new *Okiciya* Community Center opening in town. Lakota himself, he had instantly recognized the word and gone to meet the person responsible for this uncanny coincidence.

Bran continues to work for Dennis Fulton, loyal to the man who gave him his first real job, but in the kinship found with Zebulon, he is honored to volunteer whenever he can. The reverence that swims in his dark eyes depicts his love for the rituals of the culture he nearly abandoned and the renewed opportunity to impart its gifts to others.

Zebulon Paytah silently raises a drum and thumps it softly, filling the space with a low, steady rhythm. He begins to chant, releasing from his core a wordless, stirring harmony, as if channeling the many voices of his ancient ancestors.

Bran is almost halfway through his procession, focused beyond the varying reactions of those unfamiliar with this sacred ritual: Some cover their noses and look around in confusion, while others intuitively close their eyes and use their hands to pull the smoky wisps toward them as if to bathe in the healing fragrance. A smile crosses his face as he passes behind Isabeau Hirsch, Mary from St. Mary's, and a few of the long-term program participants, including Finneas Driscoll, who are accustomed to the ritual and are actively saturating themselves, soaking in the purifying clouds. A reverent brow raises as he notices the Driscoll parents following their son's lead.

The song concludes the moment Bran completes his devout revolution around the circle, and Zeb moves silently to the center, rotating slowly clockwise to make eye contact with each guest and dips his head in gratitude.

"Thank you," he says, "to every one of you who joined us here tonight to honor and celebrate the autumn equinox—the transition from summer to the fall."

His rotation completed, Zebulon takes a deep breath and exhales long and slow through pursed lips, and the trilling screech of a barn owl perched high in a nearby tree provides the perfect cue.

"I was born from a long line of gifted leaders and powerful warriors, into a culture that taught us the value of listening. To the stories passed down through generations, to the wise words of elders and holy men, to the songs sung by nature herself that are carried on the wind, inside every raindrop, by our winged friends above, and four-legged friends on the ground. We were taught that the signs, directions, and answers to our lives exist all around us. All we need to do was keep open our eyes, ears, and hearts, and listen."

Eyes falling on Finn, Zeb winks as if to remind the young man of the moment the hawk had changed the direction of a very important conversation.

"But I got lost along the way and decided that I was going out on my own. I left my community to forge my own life and spent many years chasing the dream—success, status, money, happiness. No matter how hard I tried though, it didn't happen for me. I became bitter and shook my fists at the sky, demanding to know why the world seemed set on blocking me. I was isolated and angry, unable to comprehend why life was failing me."

Most faces in the circle are glued to the storyteller, figuratively, and some are literally on the edges of their seats, anxious to find out what happened next. As is often the case with a story that hints at redemption, a few others surreptitiously roll their eyes or check their watches.

Sometimes people aren't ready to receive.

"Then one night, after another day of disappointment, I had a dream. I was being stalked by an invisible creature with a vicious growl—chased by a predator I could not see, though I could feel its spoiled breath on my neck. Each time I tried to evade it, another creature would snap its savage jaws and prevent me from escaping. When I woke, I was frightened and could not understand why I would dream such a terrible thing."

Again, his eyes find Finn's and a silent understanding passes between them.

"While I sat there, shaking in anger at all my misfortune, an idea dropped into my head, seemingly from above, and surprised me. I wasn't chasing the dream; *I was being chased.* By things I did not want to see, pain I did not want to feel. I wasn't running toward; *I was running from."*

More bodies lean into the storyteller's tale, leaving just two souls sneakily consulting their phones.

One face seems to be doing both: half-enthralled by the Lakota man's narrative and half-distracted by something internal, evidenced by the vertical crease between her brows. Perhaps Klare Driscoll is thinking about her mother, Bridget Martin, a woman who has spent her life running—or being chased—by her past. Bridget has always struggled with seeing clearly, and in her attempts to escape the unbearable realities of illness and its many manifestations, opts to view the world, and the people in it, with suspicion and disdain, for reasons unknown. For now. Perhaps Klare is thinking about her own retrogression, unknowingly perceiving the world, including her son and her husband, through a lens she inherited from her mother. Or, listening to the storyteller's tale, maybe she is thinking about her own quest to break the generational transmission of fear and secrecy.

"Let me pause here to tell you about this circle. In Lakota, this is called *Cangleska Wakan*," Zebulon Paytah articulates reverently while he sweeps his right arm in an arc from left to right. "This means 'sacred circle,' of which this medicine wheel is one. The circle represents life and considers all things in the universe as interconnected in a continuous flow of growth and evolution. Birds' nests are circular to contain life, and the sun rises and sets in a circle. A circle has no beginning or end. As one cycle completes, another begins, like the moon encircling the earth, showing us her journey in phases."

"The four cardinal directions of south, west, north, and east." He continues his clockwise rotation, pointing to each direction and adding the four seasons of summer, autumn, winter, and spring.

One of the two last souls preoccupied with time and newsfeeds turns off his phone and slips it securely into his pocket, taken in by this interesting perspective. Perhaps he is wondering why he had never noticed how many parts of life are exemplified in fours, or perhaps he knew that but has forgotten. Either way, his face shines with kindled curiosity, which leaves just one single soul seemingly uninterested.

Some people require a little more time before they are ready to listen.

Zebulon walks from the center along a line of small white rocks to stand at the point of the circle that marks the south. "It is here in the south, the season of growth and abundance, that we embrace the warmth of long summer days and rest in the compassion and love for life. Today is the autumn equinox, where we honor the fading of summer and make our way into the fall. The night my dream came, my westward journey began."

He walks to the west point of the circle, where the row of black rocks stretching out from the center ends. "The sun sets in the west, signifying things coming to an end. It is the place to draw power and strength to carry on. It was here in the west that I left behind my old life and sought out help and guidance, knowing that I could not do this alone. Then, my journey turned to the north."

The storyteller is now in the northern position at the terminus of a line of all variety of brick, henna, and vermilion stones. "In the north, we face the harsh, midnight winds of winter that teach us endurance and perseverance. It was here, with the guidance of those who had come before me, that I embarked on a vision quest, was cleansed anew by the cold winds, and had my next life's path revealed, bright and clear, before me."

He moves to the east at the intersection of the circle's perimeter and the row of small topaz, citrine, and amber stones. All around the circle, the air sparkles with bright eyes and expectant faces. No phones are checked nor timepieces consulted.

"The east is represented by the spring and holds the light of the rising sun. It is the birthplace of new beginnings and the dawn of understanding. Here, knowledge and insight are illuminated in the sunrise, along with the gift of wisdom, as we continue to move through the cycle clockwise—or *sunwise*—to align with the sun's path."

Planting his feet, he smiles as he begins to tell the most inspiring part of his story. "It was here in the spiritual seat of the east that plans for Okiciya unfolded, where my purpose of giving back to others was clear and unobstructed, and where door after door opened with ease, leading me to this extraordinary town and to the many gifted people I've met here."

He regards the faces of his guests and lingers an extra beat on the charming Isabeau Hirsch, swathed in layers of golden maple and rich mahogany. A small stone hangs from her neck on a cord of dazzling turquoise and rests lightly upon her chest. He smiles as if remembering the moment their paths crossed, the conversations they've had about the cycles of life, and the many times she has traveled around the circle. Her journey began with one that started before she was born, one that involved an escape from a tyrannical dictator determined to cleanse the world of those he deemed impure. She later learned of her parents' oceanic journey through Belgium to New York from hearing the stories told by the few who made it out with them. After a childhood rife with poverty, the inheritance of generational trauma, and no hope for a future of anything else, the next cycle began when she met a renowned psychiatrist who opened her eyes to the possibility of a different sort of life. Through the many twists and turns of her career, she migrated west and landed a job at a psychiatric hospital in Massillon, one of the first state hospitals in the United States. Commissioned by Governor William McKinley in 1892 and opened in 1898, it became known for its humane treatment of patients using an innovative community care model. Thirty-five years deep into her service to the community, she met Zebulon Paytah at the 2012 celebration of the relocation of St. Dymphna's shrine from the hospital to St. Mary's Parish. Cozy and comfortable in her current life cycle, her healing gifts continue to touch many, ushering them from their dark pasts into the brightness of the present. She inclines her head respectfully toward her dear friend and folds her hands over her heart.

He smiles and continues his tale. "My release from the binds of my past, of my pain and the pain I carried for others, came when I was willing to listen, with my heart as well as my ears. Once I was open to considering all possibilities, rather than insisting on seeing things my way—when I was willing to see with my heart as well as my eyes—I could finally find my purpose. And then, most importantly, once I was ready to ask for and receive guidance and support, I was able to fulfill it."

As if the storyteller had whistled and called out her name, Koko, black and shiny as a raven with her stunning glass-blue eyes, rises from her post at Finn Driscoll's feet and regally strides to the man she watches over, who in kind watches over her. She sits tall and leans against his leg, a gesture that radiates the loyalty and protection of an animal that knows its life cycle had originally seemed certain to be short. As a pup, she had suffered unfathomable cruelty until she escaped one night when the clasp of her overused chain randomly failed. Free but lost, Koko kept to the shadows and the woods, foraging where she could. Many miles later, she found a secluded spot behind a sprawling grassy plot scattered with stone blocks of all shapes and heights. It was empty most of the time, save for the one or two humans who stopped to leave flowers on some of the stones. Koko's instincts to watch and protect had been sparked at this sacred space, and she took up her new post behind St. Mary's Parish as guardian of those who once were. Bowls of kibble began to appear, delivered by a gentle soul with a sweet southern drawl, and Koko grew stronger. One day, the woman brought a friend who instantly became hers. She had found her charge, or perhaps he had found her, and she trailed the dark and stately man as they turned to leave at sunset, beginning a new cycle around the sun.

Zeb leans over and lovingly scratches behind his custodian's ears before concluding his story. "My journey has taught me that we gain more by giving away. That our gifts multiply when we share them with others and flourish when we bring them into a community. We are all part of this community," he says while sweeping his arm around the circle, "drawn here for a reason. To meet someone new, to show support, or perhaps to be reminded of something important that has been forgotten."

His eyes move quickly toward Finn and then hold those of Nic and Klare for a moment. As if on cue, the barn owl darts across the circle, passing Zeb's shoulder by less than a foot, taking a new seat in a low-hanging branch, her ghostly, white heart-shaped face in earnest focus.

Smiling, he continues with his final invitation. "Through my journey, I have come to believe that nothing happens by pure chance. Tonight, I invite you to reflect on where you are in your current journey. Growing in the long warm days of the south, or building strength as something comes to an end in the west? Persevering against hardships in the north, or opening your eyes to a new dawn in the east? Do you feel you are right where you are supposed to be, or do you hear a call to reposition?"

The storyteller lets his question hang in silence for several moments and then asks the group to stand, which they do without hesitation.

"If you feel content with where you are, please stay. Otherwise, I invite you to position yourself anywhere along the circle that you feel better suits you."

Isabeau Hirsch floats over and chooses a place due south, while the Driscoll family moves a few feet to their left and stops, as if suspended in the folds of a soft hammock stretched lovingly between a northern pine and an eastern fir. Cassie and Bran remain in the west; some stay where they started, and others move to a new location along the arc.

When all are settled, Zeb continues. "I encourage you to look into the faces of the people in this community—this circle reminds us of renewal and that we are not alone but part of something bigger, where connection, kinship, and gifts are abundant. If you find yourself feeling drawn to anyone in the circle, please make contact with that person..." He glances down at Koko, still pinned to his side, and smiles. "Or animal... and take a moment to share what brought you here tonight, to this community."

Several people gather around Zeb to shake his hand or ask further about the symbolism of the ceremony. A few others wave their goodbyes and follow Cassie back to the lobby, where her delicious refreshments wait to nourish bodies and souls.

Standing in the south, Isabeau Hirsch releases a young woman who had eagerly approached her for a hug and finds Finn Driscoll waiting patiently for her attention. Once given, he points to the sky and enthusiastically sweeps his arm back and forth in a wide arc. His sparkling golden-brown eyes and animated motions suggest he has just discovered, for the first time ever, the existence of the great expanse of the starry skies above. With a twinkle in her eye that mirrors his, she listens as Finn passes along a story, as originally told to him by Zeb, about tonight's surprise avian visitor. Finn explains it was nothing short of magical since the owl represents seeing the truth. There can be no deception when the owl arrives since he has the power to light up our blind side and deliver the wisdom of clear sight.

Nic Driscoll slowly backs away from the crowd, inching cautiously toward a lone man kneeling and in a seemingly deep, wordless conversation with Koko, whose crystalline eyes move from side to side in perpetual watch. With his bottom lip caught between his teeth, Nic twirls in his right hand the feather that found him. His head swivels hesitantly between the assembly behind him and the man in quiet commune with his canine friend. Suddenly, he stops, squares his shoulders, and approaches with a determined step. The man with the scar stands, says hello, and extends his hand in greeting. "Hello." Nic asks tentatively, "Is your name Bran?"

The lives of those linked by the delicate choreography of unseen forces eventually find each other, no matter how long and winding their individual paths may have been. Callings and destinies, whispered on the wind and invisible to the naked eye, are witnessed by an open heart.

38

Soft, contemporary jazz welcomed them into the new and immensely popular coffeehouse near Sippo Lake. Brick-clad walls hosted shelves of gently loved and donated books along with a section to showcase works by local and up-and-coming authors. Even on this late-morning weekday, the place was abuzz—small groups sat on plush couches in lively conversation while young children played nearby in a space filled with beanbags, blocks, puzzles, and games. Tucked into cozy, overstuffed armchairs, several readers sipped their drinks while drinking in their stories. The bright scent of espresso blended deliciously with the sweet aromas of caramel and chocolate.

A massive chalkboard affixed to the wall behind the long counter of busy chrome espresso machines and whirring bean grinders highlighted baristas' beverage favorites and tempted tastebuds with fresh-from-the-oven pastries and the day's sandwich specials.

Perusing the rows of silver-topped glass jars of loose-leaf teas, Lucy chose the smoky green dragon blend with mint and lemon on the side, and Klare opted for the customer-favorite iced vanilla chai latte with cinnamon. Milk frothers steamed and spoons clinked and stirred while Klare and Lucy waited at the end of the bar.

Upstairs and nestled in the back was a beautiful loft designed to host the working and writing visitors, where the tapping and clicking of several ear-budded patrons filled the air. Approaching four small glass-enclosed rooms available for more private conversations and meetings, the two ladies took the one remaining space, entered, and pulled the door softly closed.

"Thanks for meeting me today," Klare expressed gratefully as she settled into a soft leather armchair.

"Of course! I'm glad you called." Lucy squeezed lemon into her tea and dunked in a few mint sprigs. "I've been curious about your call with your mom."

Klare exhaled a deep *whoosh*. "You're not going to believe it."

"Mmm…" Lucy sipped her tea. "Let's hear it."

After weeks of delaying the inevitable, Klare had finally called Bridget. Her original intention was to confront her mother's secrecy—the withholding of truths that had insidiously taken up residence inside her body, lying dormant until woken, where they began bounding around like strange, disruptive entities. But within minutes, Bridget had spun herself into a blistering frenzy, firing off a barrage of accusatory deflections and feverish denials.

Determined to not back down, Klare had pressed. Bridget's sizzling verbal tirade of choppy words and fragmented sentences left Klare wondering if their connection had gone bad because it seemed only every couple of words were coming through. It took just moments to realize it had nothing to do with the phone line; Bridget was stammering and spewing so fast Klare could not grasp a coherent stream of dialogue. Straining to understand, the sharp shards and jagged pieces of her mother's rant soon morphed into a picture of heartbreaking clarity.

"My brother… never again… kids!" Bridget popped and sputtered.

"Wait, Mom! You had a brother?" Klare's heart seized.

"Gone… sent away… Scott!"

"Mom, please slow down," she implored, her heart beating as fast as her mother's disjointed invective. "What about Scott?"

"My brother!" Bridget screamed.

"Wait, what? You had a brother named Scott?"

"We were just kids." Her mother was weeping now. "Just kids."

"Okay, Mom. Okay. Please take a breath." Following her own advice, she slowed her breathing while she listened to her mom sniffling and choking on the other end of the line.

When Bridget's gasps slowed, Klare softly asked, "Mom, what happened to your brother?"

Her heart broke with each of her mother's sobs. She didn't want to push, but she knew she could not leave the conversation this way.

"Mom?"

"Damn hospital!" Bridget's voice peaked, then fell into a painful moan. "I never saw him again."

Klare's head spun as whirling bits and pieces of lost truths collided and snapped together.

"You had a brother, named Scott, who was in a hospital, and then you never saw him again?"

Her mother cried softly, sniffled, and blew her nose. "It was a long time ago, Klare," Bridget uttered, defeated.

"I never knew you had a brother. Mom, I'm so sorry." She rested her heavy head in her free hand while her heart continued its awestruck hammering.

"He was sent away. People back then didn't talk about things like this. People like him… they just disappeared." Bridget's now-monotone voice sounded flat and distant.

Treading carefully, Klare ventured. "What do you mean 'people like him'?"

"He was sick, Klare. I don't know. Not well… you know, in the head."

"Oh my god, Mom. I'm so sorry."

"They said he'd be back. But whenever I asked, they just told me not to ask again. So, I stopped. And he never came back."

Bridget had stopped crying and spoke without emotion while tears cascaded down Klare's face. She could scarcely believe what she was hearing, let alone that this private story was pouring from her mother like an open faucet.

"Do you know what happened to him?" she near-whispered, fearful of setting her mom off again, but Bridget remained worn and resigned.

"I found out after your grandparents died that he died. I found a condolence letter from the hospital in their papers. It didn't say how. He was only twenty."

A fucking letter. You've got to be kidding me. Seething anger traveled from Klare's belly to her throat—a wild and furious rage over the pain inflicted upon her mother by parents who probably believed they were protecting her—sparing her from a shame-bearing truth, blind to the fact that their secrecy, lies, and silence added to the pain, suffering, and grief that Bridget had carried her entire life.

A pain and suffering and grief that she had blindly passed down to her own daughter through the very same secretive channels.

Too soon? Klare wondered if her mom could see it. *No, it's too soon.*

"This is a terrible thing that happened, Mom. All of it." She resisted a tiny impulse to add, *like with our Scott, and with Dad.* "But I'm glad you're telling me."

Silence.

"Mom?"

"Klare, I can't. Not right now. I need to go." Bridget sounded tired and far away.

"Mom, please, wait." For perhaps the first time in her life, she did not want this phone call to end.

"I'll call you soon, okay? Give my best to Nic and Finn."

What? 'Give my best'? No disdain, no sarcasm? She could barely believe it.

"Mom?"

"Please, Klare. I need to go. I'll call you soon."

Click.

"Holy shit, Klare." Lucy's mouth hung open. "Shit."

Klare nodded her head and raised her eyebrows. Lucy never cursed.

While her friend sat stunned and seemingly trying to collect her thoughts, she took a sip of her untouched latte and continued. "It explains so many things. Hiding my brother's struggles, probably trying to protect him from the same fate. But it didn't work."

"That's so terrible. I can't imagine the guilt, the burden she's lived with—her whole life." Lucy's eyes welled up while she shook her head in disbelief.

"I have so many questions. She never really talked about her parents. They died before I was born. Of course, never mentioned she had a brother. I thought she was an only child…" Klare trailed off, distracted by an odd, tingling sensation at the base of her skull.

"What?" Lucy asked worriedly.

Klare shook her head, hoping to dispel the eerie feeling that had come over her. "I don't know. It's just overwhelming."

"What did Nic say?"

"He was shocked. Finn, of course, was sympathetic. I mean, Nic was too, but he was also angry. Same as me, I guess." She took another sip, also thinking about the conversation she and her husband had had later that evening—one that centered around the irony of three people in their family having lost brothers and growing up as an "only" child.

"How are *you* holding up?" Lucy asked, face full of care and concern.

Klare smiled and sighed. "You know, I'm okay. It's a lot, but it cleared up some things, even though I'm sure there's a lot more to learn."

Reaching out to grab hold of her hand, Lucy offered a supportive squeeze.

I'm so lucky, Klare thought, *especially after being such an absent friend.*

"Enough about me. How are you?" Klare shifted the focus.

"Oh, stop it," Lucy scoffed. "We're good, Dennis, the kids, me. Nothing new. I'm just glad you're back."

"I'm getting there." She smiled.

When Lucy excused herself for the restroom, Klare sipped her watered-down coffee. The tingling was back, vibrating in the nape of her neck and setting the little hairs on end.

What is it? She rubbed the back of her neck. *Maybe I don't want to know.*

"Yes, you do," a kinder, gentler voice inside countered. *"No more secrets."*

She smiled, acutely aware of gratitude's soft and solid presence resting in her solar plexus, seemingly immune to the niggling buzz in the back of her brain. She sighed and thought about part of Zebulon's message from the equinox ceremony.

" *... open our eyes, ears, and hearts, and listen."*

I'm trying.

Lucy returned with another tea, handed Klare a glass of ice water, and settled back in.

"I feel like I'm starting to come out of a fog," Klare shared, "and I appreciate all your support. Thank you."

"Of course. Anytime." Lucy smiled.

"It's funny," she commented, "the community center has been there for years, and I never thought about sending Finn there until this year, and he ends up with all this support when I wasn't able to be there for him. And same with Dr. Hirsch. We could have been referred to anybody, but we end up with this lovely woman who just seems to *get it*. And Finn absolutely adores her. Nic does too. It's very sweet."

"Well, seems like it was meant to be." Lucy laughed. "The universe just working its cosmic magic as usual."

"I guess so." Klare grinned warmly back at her friend.

With the busy lunch crowd filing in, the two women picked up their empty glasses and released their room to a newly arrived laptop-toting pair. Downstairs, the line curved out and around the front door, causing them to shimmy and squeeze through the lively murmur of connection and happy hugs of greeting. All of it left Klare with a warm, welcomed feeling inside. This place was not simply a coffeehouse; it was a place to gather… to belong.

"Excuse me?" bid a light, friendly voice. "Excuse me?"

Just outside the door, on the sidewalk shaded by pink dogwood trees, Klare turned to meet the inquisitive eyes of a woman with ashy-blonde hair and a kind smile.

Klare swiveled her head, but it was clear she was the intended target of the woman's regard. "Hello?"

"Were you by chance at the community center last week?" the lady asked.

"Oh my gosh. Yes, I was!" Klare replied, thinking, *What a coincidence!*

"I thought I recognized you. My name is Mary."

"I'm Klare. Do you work here?" Blushing, Klare scoffed at herself. *What a silly question—she's out here standing in line.*

Mary laughed. "Oh, no. Just grabbing some lunch. I work over at St. Mary's."

Goose bumps erupted up and down Klare's arms, sending a tickling shiver down her spine. "Oh, the big church?"

"Yes, in the shrine, to be exact."

39

As Klare and her family pulled up to the curb in front of St. Mary's Parish on Cherry Road, nervous flutters skipped between her heart and her stomach, threatening to let loose a giddy laugh caught in her throat.

This is so strange. Seriously, what are the chances? When she'd told Nic and Finn about meeting Mary from St. Mary's, who *coincidentally* had also been at the Okiciya ceremony, Nic seemed about as shocked as she was. Finn, with his knowing smile, simply stated that perhaps it wasn't a coincidence after all.

Glad for her husband at her side and warmed by the eagerness of her son several steps ahead, Klare intertwined her fingers with Nic's and smiled. Upon Mary's instruction, they kept to the right of the church and climbed the nine stone steps to enter the red brick rectory, host to a gift shop and the administrative offices for the caretakers of the National Shrine of St. Dymphna. Closed on weekends save for special appointments, Mary had arranged one for them. A long, horizontal glass case packed inside and atop with pendants, medallions, prayer cards, and booklets depicting the honored saint filled much of the cozy lobby.

Mary entered from the back offices and greeted them enthusiastically. "Hi, Klare! I'm so glad you all could make it today!" She introduced herself first to Nic and shook his hand with both of hers. "Oh!" she exclaimed with delight when she turned to meet Finn.

"Hi, Mary."

"Oh!" she laughed again and brought her hands over her heart. "Finn, right?"

Mouth agape, Klare stood stock-still, watching this curious and admittingly confusing exchange between her son and the woman she'd just met under already-strange circumstances. Nic looked at her, equally baffled, and shrugged his shoulders. Her son extended his hand to Mary and simply nodded, a clever and knowing smile spreading across his face.

"We met at the center. She's a friend of Cassie's," Finn clarified for his parents, although his eyes remained locked with Mary's.

"Well, how about that. Wonders never cease!" Mary joyously shook her head, then turned to pull Klare into a friendly embrace.

"Thank you so much for inviting us," she replied, still trying to wrap her head around this surprisingly unexpected scenario. "Uh, it's nice to see you again." Flurries abounded inside and Klare silently mused, *I feel like a kid right now… like I just made a new friend with a woman I've spoken with for all of five minutes.* She felt Nic take hold of and squeeze her hand, and looking at him, she blushed softly at his bemused smile. *Can he feel it too?*

They followed Mary outside, and she led the way to the church. Entering through a set of side doors on the east wall of the building, Mary genuflected and crossed herself, turned, and motioned for them to follow her into a beautiful alcove to their immediate right. Her voice, soft with respect and honor, enveloped them. "Welcome to our votive shrine."

In the corner of the room, behind a beautiful baptismal font, an elegant white marble statue of St. Dymphna stood elevated on a wooden table. Around her feet, rows of amber and white votives flickered and danced.

As she took in the resplendent sculpture, illuminated by a radiant golden light above, Klare gasped. As her right hand instinctively moved to her heart, the group turned to her.

"Mom, what?" Finn asked, wonder having replaced any sense of anxiety or worry he had felt for his mother over the last few months.

"We didn't see this part last time we were here. The statue… it's different than the one out in the church, right? But it's… *familiar*." Klare blinked rapidly and her eyes darted side to side, scanning her memory for something that would help this make sense. "It's so strange," she whispered.

As though she had access to Klare's internal perusal, Mary supplied the missing link. "Well, this actually isn't the *original* statue. It is a smaller version of the original, which *was* very colorful. Sadly, we lost her in the fire two years ago."

The fire?! A sizzle of reflexive panic streaked through Klare's chest, a white-hot crackle that originated involuntarily from some deep place within. Unlike in times past, it only took her a few seconds to recognize this familiar feeling as both old and unfitting for the situation at hand. She took a breath and refocused her attention on Mary, as the soft-spoken woman recounted how a fire had broken out one evening and destroyed the entire shrine.

"As providence would have it, the statue, whilst burning, fell against the door and sealed the alcove, containing the fire that would have undoubtedly claimed the entire church, since it was late and no one was here…" Her voice trailed and her eyes sparkled with reverence as she turned toward the shrine. "We were so distraught."

Oh my gosh. That's why it's familiar. This one looks like the original, the one from the cabin. The sadness of loss mingled with the relief of clarity.

Opening a three-ring binder that had been sitting on a chair in the corner, Mary explained how she'd worked at the shrine on the hospital grounds for many years before relocating along with it to St. Mary's Parish in 2012.

What?! She worked there too?! Mouth open in awesome disbelief, Klare looked at Finn, who responded with a broad, satisfying grin, as if he wasn't surprised in the least.

Mary flipped through a series of pictures that depicted the shrine's rosewood and glass enclosure from when it still stood in the fir grove. On the face of the entrance was a giant white cross, as tall and nearly as wide as the structure itself.

A prickly shiver flitted across Klare's shoulders. *Little Klare* recognized *the cabin* immediately.

"But, as devastating as that was, so much good has come out of it." Mary pointed to a glorious trio of white and gold stained-glass windows and excitedly shared how the 75-year-old pieces, along with the marble statue, had been found in storage, treasures tucked away and all but forgotten when the rosewood shrine had closed, and were thus used to replace what had been destroyed in the fire.

A magnificent image of St. Dymphna took up most of the middle and tallest glass pane, while the two flanking windows portrayed beatific angels, shimmery stars, and shining crosses, and near the bottom, images of two churches, one with a banner that read *St. Martin's Church of Gheel* and the other, simply *Gheel*.

Martin? You've got to be kidding me. Klare stifled a laugh at the association with her maiden name.

"These are so beautiful." Klare admired the resplendent windows as much as she did the story of their amazing discovery. Looking at her family, she noted they were clearly sharing in her wonder.

"Yes, such beauty, and so, so fortunate," Mary replied. "And there are more. Come, this way." She extinguished the overhead light and led them from the alcove into the vestibule, where she continued to point out glorious mosaic windows that had been reconstructed from old panels and retrofitted to replace panes that were either lost or damaged in the fire.

Walking down the center aisle, they turned left to approach St. Dymphna's statue centered on the west side of the nave, and Mary resumed her story. "After the fire, we commissioned this new statue. It took well over a year, and wouldn't you know it, she arrived here, all the way from Peru, mere hours before our two o'clock Mass to celebrate her feast day—just this last May!" Klare could tell Mary was enjoying sharing these likely little-known facts.

"That's on May fifteenth, right?" Nic had been silent thus far, and his question startled Klare a bit. *How would he know that?*

"Yes!" Mary exclaimed and clapped her hands together, visibly pleased that he knew.

"That's my birthday," Finn added quietly.

"Oh my! Well, what a special birthday to share." Mary winked.

Seriously? That fuzzy, light-headed feeling was back. *Is there such a thing as too much coincidence?*

Upon reaching the statue, an indistinct golden shroud of warmth and well-being wrapped itself around Klare, bringing a slight haziness to her senses. Rather than fight it again, she welcomed it and allowed herself to be enveloped.

Her hearing slightly obscured by the comforting sensation, she picked up only snippets of Nic's voice, " *… that following Saturday… yes, right in this very spot… still sorting it out…*" and listened from some distant place as Nic recounted Finn's spontaneous *visit* to the statue back in May.

"Oh! *You're* the young man!" Mary clasped her hands to her chest. "I heard all about that and wondered whatever happened. Well, isn't that something!"

Mary's response—wondrously astonished rather than critically skeptical—drew Klare's attention back to the present, while the calming glow lingered. *Are they feeling it too?* she wondered, noticing her husband and son seemed as relaxed as she was.

With a key that hung from a lanyard around her neck, Mary opened the wooden case beneath St. Dymphna's feet and took out an ornate golden reliquary embellished with shiny rubied gemstones.

"It just so happened our reliquary was not in the shrine the night of the fire. It was in the pastor's office—another act of providence, we believe—because had it been where it typically was, we would have lost our most sacred gift." Mary extended her arms to allow her guests a closer look at the eminent reliquary.

"It's beautiful," admired Nic.

Finn, always mindful and polite, asked, "May I touch it?"

"Of course you may!" she exclaimed. "You can hold it if you'd like."

Klare nodded to her son when he looked at her with shining eyes that beseeched permission. With everyone's consent, he gingerly accepted the gilded container, and Klare leaned in for a better view.

Oh, I recognize this too! A shimmery vibration tickled at the edges of her periphery. Her son's face was full of awe. *I wonder if we're feeling the same thing.*

After a few moments of silent communion, Finn returned the reliquary as delicately as he had received it, and Mary placed it back into its honorary home. Wistful and nostalgic, she repeated her sentiments from earlier. "That fire was devastating, yet so much good came out of it. Her statue may have been reduced to ashes, but her spirit rose from those ashes, and things are brighter now than ever."

Mary's words tumbled through Klare's mind like a vivid kaleidoscope, " *…fire was devastating… so much came out of it… rose from the ashes…*" After her most recent call with her mother, these visionary words spoke a truth that Klare, until this moment, hadn't realized.

An unrelenting buzz emanated from the pocket of Mary's maroon cardigan. She apologized, invited them to continue looking around as they wished, and excused herself to take the call outside. Klare motioned her husband and son to take a seat on the same pew they had sat during their last visit in front of the impressive sculpture backed by sky-high stained-glass windows.

"What a remarkable story. Unbelievable really," Nic said softly.

Klare watched as he and Finn looked around the church as if seeing it with new eyes.

Maybe we all are, she thought.

"You know," she spoke quietly, "what Mary just said about rising from the ashes, about good coming from devastation… it struck a chord for me."

Nic and Finn stopped their visual perusal and refocused on Klare.

"Dr. Hirsch said something once about how what parents cannot allow themselves to acknowledge, they cannot allow their children to acknowledge either. I didn't totally get it at the time, but after that talk with my mom, I think I see it now. Her inability to face what was happening made it impossible for *me* to face what was happening. But deep down, I knew the truth. There just wasn't any way for it to exist in the light of day, so it went into hiding."

Electrostatic pulses shot through the open channels of her veins, but this time, it wasn't anxiety and impending panic. It was the clear, sharp rush of sight—the kind that comes when an eternally fuzzy and distorted vision finally clears, revealing its integrated, beautiful wholeness.

Nic took Klare's hand in his, and Finn remained the picture of serenity.

His knowing, she mused and gave him a warm smile.

"That call with my mom revealed a lot. And I know there's more, but something just came to me." She took a deep breath and swallowed hard as she prepared to tell a secret she hadn't known she held.

Finn had scooted closer to her and pressed his side against hers. Nic held her hand tightly. Both of their faces were riveted with suspense.

"I heard a saying a long time ago about how some secrets need to be held, like a bird in a cage, until safe enough to be released. I feel safe here today." She paused, exhaled a whispery *whoosh,* and readied herself.

Eyes laden with memory and words that had longed for a voice to carry them out of the dark depths, she began. "Before the fire that took my dad and brother, there were other fires." Pausing to breathe, she steadied herself. "Scott had a fascination. He'd painted flames all over his bedroom walls. I remember him lighting things on fire in the fireplace and in the backyard and telling me not to tell. But I knew my parents knew." Another deep breath. "I think Scott was responsible for the fire that took them. I think deep down my mother knows it too."

As if her words had sprouted wings, they flew, gliding in the air with their newfound freedom. Her voice steadied as she connected with a truth that had waited decades to be told.

"I didn't tell the police about the other ones. My mom told me to stop making things up. So, there it is—what she couldn't acknowledge, she couldn't let me acknowledge either. I felt so guilty. I was nine years old when he died. And that truth got locked inside a little birdcage and forgotten. But now I get it. I was in an impossible situation—I wanted to tell, but I couldn't. My mom already said I was making things up… and I knew at some level that if I told, she would make me out to be the crazy one and I wouldn't be believed."

Anguish burned thick at the back of her throat, not for her own pain, but for the pain she knew she had caused her son.

Turning slightly to lock eyes with Finn, she continued. "When I came to you about leaving school early, I put *you* in an impossible situation. I pulled you into keeping a secret that was all about *my* fear and not about what was best for you. That was wrong, Finn, and terribly unfair of me."

"I understand, Mom." Finn stopped his mom's contrition with loving care. "I didn't get it then, but I figured it out. I knew it wasn't really about me."

She shook her head, once again dismayed by this wise, old soul inside his young-man body. She glanced at Nic, half expecting a silent admonishment over yet another secret revealed. Instead, she found a sympathetic smile that communicated more relief than disappointment.

Klare's eyes dampened, and she took her son's chin into her free hand. "Finn, I am very sorry. My inability to acknowledge my truth got in the way of you being able to acknowledge yours. I never want you to feel that way again, and I promise you, I am here—to listen and to help you acknowledge whatever is true for you."

Finn wrapped himself around her waist, and she held him close as Nic's arms wrapped around them both. She could hear the now-feeble protests of the newly dethroned guilt and shame trying to reclaim their places inside, but a new presence had risen from the ashes and claimed its rightful seat. She breathed into her heart, which in the blink of an eye, seemed to have grown exponentially to fill in the space truth and freedom had created for it.

Mary reentered the church with a stream of apologies for such a lengthy absence, but Nic politely interrupted her, asserting that they'd had a very meaningful discussion.

Klare smiled at her husband and winked at her son. She thought about Mary's earlier words, "*as providence had it,*" and pondered if the call that prompted Mary's departure was something of that nature.

"Did you get a chance to visit our cemetery out back?"

"No, we didn't," Klare answered.

I didn't even notice it!

The plot was massive, at least three times the size of the great church. They trailed their guide, who pointed and shared the history behind various statues and monuments. Klare, sensing a void behind her, turned to find Finn had stopped several steps back, his softly smiling face turned skyward. Following his sightline, she immediately noticed what had caught his attention, and a chill bubbled down her spine as she gasped.

A single white bird gracefully rode the high wind, dipping and looping in wide, elegant circles above the thick green of the east perimeter. Klare moved to stand side by side with her son, and Nic and Mary joined a few moments later.

In a low voice, as if to not disturb their stunning avian friend, Mary uttered, "Oh my, isn't she beautiful?" The others simply watched in silent astonishment.

Feeling her son's eyes upon her, Klare turned to meet his face. Her ears grasped his barely whispered words, "It's your bird." Her eyes dampened, and a small lump rose in her throat in response to his enchanting and resonant interpretation.

After a few moments, Mary softly interrupted their reverie. "That reminds me. You know, this is where we found our Koko… or I suppose where she found us."

Their heads snapped to attention and turned in unison to look at her. She pointed to the green below where the lone white bird continued her carefree dance and told of how it was there that they first discovered Koko—a scared and skinny puppy, pacing and skulking about. That she, but mostly Cassie, would leave food in hopes of helping the pup feel safe enough to come out. Puppy Koko had watched over the cemetery for the longest time, and they had begun calling her their resident guardian. When Koko finally emerged from the green, it was the day she followed Zeb and found her forever home at Okiciya.

Klare's head swam with the clink and jingle of interlocking stories and events that, not too long ago, she would have considered happenchance… amusing at most. She glanced at her quiet family and wondered if they could hear it too. *Finn's probably been hearing it the whole time.*

She brought her attention back to Mary, who was just then sharing about a small town in Belgium that for centuries has upheld the spirit of St. Dymphna—a place that has welcomed those with mental and emotional illness with kindness, acceptance, and belonging, where strengths are seen instead of symptoms, and people are celebrated for their gifts rather than their deficits.

"To this day," she concluded, "many residents of Geel remain committed to carrying forward the wisdom learned from centuries of their very special culture."

"Oh, wait. Wasn't that the name on the churches on the stained-glass windows in the shrine?" Klare asked eagerly, her head a touch woozy from another connection made.

"Yes, the very same!" Mary chirped.

Closing in on the completion of the tour, Mary cheerfully shared her happiness that they had come to visit, but all Klare heard was her soft chuckle and the words, " … although I am no longer surprised at just how many people… and dogs… are brought together by her. It's such a special part of her legacy."

Nic and Finn stopped to study one of the larger monuments—a stately stone slab embellished with carved trailing vines of ivy above the name *Meinhart*—standing tall next to an equally distinguished marker in honor of *Engelhardt*. As they began wondering aloud about the stories of those memorialized here, Klare walked several paces forward next to Mary.

Teetering on overwhelm from compounding concurrence, she fleetingly considered not asking the question that had been nipping at her for the better part of their tour.

No way. You can't leave without asking her. Realizing the truth of this internal reminder, she took a deep breath and ventured in.

"I know this is a long shot, but I have to ask…"

Mary's acceptant disposition shone with curiosity as she offered, "Oh dear, I think we are way past long shots, don't you?"

Klare laughed and asked her cardinal question with a renewed ease, one she had the sense she already knew the answer to.

They hugged their goodbyes, and Klare and Mary promised to get together at the coffee shop soon. Klare sandwiched herself between her two loves as they walked the path between the church and the little brick rectory house, sheltered above by the emerald arms of the leafy sycamores. When they emerged from the arboreal haven, she looked at her watch and was stunned to realize they had been there just over an hour.

"Did you guys feel like time was somehow different in there?" she wondered aloud, and her family answered with sweet laughter.

Huh, I never noticed it pointed to the east! Amused, Nic stepped over the inlaid baroque compass that graced the center of the doctor's foyer and followed his wife and son inside. The French doors had been propped wide open. Their white, diaphanous drapes billowed inward, pulled by the breeze from windows inside as if to usher them into the doctor's inner sanctum.

Like their previous visits, Nic felt like he was crossing some sort of invisible threshold between two worlds. The air in the doctor's office seemed… *different*. Lighter, crisper somehow. And the courtyard beyond the shoji screens. *That's on a whole different plane.*

"Hello," Dr. Hirsch sang out. "Please, come in!" They each returned her cheery greeting and found their familiar places.

"I'm happy to see you all," she said. It'd been a few weeks since their last visit, as the doctor had taken an extended vacation to see family in New York. "How have you been?"

"Well, thank you," Klare answered first, "and we have a lot to catch you up on." She exchanged agreeable nods with Nic and Finn.

"Oh, how exciting!" Dr. Hirsch leaned forward. "Where shall we begin?"

"Dad, you should go!" Finn exclaimed louder than usual.

Nic flushed, and he accepted his son's invitation with a broad grin. "Okay then, I'll start." He leaned back to square his shoulders and laughed. "I don't actually know where to begin." The irritating tinnitus rang especially strong today.

"Dad, tell her about Bran!"

He's certainly on a roll. The warmth in Nic's cheeks found its way to his heart. He loved his son's rarely seen animated side. *I hope to see even more of it.*

"Bran? As in Bran from Okiciya?" Dr. Hirsch's eyes glistened.

"Yes, *that* Bran." Nic began with the backstory. Almost twenty years earlier, coming to the end of his clinical rotations and with still no idea what he wanted to specialize in, Nic had halfheartedly picked an elective—ophthalmology—with the intention of returning to Cleveland afterward to figure out his next steps. "I was really lost at the time. Once I got to my rotations, nothing really spoke to me, and I started to wonder if I'd made a mistake."

The ringing ticked up a notch. *This is so annoying.* He reflexively tugged on his left ear to make it stop, although that never seemed to work.

"I was about finished at the clinic when a badly beaten young man was dumped out front. He was in terrible shape." Nic shook his head in sad remembrance. "It was late, and the only doc on-site was tied up with another emergency. It was clear this kid was going to need surgery, so I prepped him, and as soon as the doc could join me, we did the surgery together."

Nic appreciated the tender touch of Klare's hand on his thigh; he hadn't anticipated that talking about these details would stir so many emotions.

Since the young man had no one, Nic had sat with him in recovery and talked to him, even though he was still under. "And when I went to check in on him the next day, he was gone. I never knew what happened to him. But everyone at the clinic said that I had saved his eye."

"Oh, my goodness!" Dr. Hirsch gasped and slumped back into her chair, hand over her heart. "Oh, my goodness… Bran!"

Klare wiggled closer and Finn sat tall, his proud face filled with a grin that seemed to convey a secret knowledge. Nic inhaled deeply. "In that moment, I knew what I wanted to do. The idea just materialized in my head, like it had been there all along and I simply didn't see it until that moment: I wanted to help people *see*. At the ceremony, I asked him if he happened to be this same man. He said not only had I saved his sight but that I had saved his life. Apparently, he took that ordeal as a sign he needed to change. He went and got a job over at Brown Stadium…" Nic paused, and a tiny smile lifted the corners of his mouth. "Get this, working for their new facilities manager at the time, who just so happens to be my best friend, Dennis."

Dr. Hirsch's soft, cottony curls bounced back and forth as she shook her head in unsuppressed wonder.

"I went back to Cleveland, completed a residency in ophthalmology, and then joined a new clinic near Akron, where I met Klare." He looked lovingly into his wife's teary eyes. "It's so strange. You know, he said I changed his life, but he changed mine too." Nic gave a slow nod, giving himself over to the indisputable truth of his story. "It's like it was meant to be."

An awed hush fell over the group, and they paused as if in reverence to the magnitude of Nic's tale.

"Dad?" His son's mild-mannered interruption penetrated the aural racket and snagged his attention. Nic's eyes had been coaxed far away, set past the shoji screens to the garden courtyard beyond. His neck craned and his chin jutted forward as if looking for someone, or something, off in the distance. A noiseless buzz filled his head—not the same tinny, high-pitched tone he was used to, but a gentle, pleasant hum that muted his thoughts.

"Are you okay?" Finn asked.

"Oh, yeah. I'm sorry," Nic stammered as heat rose again in his face. *Ugh. How embarrassing.* He took a sip from his water bottle, hoping it would settle him.

"I'm reminded of what Zeb shared at the ceremony—the part about '*how nothing happens by pure chance.*' That seems to certainly apply here, doesn't it?" The doctor's visage radiated fresh vitality. "This is truly a remarkable story, Nic. Paths that had crossed long ago, only to be drawn back together as if it were meant to be."

Nic nodded his agreement and felt his wife's reassuring pat on his knee. "Babe, you sure you're okay?" she asked.

"Yeah. Uh, why don't you talk about our visit with Mary?" Nic smiled and gestured for her to take the floor. Relieved by the attention shift, he took another drink of water. *Why is it so hot in here?*

"Speaking of paths recrossing…" Klare readjusted to turn toward the center of the room, "it's almost beyond belief."

"Well, after hearing Nic's beautiful story, I suggest we suspend our beliefs for the moment," Dr. Hirsch offered with a sly smirk.

"Yeah, Mom," chimed Finn, "it's not that hard to believe."

Nic appreciated this entertaining exchange and, for not the first time, mused at how similar his son and the doctor were. *One and the same, these two.* He relaxed back into the loveseat to listen to his wife recount her equally extraordinary encounter that began at the coffee shop. The fuzziness continued its subtle vibration as Nic's attention was drawn back to the verdant outdoor patio. *Maybe I need some air.*

Nic dug his fingernails into the palms of his hands to focus, but his puzzling preoccupation with the courtyard superseded his efforts. Snippets of Klare's account of her meeting Mary from St. Mary's and their enlightening second visit to the church landed in his consciousness like random and disconnected words.

"… *works at the shrine…*"

"… *at the hospital…*"

"… *remembered my brother…*"

"… *knew about my mother, about me…*"

At the words, "… *my mother, about me,*" Nic snapped back, as if falling back into his body from a brief mental vacation.

"Wait, wait," Dr. Hirsch stuttered and leaned in closer to Klare. "She *remembered* you?"

"I mean, sort of," Klare clarified. "She remembered the day a woman—*my mother*—threw a fit and caused a scene at the hospital. My brother was apparently a frequent visitor of the shrine. She said she was just outside when she saw a woman drag a little girl out of the shrine. Mary said she tried to intervene, but the woman sped off, and she never saw them again."

Nic felt faint and worried he might pass out. *I need some air.*

"This is incredible," Dr. Hirsch uttered in astonishment. "Just like Nic, you crossed paths with someone from a long time ago who showed back up in your life, seemingly, right when you needed it."

Just breathe, Nic privately coached himself as a panicky unease crept into his head. *What is happening to me?* A flicker caught his eye and pulled his attention back to the courtyard. *It's just the play of the light on the water. Calm down.* He refocused his eyes on the doctor and hoped no one could detect how unhinged he felt.

Luckily, Dr. Hirsch had turned the attention to Finn and asked him if he, too, had had any interesting reunions lately.

"Yes." His report was a simple, single word. But his tone spoke an entirely different language, one that said, *Ha! What a silly question! Yes, of course I did!*

Half of Nic's attention was meandering outside in the wooded retreat while the other half watched his wife's eyes narrow in confusion and the sweetest smile spring from the doctor's face.

"You did?" Klare asked, surprised. "Who?"

Finn inclined his tawny-brown head toward Dr. Hirsch. "Her," he stated, plain as day.

I'm losing it. Nic was drifting. He couldn't feel his body. The piercing pitch was back in full force. Through its metallic timbre, he barely heard his wife's nervous giggle.

"Ha! I guess that's one way to look at it," Klare replied.

From some far-off space, Nic watched his son point to a small decorative frame on the table before them. He hadn't noticed it before, tucked between candles and the various tchotchkes that were sprinkled throughout the doctor's office. He robotically leaned forward in sync with Klare and read the quote contained within, penned in ornate, lavish calligraphy.

My heart and your heart are very, very old friends. ~ Hafez

Dr. Hirsch's laughter tinkled like tiny bells in a breeze. She leaned back and expelled a full sigh. "I agree, Finn. I think we might be cut from the same cloth, you and I."

Finn beamed, and Nic saw bright sparks and rays of golden glitter radiate from his son's shining face. *Now I'm hallucinating? I've lost it, no doubt about it.*

His son redirected his glow to him. In some sort of incomprehensible amalgamation, Nic felt both scared and comforted at the same time. *I can't breathe.*

"Nic, you don't look so good." His wife's comment came from some hazy, faraway place.

"Uh… yeah… um, I think I might need some air." The allure of the sheltered space on the other side of the screens had reached a mesmerizing level. He could no longer keep at bay the profound sense of longing, the compulsion to enter the courtyard. *I need to be out there.*

The doctor suggested Nic take a moment outside and said something about all of this being a lot to take in. He couldn't really hear everything she said, but he knew it wasn't that. Some invisible power from out there had reached in and ensnared him in its grasp. Even if he wanted to, he wasn't sure there were any words that could describe what he was experiencing.

"Dad, go outside. It's okay."

He stood and walked toward the force beckoning to him from beyond.

Nic slid through the narrow gap between the screens and stepped carefully down into the secluded yard. Crisp, clean air saturated his body and filled his lungs with purified oxygen. The rhythmic spatter of the fountain on the far side of the quad soothed his senses like rain falling on parched ground and reduced his heart rate to a slow pulse. Passing the wicker chairs and the bench he and Klare once sat upon, Nic circled around to the right and found a small section of a stone retaining wall nearly overgrown with looping, trailing vines that sprang forth from all different directions. He sat and nestled into the nook, letting the plush, leafy wall hold him vertical.

I feel so much better. One part of his brain rationally commended the decision to go outside and get some air. Yet another part knew, despite the press of his intellectual acumen, that this profound infusion of relief was not simply because of the air.

"You listened," this part whispered with confident assurance.

As if on cue, the thin, high-pitched wail returned to his inner ears. It was deafening and all-consuming and caused his eyes to rapidly fill with tears of exasperation and defeat. *Why, why, why!?* He wanted to scream, but no words came forth from his frustrated throat.

Instead, a wilted whimper leaked out, and Nic's head fell back against the abundant green behind him. *I don't know what to do,* he lamented. *What do I do?*

As if it had reached its critical mass, the shrill screech collapsed into a tiny pinpoint that situated itself between Nic's eyes, just behind his forehead. *A black hole.* He closed his eyes and watched in wonder as the speck shrunk even further, shimmering and vibrating like a subatomic particle in the world of quantum physics. And then, with an infinitesimal flash, it disappeared, leaving him not in mere quiet but in the complete absence of noise.

Within the void, Nic allowed himself to fall into the well of the black hole, surrendering to the gravity of its twisting spiral with no thought as to when, or where, it might end. With time nonexistent in this wonderfully silent abyss, Nic had no idea how long he glided before he stopped and found himself suspended in a boundless expanse of cobalt blue with streaks of deep amethyst, shimmery rose, and sunset coral dancing around the edges. The air carried puffs of warmth and left a faint salty taste on his lips. Beneath him, a flat surface sparkled with crystalline jades and emeralds in undulating cadence with diamonds and sapphires.

The ocean? Nic's heart skipped a beat. *That's the ocean. So, I'm… oh, I'm in the sky.* He rotated, trying to find any other point of reference, but the spectacular open blue continued to swirl and float around him. A distant splash echoed up to him, then another and another, until he became more acutely aware of a wet and *whooshing* pulse below. Although he remained skyward, he had come close enough to the ocean to glimpse the white sails of a miniature vessel navigating toward a stretch of secluded coastline.

He set his sight on the shore and was both surprised, and not, to find himself drawing closer. *It's so beautiful,* he marveled. From on high, Nic beheld what appeared to be a small port village, perhaps on some secret island the rest of the world didn't know about.

The miniature craft was heading toward one of the few docks that jutted out from the coastline. He strained for a better look, but to no avail. As he willed himself to get closer, the picturesque township started to dapple and dissipate, along with the ocean, boat, and the rest of the land. In a single flash, everything evaporated in front of his eyes, leaving him swathed in a colorless white. *No! No!* he wanted to cry out, but he had no voice in this mysterious place.

The tranquil sound of bubbling water drifted in from his periphery. Unaware that he had closed his eyes, he opened them and found himself nestled in the shrubbery nook next to the gurgling fountain that seemed to be spattering water on his face, as if to wake him.

Wow. What a dream. Nic sat in the cozy foliage for a moment to regain his bearings, confused by a sensation he'd never before experienced.

What's going on? Effervescent zips and sparks sizzled in his veins, sending pinpricks across the surface of his skin.

Oh my god.

The identity of the strange and unfamiliar feeling alighted quietly in Nic's consciousness, tenderly revealing the existence of a reality he had never known but had always wished for.

Silence.

Afraid to move lest his lifelong tinnitus return from playing some cruel trick, Nic was also aware that he was missing their session. He rose and moved gingerly back toward the office, a blissful stillness filling his ears and the taste of ocean air still salty upon his tongue.

41

"**E**xactly!" the animated Dr. Hirsch exclaimed. "That is precisely how it works! When topics are made off-limits, the child's feelings about those topics become forbidden. And no child wants to burden an already-struggling parent, so they tuck those feelings away deep inside and, over time, they become all but forgotten." The delight the doctor seemed to get from Klare's insights rang true in her proud voice.

While still digesting and wrapping her head around the complexities of unshelving hidden truths and reorganizing them into a more coherent storyline, Klare was grateful for the sense of freedom and clarity the doctor had predicted would come, one that had remarkably soothed the burn that had plagued her belly since childhood.

"Hey, babe." Klare paused to greet her returning husband. "Are you feeling better?"

Nic took a seat and draped his arm around his wife's shoulders, squeezing her close. "Yes. Sorry for being out there for so long. I think I lost track of time, and—"

"Oh, it's okay. It wasn't very long." Klare spun back to face Finn and the doctor. "We were just catching up on everything with my mom."

"And the bird," Finn chimed in, drawing a sweet smile from Klare.

"Yes," she laughed, "and the bird. I had no idea how much space *the birds* were taking up inside until they started being set free."

"I'm very happy for you, and proud of the work you've all been doing," the doctor praised. "And, other birds may still show up, along with some bumps and twists as you continue on this road to freedom. But I believe with all my heart that you—all of you—are on the right path."

"You've been so helpful, thank you." Appreciation flourished in Klare's heart.

"You are welcome, but I have to say, it truly takes a village, or a community, as Mr. Zeb would say. Finn and Nic are on this path with you, as am I, and Mary, your friends, all the folks over at Okiciya, and even your mother. Each of these people are in your life for a reason. All these intersecting moments have created a fabric, if you will, that links you and everyone else together by one mighty, strong thread."

"And she's the thread." Finn's declaration landed like a punctuation mark—purposeful, complete, and final—sending an unexpected buzzy surge through Klare's body.

What? Klare was confused for a moment, until she saw the doctor's sage and knowing smile, which told her she knew exactly which "she" Finn spoke of.

"She's the thread. St. Dymphna." His eyes sparkled with the awe and wonder of seamless links and harmonious connection. "I thought she came only to me. But she was there before I was even born. She's been here for a long time." Finn paused, but the little tickle at the base of Klare's neck suggested her son had more to say; she could feel the spark of anticipation crackling in the air.

"Mary said she knew of Uncle Scott because he'd go to the shrine. Then you saw her… and then I heard her. And then we end up meeting all these people who know about her or who've had contact with her in some way."

Klare rolled her shoulders to ease the tension brought on by the little part of her that wanted to protest—to set aside her son's theory as magical thinking, a fantastic stretch. But she knew that part now… the doubtful—*no, scared*—side, the heiress to a generational legacy of fear and secrecy. She wasn't interested in that old heritage; she was ready to create a new one.

She glanced at Nic, as relaxed and serene as she'd ever seen him.

I wonder what happened out there?

Klare inhaled deeply, lifted her chin, and grinned at Finn, feeling a radiant golden glow drape over her shoulders.

"Well, she's persistent, I'll give her that," Klare playfully remarked, and a collective, lighthearted sigh filled the room.

"After all these years." Dr. Hirsch chuckled. "I love getting surprised by synchronicity's magic. Finn, you are truly an old soul with an ageless wisdom inside. You have such a gift."

Klare watched her son beam and remembered Nic sharing the way Zeb described Finn the first time they had met.

"He has a powerful energy inside that speaks for him."

"He has a wisdom about him—a depth—like he is old in a young man's body."

"Finn?" Nic interjected, his voice easy and calm. "You've said that you had this feeling that you were supposed to do something but didn't know what. Do you have any ideas with all this new information?"

Déjà vu flickered at the edges of Klare's mind as she watched a wise and peaceful composure come over her son. *I've seen this before… he's in the knowing.*

Finn paused in contemplation and then spoke, his voice filled with a sentient self-possession that brought images of wise shamans and spiritual guides to Klare's mind. "We aren't done. I am not sure where we are heading. But like Zeb said, if we keep our ears and eyes open, we'll know."

Once again, all sat in reflective silence. Yellow-orange embers of calm glowed inside of Klare's body, and by the tender grins upon the others' faces, she presumed they felt it too.

She spoke the only words that rose in her mind, "Son, I believe you."

Minds saturated by the magnitude of converging pasts and paths, the group fell into easy conversation about Finn starting the ninth grade and his afternoons at the center, Klare's decision to resume part-time work, and Dr. Hirsch's recent visit to New York City. Wrapping up, they scheduled another meeting for a few weeks out.

Readying to leave, Klare nudged her husband, who seemed once again lost in thought, staring out into the distance beyond the screens. She thought about Lucy's near-giddy reaction to entering the space. *What is it about this place?*

Nic rose and then stalled again, his gaze intently focused on a framed, vintage-looking print hanging on the wall to the left of the shoji screens.

"Babe?" Klare asked, and when Nic didn't respond, she followed his eyeline to the object of his fixation.

The print looked like one of those vintage Coca-Cola posters from the 1930s. It depicted a woman in a fanciful hat and a young girl with thick, flowing red hair sitting on a dock and looking out across the ocean to an approaching ship. "*Red Star Line*" was printed across the top in antique lettering and the bottom read "*Antwerpen ~ New York.*"

A surge of bright energy burst up from Klare's feet all the way to the top of her head. *Antwerpen?! Like Antwerp, Belgium?* She recalled Mary's description of the town inspired by St. Dymphna's life. *No way.*

"Uh, I'm sorry…" Nic stammered. "Does that say Antwerp, as in Belgium? Near the town where St. Dymphna went?"

"Ah, yes. You mean Geel. As a matter of fact, it is!" Dr. Hirsch chimed in her reputable chirpiness. "Before I was born, my parents fled Nazi-occupied Germany by making their way to Antwerp and then sailing on to New York. Hundreds of thousands of Jewish people escaped this way. They were on the SS Westernland, and one of their fellow passengers was none other than Albert Einstein!"

Klare intentionally slowed her breathing to steady her thrumming heart and looked at Nic, who, slightly pale, appeared to be doing the same. Finn, on the other hand, beamed, a luminous smile stretched wide across his face.

"This picture reminds me of perseverance, hope, and salvation." The doctor continued. "All the people who fought to escape madness, who held on to hope despite their desolate circumstances, and went on to create a new and better life out of the ashes of their pasts." The doctor's voice was thick with remembrance and honor.

Nic looked at his wife, who repeated softly, "Out of the ashes."

Finn added, "Like St. Dymphna too."

"Yes," Dr. Hirsch replied wistfully. "I suppose her journey speaks to us all—leaving behind the painful parts of the past in the spirit of building a better life, establishing a new legacy focused on helping and healing. And inspiring others do the same."

Klare remembered Dr. Hirsch's earlier sentiments, " … *the intersecting moments have created a fabric… one that links you and everyone else together by one mighty strong thread…"* and imagined an infinitely wide ribbon woven together by thousands upon thousands of colorful threads. It was a comforting thought.

Then she caught Finn studying Nic's face. *The knowing. He's in it again.*

As if he could hear her thoughts, Finn smiled and nodded ever-so-slightly at his father, who casually stated, "Um, I think I know where we're heading."

ON THE CUSP of autumn completing her harvest to welcome in winter's crisp spell, the Driscolls are about to enter their own new season.

The dazzling glass façade of the Antwerp Port House ripples and dances, as if made alive by the sunlight bouncing off the meandering Scheldt River. In the distance, the gothic spire of the Cathedral of Our Lady ascends into the sky, her medieval sword thrust high in triumphant celebration. In just a few minutes, the Driscoll family will land in Brussels and make the hour-long drive to the historic pilgrimage town of Geel.

It had been evident by the time they left Dr. Hirsch's office that warm mid-October afternoon that Belgium was beckoning. Later, when Nic had shared about the mystical oceanic "dream" he'd had in the doctor's courtyard sanctuary, a laughing Finn had gleefully corrected his father, insisting that it was not a dream but a vision. His feeble attempts to dispute Finn's fantastical conclusion had been unsuccessful, and Klare had emphatically agreed with their son's impassioned campaign.

Two months of enthusiastic planning later, the Driscoll family settles into a cozy hotel overlooking the charming limestone-and-granite-slabbed market square. Conceding to their fatigue from an entire day of travel, Nic and Klare suggest a quick catnap before heading out.

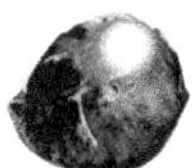

Oh! Oh, hi there. Finn welcomes back the hum and flutter of his much-missed friends. His eye stone and avian companion had slipped into a hazy hibernation through the fall months, their presence fading to phantom vibrations. Clutching his stone with his left hand, he rests his right over his heart to better feel her spirited tickle. Breathing in deeply, he closes his eyes and lets the humming purr envelop him.

Dappled images of yellow-highlighted walking maps come into sharp, fluorescent focus in Finn's mind. He has studied the various routes to *Sint-Dimpnakerk*—St. Dymphna's Church—and knows he could get there with his eyes closed. But it is not merely his mental rehearsal that has primed his confidence for a trouble-free arrival at Rijn 2. With the symphonic wakening of the buzz and flitter, Finn hears another call.

A sweet melody floats upon the tendrils of smoke that curl from the chimneys of the peaked, red-roofed homes and age-old farmsteads scattered throughout the outskirts of town. The scent of smoky vanilla hickory infuses Finn's nose and sits lightly on the back of his tongue. He knows she is close and can feel the delicate pull of her invitation.

He yields to the familiar shimmering aura that absorbs him into its soft emerald bubble. As before, he becomes weightless and feels himself floating rather than walking, shepherded by tones that soothe him. Through the hazy membrane of his suspended cocoon, Finn can make out amorphous silhouettes of what he believes are people, walking through the streets of Geel. One motionless group of figures appears frozen in dance: the taller shapes holding aloft two smaller frames as if to make a human pyramid, with another body standing in the middle, looking skyward. *I wish I could see what they're doing.* And like magic, he is standing right next to them, looking at an iron statue of what appears to be a family of five, holding hands in joyful, exultant unity.

He smiles to himself, and the images before him once again become a nebulous and blurry mass while his attention gravitates back in the direction of the church.

I hear you! I'm on my way! His declaration propels him into hyperspace; in the next blink of his eye, Finn is standing at the edge of a sprawling and ancient cemetery, looking across toward the gothic tower and the banded white sandstone fascia of *Sint-Dimpnakerk*.

From eyes squeezed tight in near disbelief, Finn turns his face skyward and tears stream freely down his cheeks.

I'm here. I'm finally here.

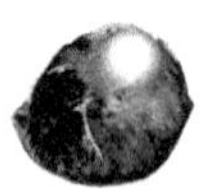

Klare's eyes flutter open with slow and drowsy blinks, and she pauses a moment to gather her bearings. Nic rouses at the same time, their internal alarm clocks in sync. He rolls over and up off the bed, stretches his neck and back, and makes for the bathroom. Klare's eyes close again.

"Klare! KLARE!"

She bolts up with a startled yelp and shouts, "What?! What is it?!" She frantically whips her head around to locate the source of her husband's emergency. With no glaring catastrophe immediately evident, she turns back to Nic, her eyes still wild and wide. "What's wrong? Are you alright?"

"It's Finn. He's not in his room," he shudders.

They rush into the second bedroom to find the bedcovers pulled tight; he hasn't slept there. They dash around the rest of the space as though he might be curled up on the little couch reading a book. He isn't there either. Klare doubles over and plants her trembling hands on her knees while Nic expels a blast of air from his lungs. She straightens and looks at her husband with pleading eyes.

They have been in this moment before. And although they are across the sea in a foreign country where they do not know the language, they do not rush into the street screaming for their son. This time, they know where he's gone.

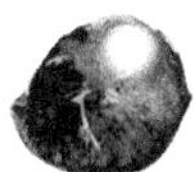

No longer afloat in cozy, ethereal suspension, Finn stands on solid legs with feet held firm by the spongy earth below. Cloudy puffs issue from his mouth in white bursts like a tiny steam locomotive trudging up a steep hill. The smell of woodsmoke still lingers faintly in his nose and throat.

"You're here. I can tell." Finn nods and whispers from his place at the outside border of the cemetery. His body vibrates, sensing himself on the verge of a threshold certain to bring him closer to understanding his part in this mysterious, unfolding, cosmic story.

A flash of black against the backdrop of mostly barren and spindly trees desperately clinging to the last few red-gold and yellow leaves seizes his attention. He wraps himself in the glittery green aura swelling around the edges of his body, rolling in like a misty fog from the sea. He cannot tear his eyes away from the sight of the furtive, shadowy streak, and a powerful, familiar surge of obligation compels him forward. Carefully, so as not to spook whatever, or whomever, is rustling and lurking in the leafy, loamy thicket, Finn approaches. Softening his already gentle voice, he murmurs, "Hello?"

There it is again! Finn's heart leaps, sending his bird into a feathery frenzy within his chest. As if picking up her signal, his stone replies with several hot and buzzy bursts, and its surface feverishly shimmers as if to say, *"I feel it too!"* Senses sharp and alive, Finn crosses the remaining space to the trees, steps around a headstone nearly as tall as he, and freezes.

A pair of crystalline globes the color of pale turquoise meet Finn's gaze with an intensity that steals his breath. He instinctively drops into a crouch to bring himself level with her regal face. Her once jet-black mane is peppered with patches of white and gray, especially around her watchful, noble eyes.

I don't believe this, Finn wonders, and another voice from deep within whispers back, *"Yes, you do."*

The elderly version of Koko slowly rises and moves a few feet to her right, granting Finn access to a sacred secluded corner of the cemetery for which she serves as sentry.

"Thank you." Finn nods to his mysteriously familiar friend and steps forward into the sheltered area. She returns to her station and resumes her guardian duties.

Centuries of elemental exposure make most of the names and dates on the ancient headstones and grave markers nearly indecipherable. Atop many of the worn and windswept slabs rest small trinkets of honor and remembrance: war medals, pendants in the shape of crosses, tarnished lockets, and skeleton keys covered in green patina. Finn's breath quickens as his body quivers in reverence and... *recognition*.

This place feels so familiar, like I've been here before. But that's impossible.

The distant voice speaks again, *"But, is it?"*

Finn hearkens back to Zeb's stories about signs and messages and how it is when one is open—not just with their eyes and ears, but with their hearts—that the path of meaning and purpose is most clear. He takes a deep breath, relaxes his shoulders, and visualizes his heart as an open container—an alive and beating repository, ready and available to receive any guidance offered.

It begins like it did days after his thirteenth birthday, hearing the call and feeling the invisible, magnetic pull reaching forward through the ages. Time slips away as Finn gives himself over to that memory, and the powerful draw surges to envelop his entire being. With a flash, it collapses into a tiny pinprick of golden light that hovers in front of him, bouncing as if eager to show him the way.

With full trust, Finn respectfully weaves around monuments and markers that have endured the long passage of time and along the path to an unknown destination that glows in illuminated clarity. A distant part of his consciousness detects a slight rustle of leaves and approaching footsteps, two sets, and he knows his parents have arrived. The image of the elderly Koko-dog emerges in his mind, followed by, *"She'll show them the way,"* and he continues his journey.

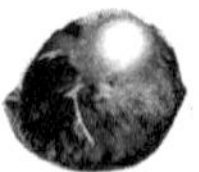

Glimpsing her son moving through the cemetery trees, Klare breathes a sigh of relief. Her belly no longer the delegate for unexpressed feelings, she takes another deep breath and exhales her anxieties to the wind.

Through noiseless ears that have remained clear and open since his oceanic adventure under the arboreal canopy of Dr. Hirsch's courtyard, Nic hears his wife's breathy release and dispels his worry in kind.

Hand in hand, they follow the mysterious blue-eyed, furry chaperone that appeared out of nowhere but seems to know exactly where their son is going.

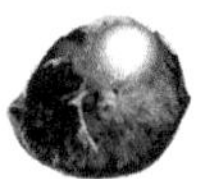

"Oh!" Finn nearly stumbles as a modest and unassuming headstone up ahead seems to emit a golden pulse. He slows his pace and tenderly approaches a space that radiates sacredness. The footfalls of his parents and the Koko-dog are closer now, but stop when Finn reaches the ancient headstone, jutting upright as if born directly from the earth.

He places his trembling hand on the face of the stone and feels a delicate vibration pulse up his arm and into his chest. His eyes scan the fragmented worn carvings, straining to decipher what it says. Using his fingers, he traces the uneven letters and numbers, and tactilely, they reveal:

Our Hart

d. 1717

~ from the ashes ~

From the ashes. His breath catches in his throat as the voices of his mother, Zeb, Mary from St. Mary's, and Dr. Hirsch swim through his heart and soul.

Finn senses the warm approach of parental and canine company just behind him. The old dog comes up on his right and leans against Finn's legs, just as Koko does. He tips back into his parent's supportive hands upon his shoulders and hears his mother gasp.

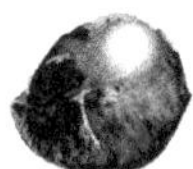

"From the ash..."

Klare's whispered words evaporate into the ether when a pixelated flash pulls her attention to the left.

The rippling mirage dances in kaleidoscopic color, undulating waves of sparkling gold and amber wrinkling the very fabric of space. Unable to fix her sight on the shiny wavelet, Klare softens her focus and just makes out the faint outline of a body.

A girl's body.

Enveloped in flowing flaxen robes.

Her breath returns to her, infusing her body with lightness.

It's you.

Klare closes her eyes and allows the golden radiance to permeate her senses. An image of Little Klare arises, and instantly she feels her younger self next to her. As one, they behold her—a young woman to Klare, a tall lady to *Little Klare*—but known to them both. She smiles, and as one, the Klares smile back, united in the sweet harmony of their *knowing*.

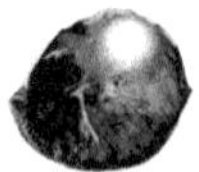

A mighty gust of wind buffets from behind them, causing Finn to stumble forward. As he instinctively catches the top ledge of *Our Hart*'s headstone to keep from falling, an electric zap sizzles through his palm. Yanking his hand back to see the source of the burning touch, he hears a rhythmic thumping that drowns out all other sounds. The deafening pulses mirror but are not coming from his pounding heart; they spring forth from the small stone that hangs from the thin leather cord around his neck.

Finn clutches the spirited eye stone with his right hand and leans in to find, resting upon the rough ledge, its twin: a matte, pale-gray stone with a small hole and veins of white running throughout. A low, resonant hum emanates from it, as if communicating with its brother, gripped tightly in Finn's fist. He listens to their elemental chatter and detects a different sound emerging from some faraway dimension. Shifting his focus to this new sound, recognition dawns golden and covers him like a soft, nurturing blanket.

She's here.

Held securely in his familiar *knowing*, Finn turns to face his parents.

Warmth sparks and spreads through his chest as he sees the smile on his mother's upturned face—a smile that speaks of love, peace, and... *recognition*. And in that very moment, Finn realizes that he recognizes her too. His mother. His *real* mother. Serene, calm, and accepting. The mother who had been temporarily replaced with another by the invisible hand of ancestral pain and loss. His mother. She was back, fully back.

He knows it. And so does his father.

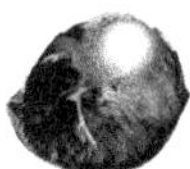

Nic watches his wife and his son in shared recognition, their faces aglow in the fresh dawn of understanding, which sets his soul alight with the hope and promise of discovery.

He leans in to take hold of Klare's shoulder and extends his free hand to Finn, who straightaway grasps it tightly. As if the contact completed some sort of invisible circuit, Nic is suddenly suffused with an electric energy that travels from the points of connection directly into his ears, igniting a brilliantly clear, honey-sweet melody that rings pure upon the breeze.

His mouth drops open and tears fill his eyes.

"Do you hear that?" Nic asks wondrously.

Klare nods and smiles at her two loves.

Finn closes his eyes once more.

Finn drinks in the ancestral song, and his nose fills with the smell of salty ocean air. He drops to his knees, overcome with sparkling veneration, sung in crystal purity, while his bird darts and dives into the harmony that fills her home. His chest feels like it has caught fire—not the painful, burning kind, but a building heat that is forcing his upper body to expand. Her glorious song is deafening. At the moment he wonders if he might not be able to contain it much longer, a distinct *crack!* rips through his chest, and he feels the pressure release.

Swallowing lungfuls of sweet oxygen, he looks up and sees her, and she looks exactly the way he has pictured her. A pale-gray head and chestnut-and-white-spotted underbelly with beautiful downy wings banded tan and black. Hatched from her cozy nest inside Finn's ribcage, she frees her magnificent wings and takes flight upon the invisible breeze. After a few tentative loops, she soars upward. Her high-pitched *kee-eeeee-arr, kee-eeeee-arr* joins an avian orchestra above. As if waiting for her, the singing band of hawks enfold her into their spiraling circle and welcome her home.

A HATCHLING TAPS her tiny beak to break through the thin shell that has nurtured and kept her warm while she grew. Now ready, she emerges, stretches open her beak and, with a piercing cry, announces to the world that she has arrived.

Epilogue

NESTLED IN THE warm hearth of home as nature sleeps under her thin blanket of snow, the Driscolls seek more from the accounts told to them by a Belgian keeper of the Dymphna legend. They sip on stories of the young woman who sought to help those who suffered like her father and who bravely advocated for those in need of dignity and compassion. They drink in the history of the revolutionary social model of mental health care sparked by her short life. They nourish their hearts and souls with tales of belonging, love, and community that have been passed down through generations for more than 700 years. And they hatch plans for how to bring its legacy home.

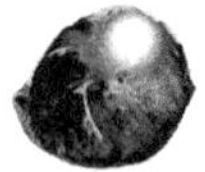

Suspended in perfect balance, the northern hemisphere begins to tilt her face toward the sun with the promise of longer days and warmer skies. Nature reawakens, setting buds bursting and blossoms blooming and calling her birds home. The pollinating legion of bees and butterflies join the yellow-bellied sapsuckers who have been invited to tap the flow of the rising sap of the sugar maples. The tiny spring peepers with earsplitting chirps emerge from their marshy beds to join nature's chorus. Great blue herons commence their annual mating rituals, a reminder of the universal practice of celebrating the magic of the turning of the seasons.

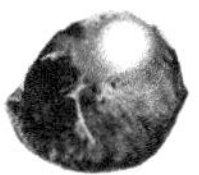

At the Okiciya Community Center, the spring equinox ceremony is underway. The east is the honoree—the place of new beginnings and home of the rising sun. It is from this position that light dawns and spreads over the earth, illuminating the path to renewal.

In the middle of the medicine wheel, a small fire pit glows. The east is the seat of fire, the powerhouse of transformation, and a symbol of strength, energy, and regeneration. There is transmutation in fire—not an ending but a rising up out of the old to burst open anew and in brilliant resplendency.

The circle is wreathed with locals, like Isabeau Hirsch, Mary from St. Mary's, and Cassie, and some who are visiting for the first time, all in some way experienced travelers on the path of changed and changing legacies. Shepherded by forces—some seen and many not—each carries a thread that intertwines with those of fellow journeyers, weaving the universal fabric, creating a pathway vibrant enough for others to follow when their eyes, ears, and hearts are open to it.

Sitting in the due east, supportively flanked by Dennis and Lucy, the Driscolls wait patiently to share their plan and are eager to discover who else might become allies on their next quest. By the end of the day, they will be surprised by the number of people who suddenly realize they have been waiting for an invitation like this to come along.

There is more that Klare is waiting for. Lucy smiles sympathetically as Klare looks expectantly to the path leading from the center to the circle. With still no one there, she loses herself in the invisible waves that ripple and dance above the firepit, where the heat from the white and gold flames rises and meets the chill of the air.

Zebulon Paytah and his ceremonial partner Bran pause as the piercing cry of a distant hawk echoes above, drawing all eyes skyward. Unseen, yet her call is heard by all and felt by the young man who tenderly pats his chest. Hand over his heart, Finn shifts his knowing smile to his mentor and then his mother.

A sharp snap and crackle of a splitting log pulls the attention back to the firepit at the center of the circle, and Lucy gently nudges Klare's arm with her elbow, tilting her head forward.

Following the direction of her friend's nod, Klare stares through the red-hot and orange embers that sparkle before fading into tiny featherlight gray ashes taken up by the swirling breeze.

Bowing to the perfection of the moment, Klare smiles. "Mom."

Author's Notes

The inspirations for this novel span centuries. While the façades and personas of the characters within are born from my own experiences and imagination, their struggles and motivations are simply manifestations of ancient and universal truths carried forward through time: a desire to be seen and understood, to be accepted wholly and held safely, to find meaning and purpose in life, to have opportunities for redemption, and to pass along the wisdom from lessons learned to help future generations do the same, but better.

Wisdom, it seems to me, exists somewhere in the space between touchable reality and that which remains unseen but unequivocally felt. It's a toss-up: fact or fantasy, real or imaginary, tangible or mystical? I'll do my best here to provide the "facts" of some of the sources that have inspired me and, therefore, the writing of this novel; it is up to you to decide where the magic lives.

Lakota Nation

My first "real" job as a clinician was with a small therapeutic community that had wrapped its philosophical approach around the Native American traditions of shared responsibility, community, and reciprocal obligation. Through the legacy of the woman who founded the program, I was introduced to the Lakota values, specifically kinship, respect, and fortitude. These became the lens through which my professional and personal worlds took shape.

Many Native cultures are rich in oral tradition wherein history, customs, and practices are communicated, often by elders to younger generations, through powerful narratives meant to teach, record history, and preserve fidelity. Below are a few of the more moving life and cultural accounts whose inspiration can be found throughout this novel. I encourage you to read, reread, and pass along these chronicles to help keep alive the history of this deeply defining culture and the profound wisdom, knowledge, and life lessons available within.

- *Black Elk Speaks: The Complete Edition* (2014), by John G. Neihardt.

- *Fools Crow: Wisdom and Power* (2012), by Thomas E. Mails.

- *The Lakota Way: Stories and Lessons for Living* (2002), by Joseph M. Marshall III.

- *Blackfoot Physics: A Journey into the Native American Universe* (2005), by F. David Peat.

"The survival of the world depends upon our sharing what we have and working together."
~ Fools Crow, Oglala holy man, nephew of Lakota visionary and healer Black Elk ~

Astounded by the remarkable healing and recovery being made by individuals in this little-known program, many of whom were diagnosed with severe and chronic psychiatric illnesses, I was curious why more places didn't know about or use this compelling approach to treatment. Well, I quickly learned that this "unconventional" method of care was not only known, but in one part of the world, had been in practice for over 700 years.

Geel (formerly Gheel), Belgium

In the thirteenth century, growing accounts of local miracles and inexplicable healing sparked a pilgrimage for those seeking a cure for mental affliction and suffering. Soon brimming with newcomers, the church, unwilling to turn people away, appealed to the townsfolk of Geel, Belgium, to take the pilgrims into their homes, effectively beginning what would become a revolutionary family-care system anchored in humanity, inclusion, and equality.

There are various accounts of this remarkable model of care where diagnostic labels are not used, "boarders" are fully integrated into family and community life, and multiple generations of families have elected to carry on a culture seeped in a welcoming and tolerant ethos. For many reasons, including the shift from agricultural to urban living, this tradition has been slowly fading; in the mid-1930s, nearly 4,000 of the 16,000-person population lived with host families compared to around 250 in 2019. While we cannot slow the passage of time nor the progression of modernized living, I invite you to read about the history of this legendary town so that we might help keep alive and pass along the valuable lessons of humanity, acceptance, and inclusive care of the Geelian culture.

- *Mental Patients in Town Life: Geel-Europe's 1st Therapeutic Community* (1979) and *Geel Revisited: After Centuries of Mental Rehabilitation* (2007), by Eugeen Roosens.

- *The Legend and Lessons of Geel, Belgium: A 1500-Year-Old Legend, a 21st-Century Model* (2003), by Jackie Goldstein and Marc Godemont.

- *Geel, Belgium Has a Radical Approach to Mental Illness* (2019), by Anne Theriault, published on Broadview. org: https://broadview.org/geel-belgium-mental-health/#:~:text=As%20this%20story%20spread%2C%20Geel,venerated%20as%20a%20local%20saint.

And no discussion about Geel would be complete without acknowledging an Irish girl from the seventh century whose life and spiritual legend are the foundation for this innovative and inspiring community.

St. Dymphna

In my imagination, Dymphna is free-spirited, benevolently wily, and precocious. Of course, having no idea what her personality was like, I imagine it was qualities such as these that helped her plot her oceanic escape from madness, establish a life of service to the suffering, and stand up for herself, even in the face of her demise.

The legend of St. Dymphna is also largely based on oral tradition. The most recognized account of her life is credited to Pierre, a church canon who was commissioned by Bishop Guy I of Cambrai in the middle of the thirteenth century. A paper published in 1893 by Father J. F. Hogan presents an in-depth analysis of various dissertations on the life and legend of St. Dymphna and can be found at https://www.omniumsanctorumhiberniae.com/2017/05/saint-dymphna-of-gheel-may-15.html (Omnium Sanctorum Hiberniae: Irish ecclesiastical record: IER, 3rd series, Volume XIV(1893), 577-589.)

All sorts of other portraits and interpretive expositions about Dymphna's story and life can be found meandering down any one of the many hagiographic rabbit holes. And while accounts of her intercession differ, it was my personal and very much unexpected experience of her divine dallying that led me to a little Midwest town in northern Ohio.

Massillon, OH

While trying to discover where the Driscoll family came from, I found myself lost in one of the warrens dedicated to our country's history of mental health treatment. Reading about some of the first state hospitals built to serve the mentally ill, I caught a double dose of synchronicity that immediately confirmed that I had indeed just found the Driscoll's hometown.

Massillon State Hospital

Commissioned by then-Ohio-Governor William McKinley in 1892 and opened in 1898, the Eastern Ohio Insane Asylum, later to be known as Massillon State Hospital, was built "cottage style" rather than in the traditional inpatient hospital-unit format common to other psychiatric institutions. Clients were addressed by their first names, given jobs as part of a work-integration program, shared in the upkeep of the grounds, and participated in farming responsibilities needed to sustain operations. In other words, it was a therapeutic community, like the one in Geel and the one I worked for in California, where clients were considered members of an extended family and treated with the same dignity and respect as everyone else.

While moved by yet another example of the practice of inclusive community care, it was actually the second strike of synchronicity's bell that really had me. One guess… Who do you suppose was chosen as the patron saint for this hospital? Yes, none other than St. Dymphna, for whom a shrine was consecrated in 1938, designated as the country's national shrine in 1957, and where it resided for nearly 75 years before relocating to St. Mary's Parish in 2012.

The Massillon State Hospital closed in 2001 and is now operated by another entity, and the glass enclosure for the shrine has since been taken down. However, a lovely account of some of this institution's fascinating history, along with some early photos, can be accessed at: https://mastahl7.wixsite.com/ archives/post/massillon-state-hospital. And I repeat my same invitation: please read up and pass the inspiring lessons along.

National Shrine of St. Dymphna

Housed within the beautiful gothic-spired St. Mary's Church on Cherry Road is the National Shrine of St. Dymphna, whose many breathtaking aesthetics are depicted in this novel. While the dialogue and experiences of the Driscoll family within the church and outside at the cemetery are fictional, Mary from St. Mary's is very much real. It was this kind and generous woman, who also worked at the shrine when it was located on the Massillon State Hospital grounds, who told of the astonishing events and discoveries related to the 2015 church fire as described in that specific chapter. Was it intercession, divine intervention, "providence," or mere coincidence? You decide.

Of course, Mary's lemonade competition with Cassie, her presence at the Okiciya ceremonies, and her chance encounter with Klare at the café are all imaginative, but she is indeed a lovely human, and when you make your pilgrimage to visit the shrine (natlshrinestdymphna.org) at St. Mary's Parish (stmarymassillon.com), please tell her I said hello.

It is true that the institutions, historical figures, locations, and traditions referenced in this novel were used to enrich the fictional narrative. However, writing this tale only further confirmed for me the existence of that great and boundless thread running through the cosmos, linking us and guiding us along our respective and collective paths toward meaning and purpose.

Thank you for reading this. Pass along whatever may have touched you in this story, and please stay tuned…

Our Hart

Under watchful eyes as crystalline as his own, a peculiar young boy is found in a burning field, unharmed beneath the soot and ashes that cover his body.

Safely hidden in plain sight by a forsaken healer, the growing boy hones his ethereal craft to help restore a town to health.

That is, until a washed-out pretender, preying on a country's instability, secures favor by denouncing the gifts of the different and guaranteeing their swift execution.

Found once more, Hart travels across the sea to escape the madness that had descended upon East Anglia. Heeding a powerful call from the east, he discovers a small farming community built upon miracles.

Carrying forward an unknown legacy, Hart becomes a steward for an extraordinary culture of care inspired by a teenaged saint dead for a thousand years.

Acknowledgments

It's a fictional story."

"Hmmm," she said.

"No, seriously. I mean, sure, parts of it are inspired by people I've met and some of my own experiences, but really, it's totally made-up."

"Hmmm," she said again.

It's amazing how one little softly muttered sound conveys so much: I hear you. I know you don't see it yet, but that's okay because you will. And I'm here to help you find it, and I will stand with you when you do but wish you hadn't, and I'll laugh with you later when you *really* get it, and I'll celebrate with you when you're ready to put it out into the world.

"Hmmm."

Amanda, you are a true oracle, and I am eternally grateful for you and your labor and delivery superpowers that helped me birth a story that is far less fictional than I ever realized. Friend, YCMTSU and I can't wait to see what's in store for us next, but I have a feeling we are going to need a much bigger feelings corner.

To Kerry, my most loyal champion. Your optimism and faith in me provided the foundation that made this journey possible. Katie, for keeping me company along this wild ride with your impressive ability to strike the perfect balance of woo and sarcasm. Hillary, my copilot in more ways than one, thank you for helping me not get lost, which is a superpower all to itself. Cuba. And to my "Kokos," my furry, leg-leaning, constant companions who always made sure to give me a little nudge when it was time to take a break.

To the Dennises, Lucys, and Cassies in my world, thank you for football in the cul de sac and cup-filling music on the Jetty. For backyard BBQs, pulling cards over brunch, and trivia nights. For 42, 501, and sitting around the firepit thunderstruck. A special thanks to Matt and Erin, for connecting me with Kristen, who introduced me to Amanda, who brought me into a cocoon of story-healing magic.

To the Zebs and Dr. Hirschs, thank you for your past, present, and future guidance. To my marathoning, celestial-singing, cosmic-dancing, wand-wielding, meandering river cocoon allies, you are inspiring AF, and you really are the fucking sun. Aaron, thank you for walking in the snow with me, and Alyssa, you can peer-pressure me into a glass (or bottle) of wine anytime.

To the Marys, the surprise connections made throughout the writing of this book, you've kept my faith in divine synchronicity strong. To my parents, godparents, and all who have loved and supported me through this journey. And a special acknowledgment to Myron, I know our spirits have been friends for a very long time, and I appreciate you sharing your stories with me. Wopila tanka.

To the Intercessors, the unseen, powerful forces who drop ideas into your head and feathers onto your path when you need them most. Thank you, Dymphna, it really has been you all along. To the shaman who lives in my soul and whispers ancient truths to me with his dusty skin, tangled hair, and eyes like my own. And of course, to the turkey. Thank you for stalking me until I was ready to hear your message and receive your medicine. I hear you, and I promise to keep paying it forward.

until then, Karlyn

About Dr. Karlyn Pleasants

As a clinical psychologist, international speaker and trainer, and leading clinical advisor, Dr. Karlyn Pleasants is wholeheartedly committed to shifting paradigms and rewriting cultural narratives about mental health, healing, and the infinite possibilities available when we believe there is always more to the story.

Fresh out of graduate school, Karlyn stumbled into exactly what she didn't know she was looking for and needed—a job in a small therapeutic community working with individuals diagnosed with multiple psychiatric disorders. Its unique philosophy of care was inspired by Native American principles of kinship, shared responsibility, and giving back. The healing that unfolded inside this community of hope, in which each member was considered an integral part of the greater system, was nothing short of miraculous for a group otherwise deemed "chronic" and unlikely to change. This remarkable experience upended everything she believed she knew about mental health and deeply formed her professional career and personal life paths around a desire to create spaces for every human to have this opportunity. For twenty-five years, Dr. Pleasants has helped create thriving therapeutic environments that have supported thousands of individuals and their families in successfully building a life of self-management, health, and independence beyond the bounds of psychiatric diagnoses.

Dr. Karlyn Pleasants is considered one the nation's authorities on working with complex mental illnesses at the individual, sibling, and whole-family levels, speaking on topics related to mental illness in families, the arc and structure of lasting change, and the importance of healing at greater systemic levels. With a clinical lens grounded in attachment theory, she prefers to walk in the world of intergenerational transmission of stories—the tales, experiences, beliefs, and traditions passed along through systems. Leaning on narrative techniques to help others put voice to that which needs to be spoken and heard, she supports the revising of family roles and personal scripts to create a new life-storyline. She holds certifications in clinical trauma treatment as well as in Jungian psychotherapy where active imagination, individuation, and harmonious integration reign supreme.

Today, Dr. Pleasants serves as the Chief Clinical Advisor at the Anew Treatment Center in Scottsdale, Arizona, with the aim of carrying on the fidelity of this deeply transformative model of individual and systemic change that promotes personal agency and interpersonal healing through belonging to a community that believes in individuals' ability to thrive and live a purposeful life.

There is Always More to the Story…

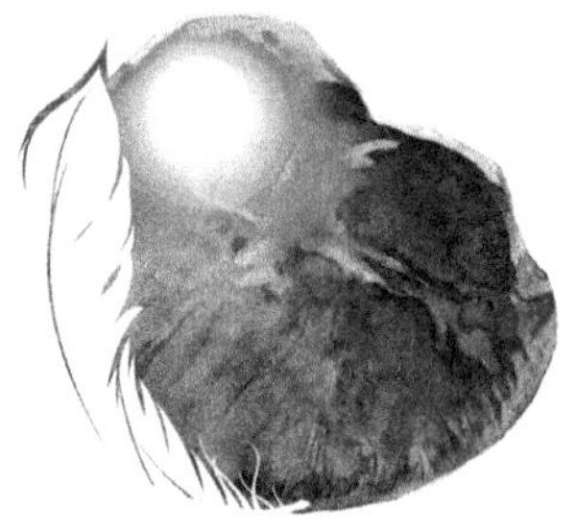

Stories…

chronicle history,
craft current paradigms,
crave to be discovered, and
call to be heard.

If this story spoke to you, sparked an idea, revealed a hidden path for you to explore, or rang the bell of synchronicity, I would love to hear about it!

Please visit my website to add your unique and special thread to the ever-growing, ever-expanding universal tapestry knitted together by story, and sign up for exclusive announcements on upcoming offerings and events.

www.KarlynPleasants.com

www.ingramcontent.com/pod-product-compliance
Lightning Source LLC
Chambersburg PA
CBHW062111290726
48975CB00001B/189